The shining [illegible] *n the cover of* [illegible] *f the story inside. Look for the Zebra Lovegram whenever you buy a historical romance. It's a trademark that guarantees the very best in quality and reading entertainment.*

LOVING ENEMIES

"It's no use, Logan. No amount of pretty words will entice me back to your ship. I may be a prisoner to your love,"—Stella inhaled deeply—"and to your touch and your kisses . . . but I'll never be a prisoner of your country."

Angrily, Logan pulled her to him. "Why are you so hardheaded? Why can't you understand what you're getting yourself into?"

"Why is it that you can work for what you believe in, but I cannot?" Stella retorted. "Are only men allowed to commit themselves to a cause? Or is it only *Yankees* whose cause is just?"

Logan pulled her even closer and kissed her fiercely, forcing her to respond.

From the beginning, he had loved her for her feisty, independent spirit—the same spirit he was now attempting to harness. That it was for her own good, he knew for certain; but it was a battle he did not expect to win . . .

TEXAS DAWN

Vivian Vaughan

ZEBRA BOOKS
KENSINGTON PUBLISHING CORP.

ZEBRA BOOKS

are published by

Kensington Publishing Corp.
475 Park Avenue South
New York, NY 10016

First printing: August, 1990

Printed in the United States of America

This Book Is Dedicated
With Love and Pride
to
Lieutenant Stephen Arnold Vaughan, USMC,
My Son

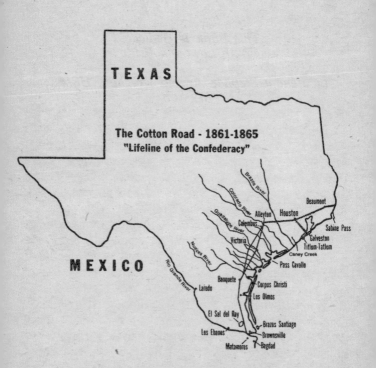

Prologue

Nottoway Plantation (The White Castle), Louisiana
June 30, 1860

"The White Castle . . . the White Ballroom . . . the Magnolia Princess in my arms." Captain Logan Cafferty, resplendent in the blue-and-gold dress uniform of the United States naval officer waltzed Stella Duval around the crowded dance floor, murmuring endearments in time with "Tales from the Vienna Woods."

"I am *not* the Magnolia Princess," she objected, breathless, nevertheless, from his eyes, his voice, his hand at the small of her back . . . from the very nearness of this handsome naval man who had stolen her heart a bare five days ago. "I'm not a princess at all. Just a Texas ranch girl . . ." *Who is madly in love with you,* she finished with her eyes.

"You are *my* princess." His eyes caressed hers, held by the excitement he saw there, by the playful teasing in her smile. Her beauty startled him still, he was sure it always would: tawny blond hair falling in soft ringlets, one seductively nudging her right eyebrow; fiery green eyes that somehow sparkled and smoldered at the same time; flawless olive skin that glistened beneath the light of at least three hundred flickering candles, inviting his lips even in this crowded room.

Although she rode a horse like the wind—outrode most men of his acquaintance—tonight, as at every moment

7

since he first met her five days ago, Stella Duval was every inch the lady. Her broad forehead stretched above naturally arched eyebrows and high cheekbones; her slender neck held her chin at a proud angle. Gowned in white silk appliquéd with green satin magnolia leaves and adorned with swags of pearls, she could only be called majestic.

"One day you will be my queen."

Her smile broke into a laugh. "Princess. Queen. I don't know what to make of you. Texans don't talk like that."

The dance ended. Logan twirled her by her fingertips, her skirt swished over its hoops, and she curtsied with the grace of one reared to royalty.

His hand lifted her arm and she rose to stare into his beckoning brown eyes. For a moment she was held captive. Her lips trembled and she pursed them together quickly.

Without another word, he grasped her elbow and escorted her through the throng of guests into the wide foyer of the mansion.

"Teach me quickly, princess."

With great effort, Stella stilled her racing heart. This man would be the end of her, yet. Or, at best, the end of her good reputation. Even now, all she wanted was to throw her arms around him and feel his body next to hers, to kiss him . . .

When she spoke, her attempt at lightness faltered beneath a quivering voice. "Teach you what?"

His hand slid down her arm to her fingers, which he brought to his lips. The green fire in her eyes ignited when his lips touched her skin.

"To talk Texan. I can't ask for your hand in a foreign language."

"Oh, Logan! Now? Tonight?"

"Now." He grinned wickedly. "Unless you want me to rip off your clothes, throw you down on the carpet, and make you mine right here in front of God and everybody. Then your father couldn't refuse. . . ."

8

Her eyebrows raised by degrees as he spoke. Glancing first right, then left, she took his hand and led him toward the staircase, smiling with delight. "As delicious as that invitation sounds, there must be a better time and place."

He glanced up the stairs, then winked at her. "Your bedroom or mine?"

"Neither."

They passed the landing with its enormous stained-glass window, turned left, and climbed a second, smaller flight of stairs. She stopped beside an open door.

He peered inside. "The music room? At least, it's empty."

Standing on tiptoe, she kissed his lips until he responded, then she drew back. "Papá is on the gallery with Mr. Ransom." She nodded around the corner. "You didn't think I was going to let you get away without asking him tonight, did you? Since *you* suggested it."

The laughter died in his eyes, leaving them simmering with passion. His hand cupped her chin while he studied her with an earnestness he rarely showed. "And you couldn't think I would let you leave tomorrow without making certain that one day you will be mine forever." Lowering his lips, he kissed her gently, purposefully.

Footsteps sounded on the stairs, and she drew back. "Go now. I'll wait here. And . . . Logan . . ."

He quirked an eyebrow.

"Don't call me *princess*. He might . . ."

"You'll always be my princess." His voice and his eyes melted her with their intensity. "But that's nobody's business except ours. Not even your father's."

His words left her quivering. She clutched her arms about her and felt goose bumps on her skin. Turning toward the music room, she sat down at the harp and began to strum the strings. Her concentration didn't last long, however, and she soon found herself at the harpsichord.

Not that she was concerned over Papá's reaction to Logan's request. She knew what he would say. She had heard it herself last night, when she visited him and her mother in their room after the other guests had retired.

In one week's time Logan Cafferty had literally swept her off her feet. At twenty years of age—twenty-one next month—she had already given up finding anyone to love. Oh, she knew she would probably marry someday, but marriage and love did not always go hand in hand.

Love for Stella had been elusive, for she was blessed—or cursed, she sometimes thought—with a handsome, daring, intelligent, and loving father. And every man she had ever met paled beside him.

Every man except Logan Cafferty. Logan Cafferty was different; she saw that the first time she met him. In fact, it was Giddeon, her father, who had introduced them.

Logan hadn't been in uniform then, but in riding clothes, when, on her first morning at Nottoway, she had hurried out of the mansion for an early morning ride with her father. There her father and Logan had stood, each holding the reins of a saddled horse, talking as if they had known each other forever.

" 'Morning, Papá." She had greeted him with a kiss, then headed into the stable to saddle herself a horse. Looking back on it, even that was foolish. No one saddled his own horse at the White Castle. Slaves did it for you. Why, she'd bet Mr. Ransom couldn't count the number of slaves he owned; there must be two per guest in the house alone. No one turned a hand here—no one except the slaves.

Her father had stopped her, though. "Here's your horse, sugar. Come let me introduce you to Captain Cafferty. He has been good enough to volunteer to ride with you today."

Twirling on her boot heels, she stared first at her father, then at Logan Cafferty. "Ride with me? When have I ever needed someone to . . . ?"

10

"Captain Logan Cafferty, my daughter, Estelle. We call her Stella."

For a moment all she could do was gape at the handsome man who stood eye to eye with Giddeon Duval. Lean, fit, and rugged, he had dark, tousled hair, and as she stared he ran a callused hand through it, never taking his amused brown eyes — rich, chocolate-colored eyes, she recalled thinking, the color of the bayous in South Texas — from hers. His brows were knit, as in a frown, but she knew the gesture well. Her father's eyebrows did the same thing. Once when she was young she had asked him about it. "Comes from squinting against the glare of the open sea, sugar."

"I was not engaged as a chaperon, Miss Duval," Logan began. Stella knew even then that she would never forget the sinking feeling she experienced at the tone of his voice — casual, as if he didn't care whether she existed at all. And at his next words, she was sure he intended to excuse himself from the chore of riding with her. "Your father thought we could provide company for one another, but . . ."

"Your mother isn't feeling well, sugar," Giddeon interrupted.

At Stella's raised eyebrows, he continued. "Nothing serious. Too much dancing last night, but I promised to breakfast with her in our suite."

Stella quickly regained her composure.

"Forgive my manners, Captain. I would be pleased for your company."

Her father handed her the reins, and the men shook hands. "Good meeting you, Cafferty. I always enjoy talking about the sea; we must continue our visit later."

"By all means, Captain Duval," Logan replied, still staring at Stella. "Don't worry about your daughter. I promise to take care of her."

Not until she was in the saddle and racing along the

11

banks of the Mississippi River did Stella question her father's motives. Serita Cortinas Duval—her mother—had never been sick a day in Stella's life. Stella couldn't recall a dance ever ending so late that Serita wasn't up and running with the first cock's crow the next morning.

Looking over her shoulder, she stared at the handsome, annoying stranger. She didn't like patronizing men. She had never needed, never wanted anyone to take care of her. Yet, just looking at him quickened her heart to a wild fury.

He spurred his mount and pulled alongside her. "Tell me something."

She stared at him and opened her mouth to speak, but the words caught in her throat. She felt unbearably warm in her crimson riding jacket, yet the sun had not risen far above the horizon. Dew still glistened on the grass beneath their horses' hooves, and the dark waters of the Mississippi River rippled undisturbed. She was the one shaken. And it had nothing to do with the pastoral setting through which they rode.

When she didn't answer, he questioned, "Are you always this . . . ah, this beautiful in the morning?"

Astonished at his word choice—she had expected him to say something like willful or angry or spoiled—she laughed. "Why do you ask such a question, Captain? Is it because you are accustomed to awakening aboard ship, surrounded by grimy sailors?"

He studied her face so intently she felt the heat from her body rise up her neck and face, flushing her skin. She squirmed, embarrassed that he could see her discomfiture.

"No, Stella. It isn't that at all. I simply want to know what to expect every morning for the rest of my life."

The remainder of the week had gone by as in a whirlwind, and by the time she approached her parents on the evening before the Magnolia Ball, it wasn't to ask their permission—she already knew beyond any doubt she

12

would marry Logan Cafferty—but to gain their approval.

That, she found, she already had.

"Logan Cafferty," Giddeon had mused, a smile lighting his green eyes. "Single, never been married, twenty-six years old, second son of an old landed family up in Connecticut, always loved the sea, graduated with honors from Annapolis three years ago, stationed aboard the USS *Vermont*. No outstanding warrants, no debts . . ."

"Papá!" Aghast, she had collapsed on the settee beside her mother.

"Don't worry, dear," Serita told her. "Your young man doesn't suspect your father has spent the entire week prying into his past. And he isn't likely to find out."

"But . . . ?"

Crossing the room, Giddeon knelt before the two women in his life. He took one of each of their hands in his own. "Your mother and I love you beyond anything else in our lives, Stella, so we decided we had best learn a few things about this Captain Cafferty, before he came to me. Which is what he intends to do, I take it."

Stella's heart stopped. "How did you know?"

Serita put an arm around her daughter and squeezed her shoulders. "When two people are so obviously in love, dear . . ."

"Mamá! You mean you could tell? How ghastly! We must be the laughingstock . . ."

"Not at all, sugar."

"You haven't given anyone cause for talk," Serita assured her. "Everyone may be green with envy—"

"Everyone except your mother and me," Giddeon corrected.

As Stella watched, her parents exchanged the familiar, loving expression she had witnessed between them all her life. Now, for the first time, she knew what that look meant, how it felt to be the recipient of such affection. Her heart swelled in her breast, and she couldn't keep from laughing with the pure joy of it all.

No, she wasn't afraid her father would refuse Logan's request to marry her, but why was he taking so long? Talking about the sea, she supposed.

Outside the music room, she paced up and down the hallway, then stared toward the window leading to the upstairs gallery, from where one could rock in wicker chairs and watch the Mississippi River roll by. Finally, she sat on one of the settees placed along the wall beneath several generations of family portraits—the Hall of Ancestors, the Ransoms called it. A couple of guests whom she did not recognize sat across the hall, and snatches of their conversation reached her: Mr. Lincoln's nomination for president of the United States and the likelihood of war, should he win the election. War. The topic on everyone's lips, on everyone's mind—everyone's except hers and Logan's.

Then a gust of wind rustled her skirts, and she turned to see him step through the open window and stride toward her. Without a word he grabbed her arm and nearly dragged her down the hall, down the stairs, through the crowded foyer, and out into the gardens. The night air cooled her bare shoulders, but inside she stewed.

"What happened?" she asked for the third time.

Finally, when they left behind the other strollers, he pulled her beneath the spreading limbs of a magnolia tree, turned her to face him, and covered her lips with his own, still gripping her shoulders in his palms.

The scent of magnolias filled the air. Strains from the quartet in the ballroom mingled with laughter and chattering voices, drifting to them on the soft night breeze. Stella heard none of it. Desperately she pulled his hands from her shoulders, her lips from his, and drew back.

"Logan Cafferty! Tell me what he said."

The evening was dark, his face in shadow, which made his silence all the more unbearable. Finally, he spoke.

"He won't give us an answer until I visit Los Olmos."

14

"I don't understand," she stammered. "He approves of you. He told me so."

"It isn't me he's worried about; it's his little girl."

She took a deep breath, incensed at the words—Papá's or Logan's, it didn't matter which. "I am nobody's little girl. I can make my own decisions, and I want to marry you, and . . ."

Logan hushed her with his lips, this time a deep, sensual, caressing kiss from which she withdrew with reluctance. The problem at hand was of utmost importance, however.

"Was he awful to you?"

"No, princess, he wasn't awful. He was honest. He loves you; I respect that. I love you, and he knows it. We'll still be married. I will visit Los Olmos at Christmas . . ."

Disappointment clouded her happiness, and she buried her head in his chest. "Then we can't announce our engagement before I leave," she sighed. "And Christmas is so far away. What if the war . . . ?"

"The war?" Gently he lifted her chin so she faced him. "Even if Lincoln is elected, there won't be a war. A few states may rebel, but it won't amount to a hill of beans. Come on now. You haven't worried over all this talk of war before. Nothing is changed."

She sighed. "I know. But anything that would keep us apart is . . . I mean, I can't bear to be separated from you until Christmas. Why don't you come home with us tomorrow?"

Clasping her face in his hands, he kissed her lips, then her nose and each eye in turn. "Desert the Navy, you mean?"

"Oh, Logan. Why can't you sail on an ordinary ship? Why must it be military? At Los Olmos we never involve ourselves in political disputes or wars."

He brushed a ringlet of blond hair back from her face. "Of course, you don't. Where else could a princess reside, but in paradise?"

He lowered his lips to hers and she gave herself up to the urgency of his kiss, to her own overwhelming need to touch and be touched, to kiss and be kissed . . . to love and be loved by this man. His lips, moist and gentle, caressed hers, awakening her body to new and urgent yearnings; his hands on her bare shoulders set her skin ablaze, as though a brilliant star twinkled from each and every pore. And when he moved his lips down her chin to her neck and cupped her body to his, she felt suddenly faint with the sheer want of this passionate man.

Logan himself had never wanted to make love to a woman as badly as he did this woman, at this time, and in this place. In fact, the only thing he had ever experienced that was stronger than his immediate rush of passion was his desire to love, to honor, and to protect Stella Duval. She was like a priceless jewel he had sworn to protect, like an ethereal creature sent to him from above, whom he would love and honor the rest of his life.

But the taste of her magnolia-scented skin proved a heady aphrodisiac, luring him further and further away from his senses. Her fingers twined in his hair, her hands pressed his lips to the base of her throat, and when her bosom swelled against him, he slipped a hand inside the low-cut bodice of her gown and lifted one breast from its nest of satin magnolia leaves. For a moment he was conscious only of the reaction of her body to his lips, to his tongue. Her labored breathing sounded like the cheering of a crowd, urging him onward . . . onward.

And his own mind joined the chorus, imagining some place deeper into the night, farther into the trees . . .

It had been done before, certainly. By lovers enjoying a moment of passion; by himself, even . . .

But never with a princess. Lifting his lips, he pulled her dress back into position.

"Don't stop . . ." she whispered. "Please . . ."

16

Logan inhaled, held his breath a moment to steady his racing heart, then exhaled. "Like you said earlier . . ."—pausing, he tried again to find his voice—". . . there must be a better time and place."

"But tomorrow I'm leaving. . . ."

"I know, princess. God, how I know, but . . ." He kissed the tip of her nose, conscious now of the strength he needed to resist making love to this woman.

She clutched him tightly around the waist and pressed her face to his chest. "Christmas is so far away. I don't think I can wait. I don't want to . . ."

Burying his lips in her hair a moment, he finally drew back and looked into her face. "It will be worth it. I promise you that."

With a finger, she traced his cheek, his nose. When she touched his lips, he took her finger into his mouth, and she felt faint at the sensuousness of it. "Then we will be married at Christmas at Los Olmos," she whispered.

Thoughtfully, he removed her finger from his mouth, and holding both her hands in his, he pressed his lips to them. "If you still want me."

"Want you? I will want you the rest of my life! What made you say such a thing?"

"Your father told me how much Los Olmos means to you. He said he and your mother got off to a rough start because he didn't understand how much she loved Los Olmos. That's why he wants me to visit the ranch before he gives his blessing."

"That doesn't make sense," she demanded. "Why would Papá . . . ?"

"It makes perfect sense," he responded. "I have never been on a ranch in my life. The sea is my . . ."—pausing, he pierced her with his chocolate-brown eyes before correcting himself—"the sea *was* my life. What if I don't . . . I mean, if I can't live confined on a ranch somewhere in Texas, what will you do?"

17

She struggled with his words, and when at last they registered in her brain, she laughed and threw her arms around his neck. "Logan Cafferty, can't you see how much I love you? Nothing will ever separate us—certainly not a ranch in Texas, nor even Mr. Lincoln and this dreadful talk of war."

She felt him relax against her. Had he really questioned her feelings? Seductively, she moved her lips to his and kissed him desperately. Then, lifting them a smidgen, she mumbled against his skin. "Now, where were we when you interrupted us with all that nonsense?"

With a heavy sigh, he pulled her to him and held her tightly against his own rampant desires, and hers. Finally, he took her by the shoulders. "It's time we returned to the ball."

"Do we have to?"

He nodded, solemn, pushing back, far back in his mind, the fact that they would not have another private moment for six months. "You did tell me dancing is your passion."

By now they were on the gravel walkway approaching the White Castle, whose windows glowed with the festiveness of the occasion. Another couple passed, and she stared wistfully after them.

"That was before I met you," she whispered.

By the time she boarded the sternwheeler *River Queen* the next morning, Stella's emotions were in a tumbled-up state. Determined that Logan's last vision of her not be one of a blubbering female, she had forced her spirits up by thinking and talking only of December, of a Christmas wedding, and not of how long the time was between now and then.

They had danced the night away, and the early morning hours as well, twirling about the dance floor in a frenzy

18

that resembled their secret — or not so secret — longings.

By morning when she awoke — if the word *awakening* applied to two hours of tossing and turning in a semiconscious state — her only thought was to dress and spend every remaining moment of her stay at Nottoway with Logan Cafferty.

Her trunks and belongings had already been carried to the levee, everything except the traveling costume she would wear today and the tapestry satchel for her nightgown and toilet articles. She dressed quickly. Then, distressed by the dark circles under her eyes, she took a few precious moments to apply a compress of cool lemon water to her face.

The costume she chose would be warm this late in the season, but she knew it looked good on her, and today that was the only consideration. The way he saw her today would be the way he remembered her for the next six months. When she descended the stairs into the grand foyer and he stepped forward to offer his arm, she knew she had chosen well.

Her black merino skirt was full, pleated onto a band that dropped to a point over her flat stomach. The rounded collar on her white chemisette was accented with a brief black satin tie and a row of small black onyx buttons. Over it went a red velvet bolero banded and trimmed with black braid. In her hand she carried a floppy-brimmed black hat.

"Are we off to a fiesta?" he teased, recalling how she had told him her part of Texas was more Mexican in culture than southern.

"You are dressed for travel, too," she replied, thinking she had never seen a more handsome man than Logan Cafferty. He looked every bit the captain today in his blue uniform, his brass gleaming, his boots polished to a high shine.

He escorted her into the enormous dining room. "Might

as well head on back to my ship."

She glanced at him when he seated her at the least occupied end of the table. Although breakfast was not a seated meal, it was rare to dine alone, since the Ransoms entertained so many guests. She had hoped, but had not really expected, to find the room unoccupied.

"I thought you didn't have to report back to the *Vermont* for another week."

He took a swallow of coffee a maid poured and tried to answer lightly. "What's a castle without a princess?"

They ate in silence. She had a million things she wanted to say to him, but not the heart to speak. Around them the other guests chattered on, as from outside an enclosure. Suddenly the whistle of the sternwheeler cut through the stillness like the swipe of a saber, and she jumped. Her cup rattled when she set it back in its saucer.

Logan covered her hand with his. "It's all right, princess." When he felt her hand tremble, he pulled her to her feet and they left the room.

In the foyer people seemed to come from every direction, headed for the levee either to board the vessel or to greet it. He led her out the front door and down the steps. Before them, she saw Giddeon and Serita, headed for the ship.

In the next moment Logan drew her behind the lilac hedge, turned on his heel to face her, and she came into his arms. Tears formed behind her eyes, but she fought them back. She would not cry. Not today. At least not until he couldn't see her.

Then their lips met and her worries fled before the rush of joy she felt in his arms. His tender, loving lips, his strong, gentle arms, his straightforward manner that often left her speechless. How she would miss him these next six months!

The whistle blared again, this time much louder, since they were outside the thick walls of the White Castle. Logan tightened his arms around her. "Time," he mumbled against her lips.

She swallowed back her anxieties and, with great effort, smiled. "Until Christmas."

He nodded, silent.

"Don't you dare not come."

Taking her hat from her hands, he put it on her head, and with earnestness in both his words and actions, he tied the ribbons beneath her chin. "Don't *you* dare not wait for me."

One more kiss, quick now lest their emotions get the best of them, then they returned to the path, where he escorted her to the waiting ship with all the dignity inherent in a United States military officer. She walked beside him, proud and happy and very, very sad.

At the levee, after she thanked the Ransoms and said good-bye to the other guests, she stood on tiptoe and without a thought to propriety kissed him on the lips. His fingers brushed her waist, steadying her, tormenting her. Then she hurried to the gangplank.

Once there, however, a last precaution came to mind, so she hurried back to him, holding her hat on her head with one hand.

They searched each other's eyes; she bit her lip to still her trembling. "I meant what I told you, Logan. Please don't . . . I mean, after I'm gone . . . please don't think I didn't mean it. *Whither thou goest . . .*"

Chapter One

Matagorda Island, Texas
October 25, 1863

Stella Duval clutched a steel beam inside the lantern room of the Matagorda Lighthouse, waiting for the muscles in her legs to stop burning from her mad dash to the top. "It must be a thousand steps, straight up," she said between gasps for breath.

"Ninety-six," responded Captain James Cummings, the lighthouse keeper. "But I don't run 'em, and neither should you. You get light-headed and fall over the edge, it's one hundred and five feet straight down."

What a boring life when one was forced to count steps and distances, she thought, concentrating on efforts to steady her breathing. The only excitement in a lightkeeper's life would likely be the threat of falling over the edge of the lighthouse or down the stairwell. Especially on a night like this, with the wind whipping around the tower like children playing hide-and-seek; a black night, eerie now, with the clouds and fog blown away in the storm. At least, she couldn't see the ground below—one hundred and five feet below.

And she certainly did not intend to step out on the walkway and chance being blown off in the gale. Such a night should keep the Federal patrol boats off the coast, though. "Has the signal come?"

"Not yet." The lightkeeper held a small lantern to reveal her face. "Are you alone?"

"My vaqueros remained below with the boat. We will return to the mainland as soon as the signal comes."

"You shouldn't have come, nohow. This business is too dangerous for a woman."

She sighed. "Are you sure we will be able to see the signal?"

"Yep. Not all the way from Half Moon Reef," he corrected. "That's near to twenty miles off; their lens is only a fourth-order, won't reach over twelve miles on a good night. Runners on the peninsula will relay the signal to the boys at Fort Esperanza, what there are left of them."

Fort Esperanza, she thought. A fancy name for the earthen works that served as the only protection for Captain Shea's artillery battery. "Where have the men gone?"

"Inland. You haven't heard of ol' Jeb Magruder's orders to destroy the railroad between here and Victoria? Thinks it'll keep the Yankees from coming ashore."

"I heard. That's all everyone's talking about." She pulled her worries back to those at hand. "The beacon won't be seen in the Gulf?"

Cummings didn't answer; he didn't need to. Both knew full well that Federal patrol boats could see the light of a swinging lantern if they were near enough; they could certainly see lighthouse beacons, and from a greater distance.

Forcibly, Stella gripped her emotions. War was war, and a determination of steel was required to carry it forth. Especially when her father's life was at risk, should the Federals capture the blockade runners this night.

If he wasn't already held prisoner on some Federal ship somewhere in the Gulf of Mexico. Giddeon was two days overdue. But of course it wasn't the first time. In the year or more since he began running cotton for the Confederacy through the inland waterways along the Texas coast, she had learned not to panic when he didn't appear on

24

schedule. So many factors were involved in his trips: Not only must he get the cotton to market in Matamoros or Bagdad, undetected by the Federals, but he must reload his schooner, the *Serita Cortinas,* with munitions, clothing, and medicine for the South. At any point along the way he could be detained by legitimate causes — or he could be captured by Federals. She tried not to think about the latter, but when she did, she prayed even harder for a speedy end to this dreadful war.

The twenty wagon loads of cotton she brought from Alleyton this trip waited behind hastily erected brush barriers along the shores outside Indianola. How long the cargo could remain undiscovered by Federal patrol boats was anybody's guess. Certainly not indefinitely.

"How much time do we have before the next patrol boat?" she asked.

"Three, four hours, I'd say. They won't venture into these sandbars and reefs until daybreak — not in a storm like this." He began to unfold the tarpaulins she brought. "Sad state of affairs when young women have to help fight our wars."

She worked with him, stretching the tarpaulins over two sides of the lantern room. "It's a sad state when we have wars at all." Sighing heavily, she thought of Logan Cafferty — her beloved Logan, whom she had not seen since she sailed away from the levee at Nottoway Plantation so long ago — and of Giddeon Duval, her equally adored father. "When the Federals fired upon our home, with no provocation whatsoever, they destroyed part of our house and killed my cousin's wife. What else were we to do but fight?"

"Head inland," Cummings suggested. "Away from the hostilities. Leastways, the womenfolk."

Stella smiled in the pitch-black room. "Papá needs me. Now that the Mississippi River is in the hands of the Federals, the South can't survive without the Cotton Road."

"Humph! The South can't survive nohow. Why, they don't even have enough horses for the men to ride. First, they dismount the cavalry to send the horses east, now I hear they're setting up a training center to teach our Texas boys how to *walk*. Beats me . . ."

"To march," Stella interrupted. "We came through Camp McCulloch on our way here."

"Bet they don't have none of Terrell's Cavalry at McCulloch. Heard them boys rode their horses home to the frontier. Said they'd rather fight Indians on horseback than Yankees afoot."

"They're calling it a mutiny." Stella concentrated on her work. Soon the two of them had the black tarpaulins attached to the east and west sides of the lantern room, shielding the six-foot Fresnel lens from the Gulf of Mexico. "Do you think it will work?"

"Should. Unless one of them Yankee captains has been tipped off. A man'd have to be looking in the exact spot to see our beam tonight."

Following his directions, Stella held a small hand-carried lamp while the lightkeeper poured fuel into the enormous lantern. "Have you seen the new Federal ship?" she asked. "The one they are rumored to have brought straight from their victory at Vicksburg?"

"Nope. Not that I recognized, nohow. My idea is they'll keep it farther east — New Orleans or maybe Mobile."

Stella laughed. "Especially since Dick Dowling showed them what we're capable of in Texas. They won't soon forget him capturing two gunboats and taking three hundred prisoners. . . ."

"Three hundred fifty," Cummings corrected.

"And him with only forty-seven men. They won't be so fast to jump on one of our ships from now on. That should make things safer for Papá and the other blockade runners."

Captain Cummings capped his jug of kerosene. "You sit

26

tight, now, while I go down and wind the mechanism, then we'll be ready when the all clear comes from Half Moon Reef. Stick your head outside the tarp so you can see the signal if it comes while I'm gone. I won't be long."

Stella sank to the steel-plate floor and stared intently toward Matagorda Peninsula. If the lighthouse at Half Moon Reef was unoccupied by Federal troops, the light-keeper was to signal with one beam of his Fresnel lens. Men stationed on the peninsula would relay the signal by hand-held lanterns, then Captain Cummings would sweep the Laguna Madre Channel south of Pass Cavallo with one beam from his larger lens, signaling Giddeon the coast was clear of Federals. By draping all sides of the lantern room except the one facing the inland waterway, they might—if their luck held—escape notice of the Federal patrol boats that had blockaded the Gulf of Mexico for the past two and a half years.

She listened to the captain lumber down the steel staircase that wound like a serpent through the inside of the lighthouse. To keep from worrying over Giddeon and the fact that Pass Cavallo was the only way into or out of Matagorda Bay, and that once he sailed inside the bay to reach Indianola, he would be a prime target for Federal blockade enforcers—especially with most of the men from Fort Esperanza away—she concentrated on the business at hand, going over for at least the hundredth time the messages she must remember to give him: Mr. Ransom needed immediate confirmation on the blockade-running ship to be built at Titlum-Tatlum near Velasco; twenty additional wagon loads of cotton were ready for shipment as soon as he could arrange for ships to pick them up; they needed more wagons; and the Dance brothers were awaiting confirmation on the order of munitions.

She patted the leather pouch hanging from a strap around her shoulder. None of these things was she likely to forget, nor would she fail to give him the orders from Gen-

27

eral Magruder. All were too important to the Confederacy.

Ever since July, when Vicksburg, Mississippi, fell to the Federals, the grapevine had buzzed with reports they were strengthening their hold on all Gulf ports. Rumor had it they were sending one of their "heroes" from the battle at Vicksburg to ramrod things along the Texas coast.

As always when this thought entered her brain, her heart froze. Where was Logan? How was he? She prayed he was alive and well and far, far from the Texas coastline. With Giddeon running cotton . . .

The thought of their facing each other in battle terrified her as nothing else could, short of losing either of them. Absently she withdrew Logan's letter from the leather pouch and held it to her heart in the darkness. Her trembling began to still, remembering his words. Dated April 1862, one month after the battle of the ironclad ships *Monitor* and *Merrimac,* it was the last communication she received from him. She no longer needed a light by which to read its message, she knew the words by heart. "My Darling Princess," the letter began. As always, the thought of him calling her "princess" brought a smile to her lips. If he could see her now, he would know she had been right that night at the Magnolia Ball when she told him she wasn't a princess. What would he say now, if he could . . . Tears blurred her vision. If he could see her now . . . *Would that he could see her now!*

Since the battle just past, my country seems to think I am valuable. Another promotion, when I would give them all to be by your side. My steadfast love for you has forced me to acknowledge the danger we would bring each other by continued communication. Should one of our messages fall into the wrong hands, who knows to what lengths either government would go. And were I to be labeled a traitor for consorting with the "enemy," such a judgment would

28

bring shame upon your beloved name. Please know that were it possible I would post a message to you each and every day, if for no other reason than to express my love for you. One day soon the rebellion will be put down; then I will hurry to Los Olmos, and we will be married on the very day I arrive.

If we have anything left of Los Olmos after this dreadful war, she thought, bitterness suffusing her loneliness. Already the Federals had sailed into Los Olmos Bay and fired at the house. Oh, it had been a strange sight, she knew, with a structure resembling the bridge of a ship sitting on its roof. Her mother had it built that way so her father would not feel so lonely for the sea. And now it was gone. Papá tried to reassure them, saying the Federals must have thought they were attacking a ship at sea, what with the way the house was built, and the fact that the land and sea often appeared merged into one on the sandy prairie stretching between the Los Olmos ranch house and the Gulf of Mexico. Nevertheless, a treasured part of their home was now destroyed by the hand of the Federals. And worse, a thousand times worse, a treasured member of their family, Alicia, her cousin Jorge's wife, the mother of two adorable children, now lay in the family plot. What a war! What a damnable war! The letter continued:

Until then, I rest easier knowing you are safely tucked away at your ranch, untouched by the strife. How far-sighted of your ancestors to proclaim their hacienda off limits to man's violence. Until we meet again, the vision of your loveliness sustains me, and I remain

Your loving husband-to-be,
Colonel Logan M. Cafferty, USMC

The vision of your loveliness . . . If he could see her

29

now—her hands as rough as the bark of a mesquite tree, her skin weathered like a steerhide . . . If he could see her now. She recalled his concern that she might not want him once he visited Los Olmos. Now she could well wonder the same thing about him.

But oh, to have the chance! If she could see him now . . .

She ran her fingers over the worn paper, caressing each fold and tear. She hoped the letter would outlast . . .

A light flickered in the darkness, once . . . twice . . . three times . . .

Then it was gone.

With one movement, she returned the letter to her pouch and jumped to her feet. At the stairs, she almost collided with Captain Cummings.

"It's clear." Her heart thumped wildly against the rough cotton of her shirt. "No Federals in Matagorda Bay."

Captain Cummings edged past her and set his lantern on the floor. "Then it's time to signal your father."

"*¡Andale, Raul!*" Stella wiped the misty rain from her face. "Hurry! Row faster! We must make Indianola before Papá!"

Within moments after Captain Cummings flashed the beam of his Fresnel lens down the Laguna Madre Channel, an answering light flashed back.

He had come! Thanking the lightkeeper, Stella had dashed down the stairs, his warning echoing after her in the hollow structure. Papá had come! The Yankees hadn't. And they still had a good three hours before daybreak.

With both Raul and Francisco rowing, they made it through Pass Cavallo and around the point of the mainland before they heard the approach of the *Serita Cortinas*. Stella didn't worry over her father's navigating the sandbar-infested channel in the dark, not even in a storm such as this. He was the best sailor she had ever known.

30

Wind tossed her short curls, and she pulled her jacket closer. A tantalizing question came to mind: Was Papá a better sailor than Logan Cafferty? Probably, she decided, but only because he was more experienced. Logan would catch up, given time.

The bow of the boat bumped against the shore; her heart thudded in her chest. *Given time . . .*

She took Raul's offered hand and let him help her out of the boat. She had given up trying to do much actual work when he was around. The son of her mother's cousin, Rosaria, Raul was one year younger than Stella herself. His presence with the wagon trains was Giddeon's idea. Stella was to oversee the cotton shipments, but Raul was to watch over Stella—Raul and her teamsters, made up for the most part of Los Olmos vaqueros.

"You can leave tonight, Raul," she said. "With luck you will be in time for the birth of your first child."

"Yes," he answered. "I shall be glad to see Carmen again. I hope the baby has waited. . . ."

"Babies don't wait. You should know that. Let's get the cotton unloaded. If we have it ready to load on the *Serita Cortinas* by the time Papá arrives, we can both get started toward home sooner."

"You will be happy to return to Los Olmos, too."

She stared toward the approaching schooner. "The only thing I will be truly happy for is an end to this war."

By the time Giddeon drew his schooner alongside the docks south of Indianola, about half the eight hundred bales of cotton had been stacked beside the Indianola wharf. Since four hundred bales was the *Serita Cortinas*'s limit, Stella planned to haul the remainder to Los Olmos and await her father's return.

Giddeon provided another solution.

"The *Nueces* is following an hour or so behind," he told Stella. "Her skipper and crew are new to blockade running, so this was a good opportunity to show them the way

31

around the sandbars and clay banks. She's carrying a light load—wool blankets and military shoes. Won't take long to unload."

Stella and Giddeon stood to the leeward side of a grove of oak trees, shielding their lantern from the wind. He perused the papers she brought, while both his crew and hers unloaded his cargo and reloaded the *Serita Cortinas* with the bales of cotton she had brought overland from Alleyton. Only it was no longer the *Serita Cortinas,* she observed.

"The *Marseillaise?*" she questioned.

Giddeon cleared his throat. "I'll be . . . ah, taking this load to Havana, under a French flag. Thought a French name . . ."

"Papá! Don't take a chance like that. Please. There are plenty of other ships."

"No, sugar, there aren't. General Magruder's report here confirms what I already suspected. The Federals have sent a new fleet to the lower Gulf, supported by a special unit of marines and a speedy flagship they call the *Victory.*"

"That's all the more reason for you not to take a chance," she argued. "Our old schooner is no match for a ship like that, no matter how many times you rename it. Please . . ."

Giddeon put his arm around her shoulders. "Don't worry, sugar. You know the neutrality laws. The Federals aren't allowed to touch a ship from a foreign nation, as long as it isn't headed directly for or away from a blockaded port. I'll leave from Bagdad and return there. . . ."

Delos, Giddeon's first mate, interrupted them. "The medicines have been loaded in separate wagons, Gid, like you asked."

With a nod Giddeon turned to Stella. "Now, young lady, I want you to get going. I'm afraid I have one more job for you."

Fleetingly, Stella thought of home . . . of her mother

. . . of hot meals and a bath and a soft bed.

"I won't be able to meet Ransom in Alleyton," Giddeon continued. "You'll have to do it for me. If there were any other way . . ."

"Now it's your turn not to worry, Papá. Alleyton may be teeming with speculators and soldiers, but they're Southerners. And since I'm the only one who can represent you personally to Mr. Ransom, besides Mamá . . ."

"Believe me, that's the only reason I'm sending you. This will be your last mission. . . ."

"Shouldn't I haul the cotton that is already in Alleyton awaiting shipment?"

Giddeon sighed. "Yes, I suppose so. Then let Ransom handle it from here on out. He should have moved his slaves and much of his business to Texas by this time." He handed her a packet of papers to put in her leather pouch. "These are the papers he will need—names and places—people who can be counted on to contribute to our cause, safe houses, alternate routes."

They walked toward the dock as they talked. Delos approached them again. "We've taken on about all we can hold, Gid. Our belly's already dragging the sand."

"Then let's sail." He turned to hug Stella.

"What about the new blockade-running ship?" she asked. "Are those papers in here, too?"

"No, that project is too valuable to . . ." His words dissolved into the stormy night. He squeezed her to him and she knew his thoughts.

"Don't worry, Papá! Nothing is going to happen to me. What do you want me to tell Mr. Ransom?"

"Tell him to order the ship. I'll send the profits from this load to cover the down payment, even if . . ."

"What?" she prompted.

"Even if I have to make a deal with the Yankees."

"Papá! You wouldn't do such . . ."

"To buy a vessel that can outrun the *Victory?* You bet I

would. One or two loads of cotton won't go far in helping the Federals win this war, but one modern blockade-running ship . . ."

Stella threw her arms around his neck. "Oh, Papá! I hate this war and what it's doing to us! I'm so afraid for you . . . and for . . ." She buried her face in his shoulder. ". . . and for Logan."

"I know, sugar, I know."

"What do you think has happened to him? How will I ever know?"

"When I get to Bagdad, I'll make inquiries. I won't return until Christmas; by then, perhaps we will have some answers. You can hold out that long, can't you?"

She squared her shoulders. "Yes . . . since I don't have a choice."

Home for Christmas, she thought, watching the newly christened *Marseillaise* edge away from the dock in the darkness. How many Christmases had she been waiting for Logan? This year she was reduced to awaiting news of him.

"Come on, Stella," Raul called. "Giddeon said to get these medicines on the road to Victoria and Alleyton."

"Send the first three wagons ahead," she told him. "Then you go home to Carmen. I will wait for the *Nueces.*"

"Giddeon said . . ."

"I know what he said," she retorted. "But I'm running this wagon train. And it's my job to ship the entire cargo. You heard him say the *Nueces*'s crew is untrained. They may need help."

She laughed, hearing Raul sigh. "Go ahead. If you hurry you might be in time to hear your first son's first cry."

"Giddeon expects me to stay with you."

"And the buyers who sent their cotton on this train expect me to return to Alleyton with their supplies. Besides, what can possibly happen to me from here to Alleyton? We will circle the bay and go through Camp McCulloch. Francisco and Beto will watch my every step, just as they have done my entire life. . . ."

"You're as hardheaded as always, cousin Estelle," Raul fussed, using her baptismal name. "That's why Giddeon wanted a family member along, instead of all vaqueros. You have always had your way with them."

Stella laughed. "I suppose I have. But this time, I promise not to get anyone into a jam—at least not one we can't get out of."

Raul left for Corpus Christi, the loaded wagons were started on their journey, and the hours wore on. The storm played itself out and daybreak threatened. Still the *Nueces* did not arrive.

"Come, Francisco," Stella said at last, "we must row over to the pass with lanterns. An unseasoned crew can get into all sorts of trouble—not only with sandbars and clay banks; they could take the wrong turn in the dark and sail into the Gulf. We certainly don't want a Federal crew to end up with blankets intended to keep our Confederate boys warm this winter."

Francisco and Beto rowed, and Stella sat in the center of the small boat. As they pulled away from the dock she glanced back at the black shadows of the freighters she had left behind to load the remainder of their cotton onto the *Nueces* when it arrived. Light from her lantern danced with abandon over the choppy waves, then flashed across the channel. Instantly she knew her worst fears had come true. Francisco had other ideas.

"Wait up, Beto," Francisco whispered hoarsely. "That might be a Federal boat."

"It is no Federal boat." Stella stared at the towering hulk of the sailing vessel they approached. Already it listed dangerously to starboard. "It's the *Nueces.* Not only did they hang up on a sandbar, but they did it right in the middle of Pass Cavallo. *¡Andale!* We must hurry to help them before daybreak."

When they came nearer the ship, Francisco hailed its crew, who, upon hearing assurances that Francisco and Beto worked for Giddeon Duval, tossed down a Jacob's ladder.

The climb up the knotted rope ladder proved more steady than Stella had expected, due, she supposed, to the *Nueces* being deeply embedded in the sand. They stepped on deck to the accompaniment of coarse oaths from the blustering skipper, Captain D.F. Moore.

"Pardon me, miss," Moore said when the light from the lantern touched Stella's face, "but this is the dangdest trip I've ever made. Once I get shut from this sandbar, I'm shucking the coast like an oyster. I'd rather fight Yankees than this here sandbar-riddled waterway."

"If we don't get you unstuck before the tide goes out, Captain, we may all be fighting Yankees right here in Pass Cavallo." She sent Beto back to the mainland.

"Bring as many boats as you can find along the dock," she instructed.

Captain Moore studied the sinking bow of his vessel. "Even in the storm your pa had no trouble. He threaded his vessel in and out around them sandbars like there was nothing to it."

"Papá has been traveling this waterway for almost twenty-five years. He is as familiar with the location of the sandbars and clay banks as he is with the resacas in Los Olmos pastures."

He scratched his head. "I picked up speed after meeting him an hour or so back. He said the way was clear on into Indianola."

It would have been, she thought, if he had kept to the waterway and not tried to go into the Gulf. She held her tongue, and two hours later, Captain Moore agreed it was the speed that got him in trouble. "Hell! This thing'll likely stay stuck till the war's over."

"Or longer," Stella agreed, thinking instead of time, irrevocably slipping away, and of the ten remaining wagons loaded with cotton back at Indianola. She couldn't let them sit there in open daylight with no ship to carry them down the coast.

Quickly then, she consulted with Francisco, who agreed they should send Beto and nine other teamsters on to Brownsville with the cotton.

"Contact Pryor Lea, Confederate agent in Brownsville," she instructed Beto when he returned with the extra boats only to find himself sent on another journey. "Tell him what happened and secure his help in getting the cotton to Matamoros. Meet us back in Alleyton when you finish."

Returning her attention to the *Nueces*, she lost no time in apprising Captain Moore of the situation.

"We are already stranded by low tide, and we cannot depend on the fog to hold more than a couple more hours," she told him. "Let's get the cargo unloaded and row as much of it as we can to shore before daybreak."

Captain Moore ordered his men to begin stacking crates beside the rail, while she called the small boats to the ship. All hands worked feverishly to unload the supplies of blankets and military shoes.

"Take them directly across the pass to the mainland," Stella instructed the men who left with the first loads. "After we unload the *Nueces*, we will find someone in Indianola to store the provisions until we can procure enough wagons."

As soon as an empty boat returned to the *Nueces*, Stella and her vaqueros, assisted by Moore and his crew, loaded it with goods and sent it back across the channel.

"We will take the most important things first," she said, as time slipped irrevocably away. "Although heaven knows, every single blanket and every pair of shoes is important to some poor soldier."

They spoke little; each person concentrated on the job at hand. The thought of a Federal patrol boat was etched on each person's brain, held in place, Stella thought, by the enveloping fog, by the din created by the surf lapping at the sides of the *Nueces* and by the instructions of the men one to another, all of which seemed to act like nails holding a coffin lid in place. Surely the Federals could hear them from whatever the distance.

The fog lifted by degrees, and before Stella realized it, she was working by a pale morning light rather than by lanterns. She surveyed the stacks of crates to be taken ashore.

"We're about half finished," Captain Moore said.

Turning, Stella looked at the captain for the first time, and what she saw caused her mouth to drop open and brought such a look of terror to her face that all who saw it turned to stare in the same direction.

Not fifty yards beyond the *Nueces* a Federal cutter churned its way toward them. The man in charge stood, legs apart for balance, staring directly at her, or so it seemed. She supposed he was the captain, for his uniform almost dripped with gold braid; she had the sinking feeling she would soon find out.

"Cover your head, señorita," Francisco advised. "Do not let them discover you are a woman."

Stella took a woolen cap from her pocket and pulled it over her head. She wished for her gun, which lay alongside her leather pouch on a hatch cover at midship. She started toward it. Then suddenly the man standing in the boat called through cupped hands.

"We are prepared to board. Throw your weapons to the deck. Consider yourselves under arrest. . . ."

Stella felt movement to her right, but before she could so much as glance that way, the officer in the boat raised his gun and fired. The explosion was deafening, and she watched in horror as one of Captain Moore's crew slumped to his knees, then toppled. A stream of blood trickled from his mouth and pooled on the deck.

No one else challenged the Federal sailors, and they boarded the *Nueces* without further incident. Under orders of Captain Blakesborough, as he identified himself, his men began a thorough search of both the *Nueces* and its crew. The captain stationed two men with carbines to port to await the arrival of any other blockade runners.

Francisco stood like a shield in front of Stella, and when the searching sailors came nearer, he whispered to her.

"Move behind me, señorita, so you can change places with those they have already searched."

The plan would have worked, she thought later, if she had been quicker . . . just as the entire operation would have worked if the fog had held, or if the night had been longer, or if the *Nueces* hadn't run aground in the middle of the pass.

The sailor who pulled her from behind Francisco was short and stout. When Francisco challenged him, the sailor backhanded the old vaquero across the face with a blow that sent him sprawling. The captain saw the commotion and came to his sailor's aid.

"What's the problem?"

"No problem, sir." The sailor spat to the deck, then pulled Stella into the open. "He was trying to protect this little reb. I wonder why?" As he spoke, the sailor began to pat her down. "What're you hiding, reb?"

Quickly, Stella sidestepped before he had no more than brushed her breasts. He wrenched her arm, pulling her back to face him. His eyes gleamed. She struggled to free herself, but he held her fast.

That one touch had been enough. The sailor yanked her cap off, revealing a head full of springing blond curls. His eyes traversed her face, then dropped to her body. "Takes more'n short hair and man's clothing to disguise so much woman. . . ."

She cringed.

"Leave the señorita alone," Francisco demanded.

"Señorita?" The sailor closed one hand over the collar of Stella's shirt. "Not with that blond hair, she ain't."

"What's going on here?" Captain Blakesborough pushed the sailor aside. He stared at Stella through the dim morning light. Even though she wore several layers of clothing—a chemise, a shirt, and a heavy canvas jacket—she felt naked before his eyes. The mist and fog, combined with the strenuous work of loading the boats, had left her wet from the skin out, and she had the unsettling feeling her wet clothing revealed too much of her body. She resisted the impulse to look down at her chest.

"He called her señorita," the sailor mocked.

"Hmm . . ." The captain stared her with such avarice that Stella began to tremble. Then he took her arm from the sailor and pulled her toward him. "Look what our nets drew in today, men. A rebel wench."

"Leave her alone!" Francisco shouted, only to be rewarded by another blow to his face.

"Take him away," the captain ordered. He drew Stella toward the light, where he scrutinized her face and ran his fingers through her hair. "Like the sailor said, it takes more than short hair and man's clothing to disguise . . ."

She winced at the feel of his hand on her skin. "I am *not* in disguise."

He pulled her hair to its three-inch length. "Not in disguise? A new fashion for wenches, I suppose?"

"A new fashion for blockade runners!" She kicked at his shin, but he sidestepped, grinning.

"We'll deal with the blockade running later. What you need right now, reb, is a bath." His mouth curled in a grin that set the roots of her hair on edge. "How 'bout if I throw you overboard and let my men wash you off for me?

40

You might taste a bit salty, but . . ."

"Captain?" The voice was polite but firm; the tone moderate, yet somehow it demanded attention.

"What is it, Jacobs?"

"With all respect, Captain, you know how the colonel feels about treatment of prisoners, and . . . well . . . he is aboard the *Victory.*"

Captain Blakesborough's eyes hardened; his hand gripped Stella's arm as if it were frozen there.

The man called Jacobs spoke again. "You know how ready he is to write up a report, never minding the black marks he puts down will likely ruin a man's career." Stella was sure she would forever recall the savage look that passed over the captain's face at the sailor's words.

"I mean, sir, a man like yourself, with such a promising career . . ."

"Enough, Ensign Jacobs! Enough!"

Chapter Two

USS Victory — *Gulf of Mexico*

Colonel Logan Cafferty heard the commotion even before Captain Blakesborough opened the door to his private quarters, unannounced, and tossed a frayed leather pouch onto the desk in front of him.

"We hit the jackpot tonight, Cafferty. Jacobs found this lying on a hatch cover, like it was nothing. Claims the documents inside look official." As usual, Dar Blakesborough's voice seethed with insolence when he addressed Logan.

There had been no love lost between the two of them, Logan knew, even before he committed the unquestionable sin of switching from the Navy to the Marine Corps; that he later received a promotion to colonel and a special assignment in the western Gulf of Mexico requiring him to be stationed on board Dar Blakesborough's ship added fuel to their discontent.

Blakesborough continued, counting off the night's take as though itemizing booty from a treasure chest. "Ten blockade runners captured — including a feisty rebel wench — and one of their ships destroyed."

"The prisoners?" Logan asked, mindful of Blakesborough's penchant for brutality.

"In the hold."

"The lady?"

Blakesborough glared at Logan. "The *wench,* you mean? You see her, you'll know, she's no *lady.*"

"Where is she?" Logan questioned, wanting instead to know *how*—what condition the woman was in following her capture by Dar Blakesborough.

"In the hold with the rest. The men call her señorita, and they're bent on protecting her." He waggled his eyebrows. "With good reason, I suppose, since she's the only female among the lot of them."

Logan's temper flared. "I agree, Captain, that any woman who involves herself in the rebellion is no lady, but I warn you, whenever I am aboard this ship, such a woman will be treated as though she were Abe Lincoln's own wife."

Without waiting to be excused or giving so much as a cursory salute, Captain Blakesborough closed the door of the cabin and was gone.

Logan stared at the leather pouch. Prisoners notwithstanding, this could be a prize catch. Unfastening the clasp, he poured the contents onto the desk and began going through them. If he could be lucky enough to intercept some of the blockade runners' plans—schedules, names, places, dates—he might be able to get a hold on this operation. As things stood, he was undershipped and outmanned, regardless of the fact that his superiors claimed the *Victory* to be the final piece of manned machinery necessary to throttle the blockade runners.

The *Victory* was a symbol, nothing more, and symbols did not crush rebellions, especially not one being waged by the die-hard rebels involved in this game of cat and mouse. Perhaps tonight he had been lucky enough to intercept . . .

A bill of sale among the pile of papers caught his attention. He scanned it—eight hundred bales of cotton. The shipper's name was familiar.

Ransom . . .

Harry Ransom.

The vision evoked by the name, however, was not of Mr. Harry Ransom, nor of his palatial home on the banks of the Mississippi River.

The vision was of a princess with golden hair, green eyes, and a passion every bit as great as that of the rebel blockade runners themselves.

Stella Duval. His body warmed, and, as always when he thought of her, the permanent ache in his heart throbbed. Had she waited for him? Would she be there when, at last, they put down the rebellion and he rode to Los Olmos to claim her for his bride? Or had she wed another?

Returning his attention to the bill of sale, he studied the destination—Bagdad, Mexico—and the method of transportation—overland by wagon train from Alleyton, Texas, to Indianola, thence by ship—the *Serita Cortinas*—to Mexico. Try as he might, the scribbled signatures were illegible, by design, he knew. At least he now had the name of a ship, which was more than he had had before.

His hand moved to the bell beside his desk; he would call Ensign Jacobs, his aide, and set into motion this very night the capture of one blockade-running ship—the *Serita Cortinas*. He admitted to himself, albeit begrudgingly, that Dar Blakesborough had been correct: They hit the jackpot tonight. The victory would be sweeter, however, without Blakesborough's ridicule, which was sure to follow.

At odds since their school days at the Naval Academy, Logan had determined to maintain a truce once the *Victory* was designated his base. Dar had other ideas, though, and Logan vowed to change ships as soon as his assignment was completed. Which wouldn't be soon enough to suit either of them.

Dar had been destined for greatness, if one believed his family history and his own assessment. His father, Brian Blakesborough, was winding up his career as an admiral in the Navy. Neither of the Blakesboroughs attempted to hide his disapproval of Logan's promotion, and Logan knew both were poised to shoot him down, given the opportunity.

He did not tread in fear, however, even though he and Dar approached the role of officer from opposite poles, as it were, a fact that was painfully obvious here on board the same ship. Logan's easygoing, relaxed brand of leadership endeared him to his men and elicited greater loyalty in times of crisis, while Dar bullied his way through, demanding, taking, leaving havoc in his wake. His reaction to the female prisoner was a case in point. . . .

While Logan was still in mid-thought, his hand froze poised over the bell and his mind switched gears. At first the folded piece of writing paper merely looked out of place in a packet of documents. Its familiarity nudged at a corner of his brain, until at length he reached to touch it.

His heart lurched to his throat, where it lodged precariously. He picked up the paper and unfolded it. For a moment the writing blurred; when he finally managed to focus, it was on the past. Quickly his eyes found the signature at the bottom of the page. Where had he been when he wrote this letter? On board the *Atlantis,* after the battle between the *Monitor* and the *Merrimac.*

As though transported back in time, he saw himself sitting in his hole, felt the deep and bitter yearnings with which he had penned this, the last letter he had written to Stella Duval.

Then, as quickly as he had been overcome by bittersweet emotions, his heart filled with despair.

How had his letter fallen into the hands of blockade runners? Had Stella never received it? Instantly he was overwhelmed by remorse. Had she spent the last two years wondering why he stopped writing?

Holding the letter closer to the lamp, he saw the smudges, the tears along the folds, the water stains. The paper gave the appearance of having been handled not once, but many times. Without warning, fear wrenched at his gut.

This letter had been folded and unfolded and read and carried and . . . By whom? What had happened to Stella? Had she been attacked . . . captured . . . imprisoned . . . or worse . . . ?

Viciously he rang the bell for Ensign Jacobs, his heart hammering against his ribs. When his aide appeared, Logan had to clear his throat and start all over, for his mouth was too dry to speak.

"What do you know about this letter?" He held it folded, so neither the message nor the signature was visible.

"Nothing, sir."

"When you found the pouch, this was inside?"

"If you found it there, yes, sir."

"Which prisoner claimed the pouch?"

"No one came forward, sir. I suppose it belongs to the leader."

"Nothing has been added or taken from it since that time?"

"No, sir."

Logan stared unseeingly at the ensign. Finally, his brain began to function. "Bring me the leader of the rebels . . . immediately . . . and do not mention this to anyone." Recalling the alacrity with which Dar Blakesborough was wont to burst into his quarters, he added, "Identify yourself when you return."

When the ensign left on his mission, Logan tried to relax, but found himself pacing the floor. Intermingled with his fears for Stella's safety was the very real threat of what actions Dar Blakesborough would take, should he discover a letter written by a Federal officer to a woman living in rebel territory — never mind the fact that neither Stella nor her family would consider themselves part of the Southern

Rebellion. He supposed he should thank God for small favors: Dar Blakesborough's aversion to paperwork had kept him from snooping in the packet . . . that coupled with the fact that the blockade runners were Logan's responsibility.

Stella followed the ensign with trepidation, uneasy at the thought of what lay ahead. After her experience with the Federal captain called Blakesborough, she had no desire to leave the protection of Francisco and her other vaqueros.

She noted Ensign Jacobs' astonishment when he called for the leader of the rebels and discovered it to be herself. Once convinced, however, he led her away, saying the colonel wanted a word with her.

They wound through a narrow passageway, past berths right and left, up a six- or seven-foot stairway where she followed Jacobs' lead and ducked to miss the low deck beams, steadying herself against the pitch and roll of the ship with palms flattened to the walls on either side.

She had lost all concept of time below decks, and when they stepped onto the main deck at the bow of this fancy Federal ship, she blinked against a blinding noontime sun. As she glanced up, the masts, though unrigged, seemed to reach to the sky, making her feel small and insignificant.

"This way," Jacobs called, leading her across the mid deck, which she scrutinized with deliberation, telling herself she never knew when a chance would come to escape. Deckhands paid no mind as she studied the motionless side paddle wheels and the engine stacks that emitted no steam. They approached the stern, where the Stars and Stripes snapped as in crisp salute, mocking her.

The inactivity above ship stopped when she followed the ensign down another steep stairway and through yet another narrow passageway, finding herself in the galley, where cooks toiled over steaming pots. They exited the galley without so much as a pause, but the aroma wafted after them, reminding her of the many hours since her last meal. Surely, they would feed the prisoners soon.

And surely a ship wasn't this large! The circuitous route gave her the feeling of being secreted away somewhere—a terrible feeling, given the nature of the captain. Was the colonel the same sort of licentious scoundrel? She felt weak just thinking on it.

Then the ensign stopped outside a closed door and rapped once, calling a name, which, had she been disposed to swooning, would have laid her out on the ship's deck.

"Colonel Cafferty, it is myself, Jacobs, sir. I have the leader of the rebs."

At the answering command, Ensign Jacobs pushed open the door to a dimly lit cabin. Stella's mind swayed. Was this how he would see her after so long a time, clothed in dirty breeches, her hair shorn to within inches of her head? The thought of facing him under such circumstances, he a respected Union officer and she the enemy, sickened her as surely as if she had been struck down with a plague. She had never had a chance to love him, and now . . .

Now, she was his enemy.

Ensign Jacobs nudged her forward. With one hand she tugged the cap lower around her eyebrows and tucked a curl beneath it in back. Her legs trembled so she could hardly stand upright on the gently rolling deck. She was thankful that the room was dimly lit. Perhaps her leather trousers and loose jacket would serve as a disguise, giving her time to devise a more appropriate way to present herself.

He stood, head down, studying a pile of papers—she gasped. Her pouch lay open on the desk and around it the records . . . the papers for Mr. Ransom, giving names . . .

"Here she is, sir," Jacobs reported. "Turned out to be the woman, the leader did."

Logan lifted his head. His eyes swept her up and down and, returning to her face, he glared at her.

"That'll be all, Ensign. Lock the door behind you."

It would have taken Stella a full year to sort out her feelings, had she been given the opportunity. Alone in a locked room with Logan Cafferty . . . with her beloved Logan! How she had dreamed of seeing him again, of holding him!

All that was of little consequence now. She wasn't alone with the Logan Cafferty of her dreams. Neither of them was the same as in that idyllic time at the White Castle. They might as well have changed their names, for all the differences between them at this moment . . .

At this unheralded, unforeseen, magical . . .

Desperate . . .

Moment—

"Explain how you came in possession of this letter."

The command was harsh; the voice rough. She strained to recognize it from her dreams. Would her voice sound as strange to him?

Her lips parted, but she could find no words to speak. Through the lantern light she stared at his hand—and in it, her letter, or rather, his letter to her.

"Do you know who I am?" he demanded.

She swallowed, nodded.

"Do you recognize this letter?"

Her heart pounded in cadence with the swaying of the ship. She nodded.

"Have you read it?"

Her mouth dropped open. Had she read it? Only every day, twice a day or more, for two long, terrible years. Only . . . Her jaws trembled and she clamped them closed.

He came around the desk. "Do not be afraid. I am trying to learn about the welfare of the woman to whom this

49

letter is addressed. I will not harm her. She is . . ."

His are still brown, she thought, *chocolate brown . . .* and she couldn't tear her gaze from them.

Logan watched the prisoner intently. In her disguise she resembled a young boy rather than a woman. At first she had been afraid, he could tell, but now . . .

Now she stared at him, bringing doubts and uncertainties. Suddenly the ache in his heart became acute. Her eyes . . .

Stella could bear the tension no longer. As in a trance she reached up and withdrew the cap from her head.

As she did so she watched him study her. Her heart pounded painfully in her chest. What if he didn't recognize her? She would die if he didn't . . .

The truth dawned slowly in his eyes, on his face, like the sunrise on an overcast morning.

"Princess . . . ?"

The whispered word rasped from his throat and in the next moment they came together, clinging desperately, while their hearts raced each against the other's, as though they had just run the longest footrace, climbed the highest mountain.

Then, reaching a plateau of realization, they drew back as one and stared at each other.

"What in hell are you doing here?"

She studied him, feeling his anguish, sharing it. "The same thing you are."

He shook his head. "No."

"Yes." She clung to him, her arms rubbing against the rough wool of his uniform—his Federal uniform. "No. You are right: I am defending my country; you are attacking it."

"But . . . ? You said at Los Olmos you never become involved in politics . . . ?"

"I spoke as a child."

"What happened?"

50

"*Your* country attacked my home. Not just the land—the house . . . where we live . . ."

"Your parents?"

She inhaled, stilling her heart. "They are fine. We . . ." She stopped, unable to finish the sentence, unwilling to accuse him of Alicia's death. Yet, wasn't he guilty . . . ? "Do you have any idea what it is like for your victims? To be sitting at home minding their own business when shells tear apart their homes . . . their lives?"

"Princess . . ."

"I am not a princess, *Colonel;* I told you that once before. Now, I am no longer a simple Texas ranch girl, either. I'm . . ."

"A blockade runner."

His voice was cold, and she tried to move out of his embrace, but he held her fast.

"Why, for God's sake? Why *you?*"

She stood, breathless, her brain swirling with the past, the present. "Let me ask the same question: Why you?"

He stared, unspeaking.

"That's the trouble with war," she told him. "It distorts a man's understanding of right and wrong. It is right and fair for you to attack innocent citizens, but it is unlawful for them to defend themselves."

"I did not attack your house, damnit! But that has nothing to do with . . . with . . ." Reaching, he stroked her short, matted hair, remembering her long, silky curls at the White Castle, curls he had felt in his dreams these last long years. "Why do you have to run around disguised as a man . . . with your hair . . . ?"

"I am not in disguise! Would you have me ride horses and drive wagons through raging streams in ball gowns? And my hair . . . !" Bitter tears rushed to her eyes, but she forced them back. Why must he see her in such a hideous state? Why did it have to be like this? Her heart ached for another time . . . for the jovial, lighthearted man she had

51

fallen in love with so long ago—for the carefree life they had known—before Mr. Lincoln and his damnable war interrupted their lives. "Long hair is for females who have nothing better to do with their time than wash it! You wouldn't believe what a nuisance long hair can be—living on the trail for weeks at a time—"

"On the trail for weeks at a time? I thought your father was a sensible man. How can he allow such a thing? Exposing yourself to all sorts of dangers. I don't mean just the danger of being shot or captured. A beautiful woman . . ."

She glared at him. "The only time in two years I feared for my *virginity* was when your men took us prisoner."

Recalling the harsh treatment at the hands of the captain released a flood of emotions from behind the dam of her discipline. Tears rushed to her eyes again, and she squenched her lids shut, lowering her head.

Logan tipped her chin gently—the first gentle moment between them, she thought. When she looked into his eyes, though, they were harsh.

"Who?" he demanded. "Who among my men mistreated you?"

She shrugged. "Only one. A captain."

She watched his throat tighten; when he spoke it sounded like air forced through a narrow pipe. "What did he do to you?"

"Nothing . . . nothing but threaten. The man Jacobs who brought me here spoke up and said the colonel—you, I suppose he meant—did not allow mistreatment of prisoners."

Releasing her, he strode to the door. "I know who that captain was, and I'll have his hide . . . so help me. . . ."

"Logan. Wait."

He turned.

"They cannot know . . . your men. They cannot know about me . . . about . . . *us.*"

Wrenched from her throat, her last word cast a spell about them, surrounding them, uniting them, melding them with the intensity of her plea. Their eyes held, seeing not the other on this day, but as he had been, as she had been—three years back in time.

With a heavy sigh, he reached for the vision and felt her heated flesh. His hand stroked her face, and she turned and kissed his palm, keeping her lips there while she willed this moment to hold, to last until the world came to its senses and they could resume life as it should be . . . as it could be. If only . . .

He moved his hand to her hair and ruffled it as one would that of a child. Her beautiful hair, he thought, how desperate she must have been. The image did not match his memory—not only her appearance, but her actions. What despicable things had forced her to join the rebellion?

His scrutiny filled her with shame and she pulled away, attempting to hide her hair with her hands. "It isn't so bad when it's clean," she said, striving to sound lighthearted, as if it didn't matter, as if she hadn't envisioned their reunion night after night. And always he had been entranced by her beauty. Now . . .

"I mean . . . I haven't really seen it, but . . . It's full of sand and saltwater." Suddenly she thought of her body, her filthy clothing, and she dropped her hands to wrap herself away from his eyes. "I look wretched," she whispered. "We worked so hard, transporting . . ." *What was she doing, telling him secrets, and him the enemy . . . ?* She pursed her lips to stop her words, to still her trembling.

Quickly he drew her to him. "Stella, it's me, Logan. I love you. I don't care if you cake your body with a mudpack or shave your head. I love you. I love you." He buried his face in her cropped hair. "I care very much about the reasons for all this, though. I hate the reasons."

53

"Logan, please . . ."

A bell sounded outside the cabin. He tightened his hold. "And if you want a bath, then, you'll have a bath." Turning her loose, he crossed to the desk where he rang a bell.

"No," she said again. "They cannot discover me here . . . they cannot know about . . . about us."

"Us," he whispered. Drawing her to him, he closed his lips over hers. She was right, of course. The *Victory's* crew must not discover the truth—especially not Dar Blakesborough. It would be the ruin of him if Blakesborough learned of Stella, now that she was the enemy.

"They will not discover you, princess. These are my quarters . . . mine alone. No one on this entire ship or on any Federal ship in the whole damned Gulf of Mexico can tell me what to do, nor can they enter my quarters unless I choose to let them. I am on special assignment, answerable only to Secretary Wells . . . and he is far away, in Washington." He grinned at her, reminding her of long ago. "I may not be able to stop the blockade runners or keep our own officers from selling us out, but I can damned sure get you a bath when you want one."

His lightened tone gave her heart. When a knock came at the door, he kissed her quickly, then nudged her toward the adjoining cabin. "Stay in there. No one will see you."

She heard him order a tub with hot water; then she heard Jacobs' voice.

"The men are waiting in the officers' mess, sir."

"Tell them to eat without me. I am busy here."

"The prisoner, sir? Shall I return her to the hold?"

"I've taken care of the prisoner, Jacobs. Just remember what I told you: No one is to know about my visit with the rebel leader."

"Yes, sir."

"And, Jacobs, send me Max."

Locking the door, he returned to find her staring out a porthole. He took her in his arms, felt the need of her course through his body, lighting a fire long dormant yet ever ready to spring to life. His lips caressed hers. With one hand he smoothed her short curls back, and with the other he stroked her cheek, her neck, her arms, as though to convince himself she was here in the flesh and not a dream left from the night before.

A second knock interrupted them. Waiting behind, she watched him disappear into the adjoining room, heard him unlock the door, then an ensuing commotion—the tub, she supposed—and a different voice, muffled by the sounds of water being poured from one container to another.

"It's Stella, Max. She's here, and . . ."

"Here?" the voice questioned. "On board the *Victory?*"

"Here," Logan repeated. "In my quarters. You must help me keep her presence from the crew. She was one of the rebels . . . the leader, actually." She heard a note of incredulity in his voice, as if he still didn't fully believe her involvement in the war. Well, she had trouble believing it herself.

"What do you want me to do?" the man called Max asked.

"Don't let anyone become suspicious when she doesn't return to the cell with the other prisoners. Tell them I don't approve of a woman's being housed with all those men." This time instead of incredulity, she heard disgust, clear and undisguised. "Her men may raise a ruckus, so assure them of her safety. And, Max, we'll need some food. Bring us a couple of trays . . . not from the officers' mess, though. Wait until the men have finished eating, then bring them from the galley, so as not to raise suspicion."

"Don't worry about a thing, Colonel. I'll take care of it. And, Logan, friend to friend . . . I know what this means to you. Glad you finally found her."

"Yeah," he responded, in a tone that implied he wasn't sure what to do with her now that he had her. When she heard the door lock, she crossed to the doorway separating Logan's cabin and stateroom. He turned at the sound.

The look in his eyes set the already swaying room to spinning. She smiled. "Now that you've found me, what do you propose to do with me?"

When finally he answered, it wasn't to address the question of the prisoners in his hold. Instead, his voice was husky, and his playful banter reminded her of their time at the White Castle. "Come, princess, I shall be most happy to show you." And in the next few hours, he did just that, demonstrating his answer down to the loveliest of details.

"First, your bath." Dipping his fingers in the water to test its temperature, he beckoned her with his eyes.

And she went to him as though it were the most natural thing in the world, because, she thought later, it was. Logan undressing her, Logan bathing her, Logan's hands on her flesh, his lips on her lips . . . all so natural . . . so familiar . . . so right . . . because it had already happened a hundred times or more . . . in her dreams.

When at last his fingers squeaked through her clean hair, he lifted her from the tub and began to buff her body.

She stopped him with her eyes, begging, teasing, encouraging, trying to conceal the urgency she felt to be in his arms. "You can't back out like last time."

He laughed. "What a fool I was!" Lowering his lips, he kissed her with the intensity she had craved these last long years, lighting her soul, lifting her spirit, setting her flesh on fire.

And she returned his kisses with equal ardor, twining her fingers in his hair, pressing her body against his, until at last she could bear the rough woolen fabric separating them no longer. When she began fumbling with his clothing, he helped, and soon they stood surveying each other through the dim light, each drinking in the look of the other, the presence of the other, the moment, savoring that which had been denied them for so long.

At last he reached to touch her chin, lifting her face to his. He recalled how startling her beauty had been back at Nottoway. He had often feared he dreamed it, but he hadn't. She took his breath away.

"God, how I've missed you, princess. Every day, every night, every moment . . ."

The lump in her throat shut out any possibility of words, and she came into his arms. Their skin touched, hers dampening his, soft yet afferent with prickles of enkindled passion. "I began to doubt — I mean, not knowing where you were . . . how you were . . . whether you were alive or . . ."

He sighed against her. "Fortunately I did not know what you've been up to. I would have been crazy with worry."

She held him close, cherishing the tender torment of his body against hers, closing her mind to the specter named war. But not for long; reality would not be denied. The truth filled the room, suffocating, displacing her calmness with desperation: They had no time to waste in quiet moments. Impatiently she placed her lips over his and kissed him without shame. She didn't want to talk about war. She didn't want to think about war.

She pressed closer to him. She wanted nothing except this man, this moment, their moment.

Logan needed no encouragement. She fired his soul as she had when they first met, and he, too, was conscious of the furtive slipping away of time. He ran his rough hand along the satiny skin of her back, molding her form to his. Clasping her buttocks, he pressed her against him, heightening his already accelerated mania for this woman . . . for her body, for her very soul.

To love, to honor, and to protect her, he recalled thinking once long ago . . . to love, honor, and protect . . .

And this was the time for love.

It was like she had dreamed, Stella thought, only so very much better — his skin heating, tantalizing her own, his

57

muscles bunched beneath her palm, his hair twined between her fingers. Her body ached with long-dormant yearnings and she wriggled against him, urgently seeking to fulfill the desire to be ever closer, to be whole, to be one, to become part of this man . . . her beloved Logan.

Her breasts nuzzled against his chest, teasing his already ragged desires. Leaving her lips, he traced kisses down her neck, over her chest, capturing one protruding nipple between his teeth.

The touch of his lips on her breast flashed through her body like a beacon from the lighthouse, and she arched closer to his loving touch.

Urgently, then, he picked her up and carried her to his berth, where he stretched her out and positioned himself with elbows to either side of her face. He stared wordlessly a moment longer. When he kissed her forehead, his lips seemed to burn her skin. "I promised you more than this."

Clasping him around the neck, she pulled him on top of her where their skin clung together, almost stinging in the electricity they generated one for the other.

"We are together. There is nothing more."

So while the waves outside rocked them in gentle lullaby, inside the cabin his lips met hers, and together they fulfilled desires long awaited, holding back nothing for a future as uncertain as the separate ones they faced.

He traversed her body with his hands, tormenting her with promises of pleasures to come; his lips followed his hands, tantalizing her skin until she thought surely this time she would swoon for lack of relief. Then, as though to double her anguish, he lifted his lips and with his tongue ran a line, singular and wet, up her belly, nuzzling her navel, over her rib cage, circling each nipple in turn, before bringing his face close to hers.

Heaving for breath, she pulled him to her. But he resisted, supporting himself with his palms beside her face.

"Please, Logan." Her hips lifted against his, begging.

"It will hurt . . . ?" Like a bolt of lightning, Blakesborough's vile aspersion struck him, and without intending to he ended his sentence as a question.

"No," she breathed through dry lips. "Not so it will matter."

Forcefully he squelched his doubts, aided by his enormous passion—and hers.

Determined now, desperate, she nuzzled him, pelvis to pelvis, until, ever so slowly, he entered her questing body, reverently, struggling to push aside all else.

Slowly, inch by slow inch, he began to move inside her, hopefully, exploring, until at length he paused—stopped by a rigid barrier. Relief washed over him, followed closely by guilt—nauseating guilt.

When he stopped, her heart seemed to stop, too; then, overcome by an urgency she couldn't explain, she raised her hips swiftly and with one powerful thrust, together they tore through the resisting barrier, and she gasped.

He held her tight, damning Dar Blakesborough, loving her. "Are you all right?"

After the briefest pain came numbness, then a swelling of passion so urgent she thought for sure it could never be satisfied. She reached for his lips, moving her body against his in signal.

At the sign of her recovery, he gradually strengthened his quest, delving deeper, faster, with a vigorousness that spiraled to a brain-splitting crest.

Crumbling on top of her, his love-dampened body clung to hers. She clutched him in a tight embrace.

After his brain steadied, he lifted his head and kissed her lips. When he spoke his voice was weak. "I'm sorry . . ."

She shushed him with a finger to his lips. "You promised me the wait would be worth it . . . and it was—it was more perfect than I ever dreamed possible."

His eyes fixed hers with the look of wonder she recalled

from Nottoway; his tongue darted between his lips and captured her finger, reminding her of that long-ago time, and her passion-sapped body languished even further.

"Thank God, you are here with me, safe," he whispered, after they had lain silently in each other's arms a while. "When I found that letter, I . . . I was terrified something had happened to you."

She kissed his lips. "I prayed it wouldn't be you."

He frowned.

"On the *Victory*. We heard rumors about the ship and the hero the Federals were sending."

"You don't want me to be a hero?"

She studied his face, tried to respond with his same lighthearted repartee, but could think only of serious, deadly serious, things.

"Not in the Gulf of Mexico," she whispered.

They stared at each other at length, each knowing the other's thoughts, neither able to change the course of the other's life, neither willing to admit as much.

"Tell me about your involvement with the blockade runners."

"There's nothing to tell."

Still as death, they stared at each other, he desperate to know so he could keep her from harm; she equally as desperate that he not discover the blockade runners' plans.

"It's Harry Ransom, isn't it?"

Her heart stopped. "Mr. Ran . . . ?" He had read the documents! He already knew! Ducking her head, she struggled to free herself from his arms.

"Harry Ransom is behind this, isn't he?"

"I won't discuss it."

"Oh, yes, you will . . ."

"Then you go first, Colonel. Tell me the position of all your ships. What are your plans for invasion?"

"You are talking nonsense, when this is a serious situation. I will not have you involved in the dangerous schemes

60

of old men!"

Kicking, she untangled her legs from his and sat up, reaching for a blanket. Logan jumped to his feet.

He pulled on his trousers. "It doesn't matter now. You are safe, and you will remain that way."

"As your prisoner? Tell me, Colonel, do you claim the same spoils from all your female prisoners?"

He whirled to face her. "You're the first—" He caught his breath, held his lips between his teeth.

She mimicked him, unconscious of her motions, conscious only of him, of herself, of their terrible plight.

"Please, Logan . . ."

Crossing the room in two steps, he crushed her to him. "You're the *only* . . ."

"Please, let's not argue." Their hearts beat wildly each against the other. "Not today . . . please. Not today."

He kissed her with abandon, rekindling the raging yearnings they had only moments before satisfied. Later she recalled this first breathtaking day together—her first experience at physical love. Not a day, half a day only, but timeless, encapsulating as it did years of unrealized dreams and hopes.

When he wasn't wearing his uniform, she could put aside Logan's station in life, and unless she searched the room, she could envision them in another time and place—at Los Olmos, at the White Castle, somewhere, anywhere, away from the war.

They ate lunch brought by an unseen Max, and later Logan dressed in his uniform and left the cabin, saying he should tend to a few affairs or the officers might mutiny. He spoke in jest, she knew. The seriousness in his voice she attributed to the seriousness of their situation.

He was gone more than an hour, she judged, and when he returned, he bore a gift of clean clothing. With grim determination she dressed in the dark blue trousers and blouse with square-backed sailor collar. She hoped he

61

would not notice the change in her.

As soon as he left the quarters, she had hurried to the desk to discover, if she could, how much he had learned from the documents in her pouch. She couldn't be certain, of course, but the pile was in such disorder she doubted he had discovered the folded list of way stations, names, and dates. Quickly, she secreted it beneath a book to retrieve later. Her letter lay on top of the desk, where he had dropped it to stare at her, and she touched it tenderly, recalling his expression when he realized who she was. Hastily, then, she had restored the pile to the same jumble as when he left the room.

Now she slipped the blouse over her head and studied the rank badge on the right-hand sleeve. She tried to sound lighthearted. "What rank did you choose for me, Colonel?"

He laughed. "You're a boatswain's mate, Duval." Taking her in his arms, he slid his hands beneath the blouse and caressed her breasts until her nipples peaked against his palms. His eyes held hers; he watched them go from bittersweet, almost sad, to the smoldering green fire he recalled from their days in Louisiana. "But in this room," — his husky voice betrayed his rising passion — ". . . in this room, you are a commander — the commander of my soul."

She laughed softly. "You always did use fancy language."

Over a supper of roast beef and boiled potatoes, served with a bottle of port that she sipped so as not to become light-headed, she broached the subject they had talked around all day. "What are your plans?"

He squinted across the flickering candles. Finally, quirking an eyebrow, he glanced toward the other room. "To spirit you to bed and ravish your body, hold you close . . ."

"For how long?"

Their eyes locked.

"How long are we to be held on board the *Victory?*"

"We?"

"My men . . . and myself."

He flung his napkin to his plate and jumped up. "I wasn't aware of your impatience to leave me."

Furiously, she rose, too. "That is not what I mean. I'm not anxious to leave you! Don't change the subject. My men are in your hold . . ."

"*Your* men! How could you . . . ?"

"How could *you?* Do you expect me to disregard men who put their trust in me? Would you desert *your* men? Of course not. But you expect me . . ."

"That's different, and you know it."

"There's only one difference here, *Colonel!* The sides of the war we are on. I'm on the side of justice."

"Justice! You don't know anything about this rebellion!"

"Don't I? How much more education do I need than to have my house attacked by the . . . by the enemy?"

"You were not attacked! You told me yourself the top of your house resembled a ship . . . or some fool thing. What did you expect?"

"I expected the commander of that ship to have more sense; I expected a country that professes to know what's best for everyone to prove it by not denying us access to food and medical supplies and free commerce."

"The rebelling states can have all those things back, and well their leaders know it. All they have to do is . . ."

"Surrender? That will be a long time coming, Colonel. . . ."

Fiercely, he jerked her arm. "Stop it, Stella. Stop this *colonel* nonsense. I'm . . ." His eyes searched hers, finding nothing but turmoil. "I'm Logan, and I love you, and I'm going to marry you."

"When?"

Sighing, he pulled her to him. "When this damned rebellion is over, if I can keep you alive that long."

Leaving Logan Cafferty this time was even more difficult than it had been when the sternwheeler carried her down the Mississippi River, away from Nottoway Plantation, away from him. But it had to be done, she told herself, even though this time she left knowing she might very well not see him again for . . . for a long, long time.

True to his promise over supper, they ended up in bed soon after, suppressing for a time their deepest fears in the passionate expression of their love.

He left the cabin once more, to make rounds before retiring for the night. While he was away, she located her own clothing—she would wear the uniform of the boatswain's mate when she left—and her boots. She pictured in her mind's eye exactly how she would retrieve the leather pouch and documents in the darkness without awakening him.

He fell asleep at last; she had thought he never would; had wished, in a secret compartment of her heart, that he wouldn't. But at last, he did.

Occupied with the success of her mission, she remembered at the last minute to take the ring of keys from his pocket where she had seen him stash them, hoping one would fit the lock to the cell below decks. The rest was easy—dressing in the Federal uniform and her own boots, retrieving the document from beneath the book, stowing her clothing and the papers in the pouch, unlatching the door and slipping into the hallway.

She strove to recall every detail of the journey through the ship with Ensign Jacobs. That he had led her on the course where she would be least likely to be observed was fortunate, for she met no one in the narrow passageways and only a singular deckhand here and there on the main deck. In the darkness her disguise went undetected.

Approaching the hold, she experienced a moment of panic, then she noticed the fouled anchor rank badge on the guard's sleeve—his left sleeve. Hadn't Logan said left-sleeve badges indicated lower-ranking petty officers? Hitching up her belt, as well as her courage, she took a deep breath and stepped into the hold, standing to the darkened side of the room. She cleared her throat and coughed as she spoke, hoping thus to disguise her voice, if for only enough time to gain her men's escape.

"Ensign Jacobs wants you."

The sailor squinted at Stella, frowned, then shrugged. "Fair by me. I hate this stinking hold anyhow. Them reb's 're the foulest-mouthed sonsabitches ever I come acrost."

At that the men in the hold set up such a racket that Stella rejoiced. As soon as the sailor cleared the steps, she struggled with the keys, found the correct one after an interminable length of time, unlocking the cell and talking at the same time.

"We will take the lifeboat amidship. Two of you wait here for the guard to return, then tie him up—use his belt and be sure to gag him. The rest follow me, but keep in the shadows. I will relieve the guard on duty beside the boat. Be ready to tie him up and lower the boat."

Within seconds, she led the way up the stairs, pausing at the corner to check ahead. Eight grateful men stopped behind her. Two others stationed themselves in the shadows to await the return of the guard.

"I did not recognize you, señorita," Francisco said. "You look different—in the uniform of a Federal."

The words sobered her. "I am different," she answered, thinking of the glorious change that had taken place in her life. She had come on board the *Victory* an unfulfilled child; she left it a woman who had known love, and now left love, leaving her more lonely and desolate than she had ever been.

Thinking, too, of her beloved Logan, lying in his berth alone—the berth where she had become his lover. Would he love her still when he awoke to discover her betrayal?

For a moment anguish overwhelmed her and it was all she could do to keep from retracing her steps and lying beside him, the war be damned. Then she thought of Giddeon and the papers in the leather pouch around her neck—papers that, if read by the Federal officer to whom she had given her heart and her body, could destroy not only the Cotton Road, but very likely her own father's life, as well.

Her choice made, she screwed up her courage and headed for the lifeboat. "I am different," she repeated. "I will never be the same again."

Chapter Three

"Trouble with you, Cafferty, you're soft on women. If you had left her in with the others, she couldn't have effected their escape."

Dar Blakesborough matched strides with Logan across the main deck. Short of miming "I told you so," the irate captain made sure the entire crew of the *Victory* knew his opinion that the escape of ten rebel prisoners plus the woman who led them lay squarely in the lap of Colonel Cafferty. "Let me head the landing party," he argued. "I'll see the wench regrets playing you for a fool."

Logan clenched his fists and concentrated on the preparations his men made to get a landing party under way. A fool he felt, but striking Dar Blakesborough would not bring Stella and the prisoners back.

"There's no need for civilian clothing, either," Blakesborough continued. "Ask me, the uniform of our country will put more fear in their lost souls than—"

"And land us in a Confederate prison should we be caught," Logan retorted.

"The rebels have abandoned their makeshift fort. There aren't any others out there to catch you, except, of course, the wench you let escape."

"In that case, we won't be gone long, Captain. During that time you will have your hands full. Have a crew in the water within the hour to capture the *Serita Cortinas*. After that, send ashore for drinking water and wood. Be ready to head for a fleet rendezvous at Brazos Santiago directly upon my return. With any luck we will intercept the cutter and prisoners from the *Serita Cortinas* on the way there."

"Carrying along *our* prisoners, as well." Blakesborough emphasized the word *our* to needle him, Logan knew, and the jab succeeded.

"All aboard, Colonel," Max called.

Logan fixed Dar Blakesborough with his best colonel's stare, gave him an abbreviated salute that disguised none of his distaste for the man, and stepped into the small boat.

"Bring that rebel wench back alive. Cafferty. I aim to see her pay for her traitorous ways. She'll soon regret . . ."

The racket involved in lowering the boat into the dark Gulf waters shut out Dar Blakesborough's final words, leaving Logan's mind free to finish the thought himself. When he caught Stella, he would . . .

He sighed. He would like to shake her by the shoulders until her teeth rattled, but that wouldn't erase the embarrassment her escape caused him among his men. Bringing her back would restore a measure of his credibility, but still, he could wring her pretty neck. What had happened to the sensible Texas girl he had waved good-bye to from the banks of the Mississippi River?

The rebellion, his mind supplied. The rebellion had happened to her—to both of them, changing them, imprisoning them, setting the course of their lives—except it had been different prisons, separate courses. Would it never end?

He had awakened a mere hour ago more at peace than any other time since that long-ago day at Nottoway, only to be immediately submersed in anxiety, as in a wintry sea. By degrees he realized she had gone for good—"escaped" was a bitter word when he recalled the tenderness they had shared only moments before she left his bed—the uniform he provided her was gone, along with her own clothing

68

and the pouch full of documents. No sooner had he lighted a lamp and stared at the barren desktop than the alarm tolled above decks.

Sinking to a chair, he clasped his face in his hands. That's where Max found him.

"They're gone, Logan. All of them," his aide and closest friend advised him, when at his pounding, Logan crossed to open the door from the inside, only to find it already unlocked. Max glanced toward the bedchamber of the two-room quarters, eyebrows raised in silent inquiry.

Logan pursed his lips and sighed heavily.

"Her, too?"

"Afraid so."

"Damn." Stepping inside, Max closed the door behind him. "What are the plans?"

Logan knew what he meant: What will we do to conceal the escape from Dar Blakesborough? He laughed. Bitterly.

"Find 'em," he hissed.

Immediately Blakesborough stomped down the hallway, followed close at heel by Ensign Alan Herbert, his own personal aide, their boots echoing in Logan's brain like the recoil of a thirty-two pounder.

If he'd had time, he later thought, he might have become angry—really angry—at Stella. Dar Blakesborough did not give him that time.

"What in the hell happened to my prisoners?" the captain stormed.

Logan motioned Max, and they sidestepped the indignant *Victory* crew members. Blakesborough and his men formed the true crew of this vessel, a fact they never let Logan and Max forget. Although he chose not to pull rank on his former schoolmate, Logan had not let the captain walk all over him. And he didn't intend to start now.

Striding past Blakesborough, he ignored the captain's protests. "Max, find Ensign Jacobs. Outfit a landing party. Choose the crew—six at most. We will travel in civilian clothes, since we don't know where we'll end up. Bring along scrip from my safe."

"How the hell did they get loose?" Blakesborough demanded at his shoulder. "Where did you have that woman, anyhow? If you'd . . ."

Logan stopped. "There have been enough 'if's' since this rebellion began to sink the entire rebel navy. Obviously, that isn't enough. Max, bring me the guard who was on duty."

"It is equally evident, Cafferty, that you know nothing about security," Blakesborough raged. "Now, all we have left are the documents. I hope there is something valuable among them."

Logan quickened his pace; his feet struggled to keep up with his racing heart. If Dar Blakesborough discovered the documents gone, he'd have hell to pay keeping his relationship with Stella quiet. And what Captain Blakesborough and his father would do with such knowledge, he shuddered to think.

"There is something valuable," Logan barked. "The name of the blockading ship the rebels loaded earlier in the evening. Prepare a cutter to go after it immediately." As they approached the main deck Logan gained confidence. "It's called the *Serita Cortinas,* destination Bagdad. We know it will keep to the inland waterway, so it shouldn't be difficult to intercept."

Blakesborough kept pace with Logan. "What else?"

"Nothing of immediate importance. After we find the *Serita Cortinas . . .*"

"You find it. I'm going after my prisoners."

Logan came to a halt. "Equip a cutter. Choose your best officer to man it. The blockade runners are my responsibility." He glared at the defiant Blakesborough. "Those orders came straight from Admiral Farragut, Captain. I suggest you follow them."

By the time he interrogated the guard and two sailors

who were found bound and gagged behind a hatch cover, Max and Ensign Jacobs signaled him from the lifeboat. Dar Blakesborough's parting words grated through the misty dawn, condemning his mission before he even got under way.

"Bring the rebel wench back alive! I'll see she pays for betraying her country!"

Although it was near dawn when Stella and her crew rowed away from the *Victory,* darkness surrounded them. Only by dead reckoning were they able to steer toward land. The eleven people fit snugly in the boat, but with four men rowing on either side, the distance they gained made the cramped quarters tolerable.

They found Pass Cavallo with no trouble: The lighthouse towered above them like a black and silent monument. After putting out the five crew members from the *Nueces* who wanted to inspect their ship, the vaqueros continued, on Stella's instructions, past the wrecked schooner and into the main body of Matagorda Bay.

"Perhaps we should head for Indianola," Francisco suggested. "The men on shore may have left horses for us."

Stella shook her head. "That's the first place Lo . . . ah, the Federals will look. The Navidad River is directly across the bay; come daylight we can locate it. Once we make the river, they will never find us."

The men agreed, of course; they always did. In the beginning she had been uncertain of her ability to lead a group of men, but as Papá had figured, they gave her no trouble. Perhaps because Francisco and Beto never left her side. But she liked to think it was because her decisions were couched as suggestions rather than as orders, and because she never asked them to do something she had not thought out beforehand. Even their escape from the *Victory* had been planned.

71

And that very fact added to her torment tenfold. That she had lain in Logan's arms, experienced his magical loving, all the while planning to betray him grieved her even more than she had been grieving during the preceding years when she didn't know whether he was alive or dead.

Before tonight he had loved her—of that she was certain, as certain as she was that the moment he awakened and found her gone, he could well cease to love her. Her escape would humiliate him in front of his crew . . . how would he react to that?

Her body trembled with such thoughts while she sat impatiently in the boat, for, although her vaqueros-turned-teamsters followed her with dedication, Francisco, and Beto and Raul whenever they were along, refused to let her turn a hand—unless, as during the evening before, her assistance was required for the safety of the group. They had accepted her help in unloading the *Nueces* because haste was essential.

That difficulty behind them, however, Stella was left with nothing to do but hold her hands in her lap. She strove to keep her mind on the future, the immediate future: their escape, meeting Mr. Ransom, ordering the blockade-running ship for Papá.

The immediate future. Not anything past tomorrow. *Tomorrow, and tomorrow, and tomorrow,* the poet had written, *Creeps in this petty pace from day to day, To the last syllable of recorded time. . . .*

Well, she didn't care about *the last syllable of recorded time.* She dared not think about it, nor about *the petty pace* with which they would arrive at such a time. She had trouble enough with today, with this minute. . . .

With this instant, actually. Logan could come at any instant, and she couldn't face him now. Not after the way she had deceived him.

She hadn't deceived him, she retorted to herself. Her escape had nothing to do with deceit. The wonderment of the love they shared startled her. Although she had dreamed of loving him, had yearned to be in his arms, to experience his unmistakable passion, she had never imagined the marvels that awaited her.

Not the least of which was her own ability to respond, to give, to participate in the miracle of their love, as though she had been born for nothing else, for nothing but loving Logan Cafferty.

Was this, then, to be all? Was her star so quickly risen to set without . . . ?

Desperately she pulled her mind away from such things. Even thoughts of war were more welcome than the wanderings of her mind tonight.

Today, she corrected, when, throwing her head back to drink in gulps of air to steady her thinking, she saw the illuminated sky overhead.

"There'll be no sun to guide their way today, señorita," Francisco said. "Likely they will give up the search on so gray a day. What good would it do them to search for prisoners of so little consequence?"

"They'll come," she sighed. "Never doubt that, Francisco. They will come."

But by high noon when the scraggly group of escaped Federal prisoners made the Navidad River, no search party had caught up with them. Francisco again voiced his conviction that the Federals would not follow them on such an overcast day.

"They'll come," Stella replied again. "But perhaps they will not find us now that we are off the bay."

"Perhaps they will get lost in this soupy weather," he suggested. "They do not know these waters as we who live here."

At that moment the resounding boom of a cannon echoed through the murky dawn. Without speaking the men at the oars increased their speed. Stella clutched the leather bag to her chest.

As badly as she dreaded facing Logan again, she knew with no reservations that she would rather him search for and find her than find her father. Although the jumbled mass of papers on Logan's desk indicated he had not gone through all of them, she knew he had seen the bill of sale with Mr. Ransom's name on it.

That same bill of sale listed the ship—the *Serita Cortinas*. She wondered whether Logan recognized that name—her mother's name—and recognizing it, whether he would surmise the ship's captain. She tried to recall whether he could have heard her mother's name at the White Castle. Perhaps not, she reasoned, since her mother was known only as Mrs. Duval to most of the guests.

But that was neither here nor there now; Papá had renamed the vessel. "I hope he comes after us instead of after Papá," she sighed aloud.

"Do not worry about Senor Capitán," Francisco told her, using the name the Los Olmos vaqueros had coined for Giddeon Duval years ago when he first came to the hacienda as a near-destitute sea captain. "He has sounding lines and a sufficient stock of hard coal; besides, he knows this shoreline as well as any fish in the sea. He can hide like a crab in the marshy inlets."

"I know, Francisco, but . . ."

"No Federal officer is a match for your papá," the old man insisted.

"I pray they never meet in battle," she sighed.

Francisco brought her back to their own plight. "We must think of ourselves now, señorita. We are nearing the place where that Confederate gunboat sank. We cannot take this vessel around it."

Immediately, Stella's mind returned to their own situation. "Then we will sink our boat; we will head for Victoria. Perhaps we can catch up with our wagons there."

It took more ingenuity to sink the lifeboat than Stella had imagined, and while the men worked at the task, she hurried behind a thicket of windswept oaks to change her clothing.

Her leather trousers could practically stand alone, so caked with grime were they, and her chemise and once soft blouse scratched her skin. She wrinkled her nose at the hot tears that sprang to her eyes. Would this war never end?

It wasn't merely clean, feminine clothing for which she longed, she told herself. As Logan had put it, it was the reasons for these dirty old things that brought tears. Her own discomfort was as nothing compared with the plight of the men in the field, with the sacrifices made by thousands and thousands of innocent victims whose homes, whose livelihoods, whose very existence had been torn asunder by the injustice of this war.

And that, she knew, even more than the death of Alicia and the shelling of their home, was why she and her father had joined forces with the Confederates.

Alicia's death had become a symbol of all the senseless destruction wrought by the dastardly Yankees. Why couldn't they wage a fair fight?

Why must they deny innocent civilians access to medical supplies? Why must they blockade ports that meant a livelihood to businessmen who had never wanted a war in the first place? Why did they insist on strangling the army against which they fought? If they couldn't beat them fairly on the battlefield, then . . .

Why must Logan be involved in this damnable war? Why must Papá?

And why must she?

"Once more you look like a reb, señorita," Francisco told her when she emerged from the thicket.

"I don't want to get shot by the Heel Flies before we get to Victoria," she told him, using the local term for the Texas Home Guard.

The overland journey to Victoria took two days, and by the time they arrived, Stella felt much like Robin Hood leading his merry men. Except her gang was made up, not only of hale and hardy Los Olmos vaqueros, but of boys considered too young to fight and of elderly, decrepit, yet determined men who were forced to support the cause of the Confederacy on the homefront.

The first group they encountered consisted of two men and the grandson of one of them, who was just under age to join the army and mindful of it.

No sooner had Stella related their ordeal than the youngster—Tommie—offered to take a message to the Home Guard.

His grandfather approved. "You folks team up with us. Tommie can alert the Heel Flies at Saluria; they'll keep the Yankees off your heels. Sure hope we haven't missed that wagon train."

The other man, a Mr. Johnson from near Caney Creek, jumped down from the wagon to give Stella his place. "You're just the little lady we was coming to see. This here wagon is loaded with twelve cases of lead bullets our folks molded from the Navidad mine."

Although she resisted at first, Stella accepted the offered seat beside the more elderly of the two men, a Mr. Samuels, who looked to be somewhere over sixty years, and who had one good leg and one peg.

"Lost my leg at San Jacinto," he told her. She grimaced, thinking of all the men—young and old—who would come home from this war missing limbs. They would be the lucky ones, she knew.

"Still and all, if they'd let me, I'd be fighting them Billy Yanks with old Jeb Magruder right now."

Mr. Samuels whipped up the mules and Stella gripped the wagon seat to keep her balance. "You are doing a necessary service for your country right here," she assured him. "Armies can't fight without bullets." Although without bullets, she thought, perhaps this dastardly war would come to a more speedy conclusion.

"And you, miss, are doing a valuable service yourself. Pity, though, when our young ladies have to get involved."

Their next stop was at Cox's Creek, where they picked up a wagon hauling salt from the saltworks there, two wagons laden with hides and tallow, and another filled with gifts from the homefolk to their boys at the front: tallow candles, shoe blacking, woolen clothing. And haversacks.

"Constructed according to Major General Magruder's own specifications," a stout, yet spunky woman told Stella. "He wrote it in the *Galveston News*—the army needs twenty thousand haversacks. He even gave the dimensions, said the quartermaster couldn't provide them, since the government has no money to buy cloth. I made these from tablecloths; they're marked for my son's regiment over in Louisiana."

A frail woman with a beaded brow handed Stella another bundle, this one wrapped in a cowhide and secured with leather stitching. "My boy's with Terry's Rangers. We heard about the snow back east . . . he ain't ever seen snow. This here's some woolen socks and other garments. If the weather gets too bad, he can wrap his feet in this old hide—it's from a milk cow he raised from a calf. Went dry, so's we thought it should be put to use. I remember hearing tell how General Washington's men got their feet froze in another war. I don't want that to happen to my boy."

Stella's heart went out to the women. "I will do the best I can to get your gifts to their destinations." When she reached for the bundles, she visualized other mothers across the land and their worries, and these women's packages took on the weight of them all, and she became more depressed than ever.

As their journey lengthened her depression deepened and finally turned to anger. What manner of men started wars? Did they have sons to fight? Wives to grieve?

Lovers to leave . . . ?

The memory of Logan's flesh burned against her own, easing for a time the irritation caused by her stiff clothing. Her heart filled with bitter anguish.

. . . or to deceive?

Were there other men like Logan, other women like herself, trapped, as they were, on opposite sides of the war? Her mind spun webs of spiraling discontent until by the time the motley group pulled into Camp Henry McCulloch, she was so out of sorts, she felt a great inclination to storm through the camp berating the soldiers who trained there, sending them home to plow their fields, to tend their herds, to make love to their wives.

Watching them march to and fro across the parade ground, she was filled with a desperate sense of the future. How many of those here would survive the war? And not only the soldiers seemed doomed to her today. Who of any here present — including herself — would live to benefit from the victories being won, or to suffer from the defeats, from the death and dying?

Who? Would she? Would Logan? Would Papá? And if they did, would the world ever be the same again?

"We won't be finding any horses here, señorita," Francisco told her. "These are the men who were unhorsed up at Richmond."

She looked around. "It further proves the absurdity of the situation, Francisco. Must have been some city slicker who decided they needed a training center to teach Texans how to *walk*. Do you suppose the men back east to whom they sent our horses know how to ride? Or must they teach that skill, as well?"

"Can't figure how a man'd live to be full-grown without knowing how to do either," Francisco answered.

They spent the better part of an afternoon at Camp McCulloch, feeding, watering, and resting the teams. Several soldiers approached Stella to thank her for the service she was performing for the cause. They were young, she noticed, almost all younger than herself. They were hungry, they told her, to go whip some Yankees. She wondered whether any of them so much as knew a Yankee.

Yet, they were eager, excited, as were all men, she supposed, faced with the prospect of going to war. And they needed her help. By the time she left their camp, she had regained much of her enthusiasm.

Captain Rupley handed her onto the wagon seat. "Don't need to tell you the gratitude the men feel for you, ma'am. Guess you noticed that. Not only in Texas, either. I received a message this week from General Lee, calling the Cotton Road the Lifeline of the Confederacy. Without the medicines and munitions, the blankets and clothing you bring our boys, we'd be good as whipped right now."

"Don't worry, Captain," she assured him. "We will not let the Federals close down the Cotton Road. If they succeed in blockading the entire Texas coast, we have other routes we can travel to the Rio Grande."

Captain Rupley tipped his hat. "Give my regards to your father," he called as Mr. Samuels whipped up the mules. "Giddeon Duval is a fearless man, and a dedicated one. Those Federal blockaders won't mess with him, if they know what's good for them."

At dusk when they pulled into Victoria, Stella smiled for the first time in two days. The wagons they had last seen leaving Indianola were in the wagon yard, their tarps in place; the oxen to pull them, in the corral. Emilio Sanchez stood guard. He approached the group with curiosity.

"What kept you folks?"

"A little matter of a Federal blockade cutter," Francisco answered. "They came upon us unawares at dawn, took us on board. If it hadn't been for the señorita, we would still be held prisoner."

A crowd gathered at their arrival to hear Francisco's story, which grew as each succeeding escaped prisoner recounted the capture in his own way. Finally, Stella drew

Francisco aside.

"I will spend the night at Mrs. Mac's. In the morning you take the wagons on to Alleyton—"

"What will you do, señorita?"

"I must get there early, so I will ride ahead. Mr. Ransom has been waiting for Papá several days already."

"You cannot go alone," Francisco insisted. "Your papá would have my hide. We will send Emilio with the wagons; I will come with you. What time do you wish to leave?"

Stella sighed, thinking of a hot bath, a soft bed, one in which she could linger. "At daybreak. Be there at daybreak. I'll have Mrs. Mac prepare food for the trail."

On the way to the boardinghouse, she thanked the Lord for Mr. Ransom. Were it not for him, she would be tempted to lie abed tomorrow, and that would serve no purpose—except to allow her time to think of Logan and of their desperate, impossible future.

Especially were he to capture Giddeon, she thought later, while she tossed among sweet-smelling sheets on a plump feather mattress. Giddeon would be considered a traitor to the Union. And they hanged traitors, didn't they?

It was midafternoon by the time Logan and his crew located the sunken lifeboat, and it didn't take much longer to discover that it had been sunk on purpose. Nor was it difficult to see where Stella had changed clothes—snags of the boatswain's uniform were caught on sharp limbs of the misshapen oaks and below them, a good-size tear from her own shirt. He scowled, thinking of the haste with which she must have dressed, of the determination that . . .

No—he spat to the ground, mentally correcting his choice of word—not determination, she was hardheaded, unruly, headstrong . . .

Following the tracks, he studied them at length, then

turned to his men.

"Max, you come with me. Jacobs, take the rest of the crew back to the *Victory*. Tell Blakesborough to set course for Brazos Santiago. Max and I will track down the prisoners; we'll meet you either along the coast or at Brazos Santiago. On your way back to the ship, leave two men — Jack and Thomas will do — at the lighthouse. We don't want the rebels returning to that fort."

"Yes, sir," Jacobs responded.

"And Jacobs . . . you'll have to finish the armaments inventory alone. Be sure to keep it quiet; secure it in my safe when you finish."

Logan and Max stood on shore and watched the boat pull away.

"They don't like it," Max said. "They wanted to recapture those prisoners."

Logan spat to the ground. "Too bad."

"Blakesborough will make trouble, you know . . ."

"Too damned bad."

Max ran a hand through his sandy hair and stared at Logan with frank, hard eyes. "She worth a court-martial?"

Logan returned his friend's stare a moment, thinking of satin skin and golden hair, of green eyes and soft, sensuous lips, of the feisty, strong-willed female who had captured his heart and now, as he had put it to her, commanded his soul. Cramming the unfamiliar felt hat on his head, he turned and began trudging along the tracks she and her teamsters had left on the sandy riverbank. "Yeah," he muttered. "She's worth it."

Chapter Four

Stella drew rein outside the teeming cotton-boom town of Alleyton, mentally catching her breath for what lay ahead. Devastating though the war was for most Americans on whichever side, the hordes of speculators in Alleyton were finding nothing but profit. No wonder so many citizens looked with disdain upon anyone associated with the cotton trade. Only the respect with which her family had been regarded for several generations kept her from being numbered among the money changers.

"Another load of cotton has arrived on the rails, señorita," Francisco observed.

Stella surveyed the seemingly endless stacks of baled cotton: Most of it belonged to the state of Texas, purchased by the Texas Military Board from farmers in exchange for seven and eight percent state bonds. The rest was Confederate cotton, purchased in the same manner, often in direct competition with the Texans. Farmers throughout the South depended on their share for financial survival; both governments depended on the proceeds to purchase supplies—supplies to wage war, to keep waging war, and to keep . . .

Mentally she strengthened her resolve. "We will need additional wagons," she told Francisco, "to replace those Beto has taken to Brownsville. If you cannot procure enough wagons for a shipment this large, we'll have to use carts. And drivers. We need skilled drivers to replace the vaqueros who are with Beto."

82

Francisco nodded in agreement.

"Do not hire men who aren't sober," she told him.

"If there are such in this town. You stay out of the path of these inebriated men. I do not want . . ."

Stella glanced quickly toward a shanty where a scantily clad female lounged on the porch; she looked down at her own masculine attire. "In this getup I don't have to worry about being mistaken for a lady of the evening . . . or any other kind of lady."

Francisco scowled. "Where will I meet you, señorita?"

"At Mrs. Beaty's. I must clean up before I look for Harry Ransom."

He studied the crowded roadway. "Perhaps Mrs. Beaty has let your room to someone with ready cash."

"Mrs. Beaty would not dare rent my room to someone else," Stella laughed. "She hovers almost as much as you."

"If I did not hover, señorita, Señor Capitán would have my hide, as he is fond of saying."

As one they sank spurs. Francisco headed for the depot and Stella for the broad oak-bordered boulevard that marked the hub of the town's activities. Only a few blocks from the railhead, the esplanade was crowded with men in wagons, men on horseback, and men afoot, all haggling, swearing, and swilling liquor, while they bargained over everything from the price of a bale of cotton—regularly bringing three or four cents in the interior, but going for as much as fifty cents gold in Matamoros—to that of an imported Enfield rifle—twenty dollars in England, fifty dollars in bulk to the Confederacy, sixty dollars each on the streets of Matamoros or Bagdad.

Nudging her horse among the throng, Stella searched right and left for any sign of Harry Ransom. If she was unable to find him, she would have to bargain with the various cotton agents, both Texas and Confederate, on her own. But she would not haggle here in the street, she decided. If Mr. Ransom had returned to his plantation in

Louisiana, or if he had not yet arrived in Alleyton, she would send messages from the safety of Mrs. Beaty's boardinghouse, where she could meet other interested agents over tea, not whiskey.

Although she had been away from Alleyton but a mere two weeks, the place seemed rougher even than when she had left. Papá said it reminded him of stories about the gold-rush towns out in California. A boomtown, created not by yellow gold but white.

Actually, it was the railhead that created Alleyton. When the Buffalo Bayou, Brazos and Colorado Railroad reached the banks of the Colorado River in 1860, the war was already upon them. No time, much less funds, remained to construct a bridge across the river to the older community of Columbus.

At the time Columbus resented the growth the railroad generated for Alleyton. Now, she felt sure, its citizens were glad to be separated from the riffraff by a river. Several merchants from Columbus put up stores in Alleyton, but none moved their families into the melee.

As she drew up in front of the boardinghouse, Stella's boots had barely hit the ground when two youngsters, no more than ten or twelve each, rushed toward her. One took the reins from her hands, while the other talked.

"We'll water and stable your horse, ma'am. Miz Beaty says to."

Stella looked toward the log cabin that served as one part of the multistructured boardinghouse. Esther Beaty stood on the porch, wiping her hands on her ample apron.

Stella grinned. "Then if Esther said to, you'd better hop to it."

"You don't need to tell us that, ma'am."

She retrieved the leather pouch she had rescued from Logan's desk and her bundle of clothing. Shyly, she wondered what Esther would say about the uniform or, should she choose to tell her, about her relationship with Logan Cafferty.

Esther would not bat an eyelid, Stella knew, but neither would she, herself, relate the story. Although Esther was more moral than most women found in church on Sunday morning, she was also a practical woman. Since she had come to Alleyton her exploits from where she had lived, down near the Nueces River, had become legends.

Stella's favorite concerned the dance hall on the banks of Papalote Creek, a round building constructed by local cowboys who traded yearling calves for the lumber. One night a relative of Esther's late husband imbibed more than his share of whiskey at a dance; when he passed out on the ground outside the building, Esther called the local preacher, who baptized the cowboy on the spot. She said she thought he had died; everyone knew better. Esther Beaty made use of any situation the Lord chose to provide.

When Stella reached the steps, Esther embraced her. Tall and strong, Esther was known in Alleyton as one tough lady, with the emphasis on lady. Miz Beaty, as she was called, was a lady all the way to her extrabig heart.

Stella returned the woman's hug. "See you picked up two new strays while I was gone."

Esther stared after the ragamuffins who had by then taken charge of Stella's horse. "Winter's coming on, and you can see for yourself, not a single shoe between them."

Inside the larger half of the dog-run cabin, Esther stopped to study Stella. "You're tuckered to the core, young lady. Why, your green eyes are so tired they look like muddy water."

Stella laughed. "Lucky for me I don't expect a gentleman caller."

Esther took the bundles from her hands. "I'll have the boys fetch you some bath water. Josie's over yonder getting things ready for supper."

"Josie?"

"The boy's mama."

"Where's Ellen? And Annie?"

Obviously chagrined at having her charity exposed, Esther answered gruffly, "They're outside finishing up the wash. Josie was . . . well, you wouldn't 've wanted me to leave her in the back room of the Dew Drop Inn where I found her, would you? Pleasuring every devil of a man who passed through here, and that with her boys playing in the dirt outside the window?"

"No," Stella sighed. "But there are too many for you to save them all. There's a huge world out there, with so many Josie's and so many . . ."

"I can only hoe my own row, Stella, but that's one row I don't intend to let weeds get a hold in."

Stella bathed in the large room with the bar lowered, locking the door from the inside, feeling for a time as though she had locked herself away from the struggling world outside this building. Although the walls of the cabin were only one log thick, Esther had hung quilts over every space except where shutters closed the windows, thereby insulating the interior of this, her private living quarters.

Before Giddeon agreed to let Stella help with the cotton trains, he had traveled to Alleyton himself and, upon meeting Esther Beaty, had immediately arranged for Stella to use her boardinghouse as a base of operations. The establishment included two other dog-run buildings out back, sufficient to bed ten men each. The other half of this cabin was used for cooking and eating. On her first trip to Alleyton, Stella had found the loft in this portion of Esther's cabin prepared especially for her own private use.

She had barely finished washing off when Esther's voice came at the door. "You finished up in there? If you are, open the door so I can bring you some clean clothes."

Stella smiled. It felt good to be back where someone worried over her. Although, she acknowledged, she wouldn't want such attention all the time.

Wrapping a muslin bathing sheet around herself, she

heaved back the bar, admitting Esther, who carried an armful of mattress ticking.

"Josie sews," Esther responded to Stella's raised eyebrows.

"So do we all," Stella teased. The nice thing about spending time with Esther was that she kept you on your toes, wondering what or whom she would drag in next.

This time it was a dress. "How do you like it?"

"Hope it wasn't *my* mattress you tore up to find work for her."

"It wasn't, but it's your dress. What do you think?"

Stella frowned. "Why for me?"

Esther shrugged. "I have enough clothes, but you . . . well, you spend so much time in men's garb these days, I thought a new getup might lift your spirits."

At the words, Stella smiled. "It does," she said. "And it's lovely." She fingered the black ribbon zigzagged around the hem of the skirt, echoed in bows at the dropped sleeves and below the chaste white linen collar. "Where did you find such original buttons?"

"They're gourd seeds dyed red with cochineal. Josie made them."

"Well, I'll certainly be outfitted proper, if ever . . ."

"You might want to read this before you put on another pair of breeches."

Stella took the paper from Esther's hands. "Thank goodness, he hasn't returned to Louisiana," she said, reading Harry Ransom's brief message.

"Said if you arrived today to meet him at that Scotsman's castle over past Columbus."

Stella sighed.

"I didn't read it," Esther hastened to add. "He told me . . ."

"Esther, you would have been perfectly within your rights if you had. No message left for me will be private — except from Federal eyes — and it might contain a message I need immediately."

The Scotsman Robert Robson's Castle lay across the Colorado River outside Columbus. Although Stella had yet to see it, she knew it had not been facetiously named, but was indeed a castle. She smiled, thinking fondly of Esther, who, knowing she would need a decent costume to visit a castle, even a Texas castle, had killed two birds with one stone, finding work for Josie in the process.

No sooner had she dressed than Johnnie, the older of Josie's two boys, escorted her to the ferry. The other youngster, Jimmie, had been sent to the castle to inform Robert Robson of her arrival, as the message instructed, allowing him time to dispatch a carriage to the ferry crossing.

"When Francisco comes, assure him I am well escorted," she told Esther upon leaving. "Tell him I will meet him at the depot in the morning."

The evening was cool but pleasant, the sky gaily lit by at least a million stars and a sliver of moon rising behind them. When they neared the castle, the road became quite crowded, and as they approached, she caught her breath.

Robert Robson, who had come to Texas from Scotland to seek his fortune, must surely have found it! The castle resembled those from storybooks in every detail, down to the moat that surrounded it. Passing into the confines of the castle yard, she glanced up to be sure—and there it was, a drawbridge to complete the fantasy, although with the traffic generated by the evening's guests there was not time to raise and lower it with each arrival.

Before she could adjust to the surroundings, a genial man around her father's age, she judged, with a brilliant shock of red hair pulled open the door to the carriage and offered his hand.

"Welcome to my humble castle, Miss Duval. It is an honor to greet so famous a lady."

Stella grinned at the formality of her host. "Thank you, sir. I came to meet—"

"Robert, my dear lady, I insist. I know your mission; I shall escort you to Nottoway Plantation's famous Harry Ransom personally. But before I allow him to spirit you away with business of the Confederacy, you will sup with us at table." With that he ushered her into his castle, which, she noted, was anything but humble.

The hallway down which he led her appeared endless, both in length and in height. Looking up, she half-expected to see the moon and stars within the confines of this Scottish castle in the middle of Texas. Colorful rugs in a pattern she had never seen brightened gray stone floors, and every ten paces or so down the entire length of the corridor heavy metal sconces attached to the gray stone walls held long tapers, their glow glistening from the brass adorning the multitude of gray uniforms, from the gaiety in the soldiers' eyes. Indeed, at Robson's castle, the war was practically forgotten, a thing of the past, over and done with—if, indeed, it had ever happened at all.

Several times on the way to the enormous dining hall, Stella felt as though she should pinch herself to be sure she hadn't traveled back in time. And with each unfolding scene, she wished for Logan. He wouldn't believe this was Texas. She could hardly believe it herself!

The dining table was of roughhewn wood, heavy and dark, the place settings pewter, the dishes large and white with an authentic-looking crest of some sort on the rim. Down the center of the table—which ran to such length she was sure she could not shout from one end and be heard at the other—light from tapers in metal candelabra similar to those attached to every wall glanced in flickering reflection from crystal goblets, three at each place. Awed, she had begun to count the guests now taking their seats when her host seated her to the left of his place at the head of the table, with none other than Harry Ransom to her own left.

No sooner had she greeted Harry Ransom than the meal began—a feast, actually, she thought, with roast pheasant, quail, duck, and venison. Her host immediately launched into an extensive oration about his unusual home, giving her no chance to pursue her business with Mr. Ransom.

"It keeps me from getting homesick," he confessed. "And, I might add, delights my guests."

"How do you keep the moat filled?" she questioned. "Does it rain that much this far from the coast?"

The Scotsman shook his red head. "No, fair lady. I pump water from the Colorado River. Indeed, here at the castle, we have running water in practically every room. Pity you will not stay the night. You might find it an interesting experience."

Harry Ransom joined the conversation from Stella's left. "I'm afraid Miss Duval is far too busy for vacations at the moment. In fact —"

"One moment, Harry," their host cut in. "You shall have her to yourself after you allow me two more whims. First, a toast." With that he stood and raised high a glass filled with champagne. "I propose a toast to a lady who is doing more than a man's share of winning this war for us and managing to remain every inch the lady in the process. To Señorita Estelle Duval — a winsome lassie, enchanting . . . tireless in her diligence to our cause."

Stella felt her face flush from the unexpected attention and, when her high-spirited host grasped her arm to draw her to her feet, her legs wobbled. "Hear ye! Hear ye!" he intoned. "Miss Stella Duval. Destined to rule a man's heart . . . and his castle. A true princess."

The word stunned her, falling from the lips of a stranger as it did; a cheer arose from the fifty or more guests, and without warning the champagne glass slipped from her fingers and crashed to the floor at her feet.

Quickly, she stooped to retrieve the glass, bumping heads with him as he bent to help her.

"I meant no disrespect, my dear. I . . ."

"I know . . . I'm sorry . . ." she muttered, feeling foolish and at the same time lost and alone. Her body trembled from the fervor with which she loved a man—the wrong man—no, she thought, a man on the wrong side. "I felt . . . a bit . . . It's nothing."

The Scotsman helped her back to her chair. He excused his guests to play cards in several rooms set up for the sport, or to dance in the ballroom. As he turned back to Stella concern etched his jovial face. "I had thought to ask for the first dance, but perhaps we should wait."

Harry Ransom hovered nearby. "If you are not well, Miss Duval . . ."

"I am fine," she replied quickly. "If Robert will show us where we can discuss our business in private . . ."

Ensconced in a study hung with ancient rugs and heavy chandeliers, Stella and Harry Ransom got down to the business her father entrusted to her alone. Music from the ball—violins, guitars, and a flute—reached them as if on the night air, adding to the illusion of being transported back to medieval times. Stella found it hard to concentrate on business—on anything except the melancholy longing she felt to be with Logan, knowing all the while that even when she did see him again, their opposing causes would surely bring more pain than joy.

Harry Ransom came straight to the point. "Tell your father my move from Louisiana is almost complete. I have secured a farm south of here and within the month will have transported the remainder of my slaves to safety there. Those already at the farm have prepared the fields and planted much of it in cotton. We will be able to meet the state's quota and our own objectives with little trouble."

"Your message to my father indicated you have cotton ready for shipment to Mexico."

He nodded. "I had thought Giddeon . . ."

"Papá could not come himself, so I will direct the train. One of my men is in Alleyton tonight, securing wagons and drivers."

Instead of carrying the leather pouch to the castle, she had transferred the papers to a black grosgrain bag Esther provided. Harry Ransom studied them while she spoke.

When she finished, he rifled through the papers a final time. "I see nothing concerning the proposed vessel."

"Papá did not want to put it in writing," she answered. "He asked me to tell you to make the arrangements. He will bring a portion of the income from his present cargo as a down payment."

Ransom shook his head, thinking. "I must leave for Nottoway at first light. I have no time to travel to Titlum-Tatlum to confirm the order. And it must be done in person. How soon do you expect your father to return?"

She shrugged. "He said December, but . . . he is taking this cargo all the way to Havana harbor."

"Havana harbor . . . ?" Ransom mused, too much a gentleman to reveal his concern. But she knew; they both knew. The prospects of Giddeon's being captured on such a trip far outweighed anything he had to date attempted.

"I can go," Stella suggested. "We will take the cotton overland to Matamoros. From there I can travel straight to Titlum-Tatlum. You can trust me with the . . ."

"Miss Duval! No need to reassure me of your trustworthiness. You have kept secrets of far greater value to our beleaguered country."

"What is of greater value to the Confederacy than a swift blockade-running ship?"

"Perhaps these." He withdrew a sheaf of papers from his inside breast pocket and handed them to her.

She took them, frowning.

"One hundred United States Texas indemnity bonds," he explained. "Face value, one thousand dollars each."

"Papá mentioned them." She flipped through the stack of official-looking documents, recalling how the Federal government issued over six hundred such bonds to Texas back in 1850 in a boundary comprise. "Are they still valid?"

"Yes, if we can find someone to purchase them. So far our emissaries have come up short. Governor Lubbock asked me to see if our agent in Brownsville—Pryor Lea is his name—can sell them to the French. I'd thought your father . . ." He broke off, studied her, then continued. "Since you will be going through Brownsville en route to Matamoros, could I trouble you . . . ?"

"Of course. I will see Mr. Lea gets them."

A satisfied smile broadened Harry Ransom's face. Rising, he offered his hand. "I have kept you too long. You are surely exhausted from your arduous journey, and already you must begin another in the morning."

"As must you, Mr. Ransom. But, yes, I am tired. I think I will return to Alleyton."

"Let me tell our host good-bye and I will accompany you."

"No need," she assured him. "He has provided me an escort to the ferry, and Mrs. Beaty's boy is waiting across the river to drive me to the boardinghouse." Before saying good-bye, she added, "Please give my regards to your wife. The time I spent at the White Castle was among . . . it was the most perfect time in my life."

Harry Ransom thanked her. "By the by, Mrs. Ransom told me some news you might find interesting. It concerns the young naval man you met at Nottoway. . . ."

Stella's eyes blinked, then, quickly, she regained her composure and smiled while her heart raced ahead of the lilting music.

"Cafferty, his name was," he continued. "On their advance up the Mississippi, the Yankees destroyed everything in their sights, as I'm sure you know. In fact, they shelled the White Castle; bullets are still lodged in the pillars out front. As luck would have it, Captain Cafferty was in charge of the assault. When he recognized our home, he commanded his men to spare the house."

93

"How fortunate for you," Stella mused, thinking instead of Los Olmos.

"He even came ashore, greeted my wife, and left a man behind to protect them against further attack."

Dry from the emotions evoked by Harry Ransom's words, Stella's lips stuck together when she tried to answer. She moistened them with her tongue. "How . . . ah, how gracious of him," she managed.

"Gracious, yes. Pity he's on the other side. We could use good men like Cafferty. Speaking of gracious, my dear, perhaps you should agree to one dance with our host before you retire. Ostentatious though he is, he is also a great help to our cause."

"And his home is delightful," she answered, grateful for the change of subject, if nothing else. "A respite from the troubles outside these walls."

Her Scottish host was not at all a poor dancer, although she imagined the experience was something akin to dancing with a bear, he was such a large, burly man. He was, however, the perfect gentleman and host, and a bit more reserved now, which she welcomed.

Holding her at a proper distance, he chattered on about the precise mixture of native lime and gravel he concocted for the construction of his castle, about the wooden pipes that carried water from a tank on the roof to various rooms, and about the guests he entertained from far and wide.

Sweeping the room with his glance, he proceeded to recite the names of those present tonight, like a cannoneer, she thought. "Zachery Pell, Jonathon Luke, Joseph . . ."

"Never mind," she laughed. "I won't remember a single name. Why, I've met so many people these last few months, I can't keep any of their names straight. Unless they are directly associated with the Cotton Road, I don't even try."

"I have the same problem, my dear lady. Names and faces all run together these days. I figure there are a good half dozen men here tonight I don't know—except by sight, of course. The only requisite for crossing my moat is allegiance to the Confederate States of America."

Stella studied the freckled skin that wrinkled around cool blue eyes. "Who are they, then? These men you do not know?"

He scanned the room, and her eyes followed. "Benefactors of our cause. The ones not in uniform are planters like Harry or professional men. Doctors. Dentists. Lawyers."

"Even so," she challenged. "How can you tell a man's allegiance by his physical appearance? There might be Federals among us—"

"No, ma'am," he interrupted, swinging her around the room, past groups of men, some talking, some watching. As one of the few females in attendance, she knew if she wished, she could dance the night away. "I greet each carriage that crosses my drawbridge. I'd know a Yankee by his look, by his talk." Holding her at arm's length, he studied her with a smile. "Why, ma'am, if there was a damned Yankee in this room, I'd know him by his smell. . . ."

As in the flash of a falling star, her host's words faded into the din of music and conversation. Over his shoulder, her eyes locked with a pair of intense brown ones, and she stumbled.

"What's the trouble, my lady? Did I go and step on your pretty little foot?"

Stella swallowed, unable to take her eyes from Logan Cafferty's. He lounged against a stone pillar. Dressed as a planter in fawn pants and navy cutaway jacket, he took her breath away.

Or was it merely his presence that left her stupefied? she wondered. Here. Here where he should not be.

"Are you all right?" her host inquired in a worried voice.

She forced a smile, feeling her joints freeze, as she watched Logan cross the room with a lazy, though purposeful, stride. Every inch the military man, she thought, desperate lest he be recognized.

When he tapped her dancing partner on the shoulder, she tensed as though he had struck her.

"May I?" Logan asked their startled host.

The Scotsman stared at his new guest, and Stella recalled his words just uttered. She pursed her lips. Not for a moment did she think anyone could *smell* a Yankee. But Logan looked so much like what he was—a military man—an officer—

When they came together, her mind swayed with the touch of him, as though she were back on board the *Victory,* his prisoner. That, she knew, she was . . . would always be . . . his prisoner. They danced effortlessly a full minute or more before either uttered a word.

"Looks like I arrived in the nick of time." His smile warmed her unbearably.

"You shouldn't have come," she whispered.

"And miss the announcement?"

"What announcement?"

"I couldn't tell, though—must have been the noise when you dropped your champagne glass—did you accept his proposal?"

"Whose proposal for what?" she demanded.

"Our host's," he answered. "To become"—leaving hers for but an instant, his eyes swept the palatial room, then captured her soft green stare again—"his princess."

"He didn't mean that."

Logan grinned. "You should brush up on your Scottish. Lassie means sweetheart, or didn't you know?"

His gentle teasing eased over her distraught senses like balm. Her left hand trembled on his shoulder, and her right hand clenched his. He returned her grip, his eyes caressing hers.

"You shouldn't have come. It's dangerous for you here in the midst of so many . . ."

"Do you remember the last time we danced?"

96

She felt paralyzed, as if the only moving parts to her body were her feet and her pounding heart, and over neither did she have the least bit of control. She nodded.

His eyes bore into hers. "We danced the night away to keep from . . ."

"You shouldn't have come."

"That was before . . ." His words died away and their thoughts mingled in the charged air between them.

"Before the rebellion," he finished.

And before . . . she thought. Suddenly, her attention focused on a man across the room. "Do you remember Mr. Harry Ransom?"

"From Nottoway? How could I forget . . . ?"

"Well, he hasn't forgotten you, either. And he's here tonight. Directly behind you, across the room."

Logan's eyebrows almost touched when he frowned. His reaction was instantaneous. "Let's get out of here."

Her wet palm slipped inside his hand as he dragged her through the nearest doorway.

"You shouldn't have come," she whispered again.

He pulled her around a corner into a darkened corridor. "Are you sorry?"

Her green eyes begged, pleaded, and she solemnly shook her head. All she could think was that he was here, they were together, a thing she had felt certain would never happen again, at least, not for a very long while. Her mind reeled, and when she answered, her voice was weak with relief, with fear. "I love you."

The stairs at their right were narrow and she followed him without knowing where they led, wondering whether he did, and if so, how. After two more flights that became increasingly narrow, they stepped out into the brisk October evening. The sky was black and the stars looked close enough to pluck from the heavens.

"Say that again," he prompted.

She stared around them, searching for ears that

shouldn't hear their conversation, eyes that shouldn't see this man, her beloved, her enemy . . . no, their enemy, never hers. The roof was deserted. "You shouldn't have come."

"That isn't what I meant." His teasing voice played on her senses. "Don't worry. I'll avoid Harry Ransom, and since he isn't expecting to see me, he won't recognize me."

"He isn't your only problem. When you approached us on the dance floor, our host had just finished telling me that the only requirement for entering this castle is allegiance to the Confederate States of America. He said he can tell a *damned Yankee* by his talk, by his walk, and . . ." — at last she smiled into his eyes — ". . . and by his smell." Clasping her arms around his waist, she buried her face in his chest, inhaling deeply. "I don't smell a Yankee . . . all I smell is you. And I love you."

He lifted her chin and gazed steadily into her sparkling eyes. "That's better, princess." Lowering his lips, he felt the tension of the last few days drain away in the passion she raised within him. "I love you, too."

Alone with him at last, Stella let her fears dissolve. She returned his kiss as if they were the only two people in the world. Caressing his shoulders, she leaned into his body, while her own took on the unquenchable ache he always caused in the very nether reaches of her soul. For a moment the war ceased to exist. For a moment the castle became their own private realm, from where she and Logan together ruled the earth and brought love and joy and peace to all their subjects.

For a moment, his hands on her back, clasping her to his hard, loving body, brought only one hope, one dream, one unbearable desire. . . .

For a moment all she wanted was to love this man.

Drawing her back, he looked into her eyes. They glistened in the light of the stars, and he knew she saw only him. "See what you missed by running away?"

"Don't waste time talking about that. We have so little . . ."

"We have the rest of our lives, princess."

She laughed. "And the castle to live in, I suppose."

He tensed at her tone. "For the remainder of the rebellion, our lives will be a bit strained, but someday . . ."

When she tried to wriggle away from him, he tightened his hold. "It's no use, Logan. No amount of pretty words will entice me back to the *Victory*. I may be a prisoner to your love"—she inhaled deeply—"and to your touch and your kisses and . . . but I'll definitely not submit to becoming a prisoner to your country."

He stared at her until she looked away, then he turned her loose, but caught up one of her hands and began to walk around the roof of the castle.

"He has a garden up here," she said at last, stalling for time, determined now to find some way to separate their relationship from the war. "Roses and vegetables and . . ."

His hand tightened painfully around her fingers. "He probably grows food for the rebel army."

A tiredness enveloped her as the night. She pulled her hand from his. "The enemy's camp is a foolish place to arrest an escaped prisoner."

"I didn't come to *arrest* you, damnit!"

"Obviously, you didn't come to love me, either, so for what reason did you disguise yourself as a Southern planter, *Colonel?*"

Fiercely he jerked her about. "Why are you so hardheaded? Why can't you understand what you're getting yourself into?"

"*I* don't understand? What about you?"

"Stella, listen to me. I've seen what combat does to people. I've seen how it destroys men and women and . . . Don't you read the newspapers? The casualty lists? Do you have any idea how it terrifies me to think of you engaging in this rebellion like any man? To know you are risking your life . . . ?"

He spoke in earnest, and her anger began to dissipate in the heat of his passion. Reaching, she stroked his jaw, feeling it clench beneath her palm. Her fingers traced his nose, his lips, and, of an instant, he captured her finger and held it sensuously in his mouth. "Is it so different?" she whispered. "You worrying about me, from me worrying about you?"

"Yes, damnit!"

"Why?" she demanded. "You don't know what I've been through since you stopped writing. If you'd like, I can quote your last letter, word for word. I wouldn't miss a single period . . . or tear stain . . . or any of the hurt. . . ."

As she spoke, tears formed and rolled down her cheeks, and he bent and kissed them away. "Princess, princess. It will soon be over. I promise you. Soon." Holding her face in his hands, he studied her intently while he spoke in earnest, desperate tones. "I didn't come here to take you back. Holding you prisoner would be worse than . . ." He stopped, gritted his teeth, then continued, "I want you to go home to Los Olmos and stay. I have to get back to the *Victory,* or I would escort you there myself. But with any kind of luck, I will be stationed in the Gulf for the duration. Every chance I get, I'll come ashore. . . ."

A heavy sigh, like a sob, caught in her chest, and she withdrew from his arms and turned away. "I can't do that. I'm committed . . ."

"Committed, hell!"

His obstinacy eased the pain in her chest, if not in her heart. She turned on him, indignant. "Why is it that *you* can work for what you believe in, but I cannot? Are only men allowed to commit themselves to a cause? Or is it only *Yankees* whose cause is just?"

No sooner had the words left her mouth than she turned quickly left then right, searching for the wrong ears, the wrong person.

100

Logan grabbed her by the shoulders, and lowering his lips, he kissed her fiercely, forcing her to respond. The disparity between their separate missions was like nothing compared with the disparity between their two wills. From the beginning he had loved her for her feisty, independent spirit—the same spirit he was attempting to harness. That it was for her own good he knew for certain; but it was a battle he did not expect to win.

Lifting his lips, he pressed them against her forehead. "Why can't you be content to commit yourself to me?"

Grimly, she moved her face to look into his. "Why can't you . . . ?"

Later, in her loft bed at Esther Beaty's, she wrapped her arms around herself and stroked the crisp cotton sleeves of her nightdress. Her lips moved gently back and forth against each other while she relived the tenderness of his parting kiss, in order to keep herself from probing their surely painful, but otherwise uncertain future.

They had parted suddenly, before either of them came to terms with the road the other had chosen to tread. Too soon other couples discovered the rooftop garden, and they had fled, both from discovery by their Nottoway friend, Harry Ransom.

After Logan's role in saving Nottoway, Stella doubted the man would turn Logan over to Confederate authorities should he recognize him tonight. However, she had no doubt his opinion of her as a reliable courier for the Cotton Road would drop considerably should he discover her in the arms of the enemy. How would he react should he catch her with her arms around a Federal officer, while she clutched the purse containing bonds to purchase a blockade-running ship for the Confederacy?

For that matter, what would Logan do should he discover the bonds . . . thereby the extent of her involvement in the blockade-running efforts?

Falling asleep at length, she smiled at one last, grim

thought. Logan didn't suspect Papá's involvement; his presence here not only assured her of his love for her, but also that he had not set out to capture her father.

Francisco arrived at daybreak with word the wagons had been procured and drivers hired.

"They are busy ferrying the cotton across the river, señorita. The job should be accomplished by nightfall." Stella thanked him, wondering at the same time whether Logan was still in town, and what her chances were of seeing him again if she ventured into the streets.

Then over breakfast Esther handed her a letter. "You said to read any message," the red-faced landlady told her. "Should have mentioned that handsome fellow was following you."

Stella's heart flipped in her chest. "What handsome fellow?" The paper seemed to burn her hands, and when she unfolded it the handwriting took her breath.

Wait for me at Los Olmos, princess.
I will come as soon as possible.

Your devoted Logan

"Thought it was that father of yours at first," Esther chattered on, "way he walks, I guess, carries himself straight, like a military man, and he has the same squint to his eyes. Course when he came close, I realized he was younger." She studied Stella a moment. "I hope he found you at the castle. You need a strong, loving man, and if I were a gambling woman, I'd wager that's exactly what he is."

Stella stared at the solemn woman a moment, then smiled. "He is . . . at least, he could be, if it weren't for this . . . this damned war!"

"Don't fret yourself," Esther continued. "If he's got the sand you have, you'll work things out. Lucky, he's coming to Los Olmos."

Stella worried over that very thing during the next two weeks, while she guided the wagon train south from Alleyton toward the Mexican border. She didn't expect Logan to turn up at Los Olmos soon. He said he had to return to the ship, and certainly his special assignment, whatever it was, would keep him occupied. . . .

Still, what if he came while Papá and his blockade runners were there? Or . . . even if he didn't encounter Papá and the blockade runners, what would he do if he should see her wagons loaded with cotton?

They had good weather; for the most part, Francisco had been able to find sturdy wagons and dependable men. It took a week to reach the Cardwell stage station on the Guadalupe River, and by that time they had crossed two other rivers—the Navidad and the Lavaca, both of which allowed her to judge the mettle of the new men.

Francisco persuaded her to spend the night at the Cardwell's, which, since it was an overnight stop on the stage line from San Antonio to the coast, provided rooms upstairs for travelers. After cleaning up, she joined the men in the central dining area, where they exchanged news from Alleyton with travelers from San Antonio, and received news the Cardwells had been able to pick up from other travelers.

For supper, Cardwell's wife served a pie made of sweetbreads, kidney, and Irish potatoes, biscuits with wild grape jelly, and coffee made from parched okra seeds, for which she apologized profusely. After the meal, Stella brought Mrs. Cardwell a sack of coffee beans, exchanging them for the meal and a night's sleep on a cornhusk mattress. Both women felt the winner. Stella promised to try to bring another sack of coffee beans when she returned.

The next morning it was raining when they started the wagons across the Guadalupe. By then the trail was so familiar, the trials so predictable, she didn't wince when the third wagon bogged into the silt and had to be dug free.

The new men, for the most part, fell into the routine, but Stella feared they would miss Beto's mastery of crossing rivers.

From the banks of the Guadalupe, Francisco pointed to a new man who stood knee-deep in the river, shoveling mud right and left. "That is the man I have been talking about, señorita. His name is Maxwell Burnsides. He is the best worker we have found outside our own vaqueros, and an intelligent man, too. We will be fortunate to keep him."

"If some Confederate captain between here and Brownsville doesn't impress him into the army," she agreed. Her success in transporting, she knew, lay largely in the fact she used Los Olmos vaqueros as teamsters. While the Confederate officers they encountered along the route were allowed to impress any man they chose, cowboys were usually exempted: They were needed to raise beef for the army, and no captain wanted to go hungry.

It took the remainder of the day and into twilight to move all fifteen wagons across the Guadalupe River. Backbreaking, exhausting, often dispiriting work, for no sooner did they get one wagon safely across than they had to tackle the next.

During the long process, Stella watched Maxwell Burnsides, grateful for the diversion from less painful thoughts. Indeed, he lived up to Francisco's assessment.

He dug the third wagon free, practically unassisted, then went in search of a more suitable crossing. That found, he advised Francisco, and together they diverted the fourth wagon, successfully crossing upstream. At the first sign of bogging, the new man shoveled gravel into the ruts, prolonging the time when they must move to a new location, which he again scouted and found.

He never seemed to tire, never complained, and never shirked the larger part of the burden of crossing the river. That evening Stella took her cup of coffee and sat on a log beside him. She rarely made such advances; Francisco, and

Beto and Raul when they were along, discouraged her mingling with the hired teamsters. The vaqueros would protect her with their lives, she knew, but she had no right to put them in such a position.

This new man was different, however. Not only did he work harder than most men they hired in Alleyton, but he was obviously a leader. More polished in manner than the run-of-the-mill teamsters, he stood straight and tall— like Papá, she thought, and Logan. Studying him during the day, she decided he was very close to Logan's age and size. And his squinting eyes—again like Papá's and Logan's. A man of the sea? A deserter?

Whatever, his proficiency at moving wagon trains made him indispensable, at least until Beto returned. She needed to keep Maxwell Burnsides, and to do so, she must let him know he was appreciated.

"You put in an impressive day's work, Mr. Burnsides."

He ran a hand through his unruly sandy-colored hair and studied her with a frank expression. "That name's always sounded a little highfalutin to suit me, ma'am. Why don't you just call me Max?" He shrugged, then turned his attention to the glowing coals of the campfire. "Work's what I'm here for."

She smiled, liking him immediately. "Sometimes new drivers are taken unawares by the difficulties we encounter. It's over three hundred miles from Alleyton to Matamoros—three hundred miles and ten rivers."

He swirled his coffee in the cup a moment, then took a swallow. "I'm used to work."

"What kind of work?"

When he tensed at the question, she thought perhaps she had crossed the line of propriety, but before she could apologize, he responded.

"I'm a man of the sea."

"The sea? So is my father, and my . . . ah . . ." She inhaled a deep breath of fresh air and camp smoke and remembered the smell of saltwater and Logan. "The sea is an important part of my life, although I have never been to sea . . . ah, except once," she added, as her time on board the *Victory* came to mind with such force she almost swayed from the image of the rolling deck.

"You put in a hard day's work yourself, ma'am. That river was as hard to cross as any ocean, and you certainly did your part."

The compliment settled over her like a warm blanket, soothing her cramped muscles. There had been times today when she thought she couldn't crack her whip another time, her shoulders ached so badly. Her hands were raw with blisters, even though she wore thick leather gloves, and her right leg cramped yet from slamming on the break so often. But every time she thought she had to rest, she saw Maxwell Burnsides shoveling gravel, digging mud while standing knee-deep in rushing water, always alert, ever ready to tackle the most difficult assignment—and he didn't have one half the stake in this operation she did. "Driving a wagon is nothing compared with . . ."

"I haven't met many men who could have done as well, ma'am, and you a woman . . . it's mighty impressive. If you hadn't been along, we'd be there still."

"Thank you, Max. I agree. We all did a splendid job today. Now, if we can hold out . . ."

"Oh, we'll hold out. Long enough to get this wagon train to Matamoros, anyhow. Bet you don't quite feel up to dancing tonight, though."

She laughed, leaned back, and stared at the stars that had come out with the clearing sky. "I could manage," she sighed. "Given the right . . . ah, circumstances, I would have no trouble dancing the night away."

106

Chapter Five

Two weeks and six rivers later they reached the Santa Margarita Crossing on the Nueces River, all wagons intact. Francisco rode ahead to locate the cable they would use to ferry the wagons across the deep river and up the steep opposite bank.

Stella sat her horse and watched him go, thinking of the others who had gone before them: her forebears, the Spanish conquistadors, who used the Santa Margarita Crossing on their entradas into this hostile land, where they came to "tame" wild Indians and to take their gold, a land they named Tejas, meaning friend.

These Spaniards, her ancestors, were the ones who planted the *deadman*—a timber sunk deep enough into the earth to anchor a series of winches by which cables were then used to pull wagons through the river and up the embankment, or down, depending on one's direction. Twenty years ago General Zachary Taylor had used the same deadman to cross his Army of the Invasion on his way to Mexico to win back the Rio Grande River as the legal boundary between the United States and Mexico. Now she was using it in the cause of another war. War without end, she thought. Amen. Pray it would not be so.

Francisco returned bearing the cable he had pulled across the river from the A-frame hoist. He sat his horse, both still dripping river water. "After this river, señorita, it will be easy going."

She laughed. "You only say that because we will be in familiar territory, Francisco. We won't have another steep riverbank, but we are only halfway to Matamoros; from here on, we will be lucky to find water for our teams."

"We will be close to home."

"*Sí*," she responded in Spanish. Though she rarely used her mother's tongue, there were times when Spanish phrases dropped from her lips, quite without design. The language expressed a deeper emotion for her than the English she had been taught to speak simultaneously as a child, and any time she neared Los Olmos, her emotions ran deep.

While Francisco swam the river, located the cable, and made sure the windlass was still intact, the teamsters had swaddled their wagons with tar cloth, thereby waterproofing the contents.

When Francisco recrossed the river with a handful of teamsters to work the windlass, Max attached the cable to the axle of the first wagon and helped heave it into the water of the Nueces. Four men worked in the water, steadying the wagon, so as not to topple cotton into the river, while the men on the opposite bank worked the wince, translating manpower to mechanical.

Stella watched Max tie a square knot in the cable, then help the driver get the vehicle into the water. "You're handy with that cable," she told him.

"Hemp rope's all the same, ma'am, whether it's used to hoist a wagon or to rig a ship."

Although the crossing was laborious, as always—a fact each driver expressed when his turn came to heave his wagon into the rushing water and hope it floated upright to the other side—they had no mishaps. As he had during crossings at the nine rivers behind them, Maxwell Burnsides worked with Francisco to aid and direct the crossing. He was a born leader, it seemed.

Unless the crossing required more men than were available, Stella was not allowed—by Francisco and since his arrival by Max—to participate beyond shouting encouragements. This she did from the bank, feeling useless most of the time. When, as now, the going was fairly simple, Max kept up an easy dialogue, and she found him both entertaining and pleasant company.

"How'd you get yourself mixed up in this business, anyhow, ma'am?" he asked during a slack in activity.

"You might say I know the right people." She responded to his question easily while not revealing anything she didn't think he had a need to know.

She trusted him, more with each passing day, and Francisco did, as well. Still, the region was rife with rumors of spies and undercover Federal agents, and although she did not suspect Max himself, he could easily let slip a word in the wrong place. She had learned early that the less a man knew, the less he could tell. And she could not afford to give away her father's position or endanger the men on this wagon train.

Thinking of undercover agents brought the recollection of Logan at Robson's Castle. A smile creased her lips. He had indeed made a handsome Southern planter. The smile slowly died as she wondered where he had gone, whether he had returned to his ship without being detected . . . when she would see him again.

When. The word had come as readily to her mind as a Spanish phrase, and with as much emotion. Contentment settled over her. She would see Logan again; perhaps he would be there when she stopped by Los Olmos on her return trip, headed for Titlum-Tatlum. It was a long shot, but she could wish, couldn't she?

She could wish, yes, but where would it all get them? What havoc would this relationship wreak upon her family? And upon Logan himself? He would surely find himself in serious trouble if he spent too much time with a rebel.

Of immediate concern, however, was getting this load of cotton to Mexico and returning to Titlum-Tatlum to order the blockade-running vessel. On horseback, she followed the last wagon, driven by Max, across the river, where they unswaddled the wagons and carts and surveyed the damage.

"No broken wheels or axles," she sighed. "This will be the first time we have arrived in Banquete without needing repairs."

"We could use some fresh oxen," Max suggested.

Francisco agreed. "If we are to make the trip with limited water rations, we must find replacements for the weakest of the lot in Banquete."

Stella glanced at the afternoon sun, pondering the situation. "Camp for the night," she told the men. "Banquete is only ten miles away; we can make it tomorrow. I will ride ahead now and arrange for animals."

Francisco followed her to her horse. "I will come with you."

"The wagons . . . ?" she began.

"Max can lead the wagon train."

"He doesn't know the land," she objected.

"He is a seaman," Francisco told her, "accustomed to finding his way on the wide blue ocean with no markers at all. Surely he can travel a trail so marked by cotton lint it resembles the frozen northland."

She laughed. "You're right. But what about the animals. Do you think he can handle them?"

Francisco studied their new teamster, who went about building a campfire in the clearing he had previously selected. "He is a woodsman, also. I am sure he will not let us down, señorita."

"I feel as you do," she admitted, thinking that this would be a good test. They were sure to need dependable men in the coming months. They should begin training them now.

Although Stella could tell he was somewhat taken aback

by the suggestion, Max agreed to do his best.

"Follow the trail of cotton," Francisco told him.

"Who happens if . . . say, a wagon breaks down . . . or some of the oxen are not up to the trip?" he asked.

"In that case, unload the wagon, or as many as necessary, and hide the bales back in the brush."

Max peered into the thick chaparral. "I can see it would work, saying a man can get in there to hide the stuff."

"If you come across any bales hidden thataway," Francisco added, "oblige the owners by carrying them on into Banquete."

In Banquete, Francisco headed for the stockpens owned by the notorious Sally Scull, and Stella stopped at the large frame building that served as an eating-drinking establishment, as well as stage station, mail drop, and general information center. As soon as she stepped through the door, she was glad she had come ahead tonight.

"Jorge! I thought you were at El Sal del Rey."

At thirty-three, Jorge Cortinas was more like an older brother to Stella than a cousin. Her mother's nephew, he had been orphaned at a young age, when his father was killed fighting in the Texas War for Independence. He was ten when Stella was born and had considered himself her protector from the first magical moment he looked upon her tiny countenance. Returning his embrace, Stella forced back tears. Would she ever get over the pain she felt for him at losing Alicia, his beautiful young wife? Alicia, her own friend. Alicia, whose death had propelled the Cortinases and Duvals headlong into this dreadful conflict.

"I have been reassigned," he answered her question. "Come, let's eat. You look as though you haven't seen the inside of a house in two lifetimes!"

"It hasn't been quite that long." She laughed with him over a bountiful—in light of the circumstances—meal of beans and dumplings, washed down with scalding coffee. "Mrs. Cardwell is reduced to okra-seed coffee," she told her cousin.

He sat back and lit his pipe. "We are all reduced to fewer than our usual luxuries. Look at you. I hope you are on your way home."

His voice held more admonition than observation, and at her answer, he took the pipe from his mouth and stared hard at her. "Tío Capitán wishes you to go to Matamoros?"

She ducked the question. "He had to send me to Alleyton to meet Harry Ransom, Jorge. You know how riddled our country is with spies these days. Papá, Mamá, and I are the only people Mr. Ransom knows in Texas who are directly connected with the blockade runners."

Jorge sighed, and they sat in amiable silence, Stella recalling another person in Texas Mr. Ransom knew and the unsettling moment when she feared he had recognized Logan at Robson's Castle. Forcing her thoughts away from Logan, she turned to Jorge with curiosity.

"You haven't told me why you left El Sal del Rey."

Eyes bright at her reminder, he leaned forward, though neither of them expected to find wrong ears in Banquete. "You have heard of Fort Casa Blanca?"

"North of here . . . on the Nueces?"

He nodded. "Until now, their major contribution has been to protect cotton trains coming from San Antonio."

"I know," she nodded. "Bandits. Farther west it's Indians and in the Gulf, Federals. The whole state is crawling with outlaws of some sort." Again, her thoughts strayed to Logan . . . to the *Victory* . . . to his quarters . . .

"We are adding to security measures at Fort Casa Blanca," Jorge told her. "Soon, we will be able to ship supplies up the Nueces River all the way to the fort; we can warehouse goods for transport to Alleyton."

She smiled in admiration. "A very good idea. Tell me, is it true about the tunnel?"

He nodded. "The fort is impregnable. It will be a safe route for wagon trains, in case the rumors are true."

"What rumors?"

"You haven't heard? The Federals are supposed to be preparing a major assault along the coast. Word has it they believe they can strangle us by sea. . . ."

Jorge's words faded in the vision of the role Logan Cafferty would surely play in such an operation. Colonel Logan Cafferty. Was it, indeed, his own scheme?

"What is it, Stella?"

Her mouth felt dry, her shoulders weak. All she wanted was for the war to be over . . . for them to have survived it; to have Logan by her side . . . and Papá; to resume life as it was . . . as it had been, before . . .

Helplessly she stared at her dear cousin, seeing instead his wife, bleeding and dying from Federal shells. They couldn't go back . . . they could never go back. Things would never be the same.

"Stella?"

Inhaling deeply, she pursed her lips and girted her resolve. "I'm all right. It's just this damned war! I hate it."

In the ensuing silence, the proprietress of the establishment approached the table. "Miss Stella?"

Stella looked into the woman's coarse face. For a moment the two women stared at each other in a kinship born of the rugged work in which they engaged, of the rugged, often coarse, men with whom they dealt. Stella nodded.

"A vaquero brung this here message for you yesterday. I didn't recognize you at first, without your vaqueros."

Stella took the letter, thanking the woman. "They will be along tomorrow with the wagons. I came ahead to procure more oxen for our trip to the border."

As it turned out, Francisco procured the oxen, waited for Maxwell Burnsides, and set out on the road to Matamoros without her.

The message was from Los Olmos. Her mother's own

handwriting, beseeching her to stop by Los Olmos, if only for a few hours.

"Something must have happened," Jorge worried. "I should have stopped to check on them myself. I did not think I had time, but . . ."

Stella took her cousin's hand. She knew his thoughts: his children. After their mother's death and since he had joined Rip Ford's Confederates, the children remained at Los Olmos in the care of Stella's mother, their own great-aunt. Miguel and little Ana were all that was left of Jorge's world. "If it were urgent, the messenger would have found me along the way," she comforted. "Mamá knows the route."

He inhaled deeply. "Perhaps Giddeon has returned."

"He won't be back until . . ." Her heart almost stopped at the thoughts that raced into her mind.

Following her thinking, Jorge refuted it. "If Giddeon had been captured, how would Serita have found out before . . . ? I mean, you or I would have heard the news before those at Los Olmos."

"I don't know what to make of it," Stella admitted. "Mamá would not call on *me* for help. She can take care of herself better than I can."

"She has a reason, if it is only a mother's wish to see her daughter. How long since you have been home?"

"A couple of months."

"Tomorrow, we will go . . ."

"No, Jorge. Tomorrow *I* will go to Los Olmos. *You* are needed at Fort Casa Blanca."

"I . . ."

Stella silenced him with a laugh. "After all the places I've been lately, the road from here to Los Olmos will seem like a trip to church. We both have jobs to do. Francisco wait here for the wagon train. I will pick them up on the other side of Los Olmos Creek."

It took a bit more wrangling than that, but finally she

114

convinced both Jorge and Francisco that she could indeed ride unchaperoned to Los Olmos without falling into the hands of bandits.

"Most of the people I meet will be vaqueros from the King Ranch or from Los Olmos. Captain King's Kineños will look out for me as surely as will our own vaqueros."

"The Federals hold Camp San Fernando," Jorge argued.

"Then I will skirt San Fernando, and the moment I arrive at Los Olmos, I will send a messenger to Fort Casa Blanca with word on what the problem is . . . even if it is merely a whim of my mother's."

Not until dawn the following day when she rode away from Banquete, with the rising sun warming her face and glistening from the stirrup-high grass beneath her horse's hooves, did she allow herself to dwell on the negative possibilities of Serita's message.

Serita Cortinas Duval did not indulge in whims. In all Stella's twenty-three years she could never recall her mother's summoning her without stating the reason. What if the Federals had come up Los Olmos Bay again? What if . . . ?

She skirted San Fernando Creek to the north, taking an extra hour by the sun to avoid the Federal camp, although she wanted badly to discover the strength of their forces.

Later, she promised herself. Somehow she would find a way to reconnoiter the Federal position at San Fernando, if her own vaqueros had not already done so.

That thought brought additional fears. Had the soldiers from San Fernando attacked Los Olmos? But if they had, Serita would not have sent word for her to come home . . . not into a trap.

Thus she traveled through the chaparral, finding and discarding fears one by one, until by the time she arrived at Los Olmos Creek twilight cast soft shadows over the house. She sat for a moment, gripping the reins in damp hands. From where she sat, all she could see were the wide veranda across the front, the deep-set windows sheltered by the overhanging porch, and the gutted top of their once lovely house.

Her fears momentarily dissolved into anger as she relived the terror of that night. To the right were the family plots, where generations of her family lay in quiet repose beneath spreading arms of the elm trees that gave Los Olmos, both the creek and the hacienda, its name. The newest grave belonged to Alicia Cortinas.

Nudging her horse into the trickling stream, her knees trembled against the saddleskirt. Warily she searched the perimeter of the compound from left to right, apprehensive yet alert. Nothing moved. All looked quiet.

She urged the horse up the incline, walked it forward, carefully now, studying the front of the house: no other horses at the hitching post, no sign of activity through the darkened windows, no lanterns . . .

A green jay screeched from an elm tree, and she jumped, then chastised herself.

A familiar squawk broke through her frazzled brain: the front door. Fear swelled in her heart. Where was Mamá?

At the hitching rail, she slid her rifle from the scabbard and dropped to the ground. Her eyes darted from one side of the house to the other, then back to the door.

And there he stood.

Or rather, here he came, she rephrased, watching Logan Cafferty saunter down the steps, dressed as she had last seen him, like any well-to-do Southern planter, looking for all the world as if he belonged here, when in fact, it was she who . . .

"What are you doing here?" Her words faltered on ragged breath.

He reached for her, but instead of coming into his outstretched arms, she fell against him, weak from expectation, from discovery.

"What are you doing here?" she repeated, finding strength to pursue her fears.

116

He stared at her, taking in her bewilderment, inhaling the great pleasure the very essence of this woman brought him. "I couldn't wait until Christmas."

She struggled against the mesmerizing effects he always had on her. She had trouble tearing her mind away from the feel of his muscles beneath her arms, the sound of his heart against her cheek. He was here at Los Olmos, where for so long she had yearned for him to be.

Here at Los Olmos . . . safe at Los Olmos . . . together at Los Olmos. "You shouldn't . . ."

"If you tell me one more time I shouldn't be where ever you are . . ." he began.

His carefree jesting caressed her frayed nerves, but her fears would not be easily quieted. She tried to look beyond him, but he held her back with firm hands.

"Where is Mamá? What have you done . . . ?"

His eyes, smoldering with desire, registered understanding, at last, and his features dropped. "No, princess . . . I am alone. This is a personal visit, not official. I would never . . . Didn't your landlady in Alleyton give you my message?"

She nodded. "Mamá?"

"Your mother is in the garden with the children." His eyes twinkled as he lowered his face. "She sent me to greet you. Now, don't I get a kiss?"

When his lips touched hers, her heart felt as if it would explode, as with fireworks on a holiday, leaving her weakened and a bit wobbly. His arms tightened around her, pulling her closer . . . and closer still. For a moment her world shrank to include only the two of them: his lips, tender and moist, yet urgent with promise; his arms, sheltering, protecting, stimulating the desires already rampant within her.

Cries suddenly pierced the air, and he lifted his face, smiling at the hunger he saw in her eyes, a hunger echoed, he knew, in his own.

"Stella! Stella!" By now the children had descended upon

them, tugging at Stella's breeches.

"You're home!"

"Logan took us riding!"

"You're home!"

"He said we could go again when you came home."

"Let's go now!"

"Children!" Serita called from the veranda.

When Stella saw her mother, she laughed with joy.

Serita shrugged. "I tried to keep them in the courtyard. But I'm afraid Logan has made quite an impression on them."

Stella stared up into Logan's face; he, too, shrugged, sheepishly.

"You took them *riding?* All five of them?"

He squeezed his arm about her waist. "They're great kids. They don't even mind that I can't keep their names straight, much less their parentage."

Stooping, Stella enclosed the children in her arms. Her heart swelled to such a degree she was sure it would burst. She tousled first one head, then another, and each child leaned forward to press a kiss on her cheek. "Dory belongs to Abril and Delos, Philipe and Gracie belong to Lupe and Felix" —she swallowed back a rush of melancholy—"this is Miguel, Jorge's son, and little Ana, his daughter."

A bell rang through the bedlam, followed by Serita's voice. "Come, children. Time to clean up for dinner. You know the rules."

Reluctantly obedient, the children turned toward the house. Serita embraced her daughter. "And this is *my* child. How lovely to have you home."

Stella squeezed her mother in return. "Thank you for sending for me," she whispered.

Serita drew back. With a twinkle in her eyes she looked from Stella to Logan. "This gentleman's visit has been long anticipated. I knew you wouldn't want to miss it. Lupe has drawn a bath for you, dear, and pressed a gown."

They dined in the comedor, feasting on sopa de elote, followed by beefsteak and tamales and carne asada, served with a sauce, rajas de chili poblano, and a delicate flan for dessert. Chatter from the children's dining room reached their ears like a backdrop of gentle music.

"Mamá, you and Abril must have been cooking all day."

"More like three days," Logan offered.

"You have been here three days?"

He nodded, and Serita answered. "I know you wanted to show him Los Olmos, dear, but . . . well, I'm afraid the children and I have already done it."

Stella stared at Logan, suddenly recalling Jorge's news at Banquete. "How did you manage to be away so long?"

He avoided the question. "I wish you had been here." His eyes held hers and she felt faint with the emotions he evoked inside her—not only physical, but emotional—and her heart felt as if it would burst with gladness . . . with sorrow.

She pursed her lips to still their trembling. "Isn't it dreadful how things never turn out as we plan?"

He captured her hand and held it on top of the table. "But things do turn out. Now that I've seen Los Olmos, your father can put his fears to rest. When he returns . . ."

At the mention of her father, Stella quaked. Her father's whereabouts, his activities, must remain a secret. "I'm glad you had a chance to see the hacienda. What did you think? Did the children drive you mad?"

He laughed. "First, I loved the hacienda. I can see why this place means so much to you. And, no, the children did not drive me mad. Quite the opposite. After a ship full of cranky sailors, five children . . ."

Stella fidgeted. Why couldn't she relax? The mere mention of the war set her to trembling. "You're lucky," she interrupted. "There are actually more than five children. The others are older . . . and gone. Abril and Delos have three married daughters who live in Corpus Christi. Dory is

119

sixteen, she will soon be leaving; and Lupe and . . ."

"We have already been through the family roster, dear," Serita broke in. "Now that we've finished dining, it is time for me to put the children to bed. Lupe has a bottle of champagne cooling; I will join you in the courtyard to toast your homecoming—both of your homecomings."

The evening air was cool, but not uncomfortable. Torches glowed from brackets attached to the eaves of the house, casting golden flecks over the water that tumbled from the fountain in the center of the courtyard.

The gown Lupe pressed for Stella was of plaid silk taffeta, with a large oval yoke extending well beyond her shoulders, from which full sleeves fell to gather onto a narrow wristband.

"You're so lovely," he whispered. "You take my breath away." His hand on her back traveled up her spine, spreading fiery tingles along the way, stopping at the chenille snood. "Trying to hide your newfangled hairdo?"

Her eyes sought his, then darted away. She wasn't sure how to act with her mother slipping in and out.

He propped a foot on the edge of the fountain and spread her fingers over his knee. Then, with deliberate concentration, he loosened a curl here and there from around her face. Satisfied, he bent to plant a kiss on her forehead, where a single curl nudged her arched eyebrow. "That's the damned curl that nearly drove me mad," he whispered. "Through the years, I couldn't get it out of my mind." He paused, and she watched his Adam's apple bob. "God, how I wanted you . . . want . . ."

The ensuing silence was so thick with emotion that, although they were but inches apart, she was sure she could not have moved through it to reach his lips had she tried. Around them the fountain splashed, and in the distance the children could be heard resisting bedtime.

"I want Stella to hear my prayers."

"Not tonight."

"Please, Tía Grande."

"No, hijo. Stella has a guest."

"He is our guest, too."

"We had our time with Logan; now it is Stella's turn."

Studiously Logan concentrated on her fingers, stroking each in turn, pressing one after the other against the flexed muscles of his thigh. "Your mother is an extraordinary woman."

"Yes. Lately she has worn many hats in addition to those of mother and wife: aunt, guardian . . ." Catching the words inside her mouth, she clamped her lips shut, and her hand inadvertently gripped his thigh.

As in a chain reaction, their eyes darted and held, lingering, fear now mingling with passion.

"Stella, you must warn your father."

Her eyes opened so wide she could feel the fall air cool them.

"He is in great danger . . . he and his men."

Her mind flittered hither and yon; she saw Logan with her mother here in the courtyard, by the creek, in the pastures . . . riding with the children.

"The children . . . ? she whispered.

He nodded.

She sucked in her breath, wanting instead to spit out her thoughts as refuse, to regurgitate her fears . . . her regrets . . . here on the courtyard . . . at his feet. Her heart pounded.

"You came to spy . . ."

Releasing her hand, he grasped her shoulders and stared desperately into her eyes. "No. I did not. I came to see you. To be with you . . . even for a short time." Catching his breath, he exhaled heavily, then continued, pleading. "I didn't ask . . . they told me; I didn't want to know." His eyebrows raised. "You know children. . . ."

With a heavy sigh, she dropped her head. Yes, she knew children. And she knew Logan. He wouldn't spy on her family. But what would he do, now that he had discovered the truth? That her own father was running the blockade?

Before she could gather her wits and ask him, Lupe set a bucket filled with ice and a bottle of champagne on the table next to them. Beside it, she placed glasses.

Quickly, Logan bent and kissed Stella's lips, soundly, as though to reassure her. His eyes, however, did not tease as they sometimes did, but remained solemn. Stepping aside, he opened the bottle of champagne.

Serita returned, talking as she came. "My, you look lovely in that gown, dear. It has always been one of my favorites. I'm sure Logan is glad to see you gowned like a lady again."

Logan handed a glass of champagne to Stella, then one to her mother. Lifting his glass, he strove to keep his voice light. "To Serita Cortinas Duval . . ." — the name tore at his heart, and he was glad she did not know what it meant to him. "Thank you for raising a beautiful daughter . . ." — pausing, he turned to Stella, and his voice, intense now, imploring, twisted knots in her confusion — "for me to love."

Quickly, Stella lowered her eyes, her heart nearly exploding with joy — he was here, he loved her — and with sorrow and with fear. She sipped the champagne, steadied her runaway senses, one thought now foremost in her mind: Her mother must not discover the disaster Logan's visit could well bring upon them.

"Actually," Logan added, "I did see her in a gown recently. At the party in Columbus she wore a lovely gown made from . . ."

Glancing up, Stella saw his admiration, noticed her mother's echoing smile, the curiosity on her face.

"Mrs. Beaty had a gown made for me," she explained. "She knew I would need it to travel to Robson's Castle. It was made from mattress ticking. . . ."

"Really?" Serita inquired. "How clever."

Despair suddenly swept through Stella. She chased it

122

with a gulp of champagne, then held the empty glass for them to see. "Not clever, Mamá, a necessity. There was nothing else to use for cloth; Josie, the woman who made it, had been rescued only days before by Mrs. Beaty from . . . from a life of prostitution. . . ."

"Stella . . ."

"Josie's little boys don't even have shoes! And Mrs. Cardwell . . . you remember her, Mamá . . . Mrs. Cardwell makes coffee from okra seeds! So do a lot of other people these days. While we stand here in silk gowns drinking champagne, everyone around us is starving. . . ."

"Stella, you know I do all I can for those around us. I don't even object to you and . . ."—Serita paused abruptly, then continued with an admonition—"You also know I will not have the war brought to Los Olmos. This is our refuge . . ."—she looked from Stella to Logan—"a refuge for all of us, and I will not have it destroyed."

Stella sighed, striving to contain her anger, her fears. "You cannot sit out this war, like you did General Taylor's and those that went before. I thought you realized that after they attacked our home . . . after they killed Alicia."

"That attack was an accident, Stella. I am responsible for Alicia's death. If I had not been so foolish as to build the house with a bridge atop it . . ."

"No attack is an accident, Mamá. The commander of that Federal ship thought he was destroying *something* when he fired at our house. Whether he saw a house or another ship is immaterial."

A forlorn expression saddened Serita's usually serene face; finally she smiled at their guest. "Forgive our manners, Logan. I raised her to be independent."

Logan laughed, then poured champagne for each in turn. Raising his glass, he again saluted Serita. This time, his voice was full of devilment. "My compliments, ma'am. You certainly succeeded." His eyes found and caressed Stella's. "But I knew that before tonight."

After another sip of the wine, Serita set her glass on the table. "The children will have me up early tomorrow, so I will say good night." She hugged Logan. "Don't mind the hour. I know your time together is short, so stay up as late as you like. I will try to keep the children from bothering you too early tomorrow."

When she hugged Stella, Stella's resentment vanished, replaced suddenly by an intense need to protect her mother from what might lie ahead for them. "I'm sorry for what I said."

Serita smiled into her daughter's eyes. "I am very proud of you, dear."

After Serita walked away, Logan and Stella stood together in awkward silence watching her douse the lanterns down the long inner hallway as she went toward her bedchamber. Stella struggled to bury her fears, at least for the few hours left of this night. Tossing her head back, she stared into the black sky that sparkled now with stars.

Logan touched her shoulder, and she flinched.

"Why didn't you tell me about Alicia?" Not a demand, his voice was heavy with despair.

"Would it have mattered?"

"Yes." His hand settled over the back of her neck, stroking, attempting to soothe, she knew.

But the vehemence in his answer had startled her, and when she turned to look, his face was solemn.

"You didn't know her," she responded. "How could it have mattered."

He squeezed her neck in a tender way that made her want to cry. When he spoke, he sounded tired. "Damnit, Stella, don't close me out. I love you. I should be allowed to share your grief."

"That's impossible, considering who killed her."

He studied her, seeing her hurt, knowing her fear, cursing the events that set them in opposition. "Innocent people have died on both sides of this conflict," he argued.

124

"Innocent families are suffering every place."

"I know." Pulling away, she crossed the courtyard to stand beside a tall, straight oak tree. She clasped her hands about its trunk and fought to retrieve herself from the depths of fear that engulfed her—if but for tonight.

Logan covered her hands with his; he felt the contrast between her smooth skin and the rough trunk of the oak tree. Bending, he kissed the backs of her hands, then moved toward her, pressing his lips against the top of her head, where he held them, until, at last, she came into his arms.

Silently they stood, while their hearts beat, not in rhythm, but out, as though they worked against each other. Like their lives, she thought, like their purposes.

Finally she drew back and studied him. At length, she spoke. "What will you do about Papá?"

He thought about the orders he had given—to Dar Blakesborough, of all people—orders to apprehend the *Serita Cortinas*—orders he could not rescind, not even if he wanted to.

He sighed. "It's out of my hands."

"Out of your hands?" She shook her head in dismay; her anger rose from crumbled hopes. "Out of your hands? You forget who you are, *Colonel!*"

"Stella!"

"Don't Stella me. I am not a Federal military officer in direct communication with the Secretary of the Navy, you are. You can keep them from . . ."

"You know I can't stop my men from capturing a blockade runner. That's my job, for God's sake! I could be court-martialed, hanged for treason; I might as well desert."

His words added to her anguish. "That's not a bad idea," she whispered, thinking now of two men . . . the two men she loved above all others in the world. "You're like gladiators, you and Papá. You are locked in mortal combat

125

against each other. And Mamá and I are forced to watch helplessly."

He slid his hands up her head, capturing her face between his palms. "No, princess. We are not against each other. We may be fighting for opposite causes, but as men, we are on the same side. Remember what I told you at the White Castle? Your father and I both love you. Your love unites us. Whatever happens, you must remember that. Next time you see him, ask him if this is not true."

Drained from oscillating emotions, she slid her arms around him and buried her face in his chest. "I don't want to remember anything. I just want it to be over . . . over, leaving us alone and safe, all of us."

"Next time you see him—"—he paused, then continued urgently—"you must warn Giddeon, Stella. If he won't stop his foolishness—which I know better than to expect—he must take great care, he and his men. The fighting is intensifying; no one can stop it, certainly not I myself. If Giddeon is captured . . ."

His voice drifted off, and he held her tight. He wished he could stop Giddeon from running the blockade, but he knew he could not. Given the same situation, chances were he would be doing the same thing.

He wished he could force Stella to remain at Los Olmos, but again, he knew he couldn't. With a sigh, he told her that.

"But you must be careful, princess. I will worry about you every moment until the rebellion is over." Quickly then, he put a finger across her lips, and grinned. "Don't say it, I know, you will be worrying about me, too."

She stared at him through the moonlight, watching the moonbeams play in his hair, dance in his eyes. It wouldn't last forever, this truce. But it would have to be enough for a while longer. He hadn't said he would protect Giddeon, but he did tell her to warn him. And he no longer argued with her over her own involvement.

Reaching, she kissed him quickly, letting her lips linger on his skin while she spoke. "Now that's settled, let's go to bed."

He nipped her lips with his, and she heard the relief in his voice when he replied, "I thought you'd never ask."

After the attack on the house, Jorge's children had taken over her room in the big house, and she had moved into one of the guest cottages that lined the far side of the courtyard. She led him there now.

"Your bed or mine?" he teased as they neared the row of one-room houses.

She laughed, remembering along with him. "Didn't we have a good time at Nottoway?"

He squeezed his arm around her shoulders. "The best. But after this is over . . ."

"Shhh . . ." she interrupted. "Remember what Mamá said. This is our refuge. When we meet here at Los Olmos, we won't even mention the war."

Inside the cottage, she lighted a lamp, and he studied her, inhaling the same sweet fragrance he had smelled at Nottoway. When he asked, she turned.

"Gardenias. They're Mamá's favorite . . . actually, they're Papá's favorite; I'm just now beginning to understand why." Coming toward him, she held a small sachet filled with dried leaves to his nostrils.

"Hmm . . ." He inhaled while staring into her fiery green eyes. "How do you do it?"

"What?"

"Cause my skin to tingle, my blood to boil, and my heart to stop all at the same time?"

His words delighted her. She set the sachet aside, laughing, and began to undo the buttons at the back of her dress. "I must have learned it from you, because that's what you do to me."

Moving forward, he reached around her. "Here, let me." But when his hands touched hers, the magic of the moment dissolved beneath the weight of her fear and she clasped him about the chest. He held her tightly, soothing her with steady strokes to her head, to her back.

Tears formed behind her lids and she could not keep them from rolling down her face. "Oh, Logan, I'm sorry. I wanted our time together to be happy . . . like at Nottoway."

"Nottoway was a long time ago. Nothing will ever be like that again." Drawing back, he raised her face to his. "Being together, holding each other, loving each other . . . like you told me, we have all we need to be happy."

She stared at him while he held her and wiped the tears from her eyes, feeling her tremble in his arms.

She sighed. "I'm so . . . so afraid."

He kissed her gently, then rested his lips on top of her head. "I know, princess. I know. But we would be just as afraid if we were all fighting on the same side."

She studied him, thinking about his words. "No," she replied at length. "At least then all I'd have to worry about is a stranger killing you . . . or Papá. This way . . ."

"Stella, don't think like that. Your father and I . . . we're not going to . . ." Heaving a painful sigh, he recalled his own orders to capture the *Serita Cortinas*. "We won't . . ." he tried again, but once more, the truth of the situation was so grave that he was unable to brush it off with pretty lies. Fiercely, he pulled her close and held her within the protection of his arms. "Don't let yourself think like that."

She pressed her cheek against his chest. "Did Mamá tell you about our family in Mexico?"

He nodded against her, silent.

"We could go there and live until the war is over."

Her voice was tentative, her tone held no conviction, and he smiled. "Even there the world is in turmoil; I hear the French are getting ready to secure another throne. Besides . . ."—he winked, quirking an eyebrow—". . . if you were to quit now, poor Mrs. Cardwell would have to drink okra-seed coffee for the rest of the rebellion."

Still she studied him, while his words soothed and re-lieved—for the moment at least—her fears, leaving her body awash with much more pleasant emotions. Finally, she kissed him. "Oh, Logan, hurry. Get me out of this dress."

With each touch of his fingers the fire inside her grew, until she thought surely she would explode from the tor-ment, the anticipation of touching him, body to body, flesh to flesh. When at last she stood inside a heap of dress, hoops, and petticoats, he struggled with the ties on her che-mise.

"Hold still," he laughed, "or I'll never get you out of this."

She drew in a ragged breath. "Why did I waste so much time?"

He glanced at her quizzically.

Her fingers played through his hair. "It's true . . . happi-ness is you and me together."

Tugging, then, she drew his shirt from his waistband and struggled to get it over his head. In the meantime, he had somehow—he wasn't sure how at this stage of the game—managed to unlace her chemise, and shrugged it off her shoulders. When it fell to the floor, he stared a moment, feeling faint at the sight of her loveliness.

Her breasts, full and firm, beckoned him with rosy nip-ples. Resisting, he untied and dropped her pantaloons, then knelt and unrolled her stockings. Unshoeing first one foot and then the other, he took her mound of clothing and tossed it all into a corner.

While he stood admiring her beauty, she lifted her arms to take the snood from her head, shaking loose her short curls. The last was too much to resist further.

Groaning, he took her in his arms; her skin burned against him. . . . Or was it his own? he wondered as her fingers fumbled with the buttons on his trousers.

Within seconds, then, they were in bed, clinging, stroking, pleasuring each other. Laughing, cuddling, tormenting, and at the last, begging.

Their bodies moved in such harmony that she recalled earlier when their hearts had beat out of rhythm, and she wondered at the difference. This, she knew, was better.

This was the way it was meant to be.

Their bodies wet and hot, outside and in, glided and slipped and slid against each other in glorious affirmation of the joy they felt in their hearts. Their breath came damp and ragged, and when it was over, they lay in sweet exhaustion in each other's arms.

"This is the most marvelous experience in the whole world," she sighed.

Grinning, he raised himself on an elbow; with his other hand, he tugged at her damp curls. "What is?"

"Making love," she answered.

He kissed her, smiling, agreeing. "*You* are what makes it marvelous."

She shook her head, serious. "No, Logan, *we* are. You and me together. But what is wonderful is that it . . . it gets better every time. Will it always, do you suppose?"

He studied her, wondering how he had ever been lucky enough to find someone who embodied a child and a woman, a helpmate and a competitor all rolled into one. "I have no doubt, princess. Isn't that the way things are in paradise?"

They loved again later, and slept. Toward morning he kissed her until she stirred. "I hate to wake you, but I promised myself I would never do to you what you did to me."

She frowned.

"Leave without telling you."

Her eyes flew open. "No . . ."

He nodded, kissed her with fervor, then before her hands could clasp in a firm hold behind his neck, he sat up and pulled on his clothes.

"Besides, I don't want your mother to discover us together."

Stella sighed. "Neither do I . . . I suppose."

At the door, he turned. Their eyes held: hers begging, his urgent. "Promise you will warn Giddeon."

The reminder stabbed at her heart. Struggling to sit, she pulled the sheet around her nude body. "I will, but will you promise me something?"

He cocked his head, waiting, hoping her request would be within his power to grant.

"If . . . if Papá is . . . if he is captured, will you get word to me?"

They stared long into each other's eyes, while their thoughts, too horrid to express aloud, traversed between them on the iron wills that separated their lives. "I promise."

As it turned out, that particular promise wasn't necessary.

Chapter Six

For a moment after Logan left, Stella lay still, one hand pressed to her lips where he had kissed her awake, the other to her heart, which beat now in frantic rhythms. The fears of last night, revived by the urgency in his voice, slashed through her brain like brandished sabers—Logan killing Papá . . . Papá killing Logan; Logan killing Jorge . . . Jorge killing . . .

Quickly, she jumped from bed, pulled on a clean pair of doeskin trousers, a chemise and silk blouse, and a pair of knee-high oxblood boots.

Running fingers though her short hair as she went, she pushed open the door to the guest cottage where Logan had stayed.

"You're still here!"

Startled, he turned, a brown leather grip in his hand. His face brightened; he reached for her.

"I'm long overdue." He bent to kiss her and felt her heart pounding in erratic beats. Gently, he stroked her lips with his. "It'll be over soon, princess. I promise."

Instead of soothing, his words only increased her agitation, and she kissed him desperately, unable to keep the dark images at bay.

Finally, he lifted his lips, held her head in his hands, and pressed his lips to her forehead. "Run back to bed. Let me leave quietly."

"You must have breakfast."

"No time. I'm . . ."

"You cannot leave without breakfast." She pulled his arm. "Bring your belongings. I will not detain you long."

From the direction of the vaqueros' quarters, a rooster crowed; they heard the sounds of an ax chopping wood. He returned her agonized stare, knowing her fears, wishing he could resolve them with a hug and kiss, knowing he could not. He teased, awkwardly. "I didn't know you could cook."

She brightened. "Come, you will see. You don't have time to eat much, and I don't know how to cook much. It'll work out fine."

The gray light of dawn had not entered the house, so she lit a lamp in the kitchen, stoked up the fire in the stove, and set a griddle on it. "Since you are in such a hurry, you slice the cheese while I make coffee."

He complied, and they worked in tense silence. She had a million things she wanted to say, but could express none of them in words.

He, in turn, wanted to reassure her that Giddeon would be fine, that he himself would be fine, but they both knew the facts. He wanted to demand that she stay here at Los Olmos for the duration, but that would only bring discord between them. It was an argument he knew he could not win.

"I'm glad I came," he said at length.

She turned smiling eyes on him. "So am I."

Reaching, he kissed her lips quickly. "For another reason, too," he whispered. "I think I understand you better now."

She set the heavy coffeepot on the stove and took a stack of yesterday's tortillas from the larder. "My fears, you mean?"

Leaving the cheese, he took her in his arms. "Your independent nature. You couldn't have grown up in this household . . . on Los Olmos . . . any other way. Look at your mother . . . she runs this ranch single-handed."

"With dozens of vaqueros."

"Granted, but she runs things."

"My father might disagree."

"I doubt it. Being a seasoned seadog, he is as independent as she. Surrounded by his compadres — Delos and Felix and . . . ah . . ."

"Kosta," she supplied.

"And Kosta. This ranch is a virtual training ground for independence. You couldn't have grown into a demure Southern belle if you had wanted to."

She laughed. "Which I didn't. I'm perfectly happy with my life. . . ." Her eyes sought his, pleading. "I was until . . . until the war kept us apart."

He kissed her tenderly, then urgently, and she responded, while the coffee simmered on the stove, and their blood ran hot and feverish.

Suddenly the sound of running footsteps shattered their absorption with each other. As Stella hurried to the window her anxiety grew. A blue-uniformed sailor stopped in front of the house, looked up briefly, then hurried toward the front porch.

"Ensign Jacobs," she whispered.

Logan headed for the door. "I told him where to reach me in case of emergency."

Following him through the dining room, she lagged a few steps behind. He threw open the door before Jacobs could knock.

"Colonel" — she heard Jacobs' labored breathing — "Captain Blakesborough is fit to be tied. We're heading south within the hour. They captured a blockade runner, sir . . . the *Marseillaise*."

Logan heaved a sigh, expelling suppressed fears. He looked toward Stella, grinned, then saw her reach toward him for support.

"It wasn't the . . ." he began, thinking she had not heard.

"Where is the captain?" she demanded of Ensign Jacobs.

Logan ushered the astonished ensign into the room, closing the door behind him. He drew Stella to his side and held her with a steadying arm around her shoulders. "It wasn't the *Serita Cortinas*."

Her mind spun in frantic spirals of fear. "The captain?" she demanded again. "Where is he? Is he alive?"

Jacobs' eyes grew round.

"It's all right, Jacobs. You remember Miss Duval." Puzzled, he repeated to Stella. "It's a *French* ship . . ."

"I know," she whispered. "He renamed it."

As though gears had been switched, Logan went straight into action, demanding to know the fate of the captain, the whereabouts of the ship.

Ensign Jacobs, obviously wary, answered in terse sentences. "His fate is unknown, sir. The ship was towed to . . ." — Jacobs eyed Stella skeptically, then continued — ". . . to ah, to Brownsville, I believe, sir."

"His name?" Logan insisted.

"He would not give it, sir."

"Wait for me down at the bay, Jacobs. I will follow directly behind you."

Awakened by the commotion, Serita came into the room as Ensign Jacobs took his leave. Displaying a calm he did not feel, Logan tried to explain the situation to the women.

"Try not to worry," he told them. "Jacobs said Giddeon, if indeed Giddeon is the prisoner, refused to give his name; that must mean he was capable of doing so, had he chosen to. I will do whatever I can; as soon as I learn something, I will send word. And . . . if at all possible, I will see that Los Olmos is spared."

"How?" Stella asked, thinking of his words the evening before, when he told her he could be hanged for treason, court-martialed. "You must be careful."

"Yes," Serita agreed. "We cannot have you both in trouble."

Stella followed him out the door, where she learned the *Victory* was anchored in the Gulf three miles out from Los

135

Olmos Bay. Hand in hand they walked to the creek, where he stopped and took her in his arms and kissed her.

He tried to make light of things. "It may work out better, us being on opposite sides. This way we can help . . ."

But her spirits would not be lifted so readily. "How will we ever get out of this war without losing our lives . . . or . . . or each other?"

He pressed his lips to her forehead, held her tightly against him, wondering the same thing, wondering, too, when he would be able to hold her again, love her again . . . and when he did find the opportunity, at what jeopardy it would be to himself. "One day at a time, princess. That's the only way. Today your mother needs you. Will you stay today . . . ?"—his brown eyes pierced hers, caressing, pleading—". . . or longer?"

She kissed him. "We will decide, Mamá and I. You must go now."

But the hunger in his eyes made her want to follow him, even as his captive. Wasn't she already his captive? And his words, when he spoke, bore straight to the core of her fears.

"Please don't leave Los Olmos," he whispered. "There is no place else for us to meet."

Francisco arrived soon after Logan left for the *Victory,* with word the cotton train had secured fresh animals and was on the road to Camp Boveda. Stella approached her mother.

"I will stay, if you need me."

"No, dear. As much as I would love to keep you at home, we would only end up worrying aloud, and the children might overhear. They have been through so much already. . . . Besides, I have plenty of work to do. And so do you. On your return trip, bring us a load of salt from El Sal del Rey. If we are to fulfill our contract to supply the coast garrisons with beef, we will need enough salt to cure it."

Camp Boveda lay but ten miles farther toward Brownsville, and they made it by dusk. Logan's words wrenched at her heart with every step of her horse along the chaparral-covered way. Now that she had left Los Olmos, how would she ever find him again?

Mamá had promised to dispatch a vaquero with news of Papá and his crew, should Logan be able to send it. But what of Logan himself? How would she know his fate? *Pray he did not have to endanger himself in order to help Papá!*

Francisco took the news about Giddeon hard. "You and the other womenfolk and children should move farther inland for the duration. Señor Capitán would wish it."

"*Sí*, Francisco. He would wish it. But he would not expect it. He knows my mother as well as . . ." Her thoughts drifted to Logan again, and she smiled, recalling his claims that her mother ran the ranch. Well, she did, and she ran a whole lot more besides. Thank goodness Logan liked strong women!

At Camp Boveda personal thoughts fled with the impact of the news awaiting them. The cotton train had not yet arrived, but others had.

The first word they received of the fall of Brownsville to the Federals came from an aide to Colonel John S. Ford, commander of the Southwestern Sub-District of the Confederacy, stationed in Brownsville.

"The fighting's been goin' on for two days now—leastways, I hope it is still in progress," the aide informed the worried Heel Flies stationed at Camp Boveda. "Them Yankee's are serious this time. 'Less you saw it you wouldn't believe the forces they're sending against us. They come off those ships, the bluecoats did, and covered Brazos Santiago like a swarm of mad bees."

After bolting down a plate of beans and securing a fresh mount, the soldier rode north to spread the news, only to have his place at the campfire taken the next morning by a steady stream of evacuating Confederates.

For three days Stella and Francisco waited at the camp,

137

tending wounded men and worrying.

Manned by a group of civilian volunteers, Camp Boveda had no more than a few rounds of ammunition and virtually no medicine.

"I am doing more harm than good," Stella told one soldier. After washing dirt from his wound, she had begun to bandage him with a strip of cloth torn from his own shirt. Angrily she cast the cloth aside. "This is too filthy to use. The air alone will serve better."

From then on, she cleansed their wounds and staunched the bleeding, then left them to heal in the open air. That night, when she sat around the campfire with a steaming cup of coffee so weak it resembled boiled water, she bewailed the lack of medicine to the captain.

He agreed. "That's why your job is so important, miss. When you fetch that cotton to market, you can bring back medicine to our boys."

She swirled the coffee in her cup, thinking, worrying. She didn't tell him—he already knew—that she would never be able to transport enough medicine to treat every wounded soldier in this damnable war. Not to mention the civilians who were left without medical attention . . . hundreds of thousands of people, in misery, dying for want of proper medical care . . . and for what?

The next day Maxwell Burnsides guided the cotton wagons into camp; by nightfall the famous Indian fighter and Texas Ranger, Colonel Ford, himself, arrived, "Down, but not whipped," he said. He brought the devastating news.

"Brownsville is in the hands of the damned Yankees. We were lucky to get out with our lives. Had to blow up half the town, though, we did. Couldn't let them get their hands on the munitions. They look to be strong as a herd of bull moose, without us adding to their store of arms."

"What are their plans?" Stella asked.

He eyed her seriously. "To take Texas by land."

"By land? What about their ships? How many did they

have?"

Colonel Ford stared into the campfire, as though he were seeing other things, unpleasant things. "Can't say for sure. The harbor looked full of Stars and Stripes, and the rumors are unfavorable, ma'am. It's folks like you who will be our salvation. Get that cotton to market and bring us enough ammunition to win this war." He glanced at her with sudden interest. "Your pa's the blockade runner, isn't he?"

"Captain Giddeon Duval," she answered. "We had word three days ago that he has been taken captive. I was hoping you might have heard his fate."

"No, ma'am, and I can't say I'm sorry. Already I know the fate of more good men than sets well."

Late that night after the camp had retired, Colonel Ford sat beside the campfire, writing. Stella watched him from her bedroll until, at length, she could not bear to leave him in solitude.

Rising, she crossed to the fire and poured him and herself each a cup of coffee. He smiled his thanks, a rueful smile, she thought, heavy with loss and sadness, then he returned to his writing, and she sat silently on a log opposite him.

He scribbled a line with flourish, then held the letter toward her. "Look at this, ma'am."

She read it, a message to the mother of one of the men he had lost in Brownsville. The signature attracted her attention: Colonel John S. Ford, R.I.P.

"I thought you were a medical doctor before the war, Colonel. What do the initials stand for?"

"An abbreviation, ma'am. I've written the words themselves so many times, I started using initials instead. Less painful that way."

Her eyes held his and at first she saw only sorrow, but as she looked, she realized that beneath the sorrow lay a determination as gritty as the sand upon which they sat. "Rest in Peace," she whispered, hearing the men call their colonel "Rip."

"Yes, ma'am. It's an appellation that will surely follow me to my own resting place, and not a reminder of pleasant times, either."

After that, she shared with him her newly made plans, now that delivering cotton to Brownsville was impossible.

He pursed his lips, nodding as she spoke. "El Sal del Rey. A wise choice. I left a company of good men guarding that mine. We cannot afford to let the Federals take our salt supply."

"From there I will send word to the Rio Grande, petitioning Captains King and Kenedy to have steamers waiting at Los Ebanos to haul our cotton down the river."

"You must hurry, ma'am. If the rumors are true, the Yankees plan to take the Rio Grande, as well as the Gulf Coast."

"But they can't," she insisted. "The Rio Grande is an international waterway . . . Mexico will . . ."

He flicked his pipe against his knee and stood up. "The Treaty of Guadalupe, signed in 1848 by the illustrious United States of America, makes no difference to them now. The army in the driver's seat can do most anything it likes."

Suddenly the thought of Logan's part in all this appalled her, for she had no doubt he was involved in the operation.

"Get some rest, ma'am. Come morning we both have jobs to do for the Confederacy."

Turning away from the fire, she became curious. Rip Ford didn't sound like a man who was through fighting. "And you, Colonel Ford? What will you do now?"

The pain in his eyes eased considerably, while he pondered her question. "First I will regroup my men, then I'll find an open flank, and then I'll rout those blue devils straight to hell. That's what I'll do, ma'am, if you'll excuse my French."

When the cotton train arrived at El Sal del Rey two days later, they found it heavily fortified with Confederate soldiers, as Colonel Ford had indicated, along with its regular contingent of civilian Home Guardsmen and members of the Texas Military Board. They assured Stella they had seen neither hide nor hair of a Yankee near the salt mine.

"But you had best set out for the river straightaway. If there's any truth in the rumors, the Yankees are heading up the Rio Grande," Agent Salinas advised. "Upon your return, we sure could use some of the munitions you will be transporting."

"In exchange for two wagon loads of salt," she agreed.

Antonio Salinas, who had been appointed by Governor Lubbock to serve as agent for El Sal del Rey, blanched at her request. "You drive a hard bargain, Miss Duval. Our once sixty-five-cents-a-bag salt now goes for twenty dollars. Two whole wagon loads . . ."

She smiled sweetly. "A fair exchange, Mr. Salinas. Ammunition for our soldiers' guns—salt to cure their beef. They cannot fight Yankees without either."

When they were ready to leave for Los Ebanos, she sent Francisco ahead. "If the King and Kenedy steamboats arrive before we do, hold them there for our cotton."

"*Sí, señorita,*" he agreed.

"And do not let them sell their cargoes to anyone else. Max and I will bring the wagons along slowly. I fear the forty miles to Los Ebanos will be difficult."

"And I, as well, señorita. We could pray for rain."

She shrugged. "Without rain the oxen will suffer from thirst; with it the trail will become muddy and the wagons hard to pull. Sometimes it seems we cannot win."

"Win or lose, ma'am, the . . . ah, the war will be over soon," Max assured her when she expressed the same sentiments two nights later over their campfire.

Max reminded her of Logan in many ways: his almost identical size, his erect military bearing, his direct approach to problems. Now he was beginning to sound like Logan. When she spoke, she did not try to conceal her annoyance. "I am sure we will regret our folly, should we pray for an end to this war at any cost, only to lose it. If it makes no differ-

141

ence whether we win or lose, we are wasting time, effort, and . . ."—recalling Colonel Ford's words, she sighed—". . . and the lives of a lot of good men."

Max shrugged. "My apologies, ma'am. I meant only to reassure you. I know you are worried over your father."

Stella pulled the heavy woolen blankets closer about her. "Yes, I am, but worrying does not give me the right to be sharp with friends. You have been tireless this trip. We are indeed fortunate Francisco found you in Alleyton."

She studied him from across the fire. A solid, steady man, always ready with a word, a hand. Even in this cold, sometimes wet norther they had encountered the last few days, he never complained. He was a good man; he had already become so much a part of the cotton trains, she could not recall how they had ever managed without him.

She told him this, adding, "But in all these weeks, I have never heard you mention your home. Where do you come from, Max?"

As soon as she asked the question, she regretted it, for he tensed as he did every time she thoughtlessly pried into his private life. "Now, I am the one apologizing. . . ."

"No need, ma'am," he replied, answering with his usual obliqueness. "My life's been spent mostly at sea."

One afternoon when the norther turned wet and icy, they made camp early in a shelter of thick chaparral. Over the campfire she decided to tell him her plans. "Since Francisco obviously told you about Papá's being captured by the Federals," she began, "you will understand. I don't intend to stand by and wait for . . . ah, to receive word on his whereabouts. The report indicated he had been taken to Brownsville, so I plan to take the steamer down the Rio Grande with our cotton. . . ."

"No, ma'am. You can't . . ." Max began.

She turned to stare. "Oh, yes, I can."

"I can't allow you to go to Brownsville, ma'am."

"I won't go to Brownsville, Max," she replied, thinking all

she needed was another nursemaid. Francisco was enough. "I will go to Matamoros. We have a consulate there. I will demand they find my father."

Max didn't like the idea of Matamoros much more than he did Brownsville, she could tell. And persuading *him* was only a test. If he, a virtual stranger, objected so strongly, how would she ever convince Francisco?

The forty miles to Los Ebanos was as difficult as she had imagined, if not more so, abetted by the unfavorable weather. That they arrived in five days without losing a single animal amazed her. She owed it all to the tireless efforts of her teamsters.

And they, in turn, she discovered, praised her. Each one, upon seeing Francisco, complimented her wise decisions on when to drive, when to rest.

Los Ebanos was an old town, named for the many ebony trees found in the area. "According to family legends," she told Max, "this crossing has been used for centuries, first by Indians, later by the Spaniards as a route from Mexico to the salt lake, El Sal del Rey. My family crossed at this very place to claim their land grant from the King of Spain back in the seventeen hundreds."

The King and Kenedy steamers waited at the docks, and while the men unloaded the wagons, loaded the steamers, then reloaded the wagons with needed goods for the Confederacy and for Texas, Stella approached Francisco with her plan.

"I will accompany you, señorita," he sighed, "since from long experience with your family, I am well aware I cannot persuade you of the folly of such a trip, short of tying you to a wagon seat."

Max had been standing beside them while they discussed her trip. At Francisco's capitulation, he laughed.

"*Con permiso,* Francisco, I will accompany Miss Duval to Matamoros. You are more capable than I of seeing the wagon train to its destination. You know which patrons along the route are entitled to what goods. I, on the other hand, am familiar with the sea, so should any problem arise while we are on the river, I will be able to protect Miss Duval. As for the language . . ."—he shrugged—". . . my Spanish may not be eloquent, but I think you will agree, it is passable."

As illustration, Max had voiced his proposal in Spanish, to the astonishment of both Stella and Francisco.

Later, she wondered whether that was the fact that won Francisco over. Whatever the reason, he allowed Max to accompany her downriver, and he himself headed the wagon train back toward El Sal del Rey.

The captain of the steamer was not so pleased with his passenger. "This is a war, ma'am. No place for a lady."

When he eyed her up and down, Max took her elbow. "The lady will take passage," he said. "Else we unload our cotton, and you return to your bosses with neither cotton nor goods."

"Besides," Stella continued, after they had boarded and stood behind the tall stacks of cotton bales. "In Matamoros I can receive payment for the cotton, then pay for your goods, and we will be finished with our transaction. That will surely please your employers."

The captain scoffed. "Won't make much difference either way, once the Yankees take the river."

Stella looked at the red, white, and green banner flying from the mast. "They wouldn't stop a Mexican ship."

"Loaded with cotton, you bet your boots they would. And they'd haul us all off to prison, that's what they would do with us."

"But that's against the Treaty of Guadalupe. Colonel Ford said . . ."

"This ain't no game of patty-cake, ma'am. This here's war, and nothing much about it is played by the rules."

Loaded with cotton and enough men to ward off an attack, the steamer had little room left for comfortable quarters. Begrudgingly, the captain offered her his, but she refused.

"I am perfectly used to the wide-open spaces," she told him, settling herself on a bale of cotton.

They arrived in Matamoros before dawn; the captain stationed half his men on the river side of the steamer, rifles trained at the far bank, while the rest of the crew unloaded the cotton.

"We are directly across from Fort Brown, so we must unload before the Yanks sound reveille," he told Stella and Max. He ushered them into a large warehouse stacked to the rafters with bales of cotton. Although the hour was early, already the place swarmed with men examining cotton, taking notes, talking in—she listened as they passed first one group of men, then the next—a number of languages besides English; she recognized Spanish, French, German . . .

"Portuguese," Max added, "and Italian."

After an hour's wait a rumpled man approached them with a tally sheet. "Eight hundred bales of cotton. Come back this afternoon and you will receive your gold."

Stella studied the paper. "What price are you quoting?"

The man laughed. "You will find that out this afternoon. The price changes several times a day."

"What is your current price?" she persisted.

"Forty cents. But you will receive this afternoon's quote." He shrugged. "You are welcome to transport your cotton to Bagdad yourself. Since the Yankees hold the river below here, we can't use lighters. We are forced to travel overland, like everyone else."

By the time they finished haggling and left the warehouse, the streets swarmed with people. Stella pulled her woolen rebozo over her head and around her shoulders. Max immediately proved his worth, if not by procuring a carriage to get them out of the wind, at least by securing directions to the Confederate Consulate.

They walked a good thirty minutes before he stopped on a

street corner and looked up and down the cross street. Finally, he pointed to a building halfway down the block. "That's it. Use the entrance on this street."

"Aren't you coming?"

He shrugged, ran a hand through his hair, then pointed to a café. "I will wait here." When she continued to frown, he added, "You know the impressment laws. They might try to induct me into the army."

"I hadn't thought of that, Max. Of course, you must wait. We can't afford to lose you as a teamster."

"Be sure to ask them to recommend safe lodging for tonight."

Again, she studied him quizzically. "Where will you be?"

"I will know where you are at all times, ma'am, but I will not get in the way. The Confederates may want to entertain you while you are in town. Matamoros is known for its social life. The new opera house is reported to be as grand as any found in Europe."

"I did not come to Matamoros to attend the opera, Max. And I should hope the Confederates in town are not wasting their time in such extravagance, either. You will wait for me in this café?"

He nodded, then added, "Don't worry if I'm not here. I will have my eye on you at all times; if you need my help I will be there. Francisco would slit my throat with that Bowie knife of his if I let harm come to you."

One step inside the Confederate Consulate told her she was not in for an easy time. The room seemed to burst at the seams with desks, people, and noise. Every desk was piled high with papers; people argued, they laughed, they shouted, but for the life of her, she saw no one who looked to be engaged in the business of state, whatever that might be.

And no one paid her the least bit of attention. Going from one desk to the next, she listened and watched, trying to decide who was in charge.

Suddenly, a voice boomed from midway down a staircase tucked in a corner where Stella had not even noticed it.

"Andale, Adalaide, bring me the report on the Yankee General Banks."

Stella scanned the room; no one so much as looked up.

The man on the stairs bellowed again; again, Stella glanced around. No Adalaide responded.

On impulse, since the man on the stairs was obviously in charge of something, Stella grabbed a sheaf of papers from the nearest desk and hurried toward the stairs.

"Where's Adalaide?"

"Sick," she mumbled. "I will explain the omissions in this report . . ."—and recalling Ensign Jacobs' manner toward Logan, she added—". . . sir."

He looked her up and down, returned the cigar to his mouth, and motioned her up the stairs.

"Who are you?" he demanded when they entered an office in quite as much confusion as the one below, except without the people and noise.

"Stella Duval, sir. And the omission from this report is my father."

The man frowned.

"Are you the Confederate consul?" she inquired.

His eyes narrowed. "Assistant."

"My father, Captain Giddeon Duval, is one of our country's most effective blockade runners. His ship was boarded by the Federals, and he and his crew were taken captive over ten days ago. They are reportedly being held in Brownsville. I have come to secure their release."

She cringed beneath his close scrutiny while she spoke, and when she stopped, he puffed several times on his cigar, took it out of his mouth, and perused its tip. "You have come to secure his release."

His attitude incensed her. Stiffening her spine, she squinted at him. "I have very little time, Mr. . . . ?"

"Morgan," he supplied.

"I brought fifteen wagon loads of cotton to Matamoros, Mr. Morgan. I shipped those same wagons back to the Confederacy, loaded with medical supplies and ammunition. This afternoon I will receive payment for the rest of the cotton and tomorrow morning, if my father is released by then, I must travel to Titlum-Tatlum, where we are having a blockade-running vessel built. It will be of no value, however, without my father to . . ."

"Enough, Miss Duval . . . enough." Mr. Morgan motioned her to a seat. "Let me see what we have on your father." Stepping to the doorway, he called down the hall, then returned his attention to Stella. "So, you are the famous Miss Duval?"

Stella bristled. Pursing her lips, she cautioned herself to remain quiet. She needed this man, pompous though he was.

"I meant no offense, ma'am. Your exploits along the Cotton Road are known to everyone in this part of the Confederacy. We are indebted to you." Again, he looked her up and down. "Obviously, you have paid a dear price to support our cause. We shall have to get your father back."

She sighed, relieved. When the aide rushed to Morgan's office, it was to inform his superior that no word had been received on Captain Duval's capture. Indeed, it was the first anyone in the office had heard of the news.

"His ship flew a French flag," Stella said. "He renamed it the *Marseillaise*."

The assistant consul's eyebrows rose by degrees. "Indeed. And you are certain the Yankees apprehended him?"

She nodded.

"Then come. We will raise hell . . . ah, excuse me, ma'am . . . we'll make those damned Yankees eat their words. They are so cocky about neutrality on the high seas."

At the door he turned. "Where are you staying?"

"I just arrived in town. I haven't found lodging. . . ."

He grimaced. "I had thought perhaps you would like to

148

. . . ah, to freshen up before we go to the United States Consulate?"

"I did not come to stand on formalities, Mr. Morgan. I came to find my father, and I am quite sure he doesn't care whether I wear a silk gown or a gunny sack."

Mr. Morgan shoved the cigar back in his mouth. "Right. Quite right. Come along, then."

She followed him at a rapid clip downstairs and out the same door she had entered moments earlier. They walked up the street, turned a corner, and climbed the steps of a building similar in size and architecture to the one they just left. "This is the United States Consulate? So close to our own?"

"Indeed," Morgan replied.

She frowned. "I wouldn't have expected the two countries to keep offices so close together. I mean . . . I . . . it doesn't seem right."

"Why ever not, my dear? Our staffs are quite harmonious; we frequent the same restaurants, the opera." He nodded toward an ornate building across the street. "Teatro de Reforma, a grand opera house. Truth known, Miss Duval, the majority of our employees are their spies . . ."

She gasped.

". . . and most of theirs, ours."

Mr. Morgan's counterpart in the United States Consulate turned out to be a congenial man who had indeed heard of Captain Giddeon Duval.

"Only yesterday, as a matter of fact, a fellow came in inquiring about Captain Duval." Pausing, he corrected himself. "Actually, it wasn't just any fellow doing the inquiring; happened to be a colonel in our own Marine Corps. Cafferty, the name was . . . Colonel Logan Cafferty."

Chapter Seven

He arrived while she was sitting at a makeshift dressing table staring into a sliver of looking glass, the scissors from her chatelaine poised above her head in an attempt to cut the first snip from hair grown too long to be short, too short to be decent.

After she had recovered from the impact of the United States assistant consul's claim that Logan had come to his office mere hours before her own visit, she tried to continue her investigation into her father's whereabouts, but to little avail.

"He is being held in Brownsville, miss. That is all I know." The assistant consul, a smartly attired man by the name of Bishop, scowled at her attire; she recalled Mr. Morgan's suggestion that she change clothing before coming here.

"Then why did Colonel Cafferty inquire for him here?" she demanded, unabashed by the way he gaped at her shock of short hair.

"The colonel was not inquiring for Duval," Bishop explained, with less patience than even she herself possessed, Stella noted. "He was inquiring after the inquiries made by the French government."

"The French . . . ?"

"Seems Captain Duval was sailing under a French flag."

"So . . . ?"

"The French are contesting his arrest. They contend his load of cotton was Mexican in origin, destined for Balize, where it was to be swapped for powder and caps for Maximilian's use in fighting Benito Juárez's rebels."

Ignoring the inflection Bishop placed on the word *rebels*, she followed up on the positive information that her father might have been released at this very hour. "Where in Brownsville can I find Captain Duval?"

Bishop shook his head. "That is confidential, miss. And since you are . . ."—again, he perused her attire—". . . since you are obviously of rebel persuasion, it would be unwise for you to cross the river. As you must know, the town has been taken back from the rebels; it is even as we speak in Union hands, and you would be considered . . . ah, need I go on?"

She glared at him, then sighed. "I cannot tell you the urgency of this matter, Mr. Bishop. Will you carry a message to Colonel Cafferty on my behalf?"

Bishop snorted his disgust. "The colonel has more on his mind than a rebel captain who claims to serve the French, miss. I . . ."

"You would be well advised, Mr. Bishop, to send this message to the colonel straightaway. I . . . ah, I assure you he will be most unhappy, should he miss the opportunity to speak with me while I am in Matamoros." Taking paper, she suddenly realized she could not expect Logan to meet her at the Confederate offices. She turned to Mr. Morgan.

"Could you advise me on a place to spend the night?"

"Perhaps Letitia over at our office could put you up," he suggested.

"What about a rooming house?"

"Well . . . there's Adalaide—the girl whose identity you assumed this morning; her mother rents rooms. Perhaps . . ."

"What is the address?"

She wrote the address Morgan gave her on the paper with a terse message to "Colonel Cafferty," saying she had come in search of Captain Duval and where she could be found. She signed her name formally, "Miss Estelle Duval."

"It probably won't be a room to yourself," Morgan had cautioned, when they stood on the street trying to avoid being splattered by mud. "A private room is impossible to come by in Matamoros today, even with all the new construction you see about us. You will be fortunate not to have to share a bed."

Stella cringed. "There is nothing else?"

"You will be lucky to get that. And it won't be cheap—a hundred dollars a night, that's the going rate."

"One hundred dollars!"

He shrugged. "Time's are hard every place."

She found Max at the café, and during the next few hours was able to push aside worries over unsavory sleeping arrangements. The situation at the warehouse called for all her attention, as well as more patience than she had been blessed with. Papá would never have had to wrangle as she did, she was certain of that.

To give credit where it was due, the agent, Mr. Yates, allowed her forty cents per pound, which came to the enormous sum of one hundred twenty thousand dollars. After subtracting payment for the supplies she received at Los Ebanos, she was left with a satchel filled with ten thousand dollars, gold. Money, she discovered, the agent had no intention of letting get away from him.

No sooner had she presented the list of supplies she would want in exchange for the next shipment of cotton than the haggling began in earnest.

Mr. Yates studied the list, stroking his mustache, amused, she thought, grimly. "Hmm . . . quinine, opium, morphine, chloroform, calomel . . ."—he nodded, then continued reading from the list—"coffee, rope, bagging . . . what's this? Ten thousand pairs of cotton hand-cards? Two thousand wool cards . . . ?"—he stared at her over his spectacles—"No wool yarn? No woolen cloth? And this machinery? What does this mean?"

What business is it of yours? she thought, furious not only with his patronizing manner but with the loss of valuable time. Logan could come and be gone by the time she dealt with this obstinate man. She couldn't imagine Papá having to explain a list so clear. "The ladies in our state have taken up spinning and weaving again," she explained, striving for patience. "Their families need the income, and our soldiers need the uniforms. The machinery at our cloth factory at the penitentiary is wearing out."

Yates nodded. "Another waste of money, if you ask me. Whatever happened to all the machinery for that cannon foundry they spent hard-earned money on?"

"As with most things these days, sir, it was a gamble. And gambles, as you well know, do not always . . ."

"Indeed, Miss Duval. Exactly what I have been aiming at. In order to place this order along with your sizable arms order, I will need security. Or at least a downpayment . . . say, the gold that just changed hands."

Stella's eyes almost popped at the suggestion. "We have never been required to . . ."

"Never is a thing of the past, miss. With the Lincoln government gaining control of the southern part of Texas, your cotton trains are in jeopardy—grave jeopardy. And even if they don't fall prey to the Yankees, your teamsters are under constant threat of impressment by the Confederates. Not a secure gamble in the least."

"My cotton trains are well protected, Mr. Yates, and my teamsters will not be inducted like the others."

He raised an eyebrow. "To the contrary, every ragged Confederate company they pass along the route can impress them, leaving your cotton stranded for lack of manpower."

"My teamsters are in no danger," Stella insisted. "They are, for the most part, Los Olmos vaqueros who have been with my family many years. They have fought Indians and land raiders; now they raise beef to fight Yankees. Los

Olmos is contracted to provide meat to Confederate companies along the coast. I assure you, sir, we are protected."

He shrugged. "Not enough, miss. I need collateral."

Stella's heart sank. She couldn't leave the gold; it was needed in a hundred different places, not the least of which as downpayment for the new blockade-running ship. But she did have the bonds. Surely Mr. Ransom would deem this a worthwhile arrangement for them. "What about indemnity bonds, Mr. Yates?"

He cocked his head. "You mean those worthless United States Indemnity Bonds? Why, every Texas politician from Governor Murrah on down has been trying to peddle those bonds from Austin to London and back again."

"They are not worthless. They are guaranteed by . . ."

"Guaranteed?" He laughed, but the scorn in his tone dwindled at the end of the word, and she wondered whether he was having second thoughts. "Nothing in this part of the world at this particular time is guaranteed, Miss Duval. On the other hand, if you have bonds, there is a man you should talk to. Mr. Pryor Lea."

"Our agent in Brownsville?"

"Was in Brownsville. After the invasion, he moved his— or should I say, Texas's—business across the river."

"Here in Matamoros? Where may I find him?"

While Mr. Yates checked on Pryor Lea's whereabouts, Stella paced the floor, not so much worried over the bonds, now—the gleam which had grown steadily in Mr. Yates' eyes told her he was interested in her bonds, regardless of his words to the contrary.

Her concern now was much more personal—and simple: Logan Cafferty. Would he come and go before she even arrived at the rooming house? She must learn the fate of her father, and Logan was the only person she could trust to tell her the truth.

And *she* had to see him.

To see him, to touch him . . .

"We're out of luck for today, miss," Yates said, returning to the room. "Lea has been in Monterrey this past week, meeting with the governor of Nuevo Leon. He is due back tomorrow; his assistant assured me he will want to confer with you. You are to meet him at the opera tomorrow evening at eight o'clock sharp." He glanced toward Max, who remained behind Stella, but within earshot. "Two tickets will arrive at your rooming house this evening."

"The opera?" Stella questioned. "Doesn't he have an office? Why can't . . . ?"

"The opera," Mr. Yates repeated. "You must visit Teatro de Reforma; it cost eighty thousand dollars to complete and is a sight to see. Not surprisingly nowadays, a good many business deals are finalized between acts. Especially in your box. You will be a guest of the governor of Tamaulipas." He scrutinized her attire in a manner to which she was becoming accustomed. "I would advise you to take some of your gold and purchase a suitable gown."

"This gold belongs to Texas, Mr. Yates," she reminded him sharply. But outside the warehouse, when the cool damp air hit her face, she rethought her hasty reaction. It was indeed Texas's gold, but she couldn't very well represent her state in the governor's box at the fancy new opera house in dirty buckskin breeches.

Leaving the warehouse with a satchel full of gold and Mr. Ransom's bonds, she thought again of Mr. Morgan's prediction that she might have to share not only a room, but a bed. Pray she would not, she thought, not with this much gold in her possession.

At the first dressmaker's establishment they came to, she pulled a reluctant Max inside. "The sign says *sastre* — tailor," she told him. "You must have something to wear to the opera, too."

Max held up his hands. "Whoa, there, ma'am. I won't be going to the opera with you. 'Specially not to sit in the governor's box. I'll wait outside the building."

"I can't go alone; I may need your advice. Besides . . ."—she inhaled a draft of damp air—". . . if I am accosted, Franciso would consider it as bad as murder or kidnaping."

Max shrugged. "I doubt you would be accosted at the opera, ma'am."

"It won't be so bad," she insisted. "I don't intend to stay longer than it takes to negotiate with Mr. Lea."

He acquiesced, and with dispatch, they chose their opera attire—a fawn twill suit for Max, and a lavender silk gown with black lace overskirt for her. The whole time she stood for the pinning, she felt guilty—she hadn't chosen this gown with the thought of conducting state business. She had bought it for Logan. If only he would come tonight and stay . . . she could slip away to the opera for a few minutes—Max would help her think of some way—then she and Logan could . . .

Could what? her singing senses demanded. Where could she and Logan possibly find a place to spend time together in this city? Even if he did come tonight—or if he had not already come and gone.

Leaving the tailor with instructions to send the costumes around to the rooming house by tomorrow, she pressed through the crowded streets, so anxious to get to Adalaide's she would not even stop to eat.

"They take roomers, surely they provide meals," she responded to Max's suggestion at passing a café.

Max tugged at his floppy-brimmed hat, and guided her by an elbow around the far side of a cluster of Federal sailors. "Do not count on them serving meals, ma'am. Besides, for a hundred dollars a room, what do you suppose they charge for a bowl of beans?"

"To be honest, I'm in a . . . ah, rather a hurry to get to the rooming house. I'm expecting word from a friend. . . ."

"A friend? You ran into a friend here . . ."—he waved his arms at the throng— ". . . among all this wickedness and thievery?" With another twist at her elbow, he maneuvered them suddenly around a corner, out of the way of a rapidly advancing cart carrying more Federal sailors.

She glanced at him sideways, scurrying to keep up with his lengthened stride. "I didn't actually run into him. But he is in town . . . at least, he had been to the United States Embassy before me . . ."

Max raised his eyebrows, and she laughed.

"Regardless of the fact that you seem to be doing your best to avoid every one of them in Matamoros, Max, all Yankees are not wicked men with pointed ears. This one is . . .well, he's . . . ah, he can help secure Papá's release," she finished. "So I really must be there when he calls. Once we arrange for your room, you can go out to eat. You don't have to stay with me at the rooming house. I'm sure Francisco would not—"

"Don't count on me sleeping at a rooming house, ma'am. I'll be outside checking on you, but I wouldn't pay a hundred dollars for a bed if it was made of down from the golden goose. Now you, that's different. A lady shouldn't be sleeping on the street."

"You can't sleep on the street!"

He shrugged. "Like you, ma'am, I have friends about."

No message from Logan awaited her at Adalaide's mother's rooming house. But the disappointment she had felt through the ensuing night fled now at the sight of his reflection behind hers in the sliver of glass, resplendent in his military uniform.

"He says he is a friend, señorita," the rotund landlady hurried to assure her. "I told him I do no think so."

Stella's eyes left Logan's but briefly to set aside her scissors. She turned from the glass and stood to face him.
"Sí señora. Es amigo."

They stood as though set in stone, staring, barely conscious of the señora informing Stella that desayuno would be served *momentito*.

"Señorita Duval will not be taking breakfast here," Logan

157

answered the landlady, who finally left, dropping the faded and patched bedspread that separated Stella's small cot from the rest of the dining room.

He tossed a brown-paper package on the cot. "Friend," he whispered. Coming to her quickly, he took her in his arms.

"Amigo," she repeated against his lips.

After a brief but welcoming kiss he raised his lips inches from her face. Her eyes glinted with delight, sending the green fire they radiated spiraling through his system. "You are bound and determined to make me a widower before I'm ever a bridegroom."

She snuggled against him. "I have no intention of doing any such thing."

"And you have no business in this hellhole, either. Smuggling cotton to the Rio Grande is bad enough." His emotions ran strong, but her presence was so pleasurable, the feel of her body against his so welcome, that though his words were severe, his tone lacked conviction.

Reaching, she kissed him again; this time her arms pulled his broad shoulders toward her and her hands pressed his face closer to hers. She felt a tremor as his muscles tightened around her.

Not three feet beyond the curtain, dishes clattered, chairs scraped against the bare plank floor, and men's voices could be heard as breakfast was served.

"How did you find this place? Surely there is somewhere better. . . ."

She shook her head, smiling. "Neither my consulate nor yours knew of anyplace else . . . whether better or not."

"My consulate? You mean the United States . . . ?"

She frowned. "That's where I left the message for you. How did you . . . ?"

His frown died slowly. "The . . . ah, the runner failed to say where the message came from, and I . . ."—with a wink he nipped her nose, then her lips in a provocative kiss— ". . . I was so furious with you for coming to Matamoros I

158

didn't think to question anything else."

"Furious?" she teased, drawing his lips to hers.

On the other side of the curtain, a man belched, another blew his nose, and the landlady shrieked.

"Get dressed," he whispered. "Let's get out of here."

"I am dressed."

He studied her, amused, then handed her the package. "Didn't figure you'd be lucky enough to find a landlady in Matamoros who would rip up her mattress to make you a dress."

Untying the string, she found a taupe wool riding skirt, silk blouse, and a heavy woolen shawl. She held the skirt against her. "How did you know . . . ?"

His lascivious smile stopped her words. When he proceeded to measure first her height, then her proportions with two hands squeezing the air for her bosom, her waist, her hips, she burst into giggles.

"Shhhh . . ." he nodded toward the curtain. "You'll call our audience. Hurry now."

Quickly she dressed, her body tingling from his nearness, but he turned his head, in defense, she knew, against the same yearnings. Within moments she was ready to leave. Scooping up her clothing, chatelaine, and hair brush, she stuffed everything, including her boots, inside the satchel on top of the gold and carried it along.

When Logan questioned her, she shrugged. "This bed may be given to another person by the time we return."

His eyes twinkled. "Regardless, I certainly don't intend to bring you back to this place to spend the night."

The words themselves were innocent enough, but couched in his seductive voice, combined with suggestively raised eyebrows, they set her skin on fire. She was ready to go anywhere with him . . . to the lengths of the earth . . . to the *Victory* itself, as long as they could be alone. Suddenly she recalled her mission tonight — the opera — her meeting with Pryor Lea. "I'm having a package delivered here, so I do have to return this afternoon."

Outside the morning was gray, but though a slight mist fell on already muddy streets, the temperature had warmed considerably from the sleet and snow they encountered on the trail to Los Ebanos.

Logan guided her around a mudhole. "That's why I chose a riding skirt," he told her. "You'll need boots for where we are going today."

"To see Papá."

Her response had been automatic, and he turned to stare with serious eyes. "I can't take you to Brownsville."

Disappointment chased the smile from her face. "Logan, please. I must see how he is . . . if he's all right."

With a heavy sigh, he took her shoulders and looked into her pleading eyes. "I went to see him yesterday. He's fine. The French are working with our people to obtain his release. It will take a few days, though."

"I want to see him," she insisted.

"Stella . . ." Logan stopped, lifting his face to the sky while he considered how best to tell her.

She could see he was troubled, and her fears mounted.

"You can't go to Brownsville," he reiterated. "You're . . . ah, you are wanted . . .you are an escaped prisoner, known to be engaged in running cotton for the Confederacy."

Her breath caught in her throat at his words; she jerked away from him. Clasping her neck in her hands, she turned away. Carts and carriages clattered by on the narrow street, splattering mud this way and that.

He pulled her against the building. In the distance, she saw Max standing on the street corner, looking off into the distance. *Some protection he turns out to be,* she thought in a disjointed fashion, her mind splintered between reality and truth. "You turned me in?" she asked.

His mouth fell ajar. "Me?"

Her lips were dry, and she tried to moisten them with an even drier tongue. "Who else knew?"

Anger swept over him at her accusations, followed by anguish. "Stella, my God, don't you know me better than that? Don't you know how I feel? Don't you . . ."

"I know this uniform," she responded, tapping a finger against his jacket.

His eyes pierced hers. "I'm talking about the heart beneath your pointing finger. The heart that . . . that loves you beyond all else."

His words were simple, his tone fierce, desperate, she thought. Truthful. Honest.

"Who, then?" she asked.

He sighed. "An enemy. Mine, as well as yours, I'm afraid." Absently he pulled at the little curl above her eyebrow, noticing how it had grown out now, almost to where it had been at Nottoway. Bending, he planted a firm kiss on her lips. "Come. We're wasting time."

With a flick of his wrist, he called a waiting carriage. When it drew alongside the curb, he opened the door to usher her inside.

"Wait. I must tell Max."

Logan quirked an eyebrow.

"The man behind us, there on the corner."

When Logan turned, Max quickly looked away.

She shrugged. "He's my . . . ah, my bodyguard. If I leave with you and don't explain, he will follow us." Taking Logan's arm, she guided him across the street.

He grinned. "And what do you suppose Max would do, should he catch up with us?"

"I'm not sure, but he promised Francisco he would not let anything happen to me. He said if he did, Francisco would slit his throat."

Logan tightened his hand on her arm. "If Francisco didn't, believe me, princess, I would."

His vehemence sent a thrill down her spine, and she looked into his playful face. Somehow, she knew his words were far from playful.

"You had better let me do the talking," she suggested. "I'm not sure why, but Max has an aversion to Yankees."

Surprisingly, Max took the news in good form. She introduced Logan as the friend of whom she had spoken and said they were going riding. Then, turning to Logan, she asked when they would return.

When Logan addressed Max directly, to Stella's relief, Max was agreeable. "We may be late, but don't worry about the lady," Logan told him. "She will be in safe hands."

Suddenly Stella recalled the opera. "I will return, Max . . . in time for . . . ah . . ." Frowning, she pleaded silently for him to understand. "I will return in plenty of time."

Max nodded, gave a reserved sort of bow, a smile playing at the corners of his lips.

Not until they were in the carriage did she ask where they were going.

"To Bagdad," came the answer. "I have business to attend to, and since you've come this far, I figured you might as well get a good look at where your cotton goes."

He refused to say more, so she turned her attention to his own welfare. "If I am a wanted woman as you say, it's dangerous for you to be seen with me."

He dropped his arm from behind the seat and pulled her to him. "It's dangerous for me to be *with* you." He nuzzled a sensitive spot on her neck, teasing it with his tongue.

"I see what you mean, and me with no home except the small corner of someone else's dining room." Her body tingled with the prospect of spending the whole day with him . . . and the night. But her worries would not be submerged. "I'm serious. We can't take chances with your life, no more than with mine."

"Mexico is neutral," he responded, knowing she knew this already, yet filling time with talk to steer them away from activities they would be better served not initiating in a carriage on the crowded road to Bagdad.

She cuddled against him while the carriage bounced along

162

the muddy, deeply rutted road. Traffic was thick both coming and going, and she was glad to be encased inside a carriage, where they had a measure of privacy. "But your sailors and soldiers are everywhere; someone might recognize me."

"The only men who know you by sight are sailors from the *Victory.* They're in the harbor, not on shore."

"You have business in Bagdad?"

"And in here . . ." he mumbled against her ear.

She squirmed. "Afterward I will show *you* something in Bagdad, if it is still there."

He questioned with his eyes.

"The saloon where my father won my mother's hand in marriage."

Located on a precipice overlooking the Gulf of Mexico, Bagdad was a jumble of new and old ramshackle buildings, warehouses, and shanties. Like Alleyton, and to some extent Matamoros, Bagdad owed its growth to the war, or rather the Union blockade of the Gulf states.

Instructing the carriage to take them to the wharves, Logan sighed.

"What is it?" She had to shout above the din of people crowding the streets. Every other building was a saloon, making her wonder whether she would be able to locate La Paloma, and with the throng of sailors and shady women, she wondered further whether she cared.

"I shouldn't have brought you here," he answered.

She grasped his hand as it draped over her shoulder. "I'm safe with you."

Taking his eyes from the streets, he studied her a moment. "I still shouldn't have. . . ."

She laughed. "Are you afraid of Francisco?"

"No. If something happens to you it will be over my dead body; then Francisco will have no throat to slit."

"Unless it's Max's. Poor Max."

His eyes twinkled suddenly. "Yes, poor Max."

When the street turned and ran along the docks, she

163

stared over the cliff to the harbor that was crammed full of hundreds of ships. An equal number of lighters plied the water from shore to the ships, so loaded with cotton that she wondered how they stayed afloat.

Logan slapped a hand on the carriage roof. "Stop here."

Alongside one of the still-new warehouses, the carriage rolled to a stop and Logan helped Stella alight. "This business won't take long," he told the driver. "Wait for us." He turned to Stella. "Can you wait until we finish here to eat dinner?"

She nodded, picked up her heavy satchel, and followed him at a military clip into a warehouse full of bustling businessmen, dock workers, and a few Federal soldiers. Logan gripped her hand, pulling her along, while he scanned the area. At length, he led her to a table staffed by three businessmen.

"What if they recognize me?" she whispered.

His hand tightened around hers. "They won't. Just don't say anything." As he glanced down, his attention focused on her alone. "Listen. Listen to everything they say. But do not say a word. Outside, I will explain, if you don't understand."

His words rang with an ominous tone, and she wondered briefly whether she imagined it or not. At the first man's words, she realized why he had risked exposure to bring her to Bagdad.

Dropping her hand, Logan extended his toward one of the men at the table. "What do you have for me this morning?"

"The *Water Witch*, loaded with one thousand bales of cotton, bound for New York Harbor."

"New York Harbor, you say?" He seemed to holler above the din of trading going on around them, repeating the ship's destination for her benefit, she knew.

"What's the origin of the cotton?" he asked.

The man shuffled through a few papers, withdrew a document, and handed it to Logan. "Columbus, Texas." Stella resisted jerking the paper from his hands to see for herself.

Instead, she stood perfectly still but lifted her head, hoping to read the paper without straining. Her fury rose when she saw the paper lowered to her own eye level.

She studied it a moment, then turned her head away, as though observing the crowd. She tried to appear casual, but her hands clutched in tight fists. She wished she could punch him with them; she wished she weren't here.

"What else?" Logan barked, taking another paper and another, holding each within her range, while he carried on a conversation with the two men, ignoring her very presence.

"Eight hundred bales, origin San Antonio, shipped on the *Espíritu Tejas,* bound for New York Harbor. One thousand bales, origin Corpus Christi, shipped on the *Rebel-Rouser,* bound for Boston Harbor."

Returning the sheaf of papers to the man at the desk, he proceeded to lead her around the room from one table to another.

"What have we seized this week?" he asked at a table near the dock side of the building.

"A load of Enfield rifles last night, Colonel," came one reply, "origination—Enfield Imports, New York."

And at another, a load of wine and cognac, and other spirits from New World Imports, New York. And at another, a load of clothing—not military clothing or even necessities, but luxury items—ladies' gloves, hoopskirts, fancy piece goods and shoes shipped from Moore Brothers, Boston.

On and on around the room he dragged her, until she seethed inside. Suddenly, she jerked away and raced through the crowd toward the street where their carriage awaited.

"Take me to Matamoros," she instructed the driver. Jerking open the door, she climbed inside.

Logan caught the door and held it open. "First, we will stop at the Valensuela Ropería," he told the driver.

Stella's satchel bumped against her legs, heavy with the weight of the gold. She was tired, sick with disillusionment.

She felt defenseless, betrayed.

"I will take this carriage to Matamoros," she told him, chin held high. "You stay here to finish your business."

"Princess . . . ?"

Her eyes narrowed on him, stopping his words. She attempted to jerk the door out of his hand, but he held fast, nudging her to the other side to allow room for himself in the carriage.

"Stella, I had to show you the truth."

She moved suddenly, and he stepped into the carriage, only to have her exit through the opposite door.

She would have made it, she thought later, except for the satchel, which caught sideways in the opening.

Without warning, Logan took it from her hand.

"My God, this is heavy. What do you have stashed in here?" His words had slowed toward the end of the sentence, and by the time he finished, his eyes were wide.

Already pounding, her heart raced; she poised, one foot on the passenger step, watching him open the satchel. He glanced inside, felt beneath her pistol and cartridges, riffled through her clothing, then quickly snapped it closed.

She saw the veins rise in blue rivers along the backs of his hands. He sat motionless, gripping the top of the closed satchel, staring at it, silent.

With trepidation, as though she were surrendering to the enemy, she climbed back inside the carriage and sat beside him. Clasping her hands in her lap, she stared at her hands while the din around them roared as the distant surf.

At length he reached outside and slapped the top of the carriage. The driver called down, "Where to, sir?"

"Matamoros," he responded.

His voice was listless and somewhere beneath her own anguish, she felt sorry.

"What in the hell am I going to do with you?" he muttered, after they were well outside the limits of the burgeoning shanty town.

166

"Give me back my satchel," she said, more a statement than a demand.

Turning, he stared at her and she looked into his serious eyes; the sadness she saw there brought tears to her own.

"I can't very well do anything else," he told her. "If I turn in the gold, I'll have to turn you in."

Of a sudden, the satchel dropped to the floorboard, and he reached for her. She came into his arms, laying her face against his chest, encircling him with her arms. But he didn't hold her close, and she didn't hold him tight; their embrace was more for support, she thought, than from passion— more to comfort than to love.

Finally they sat back, leaning against the padded seat of the carriage, he with an arm still around her shoulders, she with a hand resting on his chest.

She felt as though the bonds between them had been severed in one fell swoop, and the only way they could maintain a connection was by physically touching each other.

"Do you want to stop to eat?" he asked at length.

She shook her head. "I mustn't be late."

A few miles outside Bagdad, it dawned on her that he had not had a chance to see to his own business. When she voiced her concern, his answer restored her emotions to their former peak of anger.

"That *was* my business," he answered. "To show you the truth, so maybe you will stop risking your life in this foolhardy adventure."

"Adventure!" she stormed. "Is that what you think of *our* side of the war? That it's an adventure? Papá is imprisoned over . . . over an adventure? He risks his life on the sea for an adventure?"

"That *you* do," he retorted. "Both of you."

Shifting abruptly, she turned her shoulders toward the window of the carriage. "If you expect me to believe all the cotton we ship ends up in Yankee ports, you . . ."

"I didn't say all of it . . ."

167

The despair from what she had learned today overwhelmed her. "They might as well open the railroads. It would be more economical to ship cotton and arms directly between . . . between Georgia and New York, between Virginia and Boston, than halfway across the continent, then around the Gulf and back again! It proves once more the stupidity of this war . . . and of the men who engage in it."

"And the stupidity of risking your life," he countered.

Turning, she glared at him. "And yours."

"My involvement in this conflict is not in question."

"It never is . . ." — she swallowed back tears and anger —
". . . except to me."

They rode in silence, each preoccupied, he with his fears, she with her plans. At last her mind settled down and she began to think about the things he had shown her today. She was glad, in a way. Knowing where some of the cotton went, where some of the armaments came from, made her job much more clear. Now, it was imperative that she get to Titlum-Tatlum and arrange for the new blockade-running ship. With their own fast vessel, Giddeon could haul cotton directly to market in Havana or even the Bahamas or Bermuda, where they could be sure it would not aid the Union.

A faint memory had tugged at the corner of her mind ever since Logan showed her the first invoice with "New York" written on it. Now, it surfaced like a latent torpedo: Giddeon's words the last time she saw him. What had he claimed . . . that he would find funds to pay for the new ship *even if he had to make a deal with the Yankees.*

So, he had known, and had not taken the threat to the Confederacy seriously. Surely that proved that not much dealing of that sort went on . . . not enough to damage the war effort, anyhow.

Suddenly another thought came to mind. "Where did those invoices come from?"

He turned to look at her. "From the cotton shipments."

"Then someone isn't telling you the whole truth, Colonel.

168

Cotton shipped to Matamoros never lists a southern point of origin. It is consigned to a Mexican party; the origin is never stated."

His eyes narrowed, then a grim, rather reluctant grin tipped his lips. "What about spies, princess? Don't you think we're smart enough to engage spies?"

She studied him at length, feeling the welcome warmth evoked by the endearment settle over her frayed nerves. She sighed, wanting nothing more than to lie back in his arms and close her eyes, and . . . and to not wake up until this damned war was over. "I know you are devious enough to do such a thing."

He pulled her to him, smoothing her hair with his hand. "Not me, princess." But he thought of Max and wondered what in the world she would do when she found out.

Lifting her chin he kissed her, at first gently, then eagerly as she responded in kind. He slipped his hands under the woolen shawl and felt her skin hot through the silky shirt. His muscles bunched beneath her caressing hands and when she massaged his neck, he trembled for want of her.

But this wasn't the place, he reminded himself. Raising his lips, he kissed the tip of her nose. "I wish you would reserve your passion for me, and leave this rebellion to the men who wrought it."

His lips, his tone, his breath on her face sent shivers down her spine. "What would happen to poor Mrs. Cardwell if I gave up now?"

He kissed her quickly and after a tight squeeze sat back on the seat. "Poor Mrs. Cardwell would have to drink okra-seed coffee a while longer, I suppose."

So well traveled was the road between Matamoros and Bagdad that vendors had set up stands along the way, to the extent that the entire thoroughfare resembled a giant marketplace. After a few miles, Logan had the driver stop and he purchased tamales for them to eat in the carriage. Later, they stopped for quesadillas, and later for tamales again, until,

169

by the time they arrived back in Matamoros, they had no desire for supper.

When they pulled up in front of the rooming house, Stella searched the street and located Max leaning against a wall outside a cantina no more than a half-block away.

Logan followed her out of the carriage. "Wait for us," he told the driver who had handed Stella down from her seat.

She pursed her lips, wondering how to tell him about the opera. "I . . . ah, I have plans for tonight."

He challenged her with his eyes, and she squirmed. "I know," he responded at last. "You are coming to the consulate with me."

Her eyes widened.

"You can't stay here, Stella. Not with that . . ." — he nodded at the satchel, then a grin played on his face — ". . . especially since I don't plan to sleep on a little cot in someone else's dining room."

"But I can't go there; it isn't safe for either of us."

He cocked his head. "I wouldn't take you someplace that wasn't safe. We have an office equipped to be used as an apartment by visiting dignitaries." He shrugged. "It's safe; none of the employees stay overnight in the building."

"I . . . I still can't. There's someplace I must go tonight . . . alone."

"In this town? Absolutely not!"

"I don't mean *alone,*" she recanted. "Max is coming with me."

Again he challenged her with his eyes, this time a cold stare, and she squirmed even more. The idea of spending the night with Logan, even inside the United States Consulate, stirred invitingly, though, and she knew somehow, someway, she had to work things out so she could meet Pryor Lea at the opera and return to Logan. "I won't be gone long."

"Then let's get your package," he answered, leading her toward the ramshackle frame house.

At the door, she paused. "What about Max? I know he

won't agree to spending the night with all those Yankees!"

Again, Logan felt a pang of guilt at deceiving her; again, he worried over her reaction when she discovered the truth. "Go ahead inside and get your things. Leave Max to me."

She sat between them in the carriage, clutching in her lap the package that had come from the dressmaker and marveling at the persuasive abilities of Logan Cafferty. However he had gone about it, he had convinced Max to accompany them to the United States Consulate, and to do so without so much as a grumble.

Fortunately, by the time they arrived, the hour was late and the staff had all gone home. At the corner, Logan purchased a pitcher of water from a small, barefoot boy who sold river water out of a barrel.

Once inside the building, he showed her to an enormous room, a sitting room from the look of it. He took the package from her, set it on a chair, then went to a brocade-covered Grecian couch with two enormous curved arms, one taller than the other. Pulling the fixed seat cushion forward, he lowered it until it formed a bed. "Not much larger than the cot, I'm afraid," he said, caressing her with his eyes, "but definitely more private."

Shivers raced up her neck at his words, and she strove to keep her mind on the evening ahead.

"Let me show Max where to sleep, then I'll return," he said, going toward the door.

Hastily, she tore open the package and withdrew Max's fawn twill suit. "Take this to him."

He studied the clothing in her hands, then looked at her own lavender-and-black gown that had been wrapped in the same package. "You're going out on the town . . . with Max?"

"No . . ." she said quickly, then added, ". . . I mean . . . well, I have to meet someone, and . . ." She shrugged, helplessly, imploring him to understand. "It seems everyone in Matamoros does business at the opera these days."

"The opera?"

She nodded, then thought of the hour. "I can't be late."

As soon as he closed the door behind him, she found the black satin handbag in the package and, opening the satchel, withdrew the bonds and placed them inside it. Then she shook out the dress and petticoats, smoothed the black lace snood she hoped would cover her short hair, and opened the case with the amethyst necklace the dressmaker said she must have to wear to the opera. Suddenly the whole terrible day came back to her with a force and tears formed in her eyes.

He found her sitting at a mirror that had been hidden behind the doors of an armoire, clothed in her chemise and petticoats, the scissors from her chatelaine poised over a strand of hair she held taut above her head between two fingers.

Coming to stand behind her, he saw the tears gleaming in her eyes. "What's the matter, princess?" His hands touched her bare shoulders, but instead of soothing her ragged emotions, his touch sent sharp reminders of their predicament twisting through her tired muscles.

Tears brimmed. She gritted her teeth and snipped the ends of hair sticking up between her fingers. "It looks so terrible," she wailed. "I'll never look like a lady again!"

Their eyes held in the glass; his lips moved and she knew the words, even before he had a chance to utter them; she knew what he would say: All she had to do was go home and let her hair grow out; all she had to do was give up what he scorned as an *adventure*. But it wasn't an adventure, and she wouldn't give it up . . . she couldn't. . . .

And he didn't say the words. Instead, he took the scissors from her fingers and began cutting her hair himself. "Let me help."

Her heart lurched to her throat. "What are you . . . ?"

He grinned. "I told you once I didn't care if you shaved your head."

172

Her hands flew to her head, holding his hands against her scalp. "You can't . . ." The touch of his hands, spread wide and encompassing over her scalp, soothed, somehow, comforted, like a priest bestowing a benediction.

"Trust me." His voice was so soft, so reassuring, that she removed her hands, and he began to cut her hair.

She watched him in the mirror, intent on the task, holding up one portion after another, snipping the ends gently, as with kisses. Each shank of hair he lifted sent fiery fingers coursing from her scalp through her blood, until by the time he finished, her hair fell in asymmetrical ringlets and her body glowed with tender yearnings.

At the end, he reached around her and pulled one curl over her forehead, his eyes finding hers in the glass, holding hers as with one desire. Then in a single movement, he set aside the chatelaine and turned her by the shoulders.

"Let's not go to the opera." His fingers whispered against her skin, brushing bits of hair from her shoulders, from her chest.

With a great sigh, she fell against him and embraced him tightly. "I must."

He kissed her forehead. "Then get dressed. You said we shouldn't be late."

When he released her, she stared in awe, seeing for the first time Max's suit—his pants and shirt, at least—on Logan's body.

He shrugged. "Max wasn't all that crazy about going to the opera."

"But you . . . ?" She shook her head in amazement.

He took up her gown and dropped it over her shoulders, then began fastening the multitude of silk buttons running down the back.

"Besides, I can't let someone else take out my best girl."

"Your *best* . . . ?" she challenged.

Finished with the buttons, he came around in front of her and studiously adjusted the band of lace that nipped her shoulders and dipped to a deep vee between her breasts. Bending, he kissed her skin low, beneath the lace, leaving the spot wet from the tip of his tongue.

"My *only* . . ." he whispered, finding her eyes, watching her shiver from his kiss. "You said we don't have to stay long."

"Logan, it's too dangerous. . . ."

"No objections, princess. I'll be perfectly safe." He struggled into the fawn jacket, then took her arm. "No one will recognize me; their eyes will be only for you."

Even though the Teatro de Reforma lay directly across the street from the United States Consulate, they decided to leave by a rear door and take a carriage, approaching the opera house in a roundabout manner, so as not to call attention to their lodgings.

She didn't see Max on the way out, and although she wondered how Logan persuaded him to stay behind, the glorious feeling of going out with Logan and later the splendor of the opera hall itself took that situation off her mind.

Lamps rimmed the perimeter of the building, washing it with a soft glow. Inside, the gilt carvings and rich appointments almost took her breath away. Logan tightened his hand on her elbow.

A playbill at the foot of the circular staircase announced the current attraction: *Barber of Seville* performed by an opera troop direct from Spain.

"This is truly a palace befitting a princess . . . my princess," Logan whispered in her ear.

Regretfully, she pulled her mind back to the business at hand, and he turned his attention to the tickets. "The governor's box should be upstairs."

In spite of her attempts to remain composed, her eyes blinked in astonishment when she stepped from the burgundy-carpeted staircase onto the second floor, which was made entirely of glass bricks, through which the lights from the foyer below gleamed like a thousand glittering stars.

Logan whistled through his teeth. "So, this is what eighty thousand dollars will buy."

"We don't have anything like this in Texas," she said.

Inside the governor's box the setting was equally resplendent with gilt chairs, velvet cushions and draperies, and a view of the entire panorama below, including the other boxes with their fine appointments and distinguished spectators.

Several men and their fashionably dressed ladies sat on the front row of chairs, unaware of the arrival of the two newest guests to the box. A guard at the door studied their tickets and ushered them inside.

Logan bent to whisper in Stella's ear. "That's the governor at the far left. And Pryor Lea at the other end of the row, to the right."

She stared at the two men a moment, composing herself for her approach to Mr. Lea, wondering desperately how she could accomplish her business for the Confederacy with a Federal officer at her elbow. Logan, himself, solved that problem.

"While you do business with Lea, I will see what I can accomplish for my cause with the governor of Tamaulipas."

She frowned at him. "How do you know Pryor Lea?"

He shrugged. "It's my business to know Confederate agents." Then, realizing what he had said, he squeezed her arm. "Some better than others."

She shot him a desperate look—a plea to leave the intimacies behind, for the moment.

"First, we should introduce ourselves to our host, however." He guided her by the elbow toward the governor's chair, where he surprised her even further, causing her to wonder whether he weren't afflicted with a bent toward self-destruction.

After the governor complimented Stella on her accomplishments for the Confederate cause and introduced her to his wife, who complimented her snood and quaint hairstyle, Logan introduced himself.

"Logan Cafferty, Governor, of the United States Marine Corps."

The governor quickly regained his composure, closing his mouth and turning an inquisitive eye on Stella, who, having jabbed Logan hard in the ribs, strove to recover from his awkward pronouncement. "He . . . ah, Colonel Cafferty is helping me gain the release of my father." Her voice was weak, she could hear it quiver, and she wanted to turn on Logan and demand an explanation.

Instead, she smiled stupidly through the ensuing introductions, and finally, seated beside Pryor Lea, with Logan already in earnest conversation with the governor at the far end of the box, she began to relax.

Pryor Lea nodded toward Logan. "Odd bedfellows . . ." Then at her astonished gasp, he apologized. "My deepest apologies, Miss Duval. A turn of phrase, nothing more, I . . ."

"No harm done," Stella assured him, getting down to business quickly, lest some further interruption deter her from her mission.

Lea, she soon learned, held none of Mr. Yates' reservations about the validity of the bonds.

"You have them with you tonight?"

She nodded.

He glanced toward Logan, then again at her.

"Colonel Cafferty knows nothing about this." Turning her back to the governor and his other guests, she opened the drawstrings of her bag and withdrew the sheaf of bonds.

Pryor Lea surreptitiously slid them behind the lapels of his dinner jacket, and while the orchestra warmed up, he scribbled a message on the back of his program with a lead pencil and handed it over.

"See Governor Murrah receives this receipt. Leave Yates to me. He will order your supplies; they will be ready when you return with another load of cotton." Once more he glanced at the far end of the box, then back at Stella. "When

176

are you leaving town?"

"In the morning," she told him, "if all goes well. And . . . ah, please don't worry over my escort tonight. Being . . . ah, indebted, if you will, to my family—a matter that happened well before the outbreak of our present difficulties—Colonel Cafferty is helping me obtain the release of my father from prison in Brownsville."

Pryor Lea nodded sagely, and Stella held her breath in relief. The orchestra grew louder, people around them began to applaud, and the curtain inched its way to the ceiling.

"If you will excuse me, I should go now," she told him, turning to catch Logan's attention. "Thank you for your help, Mr. Lea."

"Thank you, my dear. You are a boon to our cause."

Outside she almost ran to the nearest carriage. Logan kept pace. "Glad to see you are as anxious as I am," he whispered, reaching for the door.

She felt a blush rise to her cheeks. Then she pursed her lips and glared at him. "You are determined to get one or both of us in trouble."

The driver took the door from Logan's hand, and when he spoke, his voice startled them.

"Don't turn around," Max said quietly. "Get in the cab." Slamming the door behind them, he climbed to the top and whipped the horses to a trot.

Logan pulled her to his side, shielding her head with his arms. She felt his heart pound against her face. Before either of them could find words to speak, the carriage swayed to a halt and Max jumped to the ground.

"What's happened?" Logan barked.

"Blakesborough," Max answered, and for a moment, Stella wondered what was going on. In the next, she wished she did not know.

"Captain Blakesborough," Max rephrased, "from your ship, Colonel. A fellow named Jacobs came to the consulate not long after you left, carrying word that Blakesborough has had a tail on you. He knows you have been with Miss Duval, and he is coming ashore to personally catch you . . . ah, consorting with the enemy."

Stella caught her breath. For an eon the interior of the carriage was so still that all she could hear was Logan's heart beating—or was it her own? she wondered.

"I brought your things, ma'am." Max pointed to the satchel on the floorboard. "I stuffed in everything belonging to a woman I could find in the room."

When Logan spoke, his voice carried the authority of his position, and Stella felt his strength flow into her own body. "How much time do we have?"

"Couldn't say. Jacobs said they were right behind him. They have surely found the consulate empty by this time."

"Then we have to get Stella out of town. Now."

"That's what this carriage is for, Colonel."

Chapter Eight

For what seemed like an eternity after Max returned to the driver's box and whipped up the team, Logan held her in his arms as though he were afraid to let her go.

Max's parting words, just before his grim countenance left the window of the carriage, had stirred fear in both their hearts — in Logan's for her, in hers for him.

"What kind of plans have you made?" Logan had asked. While they listened, Max told them.

"I've arranged for an escort; you know them, Colonel. We will travel north up the Rio Grande on the Mexican side, cross the river on the ferry at Las Rucias; from there we can take the stage inland."

"Let's get going, then," Logan had told him.

Max stared inside the carriage and his voice dropped. "Make your good-byes quick . . . ah, Colonel. We'll let you out at the next stop."

Stella's heart froze. "He can't let you out! Not on the street. What will you do?"

Logan nuzzled his chin on top of her head, before lowering his face to hers. "Don't worry about me. I'll cross the river and get back to Brownsville." He kissed her then, and she responded, knowing their evening's tryst had been abruptly, savagely, canceled.

Her heart pumped with such a violent rush it ached physically, forcing tears to her eyes. She tightened her arms around him, pressed her body to his, thinking of this man, of her ever-growing love for him, of her desperate need to be with him, to stay with him . . .

But more, of her overwhelming fear for him. "What will happen to you? How will you return to the *Victory* with the captain threatening . . ."

"Shhh . . ." he whispered, kissing her face.

But her fear was great, and she persisted. "Where will you go? When will I see you again?"

"Soon, princess" was all he would say. While the carriage thundered down the roadway, jostling them thither and yon, he fumbled with the buttons on her bodice. At last he turned her away from him, and began to work at them earnestly.

"You can't travel in this . . . not where you are going." His voice was rough, his fingers tantalizing as he unbuttoned her dress and pushed it over her shoulders.

She reached for the satchel, opened it, and in the darkness, groped for her shirt and breeches.

"Sit up," he ordered; when she obeyed, he helped her wriggle out of the gown, which she stuffed in the satchel.

He kissed the tender skin along her shoulders, her neck, while she untied her petticoats and struggled out of them. "Such a waste of time," he mumbled against her skin, turning her by the shoulders, kissing her softly along her neckline, her chest, and lower. Coaxing one firm breast from her chemise, he nipped and teased its tip, knowing all the while he should not stir up their already heightened longings, finally stopping himself with the reminder of their desperate situation.

By the time the swaying coach drew to a stop, she had pulled on her shirt and her pants.

While she stomped into her boots, he loaded her pistol. "Keep this in your lap, just in case" he advised, then added, "Max will take care of you."

With effort she laughed. Drawing his face to hers, she clasped the back of his neck and kissed his lips. "Or you will slit his throat?"

"You're damned right." He returned her kiss, frightened now of the dangers at hand.

"And what about you? What if . . . ?" she worried.

"I will be fine. And I'll be in touch as soon as . . ."—thinking of the future, he sighed—"How did we end up on different sides of this damned conflict?" His whispers teased her lips. "There's nothing we can do about that now, but . . ."—he paused, not wanting to scare her, knowing she would be better served with a little more fear in her heart—". . . for the time being, we are safe only when we are apart."

They felt Max jump from the driver's box, heard horses' hooves, voices. She tensed.

"Do exactly what Max tells you," Logan told her. "He will escort you to Los Olmos, and I expect . . ."—he inhaled a deep breath—". . . you must stay at Los Olmos, Stella. Wait there for your father; he will be released within days. Persuade him to stay at Los Olmos, too."

Max jerked open the carriage door. "It's time."

Stella clutched Logan's sleeves.

"Whatever you do," Logan continued, "stay away from the coast—and from the Rio Grande." He kissed her quickly, but firmly.

Outside the carriage, with only the stars for light, she saw only forms, but those forms terrified her. "Who are these men?"

"Friends," Logan assured her.

"Friends? With Spanish horses and crossed bandoleers?"

"Do you think I would send you off with men I do not know . . . personally?"

"But . . . ? How . . . ?"

One of the men led a saddled, riderless horse toward them.

"Now," Logan began, changing the subject, "remember what I told you about the pistol. Stay in the cab until Max tells you to come out. The escort will see you to Las Rucias; from there Max will travel with you to Los Olmos."

"You have everything worked out . . . ?"

He inhaled a deep draft of cool night air. "With luck."

"How do you know these men?"

He shrugged. "You heard Max."

She stared from Max to the horsemen. Alarm spread through her, and she tried to fight it off. Tearing her eyes from the riders, she stared, pleading, at Logan. "They look like bandits."

"That's the idea, princess." Pulling her close, he again kissed her lips and she responded, shamelessly, in front of Max and the strangers, ominously, as though it were for the last time.

Max cleared his throat. "Time's wasting, Colonel."

Logan gripped her shoulders, stared into her anxious eyes, then lifted her back inside the coach. "Remember, you must stay away from the Rio Grande and from the coast. Don't forget to warn Giddeon."

When he closed the door, she heard him address Max.

"You're sure? You can still beat Davis to Las Rucias?"

"I'm sure. Now, you get going and take care of yourself. I'm not about to let anything happen to her."

When again the coach stopped, the sky had turned a dull gray, matching her spirits, Stella thought. She heard Max conferring outside with the horsemen who had ridden beside both carriage doors during the long ride from Matamoros.

She had tried to sleep, but had been unable to for the specters raised in her mind by the events of the evening just past. Not that she was afraid for herself. Max had proven his worth even before they arrived in Matamoros. Logan's trust in him only confirmed her own. But what of Logan himself? What would this Blakesborough do to him? How much trouble could a mere captain cause for a colonel?

The most troubling aspect, though, occurred to her as the sky lightened, like a revelation she would rather not have had unveiled. She worried about Logan, of course.

But she was also . . . not angry with him, she decided,

rather, irritated . . . aggrieved, perhaps, was a better term. As much as she loved him, for as long as she had wanted him beside her, now that he was here, everything had gone wrong. It was the war, she knew. Logan had nothing to do with it; he had no more control—not much more, anyhow—over their situation than she had. It was the war. This damnable war.

But it distressed her nonetheless that from the moment they were reunited on board the *Victory,* their relationship had brought strife not only to themselves but to her entire family. Before, Giddeon had safely run the blockade; before, she had no trouble with the cotton trains.

As foolish as it was, she found herself blaming Logan. Perhaps not for the mishaps that befell them, but . . .

She sighed, exasperated—with herself, with the situation. Before Logan Cafferty reappeared in her life, she had been able to control the events surrounding her.

Now, look at me, she thought. Being smuggled out of Mexico like a criminal—like the contraband she had dealt in daily for the past year. Always before, she had been in control.

Now, she found herself being controlled. And she did not like it.

Max jerked open the door. "Ready, ma'am?"

She nodded, taking his hand. "I suppose so, since I have no choice," she answered, then bit her tongue. Max had been nothing but a faithful employee, whose skill and expertise had been invaluable to her work. She had no cause to be sharp with him. And he had gotten her out of Matamoros in the nick of time—if she were to believe him.

Swallowing her pride, for that was what bothered her, she knew, she stepped from the carriage. Max reached for her satchel, and at the same time, their eyes fell on her hoopskirt.

She blushed. "I . . . ah . . . it wouldn't fit inside the satchel."

"We'd better leave it behind, ma'am."

She nodded, smiling for the first time in hours. "What will you do with the carriage?"

"One of the men here will take it off the road. Try to mislead anyone should we be followed."

Her eyes widened. "Do you think . . . ?"

"No telling, ma'am." He took her arm. "That's why we'd best get to our side of the river."

Then she had an idea. "Couldn't we . . . ? Ah . . . why couldn't we *borrow* . . ." —she looked down at the satchel full of gold— . . . "or buy two of those men's horses? They could ride back in the carriage."

Max shook his head. "This country's rife with bandits, ma'am. We'd best take the stage like we planned. If I let you go off and get captured by bandits, Log . . . ah, the colonel would have my . . ."

She laughed at her situation. "So, now you are accountable to Logan *and* Francisco?"

He shrugged, leading her to the ferry. "Something like that, ma'am."

Once on the ferry, however, she noticed that he held one of their escort's rifles in his hands and carried a bandoleer across his shoulders. "I see you weren't above *borrowing* a rifle and ammunition."

He shrugged once more. "Times of need, a man does what a man does."

She shook her head, studying the muddy waters of the Rio Grande River, thinking how Max was beginning to resemble Logan in persuasive abilities. And thoughts of Logan called to mind his admonition to stay away from the Rio Grande.

A desperate sense of impending calamity spread over her, chilling her like the damp December air.

December, she thought. Christmas. Would they never see an end to this strife?

Strife for this day, she soon discovered, involved trudging through several chaparral-covered miles to a distant stage station.

"The stage ain't passed through here since the war broke out," the ferryman told them after they set foot on the Texas bank of the Rio Grande. They watched the riders disappear in the distance on the other side. Max ran a hand through his sandy hair. "I'm sorry, ma'am. The colonel . . ."

"Never mind the colonel, Max. We are on our side of the battle line now, and we will do things our way." But when she tried to purchase horses from the ferryman, he all but laughed in her face.

"Horses? I don't even try to keep horses anymore. Some highfalutin army man would just come along and commandeer 'em. I already donated more horses to that danged army than I set out to."

Two hours later they reached the stage road, and luck, she thought, was at last on their side. Not thirty minutes after walking up the rutted tracks, a stagecoach lumbered along, headed north.

One look inside the cab warned her it might not be luck that smiled upon her. The driver was agreeable, but the passengers were a bit reluctant to have another body added to their number.

The three transverse seats were filled to capacity—nine men, she counted. At first glance none was willing to give up the interior, which shielded them from the cold damp wind, for a seat on the equally crowded roof.

The driver was the first to recognize a lady among them. "If you geezers don't decide which *gentleman* will give the lady a seat, I'll decide for you."

When the fact registered that she was indeed female, a junior-ranking Confederate officer jumped out of the coach. He came face to face with Max.

Rolling a plug of chewing tobacco from one cheek to the other, he glared close at Max's face. "You a deserter?"

Max's eyes flared, and Stella quickly stepped in. "Certainly not. Mr. Burnsides works for the government. We transport Confederate cotton across the Rio Grande, and we have only now narrowly escaped a Yankee patrol."

The soldier shifted his tobacco, shrugged, and climbed to the top of the cab. Max followed, situating himself at the opposite end from the soldier.

The driver proceeded to find Stella the best seat. "You heard the young lady," he said, "straight from the jaws of the enemy. Let her in the middle there, so she won't have to fight off spittle from the likes of you miscreants."

The group was a varied lot, including a sheriff chasing a bandit who was thought to be on the stage ahead of this one, several Confederate soldiers, one a courier carrying news of the fighting around Brownsville to coastal batteries as far away as Galveston.

"The shortage of mounts," he responded to the question of whether it would not have been faster to travel on horseback.

"Texas with a shortage of horses! Who would ever have imagined it?" said a well-dressed businessman who claimed to be with Governor Murrah's office. "Why, this very area we're riding through was once so littered with mustang horses they were a plumb nuisance. The Wild Horse Desert, that's what this region was called twenty years back."

When they came to the Paso Real crossing at Sebastian, Stella got out and rode beside Max across on the ferry, inhaling what she hoped would be enough fresh air to last to the next stop.

The ride wasn't as bad as it could have been, she realized. Only six of the passengers chewed tobacco in her presence, and they took careful aim at the windows, so as not to splash her. Although her center seat had no backrest, only a strap to lean against, she was glad not to be sitting next to a window, where the passengers' heads were in danger of being kicked by feet of those on top, who rode with their legs dangling over the side of the cab.

And the driver showed more care than some she had ridden with. At rough or steep inclines, he made the passengers on top alight and walk, so as not to overturn the vehicle. She became hopeful that this would be one of those rare stagecoach rides on which the coach did not overturn one time the entire journey.

Along toward dusk, they neared Los Olmos. When the driver slowed at the creek, she had one of the passengers signal him to stop, and after a brief pause, it rumbled on again, leaving her and Max in its wake.

Combined with the clatter of the disappearing coach, the commotion she heard sounded so natural she didn't think anything about it until they gained the crest of the rise overlooking the house and saw a great herd of bellowing cattle being driven, not by Los Olmos vaqueros, but by men in Union-blue uniforms.

Quickly withdrawing the pistol from her satchel, she began firing in the air, while at the same time, she ran toward the house. Once she looked behind her, but Max was nowhere to be seen. She didn't have time to stop and worry about him, however, as her shot had attracted the attention of a uniformed man, who bore down upon her at full speed.

Holding her ground, her pistol aimed with extended arms, she searched behind him for activity around the house.

He jerked his mount to a halt at her feet. "I'll take that pistol."

She glared at him, arms steady. "Where are you driving our cattle, Sergeant?" Staring toward the brand on the rump of the horse he rode, she added, ". . . and our horses?"

He grinned, infuriating her with his insolence. "Brigadier General Davis is hungry for Texas beef." Leaning forward in the saddle, he reached toward her. "Hand over the gun, reb."

"The only way you will get this weapon is through your heart!"

He blinked, straightened in the saddle, and for a moment she thought he was going to spit in her face. Turning, he spat to the ground. "You women on this ranch ain't no Southern

187

ladies."

"No woman is a lady when her home is being threatened by . . . by crude invaders such as yourself. Now, take your men off our cattle at once . . . and off our horses."

In a gesture of mockery, he tipped his hat. "Sorry, the other woman on the premises . . . ah, *agreed* to let us have them . . . for the cause, of course." He turned in his saddle and whistled through two fingers. Immediately a group of people appeared on the porch of the house.

Stella stared at her mother, who was accompanied on the porch by Abril and Lupe and the children. Cautiously, she started toward them.

No sooner had she moved a step than little Miguel saw her and tore away from Serita's hand to race toward her. "Stella, Stella! These men are Yankees!"

Reaching her, he clutched at her legs. "They are stealing our cattle . . . the cattle we were rounding up for—"

"Miguel," she interrupted quickly. "Quiet, now. Take my hand and walk with me to the house."

The sergeant on the horse above her cleared his throat. "If I had reason to believe this household was aiding the rebellion by providing beef . . ."

She glared at him. "How dare you come onto our property and frighten these children!"

Serita had not, it turned out, agreed to let Edmund Davis's men have the cattle. Since they had arrived in a flourish, brandishing firearms and holding the vaqueros at gunpoint, she had had little choice.

"Edmund Davis, of all people!" Stella fumed after the Federal troops rode away from Los Olmos, driving the cattle Serita and the vaqueros had rounded up for shipment to Jeb Magruder's army on the Gulf. "Davis is a traitor, nothing more! How could he, a judge from Corpus Christi, turn on his own people? If he had to fight for the Union, he could have at least insisted on an assignment back east."

They sat over supper exchanging stories of their activities

since Stella left home. The first thing Serita — indeed the entire household — wanted to hear, of course, was news from Giddeon. Learning he would soon be released, they rejoiced.

"Thank heavens for Logan Cafferty," Serita sighed. "Without him, I fear Giddeon would be imprisoned for the duration."

"Yes," Stella mimicked. "Thank heavens for Colonel Cafferty. I wonder how much we could have accomplished without his interference."

"Stella, dear! Logan didn't capture Giddeon, he is seeking his release."

"As far as we know," Stella responded.

"You are tired, that's all," Serita comforted. "Now that you're home, you can rest up. . . ."

"Mamá! You sound just like *him*. How can I stay home and rest? How can any of us rest? The Yankees took our cattle today; what will they take tomorrow?"

"Don't join the doomsters," Serita warned. "We have enough of those already. Once your father is home . . ."

"Once Papá is home, he will only go out again. From what I learned . . ." She leaned forward to emphasize her point. "Would you believe me if I told you part of the cotton shipped over the Cotton Road is sold to New York? Part of it to Boston?"

Serita sighed. "Yes, Stella, I would believe you. I've seen war before. It does crazy . . . terrible things to people."

"That is exactly why I cannot stay home, Mamá. Once Logan showed me the truth, I realized why Papá needs that new blockade-running ship. That's the only way we can be sure the risk Papá takes with his life is for something . . . something of value — he must have his own ship, one he can sail away from the greed here on the coast. It's bad enough to think he might be . . ." She stopped, thinking of the children. "Anyway, I promised Mr. Ransom I would go straight to Titlum-Tatlum from Brownsville to order the ship. I must leave in the morning."

Serita shook her head. "I don't like you running about the country like this."

"Don't worry, Mamá. Max will take care of me. Won't you, Max? You should have seen the way he arranged our escape from Matamoros! He even had Logan jumping to do his bidding, and . . ." —she paused and grinned at Max— ". . . for some reason all his own, he has an aversion to Yankees."

Max looked down at his lap where he painstakingly rearranged his napkin. When the silence lengthened, he cleared his throat. "I'll take care of her, ma'am. I promised the colonel I would."

Stella laughed. "And Francisco. Don't forget Francisco and his Bowie knife."

During the next week Stella and Max traveled from Los Olmos to Papalote to Victoria, finally arriving at Caney Creek just north of Titlum-Tatlum on a damp and chilly December twenty-second.

At each stop along the way they heard reports of the Federals' steady advance up the Texas coast.

The first night away from Los Olmos they stopped at Papalote Creek, where a dance was in progress, although according to the proprietress, a Mrs. Oates, it wasn't with the same spirit as before the conflict.

"The teamsters are not the same quality men, if you'll pardon me for saying so, as our local boys. Not yours, now, Stella. But of course your teamsters . . ." —the old woman stopped, squinted at Max, then continued— ". . . for the most part, your men are longtime Los Olmos vaqueros."

"Max is taking Francisco's place escorting me up the coast," Stella explained.

"Francisco," the woman enthused, "that nice man brought me salt. I will love him to my dying day for that."

Stella smiled. "I'll be sure to tell him, Mrs. Oates."

The quality of men notwithstanding, the music at Papalote dance hall was as loud as ever, Stella noticed, and discordant enough to keep her awake into the wee hours of the morning.

The next day they rode hard and arrived in Victoria by sundown. At the wagon yard, Stella learned that Francisco had indeed been through, dispersing goods and, as a consequence, goodwill. She thought of Mrs. Cardwell and hoped he had saved enough coffee to take her when they passed through there.

She would take the coffee to Mrs. Cardwell herself, on her return trip. This she told Max on their way to the café.

"By the time we get back to Alleyton from Titlum-Tatlum, Francisco should have another wagon train ready to haul to the border. We will pass the Cardwells' stage station then."

Max stared frankly at her. "Colonel Cafferty . . ."

"Max, don't you start in on me, too. You can see the need around us. We cannot let these people down."

"He warned you to stay away from the Rio Grande River?"

She sighed. "He would try anything to keep me at Los Olmos. Haven't you figured that out by now?"

But the next morning when they took breakfast before resuming their journey, news arrived that disturbed them both. A young man at a center table held the attention of the entire room.

"That's what I said," he answered Stella's question. "The Yankees have taken Fort Esperanza and slipped through Pass Cavallo; they're fighting now at Indianola—fighting fierce, and it don't look good for our side."

"Guess it's that highfalutin new hero of theirs, what done it," an elderly man chimed in. "Why, just over a year back our boys held off two Federal ships in the same spot. Them Yankees had to steam out of Matagorda Bay with their tails between their legs."

"That's Major Hobby's battalion. Most of his men are Victoria boys. Any word on casualties?"

191

The young man shook his head.

"Wonder what happened to our marine artillery?" a listener asked.

"By artillery, you talking about them Quaker guns old Jeb thinks he can fool the Yankees with?"

"They got more'n wooden Quaker cannons now," a defender interjected.

"Humph! We all knew onct them Yankees got their act together, they could overpower rafts and dredgeboats."

"It wasn't the Federal navy," the reporter responded loudly enough to draw the attention of the room, once more. All eyes trained on him, expectant. He paused for quiet.

" 'Twas land forces. Led by a fellow named Banks — General Banks — operating from his base off Point Isabel. They took El Sal del Rey, then stormed up the coast lickety-split, like it wasn't nothin' more than a Sunday outing with your girl, took Corpus Christi, then Aransas Pass."

Stella had listened, relieved for a moment that Logan obviously played no part in the taking of Indianola. Then, at the young man's recitation of locations captured by the Yankees, her thoughts sped from Logan to home. "What about the ranches in those areas? Los Olmos? The King Ranch? Did you hear any mention of . . . ?"

The young man shook his head. "As I heard it, ma'am, 'twas strictly a military action. They took beeves from the ranches, but it was the military installations they destroyed. Word has it they plan to fight all the way to Louisiana, then they will have all our Texas ports in their pockets."

One man guffawed. "They make it to the Sabine, ol' Dick Dowling and his handful of Texans will chew 'em up and spit 'em out!"

"And Jeb Magruder over to Galveston. General Magruder will have plenty to say about it."

"Prince John, you mean?" one of the ladies chimed in. "If they wait a few days, they can catch Prince John Magruder at his Christmas ball."

"Now, Nettie, don't be hard on ol' Jeb. He's done us a right fine job."

"Well, it ain't time for partyin' just yet."

"I wouldn't worry too much about the ranchers south of here, ma'am," one of the diners told Stella. "Most of them have already moved inland. We've had several families a day coming through here . . . won't even stop this close to the action. Said to feel safe, they'd have to go as far as Washington on the Brazos."

The news cast Stella into a dilemma. Should she return to Los Olmo . . . or should she go forward? Max, of course, encouraged her to return to Los Olmos.

"This must have been what the colonel warned you about," he observed. "He said he would see to it they spared Los Olmos."

She studied her companion. "How do you think he can accomplish that?" she demanded. "Were he in control of a ship, he could perhaps prevent that one ship from shelling our house, but how do you think he can keep forces he is not even in communication with from ravaging everything in their path? You saw how General Davis's men took our cattle. . . ."

"They may have taken some of your cattle, ma'am, but General Banks is noted for humane . . ."

"Max, for goodness' sake! You don't have to praise the enemy to make me feel better. You don't know any more about General Banks than I do. But my mind is made up. I will hire a courier to take a message to Mamá, then bring us word of their situation. This Federal assault makes my mission even more imperative."

They left soon after breakfast and Max didn't resist further. He did, however, comb the woods for news of the fighting. When word reached them that General Davis was progressing with his attack up the Rio Grande River, Stella became despondent.

"What will we do if he reaches Laredo?" she sighed one

night when they sat around a campfire along the north bank of the Colorado River.

Max sat across from her, and his expression incensed her, reminding her of the admonitions Logan was forever giving her.

"I will not return to Los Olmos!" she declared. "One way or another I will get another cotton train through, if for no other reason now than to prove to Mr. Yates I can do it."

Max shrugged. "You can certainly try. But it would be a pity . . . what I mean to say is, you do need to take care of yourself, seeings how the colonel and you have plans for the future. This rebellion won't last forever, and—"

"Rebellion?" She laughed, her flagging spirits lifted somewhat by the absurdity of their circumstances. "We have been talking about Yankees so much you're beginning to sound like one of them."

Crossing the Brazos River the next day, they arrived at Caney Creek by midday and the sight gave her heart a lift. Sailors and soldiers and marines in every description of uniform labored steadily, fortifying the mouth of the creek to fend off a Federal invasion.

"Old Jeb ordered it, ma'am," one soldier told her while he shoveled dirt and mud in three directions at once.

"We won't let them Yankees get any farther than Caney Creek."

"They done took Galveston onct, they ain't gonna get at her again."

"If Dick Dowling can whip 'em outnumbered fifty-two to one, we can hold the whole danged Yankee army right here."

A hundred men or more worked on the earthen fortress, building rifle pits, trench works, and what they assured her would be four redoubts that would turn the entire Yankee navy.

She turned away, staring upstream where more men labored—to hold back General Banks, they assured her.

"You feeling all right, ma'am?" Max asked.

She stared at him a moment, seeing instead the battle these men were preparing to wage, hearing instead of ax and pick, Max's earlier words.

"If I needed proof, Max, this is it. Why should I protect myself for that future you talked about when . . ." — sighing, she suppressed a rising sense of doom — ". . . when *this* is what awaits . . . the colonel?"

At the encouragement of Captain Ireland, who had come up from Fort Esperanza to take charge of the fortifications, Stella and Max camped for the night under the protection of the Confederate troops. The enthusiasm of the men was high.

"More troops are arriving every day," Captain Ireland told them. "General Magruder promised me five or six thousand men in time to defend this place. I know folks speak harshly of him, but he's been biding his time, much like Sam Houston did at San Jacinto. It's a smart move; the men are ready; our fortress will be, too."

"When do you expect the attack?" In light of the captain's high spirits, Stella hoped her lack of enthusiasm didn't show.

"Soon," he told her. "Very soon. Then you can get back to doing what you do best for our cause — hauling cotton. We surely do owe you a debt, ma'am. We surely do."

"We all do our part, Captain. That's what it takes."

"Will you be going across the pass to Galveston from Titlum-Tatlum?" Captain Ireland asked.

"We have no reason to," she answered. "As soon as my business is completed with Captain Wedemeyer, I'll head for Alleyton."

"You really should go on to Galveston and take in the general's Christmas ball," the captain suggested.

Stella smiled. "I'm not sure this is an appropriate time for a ball, Captain, Christmas or not."

"Oh, but it is, ma'am. One year ago this Christmas, General Magruder retook Galveston from the Yankees. This year we'll celebrate, then we'll set about whippin' their . . . ah, winning this godawful war. You being such an important part of our efforts, why, it would be fitting for you to attend."

"Not only that, ma'am," the captain's aid said, "if I may say so, a lovely lady like yourself, well, it would do the men good to twirl you around the floor a time or two."

Stella smiled, thanked them.

"Tom's right, ma'am," the captain added. "I hope you will give it considered thought."

you with the important half the stock to hundred
as wormwood with its mechanism at the back of the vessel
Max Mason walked out in a stretch to surprise on board
bigged round to find it now beautiful
Captain Wedemeyer married Stella and told him that
seaman here hold at the same forward
Max Mason had came to see the idea there at the
to the forty
built a private professional of almost no interest and when
her to answer question the he had on the

Chapter Nine

Captain H.C. Wedemeyer's unique operation occupied most of the secluded island of Titlum-Tatlum. He had not come to the Gulf Coast to build ships but, rather, to help run the Union blockade. Once there, however, he met Giddeon Duval and together the two seamen hatched a scheme to build the perfect blockade-running vessel.

When Stella and Max arrived at Titlum-Tatlum around midmorning the day after their visit with Captain Ireland at Caney Creek, General Banks was hot on their heels, as it were, eating up the Texas coastline with his land forces. Rumors still abounded relating to a Union naval attack, and the temptation was great to succumb to the pessimistic view of the doomsters, as Serita had called them.

Captain Wedemeyer was not a doomster, Stella discovered. He enthusiastically embraced Giddeon's instructions to begin work on the vessel—and the gold she brought to help him get the project under way.

Wedemeyer clapped his hamlike hands in glee. "No time to waste. We will begin at once."

Stella surveyed the setup. Everything in sight—saw-horses, workbenches, even the ground—was littered with bits and pieces of old ships: sections of hull plates and spars, fragments of paddle wheels and smoke pipes, and things she didn't even recognize, except that all were unmistakably used . . . old. The area more resembled a dumping ground than the construction site for a new ship. What worried her most was what she did not see.

"What will you do for materials?" she asked. "With the blockade intensified and land forces to contend with, it will be difficult to bring in new materials."

Captain Wedemeyer ushered Stella and Max into a hut, equally as jumbled as the land around it. Using his massive forearm, he cleared a place on the table by raking everything to the floor.

With a flourish he unrolled a set of blueprints and called her to examine them. Unlike the surroundings, the blueprints for the new vessel were immaculate, uncluttered, and sketched in intricate detail.

Standing beside her, Max emitted a low whistle. "Estimated eight hundred tonnage!" he read. "What kind of engine are you talking about?"

Wedemeyer tapped the drawing with his pipe. "Nine hundred. With its two-hundred-foot length and low draft, the lady will skim through the bay and across the Gulf like a nymph in one of those old stories."

Stella listened, while Max questioned and the captain answered, each obviously enjoying the opportunity to share his knowledge of shipbuilding with a fellow seaman — "dual paddle wheels," "two-masted schooner rigging," "brass-covered bottom," "lead pipes," "brass fittings."

"Impressive," Max agreed. "Mighty impressive."

"And curious," Stella added.

Max studied the plans while the captain questioned Stella. "What do you not understand, Miss Duval?"

"How you intend to get hold of such fancy materials with the blockade . . . and now General Banks' land attack?"

Wedemeyer waved his pipe toward the exterior of the hut. "Out there, miss."

"You mean to use all that old stuff?"

"Old, yes," he agreed. "But not in the sense your tone implies. Sometimes *old* is *best*. As in the case of that oak hull I salvaged from a prized vessel, or the brass from —"

"Engines?" she questioned. "You have an *old* nine-hundred-horsepower steam engine lying about in all this . . . ah, among your treasures, which you intend to put in a ship for my father to risk his life in?"

Captain Wedemeyer laid an arm around her shoulders in a fatherly fashion. "Miss Duval, leave the steam engine to me. But rest assured, I would never build a ship I knew would endanger a man's life. To the contrary, the ships I build are to preserve life—lives, I should say, in the Confederacy of Southern States."

Outside, the shipbuilder led them from a pile of timbers and planks to a stack of brass plates to a keg of brass nails.

"What about armaments?" Max asked.

The captain smiled. "That, my man, is a question I'm proud to answer. You may know the Dance Brothers Armory is in the process of developing a cannon of no greater weight than that of a man—an effort on their part to arm the Texas Cavalry so they can be more effective in their hit-and-run attacks along the coast. Another use for such a cannon would be on a ship of this nature, where weight is of a premium."

"How long do you expect the construction to take?" Stella asked.

"When Kosta arrives and . . . ah, that other friend of your father's—"

"Edward Stavinoha," Stella supplied, "from Corpus Christi."

Wedemeyer nodded and puffed on his pipe, thoughtful. At last he removed his pipe. "Yes. Edward Stavinoha, the cabinetmaker. With him and Kosta . . . I should think not over three months." He held his pipe by the bowl and pointed the stem toward her. "That is, if the weather holds and we can keep the Yankees off our necks."

The talk turned to other matters. Stella told him about the fortifications being erected at Caney Creek, and of the reinforcements General Magruder had promised to augment the effort to turn back the Federal advance at that spot.

"Old Jeb Magruder . . ." Captain Wedemeyer mused. "Some call him Prince John, I suppose you've heard. You headed to that shindig they're throwing for him on Galveston Island?"

While Stella was busy shaking her head, she heard Max reply, "Yes. The troops at Caney convinced Miss Duval it is her patriotic duty."

She frowned at him. "I've decided to go straight to Alleyton. With General Davis charging up the Rio Grande, we need to get another cotton train on the road."

Max studied her with a serious, frank expression. "I realize that's important, but don't underestimate your effect on the morale of the troops."

She scoffed, and the captain spoke up. "There's two trains of thought about that ball. Some folks are up in arms because ol' Jeb's throwin' a party when there's so much suffering about. Others say it's his way of building morale for the upcoming fight with the Yankees."

"See what I mean?" Max asked her. "It takes more than guns to win a . . . ah, a war. Of course, if you . . ."

Stella sighed. "We'll go. But certainly not because I relish attending a ball."

Before they left Titlum-Tatlum, Max inquired of the captain about safe lodging for Stella in Galveston. Afterward, following him on horseback across the shallow inlet to the west end of Galveston Island, she reflected on the extent to which she had come to depend on him.

Her assessment his first day on the job had been correct: Maxwell Burnsides was an experienced leader. She smiled, recalling how even Logan followed him without question when they escaped Matamoros.

Yes, she was indeed fortunate Francisco had found such an able and agreeable man. Granted, he possessed an obvious aversion to Yankees in general, but he had never once questioned her relationship with Logan. To the contrary, his understanding of that relationship surfaced in numerous ways: his insistence that she take care of herself—how had he put it?—since she and the colonel had plans for the future; in the way he sought news of the war at every stop, so he could break each new Federal victory to her himself. She knew he was trying to cushion the blows.

She spurred her mount alongside his, and they galloped across the flat, sandy surface of the island. Everything was somber—December gray, she thought—the sky, the sand. She looked toward the sea and found it a deep, winter green. She wondered where Logan was; she wished he were here beside her.

It was late afternoon by the time they arrived at the grand old clapboard house to which Captain Wedemeyer directed them. Max advised her to send word to General Magruder that she would attend the ball, so she asked him to take care of it. Before she retired that night he brought word that the general would send a carriage for her.

Max, of course, preferred to find his own lodging. Though she often wondered where he slept, she never asked, given his obvious desire for privacy. And come morning, Mrs. Thomas, the landlady, gave her no time to think about anything other than the upcoming ball.

While Stella soaked in the last of Mrs. Thomas's rose-scented glycerine soap and scrubbed her hair and nails, Mrs. Thomas herself set out to mend and press the lavender and black gown Stella had worn to the opera in Matamoros.

Finally, in exasperation, she cast it aside. "This will never do, Miss Duval. You cannot attend the ball in rags. You will be the most scrutinized lady there."

Stella shuddered at the prospect of being examined in such a manner by the ladies of Galveston. "They will find me a disappointment no matter what I wear," she said, "if they expect me to look as if I have done nothing but knit socks for three whole years. Not that knitting socks isn't necessary; it is, but . . ." She heaved a heavy sigh, fingering the rents in the lavender silk fabric. "If it were the lace, perhaps it could be mended."

Mrs. Thomas never heard a word. She had suddenly dropped to her knees before a large trunk. After rummaging through it a moment, she stood up holding a cherry-red tissue silk dress against her ample figure.

"Perfect," she said. "Perfect for the general's Christmas ball. I wore this gown to my sister's wedding . . . ah, a number of years ago."

By concentrating on Mrs. Thomas's generous spirit, Stella kept her mind off the lady's equally generous figure, and a smile from her lips as well. "It's lovely," she agreed. "But are you sure . . ."

"Of course, I am sure. Let's see here." She turned the dress toward Stella, instructing Stella to hold it in place. Nipped to a vee at the waistline, the skirt bellowed in loose pleats to the floor. "What a lovely bertha," Stella complimented, fingering the lace-bordered gauze ruffle that would fall low across her shoulders.

Mrs. Thomas pursed her lips. "Yes, yes, it will fit nicely, but what about unmentionables? Let me see . . ." Again she stooped to the trunk and withdrew clothing, this time a crinoline and a limp petticoat, minus its hoops. "I'll send Timmy to the bayou to fetch us some vines."

Stella laughed.

"Haven't used vines for hoops in twenty years," she sighed. "Never thought we'd have to resort to the ways of our ancestors, but war brings us all down a notch."

Stella dressed for the ball with little enthusiasm, her thoughts on the blockade-running vessel, on whether it would perform as well as Captain Wedemeyer intended, hoping it would for her father's sake. Now that he was safely home, she hated to think of his ever being held captive again.

As always now, thoughts of Giddeon brought thoughts of Logan, thoughts that were like a second skin always near the surface. Wherever she went, he traveled with her, a spiritual

202

companion, as real as both sorrow and joy.

Mrs. Thomas insisted she eat a bowl of Hopping John—
"made with rabbit instead of pork, I'm afraid"—to take the
edge off her hunger.

"In these times of meager rations," the landlady added,
"the propriety of a lady not overindulging herself in public is
of even greater importance."

Well before General Magruder's driver arrived, Stella was
dressed in the red silk gown, which, after minor adjust-
ments, "fit to a tee," in Mrs. Thomas's words. As finishing
touches, the inventive landlady produced a headdress of
cherry-red silk flowers and a pair of white netted mitts.
Glancing at Mrs. Thomas's chubby feet, Stella was thankful
she had salvaged her own black pumps from her Matamoros
costume. Otherwise, she would likely have had to dance with
General Magruder in her boots.

As she prepared to take her leave Mrs. Thomas ferreted
one more item from her treasure chest: a relatively untat-
tered white rabbit cape. The fur tickled her bare shoulders
and brought a wistful expression to Mrs. Thomas's proud
face.

"Try to smile, my dear," the landlady encouraged. "Remember, your pretty face will be the finest thing these young
men have seen in many a dreary day."

Stella tried to replace her own self-pity with more appropriate duty-inspired emotions. She, as much as anyone,
wanted to do her part for the Southern cause, but somehow
driving cotton across rugged country seemed less threatening than dancing with strangers—even if those strangers
were their own boys in gray. The thought of anyone but Logan's arms around her . . . of smiling into anyone else's face
. . . No, she conceded, she would go to the ball, but her spirits would definitely not be in it.

On the short drive to the Brown mansion on Broadway,
where General Magruder kept his headquarters and where
the ball was to be held, she continued trying to shore up her

enthusiasm, and by the time the driver drew rein in front of the redbrick home, she had succeeded in convincing herself that her presence was a necessary part of the war effort.

The Brown mansion temporarily took her mind off her own plight. Ornately trimmed with wrought-iron galleries, gates, and fences, the house looked as though it had been specifically designed for the holiday season. Every window in the three-story structure glowed with candlelight. Though the evening was cool, many of the shutters stood open, allowing voices to mingle with strains of lilting music and drift toward her on wafts of the Gulf breeze.

She was suddenly reminded of another ball at another mansion — this one long ago — and of promises made there.

Of Christmases since. Lonely Christmases. And Christmases to come. Would any of them be spent with Logan?

The carriage door opened. A hand extended for her. She pursed her lips soundly to bring color, then placed her hand in that of the waiting gentleman.

She would go to the ball. She would dance with the general. Dance with the soldiers. Go home to a stranger's house. Would she ever spend a Christmas with Logan?

She grasped the red silk skirt in one hand, the firm, offered hand in her other. Steadying herself, she stepped onto the running board.

She would dance. She would smile. Perhaps, she would laugh.

The hand holding hers tightened.

She tensed.

The hand squeezed her fingers. A familiar gesture.

Familiar.

Heat flushed her body from head to foot. Belovedly familiar.

Her eyes darted to the attendant's face; she flushed at the intensity in his mischievous, adoring eyes. "You! You shouldn't . . ."

Dressed in his finest imitation of the Southern planter, Logan quickly drew her hand through the crook in his arm and escorted her toward the lighted entrance to the Brown mansion. Louder now, the music surrounded them. She imagined them floating on it, submerged in it. Her flesh burned beneath a layer of skin chilled by the December air.

"I thought I convinced you I have a right to be wherever you are."

She swallowed, her mouth dry; she gripped his hand as though she were afraid he might escape if she loosened her hold. "But how . . . ?"

She thought of all the reasons he shouldn't have come, the danger he was in, walking straight into the mouth of the lion, as it were. But his presence surrounded her with such a wondrous feeling of love, of completeness, that she couldn't even *wish* he hadn't come.

"This is Christmas . . ."—they progressed unhaltingly toward the mansion—". . . I couldn't let my best—"

Her eyes were on him, and before he completed his sentence, she interrupted. "Your *only* . . ."

His footsteps faltered, then stopped; his eyes found hers, held, and she watched a muscle in the side of his face twitch. "Don't look at me like that . . ."—his husky voice caught in his throat—". . . not until later, after you have performed your duty and danced with the general."

Although her senses were nearly rent asunder by his suggestion, indeed by his very presence, his message sustained her—*later,* he had said, *later . . . later.* Somehow she regained her composure—outwardly, at least—and entered the grand home with an air of confidence. With Logan Cafferty at her side, she could do anything, she told herself, endure anything . . . until later.

"My dear, my dear, you must be—"

Stella watched an energetic Confederate officer approach them across the massive foyer. Logan bent to whisper in her ear.

"Have you been introduced to Magruder?"

She shook her head, and in the next instant, stood bewildered, while Logan himself performed the introductions.

General Magruder was a broad-shouldered man in his mid-fifties with whiskers and mustache. He lifted her hand to his lips. "An honor, indeed. An honor to stand in the presence of so lovely and courageous a warrior as yourself."

She studied him, thinking of his nickname—Prince John. He was handsome, or at least he would be, she assumed, had he not been standing beside the most handsome man in the entire world—in her entire world.

General Magruder retained her hand. "May I have the honor of the first dance, my dear?"

When he guided her to the dance floor, she was amazed she hadn't refused and immediately fallen into Logan's arms. But this wasn't a time for herself; it was time for her country; for lighthearted repartee and polite conversation about the great service General Magruder and his men were doing, about the fortifications at Caney Creek, about the soon-to-be-built blockade-running vessel.

That she succeed in all the above amazed her, then confounded her, for General Magruder and his men *were* doing a great service to the country, and he deserved her compliments; but she—and only she, she prayed—knew these compliments came from the surface of her brain. Beneath them lay her feelings, her emotions—and they were all for Logan Cafferty, the enemy of her country.

Colonel Logan Cafferty, USMC. He stood within her line of vision at every turn, as first one, then another of General Magruder's aides swept her around the room. She laughed, she smiled, she flirted, and all with him, from a distance, a distance separated by gray uniforms.

At the band's intermission she stood beside the refreshment table, answering questions, and he was there, handing her a glass of champagne punch; she drank the punch, she asked polite questions, she recounted her exploits along the Cotton Road, and he was there, taking her empty glass.

The music resumed; she danced with the general again, and he was there, always within sight, his eyes teasing, tempting, promising.

Then, at last, when she thought the evening would go on forever, he was there, holding her in his arms, swinging her about the room, grinning into her upturned face.

"I thought you would never come," she said.

He bit his bottom lip, studying her intently. "I wanted to give you time to dance with them all," he answered, "for once I took you in my arms, I knew I could never let you go."

She didn't speak; her mouth was too dry, and her heart pounded in her throat, constricting it. He twirled her in a wide loop, steadied her with a hand firmly against her back, heating her through her very stays.

His eyes—intense and rich—never left hers. "Watching you reminded me," he continued, "although I didn't need reminding, how very much I love you."

Her arms trembled. When she opened her mouth, it took a while for the words to form. "Can we . . . ?"—she swallowed and started over again—"Can we go now?"

Without a word he danced her around the room, stopped at the door to fetch her wrap, then escorted her to a waiting carriage.

Not until they were seated inside and gripped in a desperate embrace did she question the haste with which they had left the ball.

"I should have thanked General Magruder . . ."

"Shhh," he whispered, forcing himself to kiss her face slowly, savoring the sweetness he had anticipated all evening. "It's better if we fade into the night."

"You're right." She pulled his mouth to hers and felt her lips tremble on his. The carriage moved through the darkness and she snuggled against him. His lips moistened hers; she opened to his questing kisses, felt his heart beat against hers, inhaled wonderful drafts of his familiar, intoxicating scent. The little rabbit fur dropped to the seat, and his arms

207

warmed her skin and heated her flesh.

So enrapt with each other were they, they hardly noticed when the carriage bounced to a stop. Outside the window a throat cleared; she heard Max's voice.

"We're here, Colonel."

Sitting back, she stared at Logan. "How . . . ?"

"Later, princess. Max would probably like to get in out of the cold." He replaced the rabbit cape around her shoulders and stepped down ahead of her, reaching to give her a hand.

"Here's her grip, Colonel."

Stella studied her traveling companion in the pale moonlight. "What did you tell Mrs. Thomas?"

He shrugged. "Said you'd been called to Alleyton, ma'am. She . . . ah, she accepted that."

"Fine," Stella heard herself reply. She stared at the cherry-red gown. "But what . . . ?"

"She said to tell you to keep the gown, ma'am. Said it would do her no more good and you might be able to put it to use, seein's how it looked so nice on you."

"But the cape, and the . . ." Her hand flew to her head, where she felt the silk headdress still in place, hiding her short hair in the back.

"Hey . . ." Logan tugged at her arm. "We can worry about Mrs. Thomas's wardrobe tomorrow. Let's get inside where it's warm and let Max do the same." Turning, he dismissed Max with a casual "Thanks, see you in the morning."

Not until they were halfway around the side of the house did she notice the Greek Revival mansion towering above them. "Where are we?"

"The Oaks." Logan led her to a side wing of the house, where he held open the door.

"The home of the late Mr. Menard? The founder of Galveston?" Her voice revealed her incredulity, and he laughed.

"One and the same. His widow agreed to rent me this wing for a few days."

"But . . . ? They are staunch Texans. I'm sure . . ."

"And I am a Southern planter, in town to do business with the mercantile firm of Ball, Hutchings, and Company."

"But Logan . . . ?"

"Shush . . ."—he replaced the chimney on a kerosene lamp and bent to stoke up the fire in the hearth—". . . tomorrow is Christmas—our first Christmas together. Let's not talk business, since it's the only thing we don't agree on."

Her imagination played wildly with the things they did agree on, and by the time he stood and held out his arms, her body was a-quiver with the want of him.

His husky, playful voice further sent her senses reeling. "You are lovely in Mrs. Thomas's gown; in fact, the avarice on the faces of those rebels tonight was almost more than I could tolerate." Clasping her face in his hands, he kissed her softly, then stood back, admiring, while his hands ran down her neck, caressed her bare shoulders, and his fingertips played seductively beneath the dipping gauze bertha. "But I know . . ."—as he spoke, his fingers found the buttons on the back of her dress and he began undoing them, one by one—". . . I know you are even more lovely . . . out of it."

Her body trembled, but her eyes never wavered from his adoring ones. "I've missed you so," she whispered, "your voice, your touch, your body next to mine."

As if in a daze she felt his fingers slip the gown from her shoulders. She tugged at his shirt, unbuckled his belt, and unfastened the placket on his breeches, as simultaneously they undressed each other, finally standing bare to their toes, face to face.

Her arms seemed to ache, her spine tingled, and her breasts throbbed for his touch, and when at last he reached for her, she nuzzled against him, pressing, pulling, urging. His own want for her pushed in its most tangible form against her abdomen, and she squirmed against him.

With an earthy sound, guttural and deep, his lips closed over hers, stroking, caressing, while he pressed her body to his, cupping her buttocks in his hands, molding her shape to his.

She clung to him, the fire inside her roaring like that on the hearth across the room. His hair felt soft and sensuous, like silk knots in her fists, his lips pliant and demanding against her own. Her breasts peaked, aching against the pounding of his heart, and she felt him lift her gradually from her feet. Shifting her hips, she helped him enter and fill her with the heated force of his passion.

Fire seared through her body at his touch, and when she settled over him, like a mold filled to capacity with a wondrous mixture of fiery flesh and liquid, she looked into his eyes. The combination of passion and tenderness she saw there exploded inside her.

"I loved you from a distance all night," he whispered. "This is better . . ."

"Much," she mumbled as he began to move her against him. The thrusts were short, the position awkward, but the result was dazzling, and when, in short order, it was accomplished, he carried her to the bed, where with measured movements he lowered them to the counterpane.

Wrapped in each other's embrace, he rested his lips on her forehead. Their hearts pounded audibly in their ears, gradually returning to a more normal rate, in rhythm now, she thought—in rhythm forevermore.

"I couldn't wait," he murmured. "We were too long apart."

Drawing back, she stared at him through the dimly lit room. She smiled, happy. So happy she had to concentrate on steadying her voice in order to speak. "I didn't want to wait," she answered. "Sometimes my body aches so badly for you . . . to have you inside me . . . that it's unbearable. Sometimes I think I will die if I can't touch you, or look at you, or hear your voice." As she spoke she ran a hand up and down his back, over his buttocks and around his hipbone, where he captured her fingers.

"I know. I feel it, too. Every minute I'm not with you." He kissed her lips, then moved his head back and gazed into her glistening, yet serious green eyes, studying her, watching, as he guided her hand across his abdomen and down where he circled her fingers around him. Inside her grasp, he began to grow hard again. He grinned as her eyes registered the fact.

"The best part, princess, is that we have all night." Lowering his lips, he kissed her, softly, tenderly, then urgently, reigniting their passions.

She responded with fervor, and this time he loved her slowly, moving his lips to her ear, where he sent flames streaking down her spine, firing her need for him afresh. When she shuddered, he sat back.

"Let me look at you." He positioned her head on the pillow, her torso flat on the bed. His eyes traveled her body as he worked, his face somber.

Watching, she clasped her hands behind her head and smiled. "Do I look so strange you must decide what I am?"

At her voice he raised his eyes to hers, and the smoldering embers she saw there brought a catch in her throat.

"You are so precious I must reassure myself you are real."

"Let me reassure you," she laughed. "I am real, and I want you to love me . . . now."

He straddled her body with his knees, and clasped her face in his hands, rough hands that felt gentle as he moved them down her neck, across her chest, stopping at her breasts, which he took, one in either hand.

She lay immobile as long as she could, letting him tease and titillate with his hands, massaging her breasts, his thumbs playing across her nipples, finally with his lips, his teeth, plying her with rapturous torment. She clasped his head in her hands, pressing his face to her breast, first one, then the other, twining her fingers in his hair, until at last she was afire with desire for more.

"Logan, please . . ." Beneath him her hips writhed in quest of relief from the sweet torment, in search of the pleasures she knew to expect.

Lifting his face, he kissed her lips, her eyes, then nipped at her neck. "In a minute, princess. Let me pleasure you this way a while longer."

His hands roamed her body, kneading, exploring, tantalizing. And where his hands went, his lips followed, plying her to a fevered pitch. Running her palms up and down his sides, his thighs, she closed her eyes against the intensity of her rising passion, basking in the feel of their bodies, the fiery liquid heat that covered her body, in the glorious aroma of him, of them, of their love.

When at last he entered her body, he had to struggle to keep up with her frenetic pace. Sensing her approaching summit, he was determined to give her an experience to savor in the coming days when they would be forced to part. Nudging her lips with his, he spoke in a whisper. "Open your eyes, princess."

Her body felt like a mass of frenzied desire, desperate for release. Her lids flickered open, she fixed on his smoldering brown eyes, and in the next instant she was sure the earth had exploded inside her—not only inside her head, not only in her abdomen, but from every pore in her body.

He saw it in her eyes, felt the tremor wrack her body, and the joy that welled inside him burst into his own release, separate, yet totally coupled with hers.

"Stella, Stella, Stella," he murmured when at last he lay beside her. "They named you well; you are truly a star from heaven above."

"A star?" she questioned, following nonsense with nonsense.

"An exploding star." He pulled her close with weakened arms, where their bodies became one once more, this time sticking together from the exertion of their lovemaking. Recalling her response the last time they made love, he asked, "How was it for you? Was it . . . ?"

Moving her head, she kissed his lips, his chin, his cheek.

"Couldn't you tell?"

He grinned. "Sort of. But tell me, anyway. Was it as good?"

She was so full of joy she felt silly; she was sure if forced, she would not be able to wipe the smile from her face. It was a permanent attachment, like her arms, her legs. "It's incredible . . . how every time is better. What are we going to do? One day it will be so . . . so powerful I'm afraid my heart won't take it."

"This is paradise, remember? In paradise there is no such thing as too much happiness."

They slept entwined in their embrace and awakening later, loved again. Finally, he knew he could wait no longer to talk to her. Now, while she was sleepy and vulnerable, perhaps she would listen.

After kissing her awake, he began slowly. "Have you seen Giddeon?"

She shook her head as it lay in the crook of his arm. "Mamá sent word, though. He made it home." Reaching lazily, she kissed him. "How could I have forgotten to thank you?"

He grinned, nipped her lips. "You thanked me right proper, ma'am. At least for the next five minutes or so." Then he returned to the more serious topic. "Where is he now?"

The room was lit only by the dim glow from the fireplace embers. She searched for his eyes. "I don't know. Home, I suppose."

When her body tensed at his question, he ran a hand lightly over her satiny skin, soothing. "You suppose?"

"Logan, let's not talk—"

"We must." His hand was on her breast, and he felt the rise and fall of her chest when she sighed. "I told you things were heating up. . . ."

"You were right," she responded. "They have. Up the coast, up the Rio Grande, El Sal del Rey, who knows where

213

else."

"Then you realize the danger?"

"To whom?"

"What do you mean to whom?" he demanded. "To Giddeon . . . to you, for God's sake."

"Not to you? What are you? Invincible because you are a Yankee?"

"You know better than that. It's just . . ."

"I thought you had stopped trying to force your way on Papá . . . and on me."

Playing his hands through her hair, he pulled at the soft curls, feeling their springiness, their aliveness. . . . His heart lurched in his chest. "Please, listen to me, princess."

His plea was so plaintive, her anger died in the air between them. She traced his lips with her fingers, lightly. And when his tongue captured her finger, she held her breath, absorbing the intimacy she knew would last but a second in time.

"I will listen," she whispered.

"I want you to go home and stay there."

"Logan, you can't ask that. . . ."

"I must ask it. And you must do it. This is the last thrust of fighting. I have . . . ah . . ." Suddenly the impact of what he had done shot fear through and through him. He pulled her close, held her tight, and ran a hand up and down her back. She was more precious to him than silver or gold, more important than his own life. But God, how he prayed that was not the choice he had made. He wanted to be around to love her, to live with her, to grow old with her.

He exhaled heavily. "I arranged for Los Olmos to be left alone. You will be safe there. You and your family . . . the children . . . Giddeon . . . whoever is there. But you cannot leave. I cannot protect Giddeon on the seas. I cannot protect you. . . ."

"Logan! You know what that means for you. What will happen to you if . . . ?"

"Shhhh . . ." He kissed her lips to hush her words . . . her

214

fears. "I will be all right. So will you. The rebellion will be over soon. Then . . ."

"But . . ."

"But you must stay at Los Olmos. Giddeon and his men must stay at Los Olmos."

She buried her face in his chest while visions of the blockade-running ship swam in her muddled brain. At last his hands, rough and gentle as before, soothed, lulled, and for the time, comforted, and she slept in his arms.

She knew she had slept, because it was daylight when she awoke to voices coming from the portico of this separate wing of the Menard mansion. Familiar voices. She stirred. Logan was gone. A dim light filtered through the heavy brocaded draperies. Christmas Day, she thought.

Then the voices from the portico became voices from the past. Still drugged with sleep, she saw herself on board the *Victory,* hearing voices from the safety of Logan's bedchamber . . . voices from the present . . . words from the past . . .

"It's Stella, Max. She's here. . . ."

"What do you want me to do?" the man called Max questioned.

". . . friend to friend . . . Glad you found her . . ."

Suddenly her brain cleared, as though it had been swept clean by a harsh north wind. She sat up in bed, clutching the bedcovers around her nude body.

". . . friend to friend . . ."

My God! How could she have forgotten that voice? That name? Outside on the portico, the voices continued, words from the present now, ominous and devastating.

"She's dead set on going to Alleyton, Logan."

"I may have weakened that determination," Logan's voice replied. "But I'm depending on you, Max. Keep her away from the Cotton Road; she must return to Los Olmos."

"What about Blakesborough?"

"It's not the first time I've had Blakesborough breathing down my collar," Logan responded.

215

"How well I know," Max's voice replied. "He's been after you since we were at the Academy, but this time he's firing with ammunition—this time he's close to having enough information to get you a court-martial. I've helped you out of many a scrape, old friend, and I won't abandon you now, but this one may be beyond all our best efforts."

"You just stick with Stella as you have been doing. Leave the rest to me."

Chapter Ten

Panic struggled inside her like a wild animal trying to escape, stomping in her belly, clawing in her throat, crushing her heart and lungs in the process. She slumped back to the bed while the voices of Logan and Max droned on outside the door. Incomprehensibly, she had the strange thought they might be cold.

Likely, they were, she retorted to herself. What difference did it make? She didn't care. . . .

Hot rivers of tears streaked her cheeks. The fire had been stoked and now blazed in the hearth — Logan's thoughtfulness, she fumed — but outside a winter wind blew against the windowpanes, and the drafts left her chilled.

Christmas Day. For a moment she felt even more despondent, learning of Logan's treachery on Christmas Day. Then she realized the day didn't matter; betrayal was betrayal. Betrayal turned an ordinary day into a burial day.

Suddenly, a new fear seized her. Quickly, she pushed aside the heavy covers and searched for her satchel. The cherry-red ball gown lay over a chair, but instead of bringing warm memories, it brought more tears.

She dried them, chiding herself. Later she could cry. Right now she must get away from here. Her clothes were wrinkled, but clean. Bless Mrs. Thomas, she thought.

Dressing, she stomped finally into her boots, then scanned the room for another door by which to escape. She couldn't see Logan.

Her heart stopped. If she saw him she would die.

She couldn't see Logan.

She couldn't.

But she did.

Her heart pounded fiercely, her one thought to escape before he returned. Gathering the bundle of Mrs. Thomas's clothing, she tried to stuff it inside her satchel, but the hoops made of vines would not stuff easily, and her anxiety rose.

She no longer heard voices outside the door. He would return. Soon. Any moment.

In desperation she yanked the entire bundle of clothing — hoops, crinoline, cherry-red silk — from the satchel and flung it into the fireplace.

Sparks flew, crackled, and flames leaped. She stared, momentarily mesmerized by the violence of the fire, by the violence seething inside her.

"Princess . . . ?"

Her heart constricted at his voice. The muscles in her shoulders tensed against his anticipated touch. She whirled to face him. His voice had questioned, but his chocolate-brown eyes knew.

Behind her in the fireplace, the cherry-red silk hissed, the vines crackled and popped. Battle sounds, she thought. Sounds of war.

Clamping her teeth together, she grabbed the satchel handle and . . .

He caught her wrist in his hand.

Swinging her other arm, she struck him, palm flat, on the side of the face. His eyes registered shock; deep inside a sob tugged at her heart.

"You have a right to be upset," he admitted.

Her eyes flashed. "Upset?" She jerked the satchel to free herself. "I am not upset, Colonel. I am finished."

"Stella, calm down. Let me explain."

She glared at him. "Everything is perfectly clear."

"No, it isn't. Obviously, you don't think I have a right to

protect you."

"Protect me? I don't need your kind of protection. Haven't you heard the stories? I can shoot as straight, ride as hard, stay as long as any man."

"That is not the point, and well you know it."

"Yes," she mimicked, "well I know it. Protecting me was not your goal. You sent Max to spy on me . . . on our operation."

"Damnit, Stella, you know better than that." He grasped her by the arms. "I love you. I care about you. Allow me that much. . . ."

"Don't . . . please, don't. This has nothing to do with love . . . with caring. Please . . ." Inside she felt divided in half, like their once unified country, like their once united love. Half of her wanted to run, to escape the sound of his voice, the look on his face, the very presence of him. But the other half resisted, admonishing her to savor the touch of his hands, the begging in his eyes, even the anger in his voice, to imagine in her mind's eye how things might have been. . . .

Before the war set them apart.

Before . . .

"You used me . . . betrayed me," she said.

He glared straight into her fiery green eyes. The begging in his turned to anger. "You know better than that! Your reasoning is preposterous! You're *incredible*. . . ."

Their eyes held while the word tossed on the tumultuous air between them, much as a ship tossed on an angry sea.

Tearing herself away, she turned her back to him. She stared into the still-leaping flames in the fireplace, watched the last remnants of cherry-red silk crinkle and turn black, while her mind swayed with his words . . . her own words . . . past words.

His palm clasped the back of her neck, and she had the sudden feeling he might as well have pushed her into the fire, so intense was the heat his touch ignited along her senses. Her skin curled and crinkled like the silk now gone; she felt burnt and blackened to her core.

"Don't . . ." she whispered, just above the crackling logs. "Please, don't . . ."

"Princess . . ."

The word offended her, and she tried to react, but his tone was plaintive; it licked against her heart strings like fingers of fire.

When he tried to turn her around, though, she resisted, until at length, he came to stand in front of her. Still she would not look at him.

"I did not send Max to spy on you."

Involuntarily she looked into his eyes. "Perhaps not in the beginning . . ."

"Never."

The beginning was so far removed from the present state at which they had arrived that she had trouble recalling it. At this moment Max was an enemy potent enough to destroy the entire Confederate effort along the coast. And he had always been — even in the beginning, when his company was so welcome, his aid so appreciated.

"Who is he?"

"One of a handful of men I chose for a special mission."

She cocked her head; with difficulty, she pursued the subject. "What mission? Truthfully?"

If before his voice had been plaintive, now his whole demeanor took on an air of predestined doom. When he pulled her to his chest, she was powerless to resist. "Among other things, to stop the blockade runners."

His heart pounded beneath her cheek. Out of beat again, she thought. Their hearts; not his mission. His mission was right on track: to stop the blockade runners. Well, now he could — with her help. He knew about the blockade-running vessel, he knew about Caney Creek, he knew all the stops and way stations along the route where the cotton trains found safe lodging, he knew the river crossings. He knew exactly how to stop the cotton trains, how to stop Giddeon.

"Max Burnsides," he continued, "is my oldest and closest friend . . ."—drawing her back, he tipped her chin so she had to look at him—". . . except you . . ."

Their eyes held, his begging, hers full of despair, and he continued. "We met as students at the Naval Academy; he is the only person in the world I would entrust with your welfare."

Suddenly the turmoil inside her exploded into a sickening swirl of conflicting emotions: She wanted him to hold her, she wanted him to kiss her, she wanted him to rip off her clothing and love and torment and tantalize her aching body. She wanted to be sick.

Angry with herself as much as with him, she jerked away and moved quickly out of his reach. "I'm glad to know that, Colonel, because now he holds not only my own personal welfare, but that of my father, and of every other person along the Gulf Coast, in his *trustworthy* hands."

When he started toward her, she picked up the satchel and headed for the door. "Don't come near me, and don't . . ."

"Stella. Listen to me. What Max does or does not know doesn't matter anymore."

She stopped, glared at him.

"It's over. You must go home. All that's left is the cleanup. . . ."

"Cleanup?" The fortifications at Caney Creek popped into her mind, the men there, men who had talked with her, laughed with her. Men who would die there. And he called it a *cleanup*.

He watched her expression change from anger to repulsion. He knew her thoughts; he regretted his choice of words. "Go home, Stella. You will be safe there."

Her repulsion changed to loathing. "How kind of you. I should thank you for saving *me?* What about the others? The thousands of others? What about . . . ?"—she started to say Captain Wedemeyer, but the off-chance he didn't know about the captain stopped her—"What about Alicia?"

"Alicia's dead, for God's sake!"

"You think I don't have others in my life as dear?"

He inhaled a deep, trembling breath. "I know you do."

"What about Mrs. Cardwell?" she continued. "What about Mrs. Thomas? What about General Magruder, to whom you so graciously introduced me? What about all those other men you talked with last night? What about Harry Ransom?"

He moved forward while she raged, and grabbed her by the shoulders. "Stop it, Stella! We're caught up in this rebellion whether we like it or not. There's nothing we can do about it now. Go home; go home and wait for me. Please."

This time his plaintive appeal did not sway her. She pulled loose from his hold. "No, Colonel. You put down your *rebellion;* I'll fight the *war.*"

"Didn't you hear me? The fighting is almost finished. You can't continue to run cotton; you have no place to haul it."

Defiantly, she tossed her head. "That shows how much you have to learn."

He reached for her again, but this time, instead of shaking her shoulders, his hands held her gently. "General Davis will have taken Laredo within a month's time."

At his words, her rage curiously disappeared, like smoke up a chimney, leaving her queasy from a smoldering ember of desperation in the pit of her stomach, while determination solidified inside her brain. Before she went to Alleyton, she must get word to Captain Ireland at Caney Creek, and to Captain Wedemeyer at Titlum-Tatlum. Slowly but firmly, she dislodged her arms from his hold.

"I'm going now," she told him. "Do not follow me. And do not let Max. You told me once to keep my pistol at hand to use against highwaymen. Well, I will. If I see Max again, I will shoot him on sight."

He watched her go. She strode past Max, who stood on the

portico, down the steps and away from the grand mansion of the late Mr. Menard, swinging her satchel, tossing her short springy curls in the cold north wind.

He watched her disappear down the street, leaving him devoid of every emotion except one: an all-consuming despair at having failed her. Unintentionally, but not unknowingly. Of course, he had not sent Max to spy on her; neither had he rejected the information Max passed along.

In the beginning he had not realized the extent of her involvement, the wealth of information that passed through her hands. And more than anything else—more even than the success of obtaining such valuable material—more than anything else, the magnitude of her involvement had unfolded before him in waves of terror—terror for her, terror for her loved ones.

As a consequence his primary objective had become to keep her safe, and next to that, to keep her family safe. Third in purpose was his use of the information for his own country. And from the beginning, he knew one day he would have to explain it all to her . . . and face her rejection.

He had hoped to ward off such an encounter until the rebellion was over—until the threat to her and to Giddeon had passed. At such a time, with danger in their past, he knew he could convince her of the truth—that he had not intentionally used her, as she now believed.

Max clapped him on the shoulder. "Can't blame her, Logan. She was bound to have gotten riled. . . ."

"I don't blame her. I blame myself."

"Did you tell her about Blakesborough?"

Logan shook his head. "The less she knows about that crazy man, the better. I may not be able to protect her from herself, but I sure as hell can protect her from my own enemies."

"Want me to find Jacobs to trail her, or . . . ?"

"No. Let her go. This is the way she wants it. It'll be the hardest thing I'll ever be called on to do, but I have to trust that she can take care of herself." He stepped off the portico.

Max kept pace. "She'll be all right. You should see the way the men respect her—as a leader and as a lady. No man in Texas is foolish enough to mess with her. He'd have not only you, Francisco, and me to face, but every one of those Los Olmos vaqueros. And let me tell you, that's one wild bunch of men."

"When did you say that blockade-running ship is scheduled to be launched?"

"Wedemeyer said three months. Do you want to go ahead and take out the operation now?"

"No. Let's get busy and put down this damned rebellion before then."

By the time Stella reached Alleyton three days later, a general gloom blanketed the entire state, or so it seemed to her. She wondered whether it was merely that she looked at the world through a perpetual film of despair, which began when she walked away from the late Mr. Menard's mansion with Logan's eyes burning into her back like sunbeams, although, unlike life-restoring rays from the sun, the heat that penetrated her burned and destroyed, like fingers of fire.

The guilt she felt at allowing Logan to take advantage of her, at entrusting Max with their secrets followed her to General Magruder's office, where she related the information Logan had given her without revealing her sources.

Later she wondered why. If General Magruder could have apprehended Max, perhaps they could have kept the blockade-running vessel a secret. Somehow, she did not seem capable of making the right decisions about anything anymore. She wondered whether she would ever be able to again.

Francisco and Beto, accompanied by the other Los Olmos vaqueros-turned-teamsters, awaited her in Alleyton with a train of cotton ready to leave for the border.

"Wagons are scarce," Francisco told her. "Our train is made

224

up of more carts than heavy wagons. We must try to purchase some wagons at the border."

She nodded, unhearing. "We have no time to waste. Can we ferry the carts across the river tonight and leave in the morning?"

"*Sí, señorita*. But where is our man Max? Will we not wait for him?"

Stella sighed. "As it turns out, he is not *our* man Max. He is a spy."

"¡Ah, señorita!" Francisco lamented after Stella told him the pertinent parts of the nightmare she had awakened to on Christmas morning. "It is my fault. I should not have trusted the man."

"No," she told him. "It is not your fault. He would have worked his way into our midst regardless of how we tried to keep him out. It was his mission, and he is trained well."

Leaving Francisco to ferry the cotton across the Colorado River, Stella set about collecting supplies for the trip. At every stop she added to the list of necessities the townsfolk wanted her to bring on her return. If anything, their needs were greater now than when she had last made the trip to the border.

Although subtle, the mood of the entire town was different. The docks were still piled high with cotton, only not quite as high as before; the boulevard was as crowded with speculators and bargaining, but the urgency had diminished.

When she stepped into her saddle, with one foot in the stirrup, a horseman bumped into her horse's rump. Nothing unusual about that, but the man took time to inquire to her welfare and to apologize. That was unusual for Alleyton.

"Things have changed," Esther agreed that evening after dinner when she and Stella sat in rocking chairs before a roaring fire, sipping tea from her scarce store of the commodity, their feet swaddled in blankets. "We have all changed." She studied Stella over the wire rims of her spectacles. "You most of all. The fire is gone in you, I think. The enthusiasm."

Stella sighed, her mind only half in this room. Staring into the fire, she saw the red dress, heard the plaintive pleas of the man she had loved and trusted . . . and loved still.

"Why don't you quit?"

"I will."

"When?"

Stella rocked, sipped her tea.

"Why not now?" Esther encouraged. "Tonight. Let Francisco take the cotton."

"I can't do that. This train has to get through in a hurry. This one may be . . ."—hesitating, for she knew once she broached the topic, Esther was likely to worry it like a dog with a bone until all the facts were out, she continued—"Logan said Davis will have taken Laredo by the end of the month."

"Logan?" Esther eyed Stella, brows knit, until light dawned on her face. "That handsome fellow with the message?"

Stella nodded.

After a moment's silence, Esther questioned quietly. "And who is this Logan of yours that he knows so much?"

"A Federal officer. A marine." Suddenly she felt the overwhelming desire to confide in someone, and Esther, she knew, would make no judgments, issue no unwanted directives. "We met before the war—actually, we fell in love before the war, at a plantation in Louisiana where we were both guests. At the time Papá refused Logan's request to marry me. He wanted him to visit Los Olmos first."

"Your father is a wise man."

"Logan was in the Navy then, but nobody believed war would come." Stella stared into the flames, recalling the frivolity of the times. "You are right, Esther. We have all changed. Everything has changed."

"Except your feelings for this man."

Stella swallowed the emotions that choked in her throat. "Feelings don't count in war . . . they can't."

"Feelings always count, my dear, if you dig deep enough to find the true ones. Now, what has he done to cause you such distress?"

Stella turned to the older woman, eyes wide. "His special mission is . . . to stop the blockade runners." Quickly, she turned back to the fire. How difficult the words . . . "He sent his spy to travel with me; now, he knows things . . . things that could close down the Cotton Road . . . destroy the new ship before it is even built . . . kill Papá."

"That is serious, if he intentionally planted a spy in your camp. So, now you are determined to beat Davis to Laredo, to prove to Logan you can do it?"

Stella frowned. "It sounds ridiculous, put that way."

"It is ridiculous. How will it solve the problems of his knowing too much about the Cotton Road and the blockade running? You have no right to put yourself or your men in jeopardy for a personal quarrel."

Stella's mouth flew open. "Esther. You don't think . . ."

Esther shrugged. "You said . . ."

"I didn't say he intentionally planted Max as a spy. He said he sent Max to act as a bodyguard, to protect me. I believe him. But that doesn't change my guilt in taking the man into my confidence, providing him with knowledge about . . ."

"Neither does it change the fact that you should not take this cotton train into certain danger for personal reasons."

They rocked silently while the fire warmed, then began to burn Stella's cheeks. She edged her rocker back a bit. "That isn't the reason I must get this cotton through. I assured Mr. Yates in Matamoros I would bring him enough cotton to pay for the supplies he has already purchased for us. I can't let him down. And I can't let down the people all across this country who need those supplies. Why, only today I realized how much worse things have gotten since the last time I was here. Mr. Abbott has only one sack of salt left for the entire community; and Dr. Vick will be out of morphine by week's end. I know things are as bad or worse all across the state,

227

and the Confederacy. One more train load of supplies will not go far to alleviate the suffering, but . . . but I must try. I must get one more wagon train through before Laredo falls."

When Stella finished, Esther reached over and patted her on the knee. "Go to bed now, my dear. I think you will be able to sleep after all."

Stella looked at her, questioning, then her eyes brightened. "You! You knew all the time I had enough cause to make this trip."

Esther laughed. "That I did, but I wasn't sure for a while whether you knew it or not. Sometimes it makes a burden lighter to put the truth into words."

The trip took a good month, and although the animals suffered during much of it for lack of water, Stella was grateful for the drought, which kept the riverbeds dry enough to cross. By now their routine was set and the journey relatively uneventful, but news of the war, which they received at each stop, heightened their distress and redoubled Stella's urgency to reach Laredo ahead of General Davis. Even before they left Alleyton, word reached town of the fall of Port Lavaca on the day after Christmas.

At the Cardwell Stage Station, Mrs. Cardwell's gratitude for the coffee Stella brought was overshadowed by worry about the Federal advance.

"Them Yankees are holding every port north to Matagorda Bay—Corpus Christi, Fort Esperanza, Aransas Pass, Indianola," Cardwell complained. "And ol' Prince John just sits there in Galveston doing nothing."

"Must be something in the Texas weather," replied a soldier on his way to Galveston. "My pa tells how Sam Houston run from the Mexicans back in thirty-six."

"Humph! He might have run, but it was with a purpose. Drew them Mexicans right into a trap. When ol' Sam took charge, he kicked Santa Ana in the . . . ah . . ."— belatedly, the speaker acknowledged Mrs. Cardwell and Stella—". . . in the bunions, ma'am."

"Jeb'll do the same; give him time."

"Time's running out. And so is land. If he don't stop Banks soon, that damned Yankee'll eat up our coastline clear to New Orleans."

After another bite of chili, Stella pushed the bowl aside. She pulled her woolen coat closer about her legs and wished for home—home, where the north wind didn't howl through chinks in the walls, congealing one's food and one's blood.

But her blood ran cold for more reasons than the weather; in fact, had they been in the midst of a heat wave, she was sure her trembling would have been as great.

For her thoughts were on Caney Creek, on Captain Ireland and his men, whom she had betrayed. Of course, she hadn't known Max was the enemy when she took him into their camp, but that did not alter the fact she had done so. Her ignorance could result in the deaths of hundreds . . . perhaps thousands, if General Magruder sent five to six thousand men to the area—

"You are not at fault, señorita," Francisco told her a couple of days later when she brought up the topic again. "You alerted General Magruder. He will use your information well."

What information I gave him, she thought, wishing for the hundredth time she had told Magruder about Max. He could have captured Max. . . .

What's done cannot be undone, she recalled. But if she hurried, perhaps she could beat Edmund Davis to Laredo. That, now, was the most she could do to make amends.

A week later they reached the Santa Margarita crossing on the Nueces River, posted guards to the southeast toward Corpus Christi and south along the road to Camp San Fernando, both of which were in Federal hands.

Morning arrived with no action, but Stella could tell by the expeditious manner with which the vaqueros went about breaking camp and preparing their carts for the crossing that the same thing was on every person's mind:

Federals.

While Beto swam his horse across the river, found the dead man and attached the cable, Francisco took three men on horseback downriver a mile or so toward Corpus Christi to watch for Yankee patrols.

A minimum of conversation flowed. Stella helped swaddle the carts with treated canvas, then sat her horse, watching the men haul them one by one across the river. Watching the carts, glancing periodically to the southeast.

Watching the activities, but seeing instead Max—Max, always ready to assume the most difficult job. Max, always laughing, always pleasant.

Max, always spying.

And always now, reminding her of Logan. What lay ahead for them? Much, of course, depended on the outcome of the war . . . on the tragedy that could result from the knowledge she provided him. She might as well have become a Yankee spy herself; she could not have done more damage.

She hadn't lied when she told Esther she believed Logan. She did believe him. She knew he had not deliberately set out to deceive her; but for months now he had been receiving reports from Max, and he had done nothing to stem them; he had done nothing to separate their personal relationship from . . . from his *rebellion*.

Yes, she thought, much depended on what he chose to do with the information acquired at so high a cost. Much depended upon who lived and who died in the next few weeks . . . or months . . . or years.

By late afternoon most of the carts had been crossed, and Stella tried to relax. As each driver cleared the river, she had started him on the road to Fort Casa Blanca, until by now the train of cotton-laden carts stretched for miles along the south bank of the Nueces River. They would camp for the night after the last cart had crossed the river and all had begun their journey to the safety of the camp. In this manner she hoped to reach Casa Blanca in two days.

The urgency she felt to reach Laredo ahead of General Davis was fueled by the proximity of the Federals at Corpus Christi. She knew, however, that the real tempest that drove her came from within herself—the overwhelming need to right the wrongs she had done her countrymen . . . and her own father . . . before disaster struck—one disaster wrought by another, the disaster of trusting the wrong man, of loving the wrong man.

Then Francisco galloped into sight as if the whole Yankee army were after him, and her urgency took on an entirely different nature.

His first orders were issued to Beto and the men on the far side of the Nueces who worked the cable. One cart was in the middle of the river at the time.

"¡Andale! Hurry! Get this cart across and release the cable! A supply boat is coming, chased by a Federal patrol boat."

Gripping the rifle she held across her lap, Stella glanced quickly downriver. She saw nothing. Then Francisco reached her.

"When the supply boat passes, señorita, we will get you on board. Those of us left will engage the Yankees in enough fireworks to give you time to reach Casa Blanca."

Stella's heart stood still. Her first thought was one of pure terror: being captured by Dar Blakesborough. Her second thought was of her vaqueros. She would not abandon them. Quickly she surveyed the timber on either side of the river— sparse stands of trees interspersed with thick motts of oak and chaparral.

"No," she told Francisco. "We must not slow them down. I will stay here—and fight."

Only three carts and drivers remained to be hauled across the river. Stella took them all in, her mind a whirl of activity. "Take cover behind the chaparral," she told the three drivers. "Quickly."

231

Across the river elongated shadows of men wrestled with a horse-drawn cart. Already the heavy rope cable was indistinguishable in the diminishing light. She turned to Francisco.

"How far behind the supply boat are the Federals?"

He shrugged. "A hundred yards, more or less."

A hundred yards. Enough time. Perhaps. Turning, she searched the area directly behind her. "Help me, Francisco. We need a dead man."

The old vaquero grunted. "Be patient, señorita, before the night is out we may have more than one."

"Not that kind," she replied. "Something on this side of the river to anchor the cable . . ." Her words drifted off as, in unison, she and Francisco spied a large boulder. They raced toward it. Francisco tried to roll it over, to no avail.

"What is it?" she asked. "I have never seen a stone so large in this part of the country."

"It is not a stone, señorita, but a doorstep."

Indeed, peering further into the shadows, she saw a tumbled-down chimney, and other, smaller stones, from a foundation, she supposed.

"Will it hold?" she asked.

Francisco scratched his head. "Depends . . ."

Suddenly realizing the substance of her plans were still in her head, where they would do no one the least bit of good, she hurried to explain. "If we fire on the patrol boat, we are putting our own cargo and men in jeopardy. But if we can stop them in another manner . . ."

"Yes, señorita, I understand your intention. I will cross the river and see this is done. As soon as the supply boat passes, we will string the cable across the river and secure it to this boulder."

"You did not answer my question—will it hold?"

"For our purposes, and in the dark, perhaps."

"We cannot afford to break—or let the Federals cut—the cable for so important a crossing. Position the rest of our men within firing range. As a last resort, we will open fire."

Even the words made her sick. With a heavy heart she went about the joint tasks of aiding the supply boat and protecting her own teamsters. Racing toward one of the carts, she dragged a shovel from its cargo and instructed a man nearby to do the same. Together they began spreading sand and gravel over the fresh cart tracks.

"Swim across," she told him when they finished obscuring the fresh tracks made by their carts this day. "As soon as the last cart is free of the river, cover the tracks on that side. We couldn't fool an old Indian tracker, but in the darkness we may be able to fool the Yankees."

The wait was terrible. With each passing minute the sun sank lower; anxiety buzzed through her brain, charging it, as with electricity. Finally the cart made the opposite bank. The cable was withdrawn from the river. The supply boat eased past the crossing, rippling water to each side, ripples that were heard, rather than seen, with the sun now almost gone.

As quickly as the boat passed, Francisco rode into the river, carrying the free end of the cable. Stella met him at the boulder, wrapped the cable twice around the stone, then yielded the tying of it to him.

Before the last tug was given they again heard ripples in the water. Francisco pulled the cable twice in signal to Beto.

"Beto will watch now, señorita. When the time is right, he will raise and secure the cable in a position to restrain the patrol boat."

Quickly, they took their places in the heavy brush, within firing distance of the river.

And she would begin the firing. If there was to be firing. She had said so herself, to Francisco. And he, in turn, had told the men.

"The señorita will begin the shooting. Hold your fire until she shoots first."

Sweat bathed her hands, turning cold once it met the frosty air, making the rifle hard to hold. She raised a knee, steadied her gun . . .

The rippling water neared, like a wave washing to shore, but unlike the waves along Los Olmos Bay where she had played as a child, these ripples brought danger . . . perhaps death. . . .

The lanterns on the patrol boat cast eerie shadows and even more unearthly images of dark bodies, glinting brass — buttons, she knew, envisioning the uniform she had come to know better even than the uniform for which she fought — male voices, harsh, hesitant, words couched in unfamiliar accent . . .

Except the accent was no longer foreign. She shivered against the cold, prayed the cable held, prayed even harder that the men in the boat did not try to cut it.

"Hey, what have we got here?"

"A sandbar?"

The steam engine strained.

"Where'd that damned rebel boat go?"

"If it got through, so can we. Shine the light over this way."

Stella held her breath. She watched one of the lanterns on the bow swing to the left. In its glow, she could make out forms of men leaning over the edge of the boat.

"Why'd you steer into a damned sandbar?"

"You think you can do better, have at it!"

Forms of men scurried about on deck. The engine strained again.

"This ain't no sandbar. . . ."

"Then what the hell is it?"

"Only one way to find out. Someone's got to go in."

Silence.

Stella brought her rifle sights to bear in the center of the forms on the boat. Her finger felt stiff, frozen. She fought down the image of Logan, of Max.

She felt sick.

"You, Jack. Over the side."

"Hey! Not me. I ain't fixin' to get a leg chewed off by some rebel alligator."

"Aw, Jack. There ain't no alligators in this river."

"That's what they said over at the Sabine, too. Likely that Dowling fellow wouldn't have come out smelling like a rose, at our expense, if he hadn't been playing in alligator-infested waters."

"Jack. I gave you an order."

Silence.

Stella's finger steadied on the trigger of her rifle; her eyes stung from the night air, from a thin layer of tears, which formed like cream on top of the milk jar, she thought crazily.

"I don't take orders from you, Sidele. You an' me, we're neither one high enough to a rat's ass to make it worth our time to get chewed up and spit out in some rebel river."

The engine labored as in angry reply.

Silence.

Jack's voice whined above the engine. "I'll tell you something else, Sidele. I ain't about to ask a man here to go where I won't go myself."

Silence.

The voice called Sidele spoke. "You've done it now, Jack. While you jawed about alligators, we've let that rebel boat get so far ahead we'll never catch up. Turn this thing around. If you can."

The engine sputtered; men leaned overboard with poles to push the patrol boat around in the river.

Stella swallowed the fear that had risen in her mouth and drew in a deep breath of sweet, fresh air. *Thank you, Jack,* she whispered.

Chapter Eleven

Later that night after the patrol boat had retreated well downriver, they crossed the remaining wagons, and by moonlight headed without making camp for Casa Blanca, where they arrived at dusk the following day. Scouts from the camp had ridden out to greet them, at the insistence of the supply-boat crew. Jorge, in charge of the camp now, held open the heavy cypress door, waving each team and cart inside the fortress. Stella dismounted and hugged him.

He greeted her with more than a little fatherly advice. "The whole area is crawling with Yankees, Stella. You have no business traveling the Cotton Road anymore."

She laughed. "If you had told me that last night, while I was sitting in those bushes with a rifle in my hand, I might have agreed with you."

Over supper he tried again to persuade her to return to Los Olmos. "Why don't you let Francisco take the carts to Laredo? You go home and move Serita and the children here to Casa Blanca. I sent word for them to come, but Serita refused to leave Los Olmos. She said they were safer there than here at a military installation that could be attacked at any time."

"They are," Stella responded, knowing as she spoke that Logan's promise could well hold more hope than substance.

"How can you say that?" he challenged. "Haven't you heard about the Federal advance up the coast?"

"Yes," she replied, "I've heard. But . . . I agree with Mamá. For the time being, I think they are safer at Los Olmos than they would be anyplace else. We'll keep close

236

watch on the situation."

Later, she knew he would likely have pried the truth out of her, except their conversation was interrupted by news that distressed her to the point that she pushed her plate of beans aside and had to concentrate to keep tears from her eyes. "Caney Creek?" she asked.

"We're holding them off," Jorge assured her.

"When did you say fighting began there?" she asked.

"First week in January."

"A month ago. And they're still fighting? What about casualties?"

He shrugged. "We haven't received casualty reports. Captain Ireland was prepared, I hear. Word of his preparations have been filtering in for a couple of months. . . ."

"I saw the fortifications," she said. "We . . . ah, I visited Caney Creek a couple of days before Christmas. General Magruder had promised to send five or six thousand men once the fortifications were in place. Captain Ireland was confident . . . so confident. Said General Banks would turn tail and run straight into the Gulf of Mexico."

"He isn't fighting General Banks, yet," Jorge said. "Right now, he's facing a naval bombardment."

"Naval. . . ?" She clamped a hand over her mouth to still her trembling words.

Jorge shrugged. "We're winning. That's the important thing, Stella. We're winning."

In a futile attempt to tear her mind away from the naval battle at Caney Creek, she changed the subject. "Have you heard anything about Davis taking Laredo?"

Jorge shook his head. "Farther down, though, he holds Rio Grande City. You won't be able to get your cotton down the river. Even though it is an international waterway, they aren't allowing any commerce. It's making the French fighting mad, believe me."

"This cotton is going to Matamoros by land — on the Mexican side of the river. The arrangements have been made. All

I have to do is cross the river at Laredo."

Stella could count on one hand the times her cousin Jorge had been angry with her. When he exploded now, she grinned. "Don't worry. I'm not going into Mexico myself. Mr. Yates will have representatives in Laredo, along with the supplies I ordered. In fact, if it will make you feel better, after I make the transaction, Beto can take the supply carts back to Alleyton, and Francisco and I will go straight to Los Olmos to see about the family."

When he hugged her good-bye the following morning, he kissed her cheek. "It will make me feel a whole lot better. No matter what you say, I think they should move inland. If they don't want to come here, they can go to Columbus . . . or even farther . . . perhaps as far as Washington-on-the-Brazos. A lot of coastal families are moving to Washington."

They arrived in Laredo without mishap to find the city still in Confederate hands. After her business was transacted and Beto headed northeast with the wagon train, Stella sighed in relief. Mr. Yates' agent was appreciative.

"You cannot imagine how many deals fall apart these days," he told her.

"Mine won't. Assure Mr. Yates that as long as he can furnish the supplies we need, I will deliver cotton as promised. If Laredo falls, we will travel farther north."

Unhampered by the cotton train, Stella and Francisco made good time. Although there were few stops along the way, and fewer watering places, they inquired of every person they met as to the progress at Caney Creek. Word still had the advantage going to the Confederates, but news traveled slowly, and the situation could change, she knew, and they would not hear about it for days. Her heart became heavy, weighed down with dread, as it were, and guilt over her part in that battle, over the men who could die there . . .

Because she had foolishly, recklessly . . .

Trusted . . . and loved . . . the wrong man.

Pray God, no one died at Caney Creek. If even one man

died, his blood was on her hands. . . .

One man . . .

What if that one man was Logan Cafferty?

The first night out from Laredo they made a dry camp, using the extra water bags they had filled before leaving the Rio Grande. Francisco was a silent companion, but he had a way of speaking at the right time, of calling her back from the edge of despair.

"I remember this place well," he told her. "It is the route I traveled with my family after your papá found us in Mexico, promised us a home at La Hacienda de los Olmos."

Stella recalled the old story, too. "I was born while he was away on that trip—selling a herd of mustang horses."

The land through which they traveled became more heavily overgrown with chaparral the farther south they went. Mesquite gave way to its cousin, the huisache.

"When I first came to this land," Francisco continued, "we could see our cattle for miles on end. Now, the chaparral has grown so thick we are lucky to see a few feet in front of us."

"I remember the open vistas," Stella said. "And the horses. When I was a child these lands were overrun with horses instead of brush."

"Mustangers put an end to that," the old man said.

She nodded. She wondered what the Yankees would put an end to.

The second day from Laredo they entered land once owned by the Cortinas family. "My mother always dreamed of reuniting her family's original land grant. Of course, that has not been practical—or necessary. We have plenty of land to support ourselves."

"And all the families your father brought from Mexico, too, señorita," Francisco reminded her.

The third day, they reached the headwaters of Los Olmos Creek, where they met a traveler who brought news of fighting that was much closer to home than Caney Creek.

239

"We've got 'em on the run now," the man said. "Ol' Rip's taken San Fernando with his Calvary of the West."

Stella's spirits picked up. If the Confederates could hold San Fernando, Jorge would not worry so much about his children remaining at Los Olmos. She had dared not tell him Logan's promise; in fact, she had tried to push that promise out of her mind as she attempted to repulse every other thought of Logan Cafferty that flailed mercilessly at her memory.

As far as his promise to keep Los Olmos safe, she knew he meant it, but how much could he do? He did not have control over every ship in the Gulf; no one could be sure what this captain or that—the man Blakesborough, for instance—would do.

No, Logan's promise would not ensure protection for Los Olmos; a company of Confederate soldiers close at hand might, however.

"Señorita," Francisco interrupted her reveries. "I do not like the look of things."

They neared a place on the ranch that had long been called Pablo's Resaca, after an old Los Olmos corporal who was tossed unceremoniously into the mudhole by an outlaw horse. She squinted toward the huisache and retama, growing as a thick barrier of chaparral around the waterhole. Alarm sounded like a dinner bell in her brain.

"Why would the vaqueros bring our cattle to this side of the ranch?" she wondered aloud. "And why. . . ?" She spurred her mount. "Francisco, you are right. Something is wrong. The women are with them . . . and their children."

The words floated behind her on the wind as she raced ahead. Francisco kept pace.

Dry grass crunched beneath their horses' hooves; dry, cold wind stung her face. By the time they reached the camp on the near side of the wall of chaparral, she jumped to the ground, breathless.

"What is the meaning of this?" she asked the first person

240

she saw, one of the wives who was preparing a cold meal for her family. Stella looked around at the scattered camps. No cooking fires at any of them.

"The Yankees . . ." the woman began. "They attacked la casa grande."

"Our house?"

"Sí señorita" came the reply. The woman's husband, one of the newer ranch hands, slid from his saddle.

"Where are my mother and father . . . and the children?" she demanded.

"Do not worry, señorita," the woman told her. *"La señora y los chicos . . ."*

"They were warned," the vaquero told Stella. "A rider came with word to evacuate. La señora had us bring the cattle here, to save them from the Yankees."

"But my parents? Where are they?"

"The rider took la señora to safety, señorita. To Camp San Fernando, I believe. *Su papá* . . . he left the day before, he and his hombres, Delos, Felix, and Kosta."

Anxiety stirred like a bed of angry ants inside her. "Come, Francisco, we must see what the Yankees are up to at la casa grande."

Francisco held her back. "No, señorita. You cannot go there. You heard . . ."

"I must see these Yankees for myself. . . ."

"It will do no good," Francisco argued.

She inhaled a deep draft of winter air, along with a good measure of Francisco's wisdom. "I *need* to see . . ." Her words trailed off—she wanted to see who these Yankees were. Surely not Logan; but why had they attacked? She had known he could not protect Los Olmos against all the Yankees in Texas, but . . .

"You need to see about your family," Francisco finished for her.

My family, she thought. If only the definition of that word were clear, like it used to be . . . before the war . . .

241

before she and Logan had been torn apart by this . . . this *war.*

My family. Mamá, Papá, the children, Jorge, Delos and Abril, Felix and Lupe, Kosta . . .

My family. Not Logan Cafferty.

"You are right, Francisco. I must see to the welfare of my family. But we cannot afford to lose our cattle. You remain here and oversee the ranching operations. I will ride to Camp San Fernando to find my mother."

Although he put up a fuss, she finally convinced him to let her ride alone to Camp San Fernando, since it was but a mere ten miles' distance.

"Colonel Ford has retaken the fort," she argued. "I will be perfectly safe. And Papá would prefer you to stay here and protect our herds. Perhaps you will be able to round up more of them, bit by bit."

"I am sure the Yankees are already searching for the cattle. They would not raid a ranch without commandeering every head of cattle."

"Then take care," she told him. "We would rather lose cattle than men."

"We will fight for both, señorita."

It took three hours' hard riding to reach Camp San Fernando, and along the way she encountered a number of families scurrying to leave the coastal regions ahead of Federal forces.

"The Federals have already secured the coastal ports," she contended to Jesse Martin, the father of a family of six who lived near the settlement of Riveria. "They even raided Riveria last December. Why are you leaving now?"

"We survived the raids before, because the Federals intended only to destroy the cotton trade and stop the blockade runners; they weren't interested in harming defenseless citizens. Things are different now."

"How do you mean?" Stella asked.

"Different," the man answered, close-lipped.

242

"I'll tell you the difference," Mrs. Martin spoke up. "Except for a few head of beef once in a while, or water, or fuel for their ships, they left innocent citizens alone. Now that they've bottled up the coastline, though, they are becoming restless. And restless sailors or soldiers, even on our side, aren't the kind of men I hanker to be around."

"You mean. . . ?" Stella stopped, not wanting to put into words the thoughts the woman's accusations brought to mind.

"She means," the husband added, "that a woman ain't safe in this country anymore." He gave Stella a hard stare, then returned his gaze to the trail ahead. "You should take heed yourself. A woman ain't safe, running around the country alone like you're doing."

Stella blanched at the man's warning. She recalled Logan voicing the same concern on board the *Victory,* and her own response that she had never feared for her safety until meeting up with his crew. It was true, but perhaps only because she had been constantly under the protection of either the Los Olmos vaqueros or later . . .

Max . . . The thought of Max unsettled her, and she responded in a more severe tone than she intended. "I am usually accompanied by a trusted vaquero from our ranch. But we were attacked by Federal forces yesterday, and Francisco needed to stay to keep things together. I am trying to locate my . . . my family."

Her first glimpse of the Confederate soldiers at Camp San Fernando gave her cause to think about Mr. Martin's warning. Even though they were friendly—too friendly, judging by the unrestrained leers of a few of them—she thought inadvertently of the Martins' claims that soldiers from both sides were known to have pillaged along the coast.

Upon hearing of her arrival, however, Colonel Ford came out to greet her, and she forgot about security in her quest to discover the whereabouts of her family.

"Your mother and her group of women and children have

243

gone on to Banquete; they plan on traveling from there to Camp Casa Blanca," he told her over a plate of beans and corn bread.

"I do not understand what the Federals are up to," she confessed. "With the coast secured, I thought they would concentrate on taking the Rio Grande."

"Do not let these skirmishes deceive you," he replied. "They are nothing more than retaliation for Caney Creek."

She raised her eyebrows, questioning, while her heart pumped dread through her body. He continued.

"Our boys whipped up on 'em at Caney Creek. The Federal Navy turned tail and ran like a dog in a blue norther."

Stella concentrated on the steam rising from her coffee cup. The cold weather was nothing compared to the blood in her veins. "We won at Caney Creek?"

"Whipped the socks off 'em," Ford replied. "General Banks didn't attempt to bring up his land forces. Rumor has it he is busy even now loading them aboard transport ships; no word on what to expect from him next."

"What about the Rio Grande?"

"You mean that traitor Davis?"

She nodded.

"I'm keeping my eye on him, ma'am. Don't you give him another thought. Just keep the supplies rolling in, and we will be eternally grateful to you. That's your part in these difficulties."

As the hour was late, she stayed until morning—the colonel procured a tent for her to sleep in—and long into the night she thought about her role in the difficulties. What would Colonel Ford say if he learned she had supplied the other side with ammunition to equal anything she had brought to her own side? Perhaps things had turned out well enough at Caney Creek, but Caney Creek was only one small part of her unwitting role as a traitor.

Her sleep was restless, with thoughts of battles ever on the surface of her brain: battles at Caney Creek, battles at Los

Olmos.

And in the midst of both—Logan Cafferty.

Logan, who promised to protect Los Olmos.

Logan, who had surely been involved in the fighting at Caney Creek. She had not dared ask Colonel Ford about casualties. She doubted he would know whether a Federal colonel numbered among them.

By midmorning the following day she arrived in Banquete to find her family gone, not to Camp Casa Blanca as Colonel Ford had thought, but to Corpus Christi, where they would stay with family members.

Even though the Federals held Mustang Island, off the coast of Corpus Christi, and the entire stretch of inland waterways from Brownsville to Indianola, the town of Corpus Christi was thought to be as safe a place for a civilian as could be found along the coast.

With a heavy sigh, she thought of Los Olmos, which, until two days ago, she would have considered among the safest places in . . . in the state. Nothing was certain in this topsy-turvy world.

Nothing, she thought, when, just after her arrival in Banquete, a runner from Corpus Christi stopped on his way to Camp San Fernando with word of a Confederate attack on the Federal fleet off Mustang Island.

Her mother was headed directly into the battle. Serita Cortinas Duval was a levelheaded person who made sound, sensible decisions. Usually. This time she had taken herself and the children into the heat of battle.

Unwittingly, of course, Stella knew. Perhaps when she heard about the fighting, she would turn back.

The fighting was fierce, the runner added; Major Hobby's troops needed ammunition and medical supplies.

Before leaving for Corpus Christi, Stella directed the young man to a point beyond San Fernando where she was certain he would intercept the wagon train. She suggested he take pack animals from San Fernando to carry the supplies.

"Bring them to Corpus Christi—to the general mercantile firm of Pepe Cortinas. He is my mother's uncle; I will have someone there to help you deliver them."

From Banquete Stella rode east the fifteen or so miles to Corpus Christi with the sun behind her. She steered her mount in and around thick stands of chaparral, hit the Nueces River about halfway there, and thought of the last time she had seen this river.

Her arms trembled yet, feeling the rifle in her hands, watching the Federal patrol boat chase the supply boat up the river. She quaked at the memory, still fresh, of blue uniforms in the sights of her rifle. She wondered whether anyone ever realized the horror of war when they entered it.

She certainly had not; yet, she couldn't say she would change her role had she known. She would not change *her* role, but she would certainly like to change Logan's.

At that she sighed. Such a thought could have come from his own mind. Didn't she always accuse him of making allowances only for his participation in this war?

Would that neither of them had a role in it! Would that there were no war. But there was, and Logan's claims that it was on the verge of being over appeared to have been nothing more than over-confidence on the part of a Yankee.

Or a ploy to send her home. . . ?

The sun set behind her, leaving the air chill with its absence; ahead the sky flashed with repercussions of distant explosions. Before long, the roar she had begun to hear miles back could be identified as cannons and gunfire.

Approaching the town, she encountered throngs of people pouring forth, redoubling her fear for her family's safety. She urged her mount past them—old men pulling carts loaded with household goods; women with bundles strapped to their backs, leading children whose lifeless eyes echoed the fear in the eyes of their mothers.

She searched for familiar faces; her family in Corpus Christi was large—her mother's uncle Pepe Cortinas had thirteen children who had all married and now had children of their own. She wondered about Raul, the son of her mother's cousin, Rosaria, whose wife Carmen had surely delivered their first child by now.

"What is happening?" she asked an old man who whipped a mule that carried not only belongings but also his elderly wife.

"The Confederates are taking back the island."

"Then why are you leaving?" she inquired.

"War is war, ma'am. Don't matter to civilians who is right, who wrong. We're in danger, either way."

"Did the Confederates order you to evacuate?" she asked, mindful of both Galveston and Brownsville, where the Confederates negotiated a time period in order to evacuate civilians and detonate the munitions they did not want to fall into the hands of the Federals.

Again, a head shake, a shrug.

She rode steadily on. Smoke, black and ugly, billowed into the pale sky, and her fears rose with every passing mile. She saw no damage at the outskirts of the city, but the houses were either already deserted or in a state of being abandoned.

She headed for Tío Pepe's house, which lay in an older section of town, nearer the center. As a child she had often played in the sprawling yard beneath the oaks and towering palm trees. But always with a multitude of cousins. Never alone.

Standing alone now in the empty yard, she stared at the lifeless house and felt panic rise within her.

She hadn't seen any of her family on the road. But in the crowd of evacuees, she could well have missed them.

Gathering her wits, she proceeded into the house, hoping to find—she knew not what—some indication of where they had gone. Nothing. No sign of any relatives; no evidence her mother or the children had ever been there.

Idly she ran a hand over the cookstove—still warm. She

lifted the iron kettle and poured a cup of lukewarm coffee into an earthenware cup. The kettle was nearly full. They must have left early—

But where? She drank the coffee, rinsed the cup at the handpump, and found a cold tortilla in a tin box. She hadn't realized she was so hungry.

The shelling continued from the direction of the bay, sporadic at times, followed by a burst of cannon, then intensified volleys, which seemed to come closer with each round.

Or had she simply traveled closer to the fighting? The thought brought a cringe to her spine, and a desperate desire to find her family.

Assuaged by the meager meal, propelled by the resumed bombardments, her mind finally began to function, and she ran from the house.

The church. La Iglesia de Santo Pablo. Of course. Not over a few years old, the church was one of the strongest structures in town.

And as a place of worship, wasn't it also a sanctuary? Of course, the church.

By the time Stella reached La Iglesia de Santo Pablo, she prayed her family would be inside. Although she had supposed the fighting to be isolated along the bay, such was not the case, and she berated herself for playing the ostrich. Why would the townspeople have been racing from their homes if the fighting were contained? The Confederates might be the aggressors, but as the old man along the route told her, it really did not matter which side one was on: A bullet, if fired one's way, did not stop to inquire one's politics before striking one's person.

So frantic were the men running about in the streets that, upon arriving at the church, she searched for a place to leave her horse, knowing full well were she to hitch it to the rail, it would be gone in a matter of minutes. Leading him by the reins, she pulled open the heavy oak church door and peered into the narthex.

Footsteps from behind alerted her, and she turned to see a man clad in Confederate gray trousers and a tattered homespun shirt bound up the steps. He grabbed for the reins; she held them fast.

"Come in, come in," a gentle voice urged from the open church door. "The Lord does provide. We prayed for a horse. . . ."

"Give 'em to me, lady," the soldier begged. "I don't wanna hurt you."

Stella felt the horse move. First backward as the soldier pulled at the saddle, then forward, into the open door of the church.

She watched the nun tug at the harness, her habit billowing like a black cloud in the wind. "Do hurry, my child. We prayed for a horse, and the Lord sent you with it. We cannot let either of you get away."

Stella stared wide-eyed but a moment longer. She glanced back at the struggling soldier. His feet slipped on the stone steps; his eyes registered an expression of disbelief.

Stella helped the nun.

"You are welcome, too," the nun addressed the young man. "But you must leave your weapon outside."

The soldier frowned, his hands faltered on the saddle, and the nun dragged the horse into the darkened interior of the narthex. Stella leaned heavily against the door.

A gentle odor of beeswax and incense soothed her senses in its familiarity. From the nave she heard sounds of people saying their prayers. She felt tension drain from her shoulders. This was home; here she was safe. Idly she watched the nun lead the horse with faltering steps across the tiled floor to the stairway, where she secured the reins to the railing, then turned back to Stella.

"Come, my dear, you must have refreshment. Then you can help tend the wounded."

At her words, Stella's ears somehow became more attuned to the murmurings inside the church—murmurings she had taken for prayers.

Inching forward, she stopped at the doorway of the nave and the sight hit her like a slap in the face, filling her with a deadened sense of doom. The pews, row after row of them, were full, but not of worshipers — these communicants were the wounded, stretched out on pews in place of beds; the prayers she had heard were the painful moanings of the injured.

The isle ran a good twenty-five feet to the chancel, where candles flickered. Their shadows danced against the golden adobe walls surrounding the altar. Her eyes took in the commotion, scanning the pews from back to front, row by row. Women stooped here and there, tending the wounded. Then one of the women stood up, pressed fingers to her aching back, and her eyes caught Stella's.

Like lightening, Stella raced down the aisle.

"Mamá! Thank the Lord you are safe."

"And you, my little Estelle."

Serita rarely used Stella's Christian name, and when she did so now, the sound soothed Stella's earlier distress. Abril came up then, followed by Lupe, and later Stella went into a side chapel to find the children. All were safe.

"Tío Pepe's family is helping at the hospital set up in the Britton house on the bluff," Serita told her. "Mary Stavinoha is there, also. And Tío Pepe is trying to keep us supplied with medicines and food. A hopeless task, I am afraid, if this fighting continues much longer."

"What of Papá?" she asked Serita over a cup of broth the nun insisted she drink. Reward for bringing the Lord's gift of a horse, she supposed.

"He left the day before the attack. He had received word from Captain Wedemeyer at Titlum-Tatlum that with the help of Kosta and Edward Stavinoha, work had gone rapidly; the ship would be ready to put in the water sooner than expected. Captain Wedemeyer's message arrived two days before Max came for us."

"Max?"

"You know . . ."

"I'm afraid I know more about Max than you. . . ."

Serita shook her head. "He came in uniform. In the nick of time, too. He escorted us to San Fernando, close enough, that is, for us to make it safely on our own."

Stella stared into the forgotten broth. Her body trembled so, she dared not attempt to lift the cup.

"I asked him about Logan, dear. . . ."

At the name, Stella abruptly lifted her face to her mother's, waiting.

"He said Logan was not on board the *Victory* when the captain decided to sail for Los Olmos Bay, that Logan didn't know about the raid on our home. It is fortunate you had brought Max to Los Olmos with you. Otherwise, he would not have known it was your home, and we might have all been . . ."

For the rest of the day and throughout the night, they tended the wounded and Stella thought about Logan . . . and Max.

As things stood perhaps she had slipped by without endangering the Confederates after all. Captain Ireland had won the battle at Caney Creek; Captain Wedemeyer had finished the blockade-running ship much sooner than expected, so if the Federals raided his place in three months, they would find neither Papá nor the vessel; and Max had saved her family from being taken prisoner.

"The vaqueros and their families were safe on the north side of Pablo's resaca," she told Serita that afternoon while they fed the children. "They had many of the cattle with them; I told Francisco not to endanger any ranch hands in order to protect the cattle."

"Thank you, dear. I am glad to know they were safe when you came along."

"I worry about the house, though," Stella said. "No telling what those sailors will do to it."

"The house? We have nothing except our lives that we cannot replace when this dreadful war is over. I learned that long ago. Before you were born, our house was destroyed by a wicked kinsman, and we rebuilt; this time, if we lose every material possession, we will know it was in retaliation for . . ."—Serita grinned sheepishly—". . . for having served our country. If we come to the end of this war without losing any more of our family, we will count our blessings."

Fighting continued sporadically for several days; every time the women stopped to rest, more wounded were carried in for them to treat. By morning of the third day, the supplies were dreadfully low. One of the nuns spent her time unraveling silk from the altar vestments to use as sutures, and another boiled willow bark to make tea to replace the quinine when they ran out.

"I must go to Tío Pepe's," Stella announced one morning at first light. "The runners could arrive today, and I promised to show them where to take the supplies. Make a list of things I should bring back from the store."

Serita shrugged. "I doubt he has enough left to require a list. Use your own judgment and bring whatever you think we need."

Although the mercantile was over two miles from the church, she chose to walk instead of ride the horse, which they all considered church property now. Since Sister Patricia, as the nun who helped her into the church was called, had prayed for the horse, Stella would hate to lose it to the first soldier who came along. And of even more importance to her personally, she did not relish the attention riding a horse through a throng of soldiers might bring her.

With her woolen cap and breeches, if she bundled up and did not stop to talk, she figured she could pass through the streets unmolested by either Confederate or Federal. She walked briskly, somehow kept herself from running, and held her rifle in both hands.

The extent of the destruction through the business section

of town dismayed her: A number of buildings had been hit full center and now lay in heaps of lumber and mortar; piles of rubble smoldered, sending slender spines of smoke curling toward the gray sky. Throughout the shelling she had been so busy that she had not given thought to what was happening to the town—only to the men. Now, she wondered what devastation she would find when she located Tío Pepe's mercantile.

The mercantile stood one block back from the street that fronted the bay, so she decided to enter from the rear, thereby taking less risk of discovery. When at last she found it, with "Pepe Cortinas Mercantile" stenciled above the back loading dock, she sighed with relief.

She had come early to escape the melee she knew would fill the streets later, and now she was glad. Voices from inside warmed her with the expectation of seeing Tío Pepe and her cousins again.

Once inside, she berated herself for her haste, however. The back room into which she had entered seemed to crawl with men. Since they were not dressed in uniform, she paused, trying to recognize a familiar face. By the time she realized there were no such faces in this crowd, it was too late.

"What'd you want, boy?" a voice barked.

She didn't so much recognize the voice as she did the accent, and with that recognition came fear, cold and paralyzing. And the memory of another dawn—off Fort Esperanza—and the Federal cutter that took them prisoner.

Instantly, she ducked her head and turned to leave. A rough hand caught her arm. She jerked, but the arm pulled her stumbling back into the room. Another arm pulled the cap from her head.

"This ain't no boy, Ernie. Don't you remember this face? It's a face I won't never forget . . . never."

Chapter Twelve

Alone in the dark bowels of the *Victory,* Stella knew she would be forever in debt to Ensign Jacobs, who had come to her rescue again as he had done the first time she was captured by this crew, the time Captain Blakesborough threatened to throw her overboard and let his men "wash" her clean for him.

She shuddered yet at the thought of it. And at remembrance of the day just past—or was it two days or three? With nothing to break the solid blackness below decks, she lost track of time. Twice someone had brought a crust of bread for her to eat, and a cup filled with a foul-smelling liquid. The stench of the place was nauseating enough; the mere thought of what they might send her to eat would have caused her to retch in her cell, had there been anything left in her stomach.

She was fortunate, she supposed, that she had left the church before eating anything. . . . How many times had that thought run through her mind? And each time it called to the front of her haze her mother, left to wait and worry.

She shivered against the rough deck. So many terrors vied for her attention that she had trouble sorting out one in particular on which to concentrate. Only when the scratching sounds of rodent claws approached did her mind clear, trained then on her own survival.

Quite by accident she had stumbled over a loose plank at the rear of the small cell and with diligence had pried it free. Afterward she sat against the back wall of the cubicle, curled her legs beneath her, and swiped the plank back and forth in a circle on the floor around her, hoping to discourage the rodents from coming too near.

Often she berated herself for having burst into the mercantile so carelessly. If it had not been for Ensign Jacobs . . .

The thought of that morning always brought to mind the most terrible image of all: Tío Pepe's body, lying bloody and lifeless, in the doorway leading from the storage room to the front of the mercantile. Tears rolled down her cheeks, even now, remembering. Such a kind and gentle man; more evidence that war crushed lives unrelated to politicians and warriors.

She pulled her coat tightly about her chest, recalling what had transpired afterward. In her distress at the sight of her uncle, she had momentarily forgotten her own plight. Before she knew what had happened, her coat had been pulled off, hands clutched at her blouse, at her breeches.

"Unless you intend to desert as soon as you finish with her, you'd best leave her be."

More even than the hands on her body, the voice had brought her back to the present. Ensign Jacobs. His voice had not relieved her panic, however. How could one lone man save her from such a mob?

In the next instant, she discovered the answer. As before, Jacobs remained calm. "Captain Blakesborough has had his eye on this rebel wench for a long time. You know what the bastard will do if you take her first."

"Who's to tell him?"

Stella's heart had nearly stopped with Jacobs' words; now it raced rapidly forward. She had scanned the room—six, maybe seven, sailors. What could one man do to save her?

"Look around" came Jacobs' reply. "You know well

255

enough, rumors hit the captain's desk thick as buzzards on a rebel's carcass, and travel there as fast. Take this wench if you must, but you'll have to kill every man-Jack here present to keep your secret safe."

Stella's mind reeled in the ensuing silence.

"Besides," Jacobs continued, "fighter that she is, do you think you could satisfy yourselves—all of you—and leave her unmarked? Blakesborough would know, rest assured of that."

It didn't happen immediately, but at length Stella felt the men's hands, grip after grip, loosen by degrees, until she stood untouched among them. She shook the murky shadows from her brain and tried to remain alert to the first chance to escape.

But although Jacobs had stayed beside her, protecting her from the mob, he did not allow her such a chance. When the time came to leave the mercantile, her feet and hands were bound, and she was cast into the back of the wagon along with the supplies, all of which were later loaded into a skiff and rowed to the *Victory*. She tried to console herself with the hope that Logan would greet her when they carried her aboard.

The next flash of memory terrified her still with its ominous portent of what lay ahead. When they arrived at the *Victory*, Jacobs immediately spirited her toward a passageway, which, she recalled, led below decks, but the commotion raised by the men alerted Captain Blakesborough. If she had thought herself doomed before, the sight of Dar Blakesborough, rubbing his hands in anticipation, sent terror chasing fear through her limbs.

The last ounce of sanity she possessed focused on one question: Where was Logan? Was he on board the *Victory*? Where was Logan?

"So! The rebel wench! We meet again." Blakesborough pierced her with his eyes, freezing her blood with the menace in his voice. He scanned her body, scowled at the bonds. "Unshackle her."

Two men rushed to obey. In the background she heard the tittering of expectant sailors.

Blakesborough came closer, grasped her chin with thumb and forefinger, jerked her jaw this way and that, inspecting.

The bonds dropped from her ankles; she shifted her weight from foot to foot. At her back she felt the tug of ropes being loosened. She gripped her hands into fists.

"You've given us a lot of trouble, reb." Blakesborough's voice, low and dangerous, rasped her fear to a sharper edge. "But I suspect without the aid of lover-boy Cafferty, you're nothing but a pussy cat. . . ." He paused; she watched him search for, then find, approval from his men.

". . . waiting for me to declaw you." The tittering increased in volume.

Never mind that her parents often accused her of being quick to anger, of late Stella had begun to take pride in her self-control. With Blakesborough's suggestive words, however, blind panic overtook any restraint she had learned, and she struck at him, kicking him in the shin. The taunt of amusement vanished abruptly.

He struck her across the face; his gray eyes fixed her with an ugly promise. "I'll soon learn you some manners, reb." He turned to his aide. "Bring her to my quarters!"

Jacobs cleared his throat. "Captain. . . ?"

Blakesborough turned on the ensign, his brows furrowed. "Yes?"

"In my judgment, sir, the prisoner should be confined in quarantine for a few days before . . . ah, before you . . ." Jacobs stopped, shrugged. Blakesborough's eyes registered the ensign's meaning.

"Go ahead, ensign. Explain this to me."

"She . . . ah . . . she was sick on the way over."

Blakesborough's expression lightened, his tone mocked Jacobs. "Seasickness is not contagious, Ensign. Nor will it last long enough to be a . . . ah, a hindrance."

Stella shuddered.

"It was not seasickness, sir," Jacobs contended. "When I touched her, her forehead felt feverish."

Instantly Blakesborough's eyes went to his fingers, which only moments before had clutched Stella's chin. After a brief hesitation, he placed the back of his hand gingerly against her forehead. "I don't feel . . ." His words died beneath a quizzical expression that took the place of his former belligerence.

"With the rumors what they are, sir, about her visits to Bagdad and Matamoros . . . well, a few days in quarantine should tell the tale."

While Jacobs argued her case, the captain had seized a shank of her hair and held it up for inspection. "Lice, perhaps," he fumed, angry, she knew, with the doubts Ensign Jacobs raised in his mind.

In the silence Stella heard her heart beat in her ears. She watched Blakesborough struggle, then finally make his decision.

"Quarantine her, then," he bellowed. "Twenty-four hours." Turning, he glared at her with a viciousness Stella knew she would remember the rest of her life. His voice, when he spoke, roared like a savage. "After that, you're mine, reb."

Footsteps echoed now along the dark passage between the cells, most of which she ascertained to be empty, by reason of hearing no voices for hours on end. She tensed as the footsteps, accompanied by a pool of yellow light, stopped before her cell. A key rattled in the door; the hinges squawked in protest of being opened.

She swallowed her fear and gripped the plank in both fists, ready to swing at the first provocation. If she must go to Dar Blakesborough, she would not go untouched. Perhaps, if she fought hard enough, the resulting damage to her appearance would deter his amorous intentions.

"Stella, it's me, Max." He lifted the lantern to reveal his features in the undulating light.

Her throat tightened and her head spun. She didn't want to see Max. Yet, traitor that he was, at least she wasn't afraid of him. His presence was familiar and brought a flimsy kind of hope to her heart.

"Are you all right?" he asked.

When she didn't answer, he squatted on the floor and held the lantern to her face. She closed her eyes against the first light she had seen in . . . how long? she wondered. Were her twenty-four hours up?

"I just came aboard . . . I . . . ah . . . have they hurt you?"

She inhaled a deep breath and shook her head.

"Jacobs said he had managed to keep them away from you . . . so far. Can you hold out a bit longer?"

Her eyes darted to his, questioning.

He lowered the lantern to the plate of food in his hand. "I brought you something decent to eat—as decent as can be found aboard ship."

She stared at it.

"You need to eat."

Rats scratched in a cell behind him, and he coughed. "I'll sit here with you." He extended the plate toward her until she took it.

"Like I said," he continued, "it isn't much, but I'll wager it's better than what they've been giving you."

Again she looked at him. Then she took a bite of the beef stew. She did need to eat—for strength—and if he stayed here with the lantern so she could see what she put in her mouth . . .

"Logan isn't here," he said. "When he learned about the attack on Los Olmos, he went directly there to find out about you . . . and your family."

She took another bite of stew, thinking how it was very

259

likely Los Olmos beef she was eating.

"Did they make it to San Fernando safely?" he asked.

She nodded, swallowed, and spoke for the first time, her voice hoarse from disuse. "Thank you for helping them escape."

She ate and he kept his silence a bit, then he spoke again, after clearing his throat.

"I know how you must feel about . . . well, it was a hard thing you discovered back at Christmastime. But you've got to believe the truth, Stella. Logan and me, we go back a long way. We went through school together . . . and training. He sent me along with you for only one reason—to protect you. Nothing else was in either of our minds, especially not at the beginning."

Her throat constricted with the earnestness of Max's voice . . . with the truth he expressed. She swallowed the beef in her mouth with difficulty.

"You're more important to him than just about anything in the world, Stella. He would never get over losing you . . . he wouldn't even try."

"I know," she whispered. "I don't blame him . . ."—she sighed heavily—". . . or you. Not any more than I blame myself. I was the stupid one, sharing our secrets . . ."

"Yeah . . . well, ah . . ."

"I'm just thankful neither of you was hurt at Caney Creek." She shrugged in the darkened cell, thought how Giddeon had already gone to get the blockade-running vessel, then laughed softly. "All the secrets you discovered are obsolete now, so I don't suppose there's any sense remaining angry." She handed him the empty plate. "Thank you for bringing me something to eat . . . and for staying . . ."

He took the plate, then stood. "I hate to go off and leave you down here, but for the time being, it's the safest place for you."

At the mention of her ordeal, she took a deep, quivering breath and held it.

"It won't be long," he assured her. "I'm going after Logan. As soon as I find him, he'll get you out of here. In the meantime . . . I'll leave the lantern; maybe it will help discourage any unwanted . . ."—he glanced right and left, into the darkened corners of the cell—"visitors."

"Thank you." Although she tried, her voice quivered, and she was unable to conceal her fear at being left alone in this dark cell; knowing even so she would rather be here than above decks with the captain.

Max closed the cell; she heard the key turn in the lock. "I'm not locking you in, Stella. It's just . . . not many people have a key, so this lock is your protection."

She nodded.

"Jacobs will take care of you," he told her. "But you must realize, everything he does for you endangers him, too."

"I know," she answered. "I'll be fine . . . but hurry."

Max's visit restored her well-being in a way she would not have imagined. After it, she dared to hope. After it, she made a concerted effort to keep track of time. But, of course, with nothing to judge it by, such a task was impossible. While the kerosene lasted in the lantern, she felt safe; she could see the food they brought her, which was as she had suspected no more than bread crusts and a broth she hesitated to drink. By holding her breath and keeping her fears at bay, however, she succeeded, determined not to face Dar Blakesborough, should worse come worst, too weak to defend herself.

The kerosene didn't last forever, though, and she did not ask the sailor who brought her food for more, hesitating to call attention to herself in any way. In the darkness her fears returned, and she held herself vigilant against the unexpected: scurrying rodents, whether of the four-legged variety . . . or two.

She could not remain awake forever, either, and in time—

whether hours or days after Max's visit, she did not know—she drifted off to sleep. Once she was awakened abruptly by a scratching sound from somewhere near her right leg; a terrifying image formed in her brain.

Clutching the plank she still held in her hand, she swung viciously, clubbing the deck over and over again. Her blows resounded through the empty cells, reverberating against her taut senses like a bow rasping discordant notes across untuned fiddle strings. Shrill, slight noises, accompanied by scurrying clawed feet drew her nerves even tighter. As the noise died away, tears rolled down her cheeks.

She sank to the floor of the cell, and with the plank still grasped in one fist, she held her trembling arms and wept. Again, she drifted off to sleep, but this time the sound that awakened her brought a terror totally unassociated with rodents—boot steps.

The echo of them faded beneath the clanging of a key in the lock. The hope it might be Logan . . . or Max . . . or even Ensign Jacobs died with the first human sounds she heard.

"Get on out of there, reb. Captain's ready for you."

She made the sailor come after her, but in the end, she wasn't able to offer much resistance, since the first thing he saw was the plank she swung at him. He caught it deftly in a clublike hand.

Her one brief respite came from what at any other time in her life she would have considered an outrage. When the burly sailor dragged her into Captain Dar Blakesborough's cabin, the fear of the captain's touch dissolved beneath the expression of repulsion in his eyes when he looked at her.

"Bring a tub of water," he ordered, "and some kerosene. She'll have to be deloused."

If she hadn't been so frightened, she would have laughed, she thought later. But humor was not close to the surface—only fear, and a loathing for this man so powerful she felt as though she would explode with it.

The door closed behind the departing aide, and Dar Blakesborough turned his head from her. In that moment, she swore to make him regret his attack on Los Olmos, his vendetta against Logan, his perverse intentions against her own person.

As one possessed, she hurled herself at him, pummeling him with her fists, unmindful of the danger to herself. The expression in his eyes when he turned to ward off her attack was worth at least a flogging, she decided, and if she were to be reduced later to nothing more than a slave beneath his laboring body, she would need to hold such a triumph in her heart in order to survive.

"I wish I had lice," she hissed at him. "Or even a gentleman's disease! It is more than you deserve." When he tried to pull away from her grasp, she yanked his hair.

He struggled, kicking at her, attempting to trip her. With aversion strong on his face, he shoved her away from him, but she held tight to his jacket.

"What's the matter, Captain? I thought you wanted me close."

He twisted out of her grasp, reaching toward his desk, where in her peripheral vision a letter opener gleamed in the light of the brass lantern. Her mouth went dry.

Desperately she tugged at his sleeve with one hand, and at his head with the other. He struggled; she persisted. When his knees flexed in his effort to reach the letter opener, dipping his head away from her, she leaned forward and bit his ear.

"Oww. . . !" He shook free of her and clasped a hand over his ear.

Instantly she leaped toward the door with one thought: to get away before he regained his senses and came after her, for she doubted not, this struggle was far from over.

But she reached the door only to have it burst open in her face, knocking her back toward Blakesborough, who now stared behind her, one hand clamped over his injured ear.

"What'd you want? I sent for a tub and . . ."

"Yes, sir, but . . ."

Jacobs' voice, welcome as it was, was followed by one even more welcome.

"Get out of here, princess."

Weak with the relief of it, she turned and fell against his taut body, but Logan Cafferty had eyes only for Dar Blakesborough. And the message they imparted could not be easily misunderstood.

"Go with Jacobs," he instructed, his voice softer than his eyes, but nevertheless containing little vestige of the voice she had longed to hear during the silent days spent in darkness.

As in a trance, she let Ensign Jacobs unloose her hand from Logan's arm; she felt Jacobs pull her backward. The instant he was free of her, Logan lunged at the captain.

"This is the final straw, Blakesborough. You crossed the line with me years ago; now you've . . ."

"You're the one who crossed the line, Cafferty. I have enough on you to seek and win a court-martial."

Logan jerked the captain by the collar of his crisp uniform. His eyes, hard and cold, stared hatred straight to the man's soul. "In case you don't," he hissed, "let me provide you with a little more." The force with which he hit Blakesborough's jaw resounded through the room.

The captain stumbled, and Logan drew him to his feet and hit him again.

Stella had just entertained the notion that the fight was over, when Blakesborough rose to the occasion. She hadn't realized the man was left-handed, until he landed a powerful jab with his left to Logan's throat; it sent Logan scrambling for his footing. Before he found it, Blakesborough slugged him again, this time with his right fist.

Logan stumbled backward, found his feet, and lunged. Blakesborough met him with a blow to the left temple. Logan countered with a left of his own, this one to the captain's midsection. For a moment they swayed, groping jabs at each other; then the clench broke, and they tottered apart.

"I told you to get her out of here," Logan hissed at Jacobs before Blakesborough plunged forward, clasping Logan about the waist and propelling him out the door.

Jacobs pulled Stella down the narrow hallway. The men sprawled on the floor, Logan on the bottom. Stella gripped her hair in her hands, terrified at the outcome. In the beginning she had thought Logan would best the captain in a couple of punches and that would be the tale of it.

But Dar Blakesborough was no amateur. "He fights like a professional." Her words were soft, she hardly knew she had spoken, but beside her, Ensign Jacobs agreed.

"Blakesborough was boxing champ at the Academy. . . ."

Stella chewed her fingers. What had she gotten Logan into? A boxing champion? Blakesborough could . . .

Suddenly, Logan drew his feet up and kicked Blakesborough in the abdomen, sending him flying down the hallway. Of an instant, Logan was on his feet, and this time he did the pouncing. Instead of falling on top of the captain, however, he knelt in the man's stomach and punched him hard in the face; after which he jerked the captain to his feet and proceeded to whip him back and forth across the face with drives to the right, to the left, to the right, giving Blakesborough no time to get his bearings.

". . . our first year," Jacobs finished, his sentence having been interrupted by the desperate action they watched. "The colonel beat him out of it every year after that."

A crowd of sailors had gathered at the top of the narrow stairway, their actions indicating their preference for Logan, even if their voices were stilled by fear of their captain.

Logan's last slug carried Blakesborough up the stairs; bending over the man, he seized him by the shirt and pitched him up to the main deck, scattering sailors in his wake. Logan climbed up and straddled the captain's limp body. "If you ever so much as *look* at her again, I'll kill you. Don't you doubt it."

Turning, he took a handkerchief from his pocket and began to wipe his face. Stella hurried to him, and he placed a limp arm around her shoulders. She clung to him with both hands.

They had taken but a couple of steps when Dar Blakesborough struggled to a sitting position, from which he called after them. "Your ass is burned, Cafferty. I'll see you in prison for the rest of your stinking life."

Logan stopped, turned, and stared at the man he had known since both were reckless, competitive youths — known, but never liked. He clenched a fist and looked down at his own bloody knuckles, then he glared at the captain, still on the deck. "If so, Blakesborough, it'll have been worth it."

Logan leaned against the closed door of his cabin and pulled Stella to his side. Anger and fear, which had built inside him from the moment Max told him of Stella's capture, still pounded through his veins, reluctant to release him from their grip.

He stroked her head; her springy curls, familiar and reassuring, soothed his rough palm. Her cold body began to relax against his, bringing comfort, and finally warmth.

Lowering his lips, he kissed the top of her head, then gently held her back. "Are you . . . ? Did he . . . ?" His voice broke with the intense emotions called forth by her presence, by his fears. "Did any of them hurt you?"

She shook her head, still struggling to shed the multiple layers of terror that covered her like a shroud: the terror of her imprisonment in the darkness below this very deck on which she now stood; the terror of Dar Blakesborough's intentions toward her; the terror of his fight with Logan;

and the most frightening of all, now that the other fears were behind her, the terror of Blakesborough's threat against Logan—his promise, actually.

She stroked the rough growth of dark stubble on Logan's cheek. A muscle contracted beneath her fingers. "You shouldn't have . . ."

Their eyes locked, hers smoldering with concern and passion at the same time. He grinned, then she did, and their concerns fell away like layers of old skin.

"Some things never change," he whispered as they came together in glorious reunion. "Thank God for that."

It might have been Nottoway, the White Castle, she thought, for the complete, giddy happiness she felt in his arms. Even her hurt over the situation with Max vanished, and in that moment she knew their love—not only hers for him, but his for her, as well—was stronger than anything they had yet faced; than anything they would ever face.

He lifted his lips a hairsbreadth. "We'll whip this damned rebellion, yet."

A rap at the door startled them back to the present.

"Who is it?" Logan demanded.

"Me," Max's voice responded. "Sorry to intrude. . . ."

Logan jerked open the door, then locked it behind his friend.

Stella studied Max a moment before throwing her arms around him. She kissed his stubbled cheek. "Thank you. I don't know how I'll ever repay you." She felt Max stiffen; the heat of his blush warmed her cheek. She stood back against Logan, who drew her to his side in an overtly protective gesture.

"Hey. I'm not sure I approve of this familiarity—especially with a man you've spent more nights with than me."

As he joked Stella watched the blush deepen to crimson on Max's face.

Max ran a hand through his hair, but embarrassment did not dull his humor. "Just doing what you ordered,

Colonel."

Logan kissed the top of Stella's head. When he spoke his voice had gone from playful to serious. "And you did it very well, friend."

For but an instant the moment hung suspended, and in that brief period Stella felt the bond of kinship tighten from friend to friend to friend . . . —she squeezed her arm around Logan's waist—. . . and lover.

In the next instant the deck swayed beneath their feet, taking her breath with it. Old seamen that they were, Logan and Max retained their balance without faltering, and just as instinctively, Logan kept her upright, too. Her heart swelled with love for him.

"Where are we headed?" Logan asked.

"That's what I came to tell you. The fighting on land is over. Admiral Farragut sent word to let the rebels have Corpus Christi. We'll retain Mustang Island, but since the rebs destroyed the lighthouse at Aransas Pass, we need to get out of the bay before dusk."

Even the silent exchanges of communication between Logan and Max did not dim Stella's newfound security, but when Logan followed Max out the door, she resisted.

"Will you be safe . . . out there?"

"Blakesborough can't hurt me. His orders specifically state that I am to proceed on any front, as I see fit; he is not to stand in my way, either on board this ship, or on land." Bending, he kissed her quickly. "He won't get to you, either, princess. Jacobs will stand guard outside the door until I return. I won't be long."

Before the door was closed, Jacobs ushered inside two men carrying a tub of hot water. "It's just water, ma'am," he said, calling to mind Blakesborough's orders to bring a disinfectant along with her bath water.

"I owe you my life, Mr. Jacobs," she said when he prepared to close the door behind himself. "Thank you seems dreadfully inadequate."

"No need for that, ma'am. I'm sorry I had to say such awful things about you . . . to the captain. But that's the only language he understands."

"Do not apologize; you did a splendid job of saving my life."

Jacobs shuffled nervously. "I'll go now, ma'am. . . . You call when you finish with the tub . . . or if you need anything. I'll be right out here."

After he closed the door, she surveyed the wonderfully familiar room—the desk, the tub, and beyond, the berth where first she and Logan made love.

It took several scrubbings to remove the filth from her time spent in the cell below. The stench remained in her nostrils, and after she dressed in the baggy blue pants and shirt Ensign Jacobs left with the tub, she searched out the bottle of port Logan had poured from on her last visit here. It took little more than a couple of swallows of the fiery liquid for her eyelids to droop, heavy with lost sleep and heightened emotions. She lay on the bed, thinking to rest until Logan returned, but when next she opened her eyes, he was there—sitting in a chair beside her, studying her face with an expression that made her heart flip.

"How long have you been watching me?"

He had bathed while he was gone, and was now attired in clean but casual clothing, much the same as her own. When he leaned over her, she touched his face and found it smooth. He smelled clean and spicy.

She inhaled deeply. "You're the best thing I have smelled in . . . I don't know how long."

Lowering himself to the bed beside her, he nuzzled her neck with his face. "Probably the cleanest, too," he whispered.

His breath tingled over her skin, blazing moist trails of desire to the nether reaches of her body.

With his words, though, her concern returned. "Logan, what are we going to do?"

He lifted his face, and in the dim light of the cabin, his chocolate eyes ran hot and hungry over her face. His fingers found the buttons on her shirt. "What we do best, princess . . . love each other."

She squirmed beneath him. "I mean about the captain — about his threat to have you court-martialed."

He concentrated on the buttons, which by now he had undone. With leisurely yet tormenting precision, he pulled the two parts of her shirt aside and ran his hands over her breasts, cupping them tenderly in his palms.

Her heart beat faster. "Logan, I'm worried . . . about the captain. Can he really have you court-martialed?"

"Yes," he whispered, lowering his lips to an aching nipple.

She inhaled, unconsciously lifting her breast toward him. "What will we do about that?"

At last, he turned his attention to her troubled mind. His thumb replaced his lips over her nipple, tormenting still, as the danger Dar Blakesborough posed to him tormented her mind.

He lifted his eyes to hers. "Nothing. Not right now. He can't do anything about it before the rebellion is put down — the officials in Washington have more important things on their agendas. Afterward . . ." — his words trailed off, and she watched concern cloud his confidence — ". . . a lot of things can happen between now and then, princess. He won't get me . . . I'll make sure of that."

"You'd better," she sighed, reaching for the buttons on his shirt, fumbling in her haste. "Hurry, Logan. Please hurry. It's been so long. I can't wait another minute to feel you . . ."

He grinned at her, obliging by stripping the trousers past her hips, down her legs, and tossing them to the floor. "I know, princess. . . ." he mumbled against her skin. The eternal flame she had kindled inside him at Nottoway Plantation flared as always in her presence, and grew now with her innocent passion, scorching his body as with a torch.

At last they lay body to body, skin to skin, heartbeat to heartbeat. His body grew as she nuzzled, desperately seeking, against him; he held her so tight their hearts beat as one.

". . . your body against mine . . ." she whispered in his ear, shivering with desire as his hand cupped her to him, pressing her against his own obvious arousal.

". . . inside mine . . ." she whispered against his lips, delighting when he shuddered against her.

"You don't make it easy to hold off," he teased, not teasing at all, kissing her lips, devouring, exploring, questing. But when he raised his lips to slide his tongue down her neck, her response stopped him.

"Then don't . . ." She trailed her hands along his back, cupping him closer to her, in imitation of his own earlier gesture. "The night has just begun—"

Her sentence was cut off in one intense moment when he slid inside her. She raised her hips against him, drawing him deeper into her aching chamber. Poised to continue, they held the pose, indulging themselves in this moment of perfect communion.

"How're we doing so far?" he whispered against her lips.

"It's magic. . . ." Gradually, she began to move against him, initiating their chase toward a oneness, which, though unattainable, always at this point seemed within reach.

And upon finishing, as she had predicted, they found themselves on a higher plateau than they had ever reached before. This she knew was the sweet bond of love; an atonement for all that had transpired between them since they last joined; a confirmation that their love would see them through the trying times ahead.

Toward midnight, after they had exhausted themselves yet again in physical and wonderful expressions of love, they dressed, and Logan led her to the bridge, where he conferred with the officer at the helm. She stood by the rail, absorbing the gentle rock of the ship, enjoying the feeling of contentment that soothed to some degree the myriad conflicts still moiling beneath the surface of her emotions. At least a million stars glittered from the sky above, and she knew she could count a blessing for every one of them.

And every blessing began with Logan's name. He had even promised — it was he who suggested it — to send a ship ashore in the morning with word to her mother of her safety.

Snatches of the conversation between Logan and the helmsman reached her, but those words only added to her list of blessings.

". . . blockade runners . . ."

She sighed. Papá should be at Titlum-Tatlum by now, preparing to launch the new vessel, if he had not already done so, and here they were, hundreds of miles away in the southern Gulf. Blessings. Fleeting, but to be counted nonetheless. Papá and Logan would not meet this trip.

She felt a subtle change of direction as the bow tacked to the left; then Logan stood beside her, slipping an arm about her waist, squeezing her to his side.

Blessings.

The greatest of them stood beside her. And he had come in time to save her from Dar Blakesborough.

But at what cost to himself?

Laying her head against his chest, she felt his hand slip from her waist upward, until finally he cupped it around one of her breasts. She snuggled against him, feeling luxurious and a bit wicked here in the open, even though they stood in darkness.

"Where are we headed?" she asked.

He shrugged and continued gently plying her breast through the rough fabric, working her nipple now between his fingers.

She located the North Star and studied it absently, giving

272

herself over to Logan's sensuous manipulations, knowing she was like clay in his hands; knowing, too, she had the same delicious effect on him.

Turning to him, she had just started to entice him to return to bed, an invitation she knew he would accept with pleasure, when the situation dawned on her. While he stood, lovingly seducing her, the ship had progressed at a steady clip . . . farther and farther . . . north.

"We're headed north. . . ." she whispered.

He shrugged.

". . . north to . . ." She didn't finish the sentence; she couldn't, for her throat constricted with remembrance of words she had heard spoken earlier by the helmsman, heard but not attended—

"blockade runners . . ."

". . . near Galveston."

Near Galveston. Titlum-Tatlum was near Galveston. Papá was near Galveston.

Chapter Thirteen

The North Star led them on, as it had done countless millions of travelers in ages past. But rather than pointing toward a secure port somewhere in the black of night, the star tonight guided her toward certain disaster.

And rather than something she could discuss with the man at her side, the man whom she loved as life itself, the fear instilled by the *Victory*'s heading was something she dared not mention to him. She shuddered with the prospect of dealing with her fears alone.

He wrapped her in his arms, kissed the top of her head, and turned them away from the rail. "Come. You're getting chilled."

Inside, her turmoil echoed the churning water in the *Victory*'s wake. Were they heading toward Titlum-Tatlum? Did he intend to attack Giddeon—with her at his side, for God's sake? Worst of all, she dared not ask, for if Titlum-Tatlum wasn't their destination, she could well plant the idea by mentioning it.

He knew about Titlum-Tatlum, of course. Max would have told him everything. But the time schedule Captain Wedemeyer gave them had been moved up. Logan couldn't know Papá had already gone there . . . could he?

The night passed and the following day. Logan left her infrequently and at those times stationed Jacobs outside her door. Like a skein of yarn, her anxieties knotted into a single jumbled question: What was the *Victory*'s destination?

Logan did not appear to notice her turmoil, which curiously did not interfere with their relationship. That bewildered her, since the two were irrefutably connected: her love for Logan, his assumed—she reminded herself—pursuit of her father, her love for her father. A circle of anguish, beginning without beginning, end without end.

At least, for her the end was not in sight—certainly not an ending designed to fulfill all her hopes and dreams.

Time dragged by inside the cabin, while outside she knew it traveled at whirlwind speed. And that, after all, was the only time that mattered: outside. How fast was the ship traveling? How far were they from Titlum-Tatlum? How far from there was her father?

Max brought food; Logan and Stella ate, they loved, they talked.

Logan told her about Los Olmos. "The house is fine," he said over dinner the second night after she had seen the star. "The vaqueros have returned to their quarters. Francisco is in charge."

"Francisco," she mused. "I don't know what we would do without him. Papá brought him to Los Olmos years ago—the year of my birth; he has been a faithful member of our household ever since."

"I can see you were in good hands with him," Logan confessed. "That knife of his . . . well, I'd hate to run into him on a dark night. I have no doubt he would slit any man's throat he judged a threat to you." He studied her solemnly through the dim lamp light. "A man I can trust."

She held his gaze, feeling her body stir at the sincerity in his eyes. "So you did not need to send Max, after all."

Still he stared into her green eyes, and she could see nothing there but love. "That was my best judgment. You can't fault me for wanting to protect you. Even now, I wouldn't allow you to travel that bandit-infested trail without someone I know along." He took a sip of wine. "But that's behind us. It's almost over."

His reference to the war's end activated the fear for her father, which lay always near the surface of her emotions. "You told me that months ago. In Galveston you said the war was in its last throes, and look what has happened since."

"It took longer than I thought," he admitted. "But it is winding down now. General Davis just took Laredo."

She gasped.

"You escaped there in the nick of time, princess." Although his voice held more relief than anger, his paternal tone irritated her.

"I had no trouble in Laredo." She glanced about at the four walls of the cabin. "On hindsight, General Davis wasn't the threat."

Instantly Logan rose and pulled her to her feet. His arms soothed, as did his voice. She sighed against him.

"How is it," she asked, "that you so quickly take command of my senses?"

He kissed the top of her head. "I told you once, the rebellion is the only point of contention in our lives. And we're almost finished with that. Very soon now you will live like every princess should . . . happily ever after."

She wanted to ask him how it would end—since he knew so much. Where the final blow would fall, where the last shot would be fired. Happily ever after for her depended on the ending—on who was left alive at the finish.

Most of all, she wanted to ask him where they were headed, even now. She wanted to ask him, but she did not want to hear the answer.

She did not want to hear: *an island called Titlum-Tatlum, small and unimportant—except for one man who might be there—except for Papá.* That thought added to her anxieties. Could this war have numbed her to the point that, of all the hundreds of thousands of men involved in it, only her father's life was important? Did she care for the safety of her father above all other men?

Logan drew her head back, lowered his lips, his chocolate eyes compassionate, loving, stirring now with passion. *Above all other men, except one,* she thought, giving herself up to his demanding kiss.

After that they loved—gently yet passionately, slowly and completely. And when he drove deep inside her, she held him motionless with her thighs and knew once again that this was the true meaning of being at one with another human being. Attached to him, as with the cord of life, she knew that as one they would survive this war . . . or rebellion . . . or whatever dastardly name one dared to call the game of men killing men.

This was life, not death.

This was life, not destruction.

This was life, and liberty, and freedom, and commitment . . . atonement for all that separated them.

This was love.

And when his life-bearing seeds erupted inside her, her spirits soared free in the glory of the moment, with the promise of the future.

"I wonder if we'll have a baby soon," she whispered against his damp temple.

He rubbed a hand over her nude belly. After a while, she felt him staring at her. When she opened her eyes, she trembled at his loving expression.

"We must get married."

She smiled, pleased, curious.

"I won't take a chance on disgracing you or our child, should you become pregnant before the rebellion is over."

She clasped him about the neck and pulled his face to hers, rested her cheek against his own, and thought she might cry. So loved, she felt, so secure. She started to tell him there was no rush, since in his words the war was about over. But that would spoil the moment, and she would not spoil so special a moment . . . not for any reason . . . not even for the truth.

"Of course," he continued, "if I were on better terms with Blakesborough . . ."

"No," she laughed. "To be married by such a man would be more disgraceful than bearing a child out of wedlock."

He held her then, soothing her, assuring her neither would be necessary, and she felt, briefly, that the world was spinning peacefully along.

Such, of course, she knew, was not the case.

Later, while they dressed, she suggested, "Let's go on deck and watch the stars."

At her suggestion, he stopped in his efforts to stuff the tail of his shirt into his breeches and studied her. "There aren't any stars tonight. A storm is brewing."

A storm! she thought. A storm meant dark skies. If Papá were still at Titlum-Tatlum, he could escape in the darkness of a storm. If he were still there . . . if . . .

Crossing the room, Logan took her by the shoulders and held her with both hands. At his touch, her mind returned to the cabin.

"Is he there?" He studied her intently now.

She swallowed, tried to shift her gaze, then thought better of it.

"Is he there?" he repeated.

"Who?"

"Is he there?" he asked once more, emphasizing every word.

She inhaled a deep, tremulous breath, held it. When she answered, it was in a whisper. "I don't know."

His grip tightened on her shoulders. "Could he be there?"

Holding his gaze, she clasped her bottom lip between her teeth so hard she felt the blood pool, willing herself to lie. Finally, however, almost imperceptibly, she nodded.

For an eon they stared, each at the other, while time

stood still and their hearts raced. She tried to read what she saw in his eyes: compassion and love, certainly.

And truth.

Truth.

And he saw the same in hers. At last, he pulled her into a rough embrace and held her fast.

By morning she was in almost as wretched a state as the weather. The storm had materialized during the night, tossing the ship about like a child's swing on the end of a tether. She rejoiced with each rock, with each roll; but likewise when Logan tightened his loving arms around her, she rejoiced with that, too. She must save her father; but she would have to escape from Logan to do it.

Escape, when she never wanted to leave his side again.

Come morning, she broached the subject. "If you are right about the war being over soon, what reason could you have for . . . for attacking my father?"

He set his coffee aside and took her in his arms. She trembled against him in imitation of the tossing ship.

"What good will one more victory do?" she demanded.

"What do you think brings conflicts like this to an end?" he countered. "The rebels won't simply decide to stop fighting. They must be shown they have no other way out. They must learn they have more to lose by continuing. . . ."

"More *lives* to lose, you mean. Lives. Like Papá's."

"Don't, Stella. There's no sense . . ."

Pulling away from him, she was suddenly overwhelmed by the situation. "I knew it would come to this. Didn't I tell you so . . . long ago . . . at Los Olmos? Didn't I . . . ?"

He caught her arms, held her against her struggles to escape his grasp. "Look at me, Stella. Look at me."

She didn't comply, and when he spoke again, his voice

279

was tinged with discontent. "It hasn't come to anything, yet. You needn't work yourself into such a state. . . ."

She looked at him then. Furious eyes found his. "I needn't concern myself with things I cannot control?" she mocked. "Is that what you mean? I needn't be concerned over the approaching death of . . . of my father? Or, perhaps, he won't die. Perhaps he will win the battle. Then all I'd have to concern myself with is . . . is *your* death! But other than those two insignificant matters . . ."

"I didn't say they were insignificant," he argued. "And . . . I was wrong . . . you have every right to worry." This time when he pulled her to his chest, she did not resist. "I'm worried, too," he whispered, kissing the top of her head. "But I'm going to work it out"

Somewhere about midmorning, he left the cabin for what had become a routine meeting—with whom, she did not know. This time, however, she knew well enough what the subject of the meeting would be.

After he left, she tried to contain her emotions; he was right, she told herself, she must not work herself into a state where she couldn't respond. He had said he would work things out, but she dared not hope . . . dared not rely on such a promise. What could he do, anyway, short of turning the ship around? That she knew better than to expect.

No, she must keep her wits. Papá and his crew were at her mercy; she must find a way to save them.

Suddenly, she flung the ebony-handled men's hairbrush across the room, watched it bounce off the berth and land on the floor, where with the tumbling ship, it slid across the room. If she didn't learn something soon, she would go mad! If she knew how close they were to Titlum-Tatlum . . .

Quickly, she unlocked the door and stepped into the hallway, only to be thrown against the opposite wall by the pitch of the ship. Ensign Jacobs came to her aid.

She regained her balance and started past him. "I am going on deck."

"Miss Duval, I can't let . . ."

"If I don't get some fresh air, I will be sick," she told him as he struggled to keep pace with her.

"But Colonel . . ."

"The colonel would not want me to be sick in his cabin, Mr. Jacobs."

When she stepped onto the main deck, the wind hit her with such a punch she recalled the powerful blows Captain Blakesborough had thrown at Logan. Her hair tossed and whipped, and her clothes clung to her body like a second skin. She hoped the captain was nowhere about.

Regardless, she must discover how much time she had to plan an escape—and what she would do once she managed such a feat.

Escape. The very idea sounded so ludicrous she cringed at the probability of failure. She had escaped the *Victory* once before, but only because she had ten men to help execute her plan.

Ensign Jacobs accompanied her without further argument, taking her elbow as she worked against the wind. She got her bearings and strode awkwardly toward the bow. At the rail, she had to hold on with both hands to keep from being blown backward. Icy water sprayed her face. A north wind, she thought. A March storm. As yet no rain fell, but the sky was beautifully overcast. She stared toward the west, where she should see land, but was able to discern nothing more than a mingled grayness. It reminded her of Los Olmos; on overcast days the sea and land were often indistinguishable from the bridge her mother had built above their house.

From the bridge the Federal cannons destroyed when they attacked the house and killed Alicia. Beautiful Alicia. Stella gripped the rail so tightly she felt permanently attached. She *would* escape; somehow she would. She would get to that island, and she would warn Papá. The Yankees were not going to take another member of her family.

Staring into the haze, she willed her mind to work. The cold wind whipped her body, leaving a layer of icy skin beneath the loose-fitting uniform. She couldn't do anything now, but when the haze lifted she could see the shore. . . .

She glanced toward the life boats. She would never be able to take one of the boats. Not alone. But if she chose the right place . . . In many areas along the coast, the water was shallow. If she chose her time well, chose the right place, she wouldn't have far to swim before she reached shallow water, where she knew she could . . .

"Well, well, the rebel wench."

Her spine stiffened. Quickly, she looked to Ensign Jacobs, who took her elbow. "The lady needed a breath of fresh air, Captain," he said. "She's headed back in, now."

"Not so fast." Blakesborough dismissed Jacobs with a glance before turning his attention to Stella.

"What interests you out there . . . to the *north?*"

She remained silent.

"That's all right. I wouldn't expect you to tell me. But you told Max, that was enough."

She gritted her teeth and started to turn loose the rail in order to retreat. Jacobs' hand tightened on her arm.

"Aren't you even a little curious why I let the colonel have you?" Blakesborough barked.

She paused but still did not answer. She didn't want to hear whatever lurid tales he might spin.

"Or why I haven't confined you both to cells below deck?"

He couldn't do that . . . could he? Her eyes asked the question she had not intended to voice.

"Oh, I see a spark of curiosity . . . or is it fear?"

"I am not afraid of you, Captain. You have no authority over Colonel Cafferty . . . and you most certainly have no authority over me."

"That's a matter of opinion, reb. I'd say, as my prisoner, you'd be well advised to keep your opinions to yourself. But, I know . . . I asked you. So, this time, I will let it pass. Back to our conversation. You might find my reasons interesting. You see, I want nothing—not even to whip you gray-bellied rebels—as badly as I want to get even with Logan Cafferty. And I've found the perfect way to do it. Now. Not after we put down the rebellion. But now."

Stella realized suddenly that she had lied to Dar Blakesborough. Watching him now, his eyes darting to and fro, his words were as ominous as this stormy day, as threatening as their sure approach to Titlum-Tatlum.

She had lied. She *was* afraid of Dar Blakesborough. Not for herself, but for Logan. The captain was insane.

"What did Logan ever do to you?" she asked, careful to keep her voice calm.

Blakesborough stared out at the swirling sea. "Do to me?" His inflection keened with the wind. Turning, he glared at Stella. "He stood in my way!"

Stella frowned. "In your way for what?"

The insanity in the captain's eyes pooled and eddied and his voice calmed. "Of course, I will certainly press the court-martial when the rebellion is put down. He deserves that, consorting with the enemy as he has done. But I have a way of whipping him *now.* After this week, he won't care whether he spends the rest of his life in a Federal prison or not."

In spite of the cold salty mist, Stella's lips were so dry they stuck together. She wetted them with her tongue, scarcely daring to listen to the captain's madness. At the same time, she wanted to know his intentions.

"What do you plan to do?" Her voice, weak and trembling, was lost on the wind. Captain Blakesborough, however, gave no sign of letting her go without revealing the gruesome details of his plan.

"You are the key, reb. Who would ever have thought a model Academy graduate like Logan Cafferty could be done in by his affection for the enemy."

Stella started to protest, but he gave her no time. Her words would have been lost on more than the wind had she expressed them, however. Dar Blakesborough was far beyond the ability to reason.

He smiled with glee. "He took everything I wanted in life, now I'm going to take what he prizes most. When I kill your father—Face it, reb, you will hate the man responsible for your father's death, now won't you?" He perused Stella before continuing. "Everything he wants in life . . ."—he kissed the tips of his fingers, then flung his hand to the wind—"gone, poof, vanished, before his very eyes. I have been watching for something like this, waiting. Losing you is the one thing from which he will never recover."

Stella fought to retain her composure. "If that is your intention, Captain, why don't you simply kill *me*. Your killing my father will have nothing to do with Logan."

Blakesborough smiled, a thin, curved line, nothing more. His eyes danced with madness. "Oh, yes it will, reb. Logan Cafferty gave the order."

When Logan returned he could no longer ignore Stella's wretched state of mind. At the sound of the door closing, she stopped pacing and turned on him, her eyes deep and dark in the recesses of their hollow sockets.

"Jacobs said Blakesborough confronted you." He tried to take her in his arms, but she pulled away. "You should have waited for me to go on deck with you. He wouldn't have dared . . ."

"How did he know Papá is at Titlum-Tatlum?"

284

Logan flinched. "What did he tell you?"

She held her ground. "How did he know, Logan? You and I were the only ones . . ."

"He doesn't *know*. He may suspect, but he doesn't know."

"He told me . . ." The words Blakesborough had spoken were so horrible she couldn't repeat them. Covering her face with her hands, she turned her back on Logan.

When he took her shoulders, she jerked away, but he was prepared. Holding her fast, he pulled her back against his chest. "What did he tell you, princess?"

His appellation, usually so welcome, irritated her. "Do not patronize me, Logan Cafferty. I am neither a child nor a helpless female."

He sighed heavily against her head. "What did Blakesborough tell you?" he repeated.

"He said you ordered him to kill my father."

The only indication he heard her was when he clenched his fists around her arms. At length, he turned her to face him, and she stared, questioning, waiting.

"I did no such thing." His words were simple, his tone calm.

"I know," she whispered.

"I planned the attack for now—before the ship was scheduled to be finished, so we could take it out before Giddeon arrived. I didn't think about it being finished early."

She stared, unseeing, somewhere around his Adam's apple. "That doesn't lessen our guilt. If he dies in this attack, we will both be responsible. I, for trusting Max; you, for using the information."

"What was I supposed to do, for God's sake? Do you expect me to let a new high-speed blockade-running vessel get past my post? For that I *could* be court-martialed, and I would deserve it."

"But he's my father . . . he never did anything to you."

285

He shook her shoulders firmly. "I told you to keep him from running the blockade, damnit. That's all I could do. I thought you understood that."

"I did . . . I do. But, he's . . . determined."

"Listen to yourself," he said, more softly again. "He chose what he's doing. We all did. We may not like it now, but we chose to play this game."

She attempted to pull away from him. "I can see there's no use talking about it."

Moving his hands from her arms, he clasped her head and tilted her face to his. Her distress distressed him; her anguish filled him with more of the same. He kissed her unresponding lips. "I can see we have to."

His gentleness brought tears, which she fought, to the end that her eyelashes glistened, but she succeeded in keeping them from flowing down her face.

It wasn't a matter easily resolved, but he was right; it wasn't a situation they could run away from, either. In days, perhaps hours, they would encounter it head on. And the result would depend on what they did now.

She already knew what she intended to do. How to go about it was the question.

Max brought lunch—beef stew, as usual. More Los Olmos beef, she supposed. She could barely swallow it, for the fears choking in her throat. Inside the cabin, the atmosphere was as chilly as the early spring wind that blew outside.

As soon as they finished eating, Logan left, taking the tray of dishes with him. Sometime later rain splattered against the portholes, and she rejoiced. Rain. After the rain, the sun always shone. After the storm, she would be able to see the shoreline . . . to get her bearings . . .

As she sat alone in the cabin, her anxieties grew into obsessions: She must discover how far they were from Titlum-Tatlum; she must find a way to escape the ship without Logan stopping her.

She must save Papá. She must.

Then he returned with a solution to her dilemma.

"As soon as the weather clears," he told her, "I'll send a man in to warn Giddeon." When he took her in his arms, she did not resist. Instead she leaned against him, glad for his strength, thankful for his presence.

He kissed the top of her head, then tipped her chin toward him. "Now, do I get a kiss?"

She hesitated, knowing the argument was far from over. She would have a hard time persuading him to let her go ashore with the man he sent. But he would agree. She knew that, now.

"You mean you went to all that trouble for a kiss?" she teased.

His jaw tightened, while he held her gaze and considered the various answers that came to mind—on the lewd side definitely, designed to bring a smile to her lips. But this was not the time for levity. She needed tenderness . . . and truth.

"I did it for you," he whispered before his lips covered hers in a kiss so tender it brought tears to her eyes, so urgent her heart almost burst for love of him, so demanding she responded with the full magnitude of passion that had been held temporarily behind the wall of her anxieties.

Without breaking the seal of their lips, he lifted her in his arms and carried her to a chair, where he sat, holding her on his lap. She snuggled against him, feeling comfortable, at home, where she always wanted to be.

"Do you know what Captain Blakesborough's real motives are?" she questioned. "He wants to get even with you for something. He thinks by killing Papá, he can cause me to hate you, and that will destroy your will to live."

He sighed against her. With a forefinger, he traced the contours of her face, then down her nose, around her lips. Her tongue darted sensuously out and captured his finger.

"He's probably right," he responded, his voice hoarse with wanting her.

"No, he isn't," she said quickly. "I would never hate you, because it was my fault . . . too."

He shook his head. "We have lots of spies out there, Stella. Without Max—without anyone following you at all—we would have learned of the vessel being built at Titlum-Tatlum. This very day we received a report confirming your suspicions that Giddeon is there."

Her eyes widened; fear returned. "If everyone already knows he is there, how will you be able to get me . . . ?" She clamped her lips over her words. Now was not the time to tell him her plans. Not now. She clasped her arms around his neck and held him tight, cheek to cheek.

He soothed her with strokes over her head, down her back. "Don't worry so much. I'll find a way to get him out. And you will be the first to know when he is safe."

Unlike the previous meal, when dinner came, they shared it in harmony, and afterward Logan left to attend to matters concerning his job. She didn't ask what they were; she didn't want to know.

She wanted nothing to ruin the rest of their evening. At least, not until she told him her plans. This would likely be their last evening together for a while, and she resolved to make the most of it.

By the time he returned, she had dimmed the lamps, discarded her clothing, and crawled into bed. When he saw her there, his eyes ignited like one of the *Victory*'s own cannons.

"The storm has let up"—he hastened to strip away his own clothing—". . . I'll be able to get a man out by morning."

"Good." She reached for him, pushing everything but this man out of her mind.

"Good," he mimicked, coming into her arms. "You feel good next to me."

She snuggled against him, pressing her breasts into the furry covering of hair on his chest. What a foolish thing Dar Blakesborough had said. Obviously he had never loved anyone the way she loved Logan Cafferty. She couldn't imagine not loving him; it was as though she always had; she knew she always would.

His lips teased and tempted, devoured and excited, fueling her passion with urgency, whether from relief at having their past discord behind them or from knowledge of the conflict that lay ahead . . . or both, she wasn't sure.

Without pausing to contemplate further, she returned his fervor with ardor of her own, running her hands across his shoulders, down his back, lingering, pressing him against her in a seductive gesture that elicited a groan of pleasure from his throat, followed by a simultaneous attack, each on the other's senses.

He nibbled at her neck; she ran her fingers around his hips; he moved his lips to her breast, she played her tongue around the rigid rim of his ear; he massaged her skin, her heated flesh, her inner core; using her hands, she guided him toward the center of her craving.

She whispered seductively into his tormented ear. ". . . inside me . . ."

Leaving her breast to cool in the air, he lifted his face to hers and watched her expression as he followed her instructions, fulfilling both their wishes, as one. "How's this?" he asked with a grin.

She smiled, pleasured beyond the ability to speak. Then she lifted her lips to his, her hips to his, and closed her eyes, while their bodies, as one, rode the swells of passion, as a ship tossed by hurricane winds at sea.

Afterward, still reluctant to break the magical spell of their loving, she clung to him, and he to her. Finally, their hearts returned to a more normal pace, and she knew she could wait no longer.

"When your man goes ashore in the morning, I am going with him." She had splayed her palms across his shoulders, filling her hands with his muscles, her mind with the feel of him. When her intention registered on him, she felt his muscles flex.

"No . . . you're not."

She moved her hands in a comforting manner across his shoulders. "Yes."

He pushed away from her.

She pulled him back.

"No."

"Yes."

This time when he moved, he was determined, and she couldn't hold him. He stood above her, hands on hips, staring down at her.

His body was beautiful, she thought. A knifelike poignancy pierced her heart; she hated to disagree with him.

But it was his fault, she countered, rising. She looked up at him. "I am going, Logan." He started to protest again, but she placed her fingers over his lips, shushing him. This time he did not take one into his mouth, and she was sorry.

She hurried on. "I would have gone, even if you hadn't decided to send a boat. I would have escaped . . . ."

"How in hell would you have done that?"

They stood mere inches apart; the sheen of lovemaking still glowed on their skin. Her lips were still full . . . from his kisses, he noticed. They beckoned him now.

His body responded, but he knew she would resist his touch.

"How?" he demanded again.

"I would have found a way. When we got close enough, I could have swum ashore."

He glared at her. "That's the stupidest idea I have ever heard! You would have drowned."

"Perhaps," she retorted. "But it would have been worth

it to save Papá!"

"How could you save your father if you drowned . . . ?"

"Logan. That's all in the past. We are arguing over something that has been settled. You are sending a boat . . ."

"With a trained crew," he finished. "Not with the woman I love on board."

Her breath caught at his words, at the husky tone with which he spoke them. Did he know how hard it was to resist him, standing here . . . ? Her eyes started to roam his body.

She stopped herself. "I must go. No one else can convince him to leave."

She waited for his response, but he made none, so she hurried on. "If you send a Federal crew, he will stay and fight. He won't leave that ship to be confiscated—or destroyed—by the enemy. No one else can convince him to leave—no one except someone he loves. If I go, he won't take a chance with my life. He will leave with me."

She watched him closely, saw the firm line of his jaw tighten around clamped teeth, saw the decision take form in his eyes.

"Then I'm going, too." He pulled her to him as he spoke, and she gasped at the mutual heat of their bodies, at the state of readiness of his . . .

. . . and of her own, as he slid his hands down her sides to her waist, then lifted her to a height where he could slip her on top of his extended flesh.

Lowering her in place, he clasped her to him, his face pressed between her breasts. She wrapped her legs around his hips and held his head in her arms. As one they trembled at the surge of passion that charged through their bodies.

His hands on her hips, he began to move her rhythmically over him until their passions were honed to the finest edge, at which time he cradled her in his arms and moved toward the berth, where he lowered them, and with a final flurry of thrusts, brought them to the height of ecstasy they had sought.

His body and mind weakened by spent muscles and emotions, he collapsed beside her. As in another dimension, he felt her snuggle against him.

Finally his eyes found hers. "Is that why you went to so much trouble to ravish my body tonight? To get your way with me?"

She grinned, remembering her earlier question to him. "I ravished your body because I love you." She kissed his lips; her eyes twinkled. "But it worked both ways, didn't it?"

He pulled her close with practically useless arms. "I have no doubt it always will, princess." After a soft, lingering, reassuring kiss, he swatted her bare bottom.

"Get dressed while I go make preparations. We will leave tonight, so Blakesborough will not know you are gone."

Chapter Fourteen

They cast off after midnight—three of them, Max, Logan, and Stella—into a placid sea of darkness, on a mission she dared not think of as anything but one of hope. Although the storm had passed, the sky remained overcast, and they kept their heading by compass readings—and by dead reckoning.

When Logan returned to the cabin after making preparations, it was with Jacobs in tow. The tone was business, she saw at once. No emotions; serious, deliberate actions; nothing more, nothing less.

"Max is readying our boat," he told Jacobs. As he spoke he scooped a handful of papers from the desk drawer and stuffed them into a waterproof metal box.

She watched him remove a shelf from the bookcase, revealing a hidden compartment into which he secured the box, locked the door, then replaced the shelf. He handed Jacobs the key. "These are the inventories and the background material we have been working on. If anything should happen . . . be sure they get to Admiral Farragut. We may not have enough for a conviction yet, but it will make the scoundrel mighty uncomfortable."

"Yes, sir." Jacobs buttoned his pocket over the key.

"Remain by the door, as though she were still inside," Logan continued. He turned his attention to Stella. "Stuff in your shirt. Here's a belt." In addition to the belt, he handed her a cap and a heavy coat. "Wear the coat, and tuck your hair . . ."—his eyes lightened a bit and he winked at her—". . . what there is of it, beneath here. We don't want blond curls shining in the lantern light."

His precautions produced a swirl of anxiety in her stomach, but she did as he said, then followed him out the door.

"Max and I should return before daybreak," he told Jacobs. "If Blakesborough questions our absence, tell him we went to reconnoiter."

Max and Logan rowed, and Stella sat rigid in the center of the small boat. She drew the coat around her shoulders, wondering whether she shivered from the weather or from the prospects of what lay ahead.

Mostly from the day's hours ahead, she knew. If Papá was at Titlum-Tatlum, could she persuade him to leave? Although a compassionate and loving father, he had always had the last word with her. She had never been able to sway him, unless he agreed with her anyway—never against his will. Never. This time it would be imperative that she succeed.

As Max and Logan pulled the boat through the water Stella peered into the darkness and rehearsed what she would say, how she would approach him.

All the while, she prayed he would be gone, that he had taken the new vessel and traveled to Los Olmos. . . .

Suddenly the boat collided with a sandbar near shore, jolting Stella out of her deliberations. A hand groped for her in the darkness—a beloved hand, cold and wet now from the elements. It stroked her cheek with a rough sort of tenderness that brought a lump to her throat.

The boat swayed as a body left it, and ahead of her she saw the circle of Max's lantern light the lead rope. "The water's no more than ankle deep," he called in a hoarse whisper, "but it's cold enough to freeze your toes."

She scrambled to her feet; Logan took her arm. They exited the boat without speaking. At the feel of the cold water creeping up her pant legs, she gasped, and he chuckled beside her. She jabbed him in the ribs with her elbow. His hand tightened about her arm, then released her to help Max.

Tenderness. Intimacy. *Damn this war,* she thought.

Once they had the boat well out of the water, Max doused the lantern. Darkness closed around them. The few shapes she had seen beyond the glow of the lantern disappeared as down a well. She felt totally lost.

Logan dropped an arm around her shoulder. "Lead on," he whispered in her ear.

She leaned against him; his body warmed her shoulder; he smelled of sweat and saltwater, like a wet dog, she thought. She grasped him around the waist.

"I'm not sure where we are," she admitted.

"What do you think, Max?" Logan questioned.

"Galveston Island should be to our right," he paused. "Not far, from the sound of the surf . . ."

While he pondered, so did Stella. The small island of Titlum-Tatlum should be partially concealed by this mound of sand on which they stood. By daylight, however, the masts of the new vessel, if it was still there, would be visible, plain as the sun in the sky. "I know where I am now," she told Logan. "Go on back; I'll make my way."

"No chance, princess. Do you think I would leave you alone in the dead of night on an isolated stretch of sand?"

"You're not coming with me," she objected.

"I'm coming further than this. I don't intend to leave, until I'm sure where you are . . . and who is around."

She sighed. "You would think I had never gone anywhere on my own."

"If I'd had a say in it," he retorted, a bit too seriously to suit her, "you wouldn't have."

His over-protectiveness both soothed and irritated. "Fortunately," she laughed, "you didn't. If I thought that attitude was a portent of things to come . . ."

The darkness had isolated them from Max's proximity; it

was almost as if they were alone on an island in the middle of nowhere. Logan moved a hand seductively up her back, beneath the oversize cap, and clasped her head, ruffling her silky curls. Then he pulled her face to his and kissed her, finding her lips by instinct in the darkness.

His lips were warm, his kiss wet and wonderful, and she responded for a moment, knowing this was a feeling to take with her into the lonely days ahead.

"Time to go." She dropped her hand from his waist, found his hand, and pulled him forward—as nearly as she could determine forward—across the sand. "Keep quiet, and promise you will leave when I tell you to."

"Yes, sir," he whispered near her ear.

She stumbled over a sand dune, caught her balance. "I wish I had time to show you what I think of your attitude," she hissed good-naturedly, yet meaning every word.

He squeezed her fingers. "So do I, princess."

From the top of the dune, she saw a fire in the distance. "That's the camp."

"How do you know?"

She shrugged. "Why don't you believe me? Max, tell him where we are."

Max caught up with them, from where he had trailed at a discreet distance. "That's Wedemeyer's camp, all right. See those shapes at the fringe of light? That's his . . . uh, junk."

Silently, the three of them stared at the camp, not over a hundred yards in distance.

Logan spoke first. "How do you get there from here?"

"Walk," she responded.

"Through what?" he wanted to know. "Sand? Or water?"

She sighed against him, then encircled his waist with her arms and kissed his lips. "I said walk, not swim."

During the past months, she had gotten over the awkwardness she initially felt at sharing their intimacies with Max. They had had no choice, except to remain aloof to each other, and that had not been a choice, not for either of them. In the last few days aboard the *Victory,* while she shared Logan's cabin in front of the entire crew, she had forcefully put aside the fact that every man of them knew—and likely discussed—the intimacies taking place inside that cabin. She and Logan talked about it from time to time, but neither of them knew a better way; neither of them was comfortable with the idea, but it was the only way to be together—and, at that particular time, the only way to keep her out of Blakesborough's clutches. The alternative was unthinkable. The solution heavenly, for the most part.

"That's one more reason we must get married the first chance we find," Logan had said more than once.

And she agreed. But the chance had not arisen, so now she kissed him good-bye, clung to him a moment, then stood back.

"Go on, now," she urged. "You must return to the *Victory* before dawn."

"Then you'd better hurry. I intend to stand right here until you emerge into that circle of light. Call to the camp, so someone will come out to greet you. I'm not leaving until I see a friendly face. . . ."—he stroked her cheek with the back of his hand—". . . *another* friendly face."

She pressed his hand close to her cheek. "I'm going."

"Twenty-four hours," he reminded her retreating figure. She turned, listened. "I promised you twenty-four hours to get away from here. Be damned sure you do it. I'll have hell to pay, keeping Blakesborough at bay longer than that."

She blew him a kiss and turned to go, but he stopped her again.

"Remember . . . if Giddeon *won't* leave, rig a white flag on something tall enough for me to see it—the mast of that damned ship, or something—and I'll come in to get you out."

* * *

The metallic noise of a rifle being cocked was only degrees louder than her thumping heart.

"Hello, the camp!" She approached the circle of firelight with determined steps. Her spine nearly tingled at the thought she might be shot for a thief—or worse, a Yankee—by her own father.

"Where did you come from?" a young man's voice challenged.

Giddeon came out of Wedemeyer's hut like grapeshot out of a cannon. "Sugar! What in tarnation are you doing here?"

She fell into his arms and clung to him, allowing her pulse to resume its normal pace. Then she turned and stared into the blackness across the sand. She hadn't heard Logan leave; she wouldn't be able to, she knew. She hoped he had, now that Papá had shown himself.

After another moment, she went inside the hut with her father and the young man—Carl, Giddeon introduced him as—where she held the two of them and Captain Wedemeyer captive with her tale of being captured and rescued and now set free, all by Yankees.

Finally, drawing a deep breath, she stated her mission. "Logan promised me twenty-four hours to get you away from here. Then they will blow this . . ."—she swung her arms wide to include the multitude of Captain Wedemeyer's treasures—". . . everything . . . to kingdom come."

They stared wide-eyed: Carl into the fire, as though mesmerized, she thought, by the idea of his own demise; Captain Wedemeyer dispiritedly at his treasures; Giddeon Duval with admiration at his daughter.

"Twenty-four hours . . ."—he thought aloud—". . . that should give us enough time."

She exhaled, relieved at how readily he accepted her report—relieved, only to find moments later, she should have been skeptical.

"Where are Delos and Felix?" she asked. "And Kosta?"

"They've gone ahead," Giddeon told her. "Edward Stavinoha is with them; he'll continue on to Corpus Christi to see about his family." Behind them, Captain Wedemeyer worked feverishly, gathering equipment to take along, she supposed.

"They took the . . . ah, the vessel down the coast when the storm hit. Carl here had gone to Los Olmos to bring me word of your mother, so I waited for him to return. The women and children have gone home, by the way. With our side holding both San Fernando and Corpus Christi, the Yankees pulled out of Los Olmos—taking most of our cattle, of course."

"Of course," she sighed. "But what about the vessel? How far away is it?"

"They should have gotten as far south as Velasco by now . . . perhaps even to Jones Creek."

She frowned.

"In twenty-four hours we can easily make the northern reaches of Matagorda Bay, don't you think, Wedemeyer?"

Wedemeyer grunted. "If we can fool the Yankee scoundrels long enough."

Stella's frown deepened. "What are you planning?"

"For you, a horse ride," Giddeon told her. "I want you to take a message to Colonel Shea. Tell him we need support from whichever steamer is nearer the north end of Matagorda Bay—the *Lucy Gwin* or the *Cora*. That we're coming down the coastline . . ."

"Papá!"

He stared at her silently . . . then continued. "Tell him to get some Heel Flies out to the islands, and to dismount the lighthouses at Half Moon Reef and Matagorda."

Stella could hardly believe what she was hearing. "You're going to *draw* his attack? Deliberately?"

"Sugar. We'll be well out of reach by the time the *Victory* crew bombards Titlum-Tatlum."

"Then why do you need military support?"

He shrugged. "To buy time. A dozen Federal ships sail the Gulf waters. . . ."

"Please, Papá."

"Sugar. You know the importance of the *Stella Duval*. . . ."

Her eyes widened. "The . . . what?"

He grinned, sheepish. "Didn't I tell you?"

She shook her head.

He shrugged. "What better name for a rebel-rousing blockade runner than that of the heroine of the Cotton Road?"

"The heroine of the Cotton Road?" she questioned.

"You bet."

She glared at him, hands on hips. "Then why am I the appointed message bearer? If she's *my* ship, I am going to sail on her. Carl can carry the mail."

Giddeon cast his eyes skyward. "Women! Are you all alike? Just when I was hoping to steal a part of my heart back from your mother—not much, mind you, just a little bit—you come along. The gods don't play fair. If a man has but one child, it should be male."

She frowned. "Papá! You have never said such a thing to me before!"

Grinning, he tousled her hair, studying the short curls a minute. When he spoke, his voice came from far away. "A girl-child dooms a man, sugar. You are too much like your mother; I have never been able to say no to her, either."

His words recalled Logan's, and she threw her arms around his neck. "Oh, Papá, we're going to have a wonderful life . . . after the war."

"That we are; I have no doubt about it. Now, if you're coming with me, get a move-on. The sooner we finish up this war, the sooner we can get started on that wonderful life."

Captain Wedemeyer interrupted them with his enthusiasm. "Yee-haw! I have the perfect plan."

While daylight grew as an increasingly bright reminder of their twenty-four-hour grace period, Wedemeyer led them around his yard of treasures, ordering them to carry this and that, until at last his plan began to take shape.

"To destroy the vessel by cannon, if that's their intent, they won't come within more than fifteen hundred, two thousand yards of the shoreline. From that distance, this mast will fool 'em, sure as shooting."

Stella stood back and surveyed their work. A tall mast, accompanied by the two shorter ones they had dragged from other places in the yard, now stood spaced to Wedemeyer's instructions, partially rigged. Yes, they did resemble a sailing ship—or perhaps they would from a distance. "How long do you think it will fool them?" she asked.

Giddeon tied the last square knot and turned to study her. "We'll have your namesake hidden behind the barrier islands before they discover the ruse, if they ever do."

"They will," she said quietly. Logan wouldn't bombard the island, then leave without inspecting the destruction for himself. He would want to know they all escaped. And they would have, she thought, thanks to Captain Wedemeyer's scheme.

By the time the three of them saddled up and headed overland to Matagorda Bay, Carl had long since left with his message for Colonel Shea. With luck everything would turn out all right.

She watched Captain Wedemeyer survey his property one last time. Almost everything, she recanted. The captain would lose all he owned here. It might look like junk to Max . . . to her, even. But to the captain, these treasures represented his whole life. Flicking his hand in a brief salute, he turned in the saddle and led the way to the mainland. Stella followed, subdued by the loss he shouldered so willingly.

* * *

They reached the mouth of the Colorado River by night-fall and found the *Stella Duval* anchored in a snug cove inside the protection of the peninsula.

"We will await word from Carl," Giddeon told them. "We don't want to head into the bay if the Federals have retaken Pass Cavallo."

Stella stared at the sleek ship. Her name glistened in bright new paint from its hull. Her name. On a ship. And such a glorious vessel it was.

"Oh, Captain Wedemeyer. This is a magnificent vessel."

His smile reached from ear to ear, and the expression in his eyes told her more than he could ever have said in words. He might have left the majority of his treasures behind on Titlum-Tatlum, never to see them again. But here, in front of him, stood his pride and joy, like a new child, his hope for the future; that left behind, already sloughed off like old skin.

Delos, Felix, and Kosta came on deck to greet them. "We heard the fighting was fierce in Corpus Christi," Delos said. "What do you know of our families?"

Stella recounted the details she had earlier told Giddeon, although she omitted Logan's part in it. "They left Los Olmos ahead of the Federals. I saw them in Corpus."

"Carl's news was worth waiting for," Giddeon put in. "The womenfolk and children have returned to Los Olmos. The Confederates control the entire area now."

"We should have smooth sailing," Felix said. "Word has it General Banks has moved his land troops to Louisiana."

"Ha!" Wedemeyer shouted. "We scared 'em off at Caney Creek. I knew our fellers had it in 'em."

"What about the islands?" Giddeon asked. "Matagorda and Mustang?"

Since no one knew the answer, the consensus was to wait to hear from Carl. "While we wait," Kosta told them. "We have a little untended business . . . now the señorita has

302

arrived."

Stella frowned, questioning.

"I have never built a ship that sailed without being duly christened."

A spirit of camaraderie followed, with Kosta producing a bottle of questionable liquor—questionable only as to its contents, not its suitability for breaking across the bow of a ship. Stella swung mightily, once . . . twice . . . and on the third blow she splattered them all with thick glass and amber liquid.

"Lucky we don't have to drink the stuff," Felix moaned.

"Unlucky we don't have something else to drink."

Lucky we're here, safe from the Federal ships, Stella thought. Unlucky she was here without Logan Cafferty.

They spent the night on board the *Stella Duval,* on deck, beneath a sky full of stars, wrapped in blankets Captain Wedemeyer saved from destruction back at Titlum-Tatlum.

Stella lay awake into the morning hours thinking of Titlum-Tatlum. They hadn't heard cannons. Should they have? Giddeon had sat as long as the light allowed, looking out at sea through his telescope, but he hadn't seen sight of pursuit. Should he have?

Did the Federals know their ruse? Were they keeping out of sight until the moment of attack? And where was Logan? On board the *Victory?* Or had he gone ashore . . . and stayed? Would he follow them?

And if he did, would he discover their trick?

And if he discovered the trick, what would he do about it?

The questions were endless, but not the night. Morning came with no sign of the Federals; Carl arrived with word the coast was clear past Indianola and Pass Cavallo.

At Indianola they took on cargo—six hundred bales of cotton sent by Mr. Ransom, along with a message of praise on getting the new ship in the water in record time.

The first report of trouble came from Major Hobby's

troops at Fort Esperanza after the *Stella Duval* glided undetected across Pass Cavallo: From the darkened Matagorda lighthouse, Federal ships had been sighted moving steadily along, as if scouting the area, with a purpose in mind.

"I'll send the *Cora* into Matagorda Bay as a decoy," Major Hobby told Giddeon.

"Much obliged. We will take cover in the reeds today, then move south under cover of darkness."

Stella couldn't remember a longer day, unless it was when she had been confined to the dark cell below decks in the *Victory.* At first it was fun, exploring her namesake vessel, but by noon, when they heard shells exploding in Matagorda Bay, the novelty of hiding behind reeds hoping the thin spires of their masts would remain invisible to Federal telescopes that were surely trained on this reef of islands — and beyond — wore distressfully thin.

By nightfall, when Giddeon called them to man their posts silently, not a steady heart beat among them, she suspected. Using long poles, the men positioned themselves on either side of the sleek new vessel, propelling it forward without the help of its nine-hundred-horsepower engine, of which Captain Wedemeyer was so proud.

The moon rose, pale in the dark sky. Stars shown in their patterns, guiding them. She looked for and found the North Star. The portent it held for her earlier had diffused now that they had safely escaped Titlum-Tatlum. She wondered what had happened on the little island. No matter, she thought, lives had not been lost.

Frogs croaked from rushes nearby, fish jumped in the waters ahead of them, and far to stern, Felix hummed a poignant, almost mournful tune. Giddeon held the wheel, his eyes trained on the narrow channel.

He called softly to her. "After we leave Corpus Christi, remind me to show you where I took your mother on her first boat ride."

"Was that when you brought her the little colt called

Navidad?" she asked.

"Yes." He grunted then, in obvious disgust. "Don't know what made me speak of that trip. It was far from pleasant."

"Was Mamá seasick?"

"No, the trouble was me. I acted like a damned idiot. It's a wonder she didn't give up on me after that."

Stella could see only his profile, rigid against the lightened sky, as though his head were sculpted from black marble. She had heard the stories, how her father intended to live with her mother only long enough to sell Los Olmos for money to salvage a ship he had lost at sea. The cargo of that vessel, rumored to have been thousands, perhaps millions, in Mexican gold and jewels, remained a mystery deep in the waters off Bagdad to this day.

"Have you ever regretted not salvaging the *Estelle?*"

Giddeon laughed softly, then answered in a firm voice. "Not a day, sugar; not a single day. I'm a real lucky man."

His sincerity strummed a chord of poignancy in her heart, and she suddenly became very lonely — lonely in a wonderful, positive way. She hoped Logan would be as sure of his decision twenty years from now. Then, for fear of cursing the future with too positive an outlook, she recanted — she hoped they made it past this war first, then she hoped he never regretted loving her.

She was certain she would never regret loving him. Like Papá, not for a single day.

By daylight they had made it as far as San Antonio Bay, where they were able to hide in a deep cove, more protected from the barrier islands, thus from Federal eyes and guns, than during the previous day.

The following night they were equally successful, passing unmolested from the waters behind Matagorda Island to the cover of Saint Joseph Island. That night, they found another deep cove in Aransas Bay for protection.

Although they had neither seen nor heard sign of Federal pursuit, their nerves were wearing thin.

305

"When we get to Corpus Christi," Giddeon told Stella, "I want you to hire a horse and ride straight to Los Olmos. Carl can go with you."

"Let me ride with you as far as Los Olmos Bay," she pleaded. "I won't ask to go farther."

"No," he responded. "We have taken too many chances with your life already. It's time for you to go home. When the war is over . . ."

"You talk just like Logan," she said furiously.

He tousled her short hair. "That young man and I have a lot in common, sugar."

That evening they made it as far as the town of Lamar, where the Heel Flies called them ashore.

"Thought you might like to hear about Colonel Ford's victory," the Home Guard commander, a Captain Granger, told the crew. "His Cavalry of the West has retaken Laredo."

Cheers erupted from the crew of the *Stella Duval*.

"He's headed down the Rio Grande," the captain continued. "That old Indian fighter's got 'em on the run now. We'll have Brownsville in our hands by the time you get there, Duval."

Since the town of Lamar sat directly behind Saint Joseph Island, Giddeon decided to spend the next day in hiding there. He sent Delos and Felix ashore to refill barrels of drinking water.

The news the men brought back confirmed Captain Granger's report.

"Yee-haw!" Wedemeyer whooped. "We finished this baby in the nick of time. The rebs are about to retake the whole coastline and the river. And we, men, will have clear sailing! What a ship! We'll whip those Yankees yet!"

Stella watched the others join the cheering, including Giddeon. She turned and walked to a secluded place at the far end of the ship. Giddeon came after her.

"I didn't mean I want the war to continue, sugar. It's

just . . ."

"I understand, Papá." She sighed. "Logan feels the same way. What I don't understand is how you—any of you—can enjoy war."

"It isn't enjoyment." He stared into the bright afternoon sky. "I suppose it's the adventure. . . ."—he shrugged as if not wholly understanding the phenomenon, himself—". . . some of us have adventure in our blood. That doesn't mean we enjoy war."

She studied him, not understanding him any more than she did Logan. All she knew was that she loved them both, and adventure or not, she intended to do everything in her power to keep them both alive until this "adventure" was over.

The first sign of real trouble came when they weighed anchor and began the first leg of the journey that would carry them through Aransas Pass before morning. They had progressed fifty feet or so from the dock when the first bomb struck, exploding on the main deck near the stern with a jolt that sent all hands scrambling.

"We've rammed one of the torpedoes," Delos called from the bow.

The second bomb struck amid ship, splintering the deck and tearing through the opposite side of the hull, leaving no doubt as to its origin.

"Abandon ship," Giddeon yelled above the shrill whine of shells. "Get to shore." With a heave, he tossed Stella into the water. "Swim to shore and don't stop running."

"Are you coming?"

His answer was to jump into the water behind her.

She swam furiously almost the entire distance. When her knees struck the sandy bottom, she struggled to her feet and clawed through a tangle of reeds, her path lighted by the flash and flare of exploding cannons.

The acrid odor of gunpowder stung her nose; she wondered whether it was merely the terror of being struck by exploding shells that brought the smell to mind.

On shore she discovered things were not much better. If the Federals had intended to destroy only the *Stella Duval,* they had since changed their plans. Like wolves with the taste of blood in their palates, the Federal attackers proceeded to shell the small town. Giddeon took her arm.

"This way."

He half-dragged her toward a grove of windswept oaks; she gained her footing and shook loose from him.

"Lead the way, I'll follow," she shouted above the din, which now included not only exploding shells and splintering wood, but running feet and frightened voices.

"No," he answered. "Take cover in there; I'm going to find Delos, and . . ."

Before she could respond, he shoved her into the grove of trees and retraced his steps.

Half dazed with the suddenness of the attack, she watched the melee around her. The people of Lamar ran from their homes like ants from a bed stirred up by a child. And in the nick of time for some of them. Houses splintered like kindling; fires sputtered in the dusky damp evening.

She tore her eyes away, looking back toward the bay, where Papá had by now disappeared. She searched for the *Stella Duval,* but could find no sign of the ship in the growing darkness.

The attack had come upon them so suddenly she had not had time to grasp a weapon before Giddeon flung her from the ship. Now she sat, helpless.

Felix found her. "The Yankees are coming across the bay," he shouted. "Let's get out of here."

"Where's Papá? I won't leave . . ."

Felix grabbed her arm. "Come on."

He pulled her away from the grove of trees, dragged her across a clearing, and found shelter behind one of the few houses left still standing. "They're going to sack this town,"

Felix predicted under his breath.

"Where's Papá?" She searched the rushing crowd.

"Wedemeyer was hit; Giddeon and Delos are bringing him to safe ground."

Stella's heart missed a beat. "He can't . . ."

"He'll be all right. Come on. I promised him I would get you out of here."

For a few yards he dragged her resisting body away from the crowd. Finally, he stopped. "Look. I can't drag you all the way to safety. You're going to have to cooperate . . ."

"I will not leave without Papá."

He sighed. "I'd have thought one stint in that captain's dungeon would have been enough . . ."

Stella's mind shut out the rest of Felix's harangue. Things had happened so suddenly she hadn't given thought to who the Federals were . . . to what ship attacked them. "Is it the *Victory?*"

"Doesn't matter . . ."

She pulled from his grasp and dashed back into the crowd. It mattered to her. Although the last thing she wanted to think about was Captain Blakesborough and his dungeon, as Felix called it, she had no intention of standing by while Papá was taken prisoner by the man.

Suddenly she saw them—the whole group of them, two men supporting a third whose left leg appeared to drag even in the growing darkness. Behind them, two others searched protectively.

But it wasn't Captain Wedemeyer who was injured.

"Papá!" She rushed to him, skidded to a stop inches from embracing him. Suddenly her mind raced to a halt as well, then changed gears. "Follow me," she instructed.

Somewhere inside her, panic raced rampant. But she would not let it reach her brain. Her father was wounded, how badly she did not know; she had to get him to safety.

People ran this way and that, but their cries faded to the recesses of her mind. She looked back at the men helping her father. *Hurry,* she thought. *Please, hurry.*

"Pick him up," she called. "You'll make better time if you carry him." She scanned the area for a horse . . . for a carriage . . . for anything with which to get Papá away from the fighting.

She saw a barn. "Felix, open those doors, quickly."

Inside, she choked on the thick musky odor of hay. Noises from behind them clamored in her ears—voices, distraught voices, desperate voices. "Close the doors," she ordered. "Lock them, quickly."

As in shock, she observed the scene: Kosta and Carl swung the double barn doors closed and Felix dropped the bar in place. "Check the opposite end," he instructed Carl.

While Delos and Wedemeyer set Giddeon on a bale of hay, Stella took a lantern from a hook and, using sulfur matches she located in a little packet inside Giddeon's own waterproof jacket, she lighted it. The only image in her mind, one of childhood, was of the matches he had always carried in the little bag. "A habit from my years at sea, sugar," she heard him tell her.

Kneeling before him, she squinted into his face. His eyes were closed, his jaws slack. Alarm spread like lighted kerosene. She patted his cheek—gently.

Delos cleared his throat. "He's just passed out, Stella. He's not . . . yet."

Yet! Quickly, she set to work.

Taking the knife from his own scabbard, she cut away a portion of his bloody trousers. Her heart beat frantically in her ears, shutting out all sounds except that of her own terror, which clawed inside her as she stared at the unrecognizable mass that had been the calf of his leg.

Suddenly she knew only one thing mattered . . . only one. To get him home. In panic she slit one of her own sleeves and ripped it from its socket. Giving no thought to gentleness, she bound his shattered leg tightly, pulling the cloth around and around, as many times as it would go.

She had to staunch the flow of blood. She had to get him home . . . to her mother. Her mind swirled with fear, leaving room for only one vision . . . her father and mother . . .

Together.

She had to get him home. She could do nothing for him here; possibly no one could. If he must die, it had to be in the arms of the woman he loved . . . her mother.

That, she knew, is where she would want Logan Cafferty, if such a horrible disaster should befall him. And that is where he would want to be—in the arms of the woman he loved.

Logan Cafferty sat in his cabin on board the *Victory,* rereading Secretary Wells's dispatch for what seemed like the hundredth time:

> Report confirmed. Advance to
> Brazos Santiago with *Victory.*
> Verify facts before proceeding.
> Report to Admiral Farragut.
> Good luck.
>
> Gideon Wells,
> US Secretary of the Navy

Although cryptic, the message was as clear as Stella's green eyes. Secretary Wells "confirmed" his own suspicions about Dar Blakesborough's dealings with the French. But he required positive proof before he would allow Logan to step in. As disappointing as it was not to be able to put the man away, Logan understood the secretary's concerns.

Blakesborough's father would have every star and bar and oak leaf—he glanced down at the silver eagle on his shirt—and eagle in the Navy and Marine Corps, if charges were brought against his son, then proven false.

Logan sighed, satisfied. It was no less than he had hoped, no more than he had expected: the opportunity to finish this investigation of Blakesborough's dealings with the French. Wasn't that why Secretary Wells had placed him on board the *Victory* in the first place?

At a knock, Logan stuffed the communiqué into a shirt pocket and crossed to the door. Max entered, followed by Ensign Jacobs. Logan frowned at their equally earnest demeanors.

"What's ailing you two?" he joked. "We've got Blakesborough on the run." Besides that, he thought, the fiasco at Titlum-Tatlum was over; Stella was well on her way home with her father. . . .

Well, he conceded, knowing her, she might not be on her way home, but what better hands to leave her in than those of her own father. He smiled, remembering the exuberant embrace he had himself witnessed between the two before he and Max retreated from Titlum-Tatlum.

Max cleared his throat and thrust what appeared to be a piece of kindling toward Logan. "This."

Logan squinted at the splintered plank, at the newly painted letters: *Stella Duval*. His heart stopped at the sight; gingerly, he took it in his hand. "What the hell is this?"

"One of the crew from the USS *Constitution* brought it on board," Jacobs told him. At Logan's continued frown, Max finished.

"The *Constitution* bombarded the town of Lamar, back of Saint Joseph Island three days ago. When we passed by there in the night, some of the crew members were stranded on the island."

Logan frowned; his brain struggled to grasp the facts—his mind shied away from learning the truth.

Max continued his explanation. "The fellow who had this on him said the fight started when the *Constitution* saw a blockade runner shoving off down the channel; the battle leveled the town. The *Constitution's* captain filled his cargo hold with prisoners; that's why some of the crew was left behind, to make space for more prisoners."

"Casualties?" Logan whispered, unable to speak louder.

Jacobs and Max shook their heads. Jacobs answered. "No way of knowing, Colonel."

Logan's mind swayed with the image of Stella, held prisoner again. Yet, wasn't that the best he could hope for? "Where is the *Constitution* now?"

"Headed for Brazos Santiago," Max said. "Just ahead of us."

Chapter Fifteen

Later, after they escaped the burning town of Lamar, Stella realized she had higher aspirations for her father than for him to die in her mother's arms.

Her greatest desire of all was to save his life. Fortunately, the actions she had undertaken in a state of near shock had served both purposes.

As soon as she finished tying her shirt sleeve in place around his leg, she glanced about the barn. From outside, shouts of frightened evacuees filtered through the thin barn walls, like a howling winter storm. She listened for sounds of cannon, but those had ceased, although sporadic gunfire still erupted, turning shouts to shrieks.

"We must get out of here. Quickly. We cannot allow the Yankees to capture Papá—or any of you."

A wagon stood at one end of the barn partially filled with hay; from a stall a horse nickered.

Stella jumped to her feet. The horse trampled in the stall, frightened, she knew, by the unnatural panic surrounding him.

"We'll take the wagon," she said. No sooner were her words uttered than the men grasped her meaning.

While Kosta and Felix prepared Giddeon a bed in the wagon, Wedemeyer searched for and found harness and tack, and Delos brought the horse around. In no time, they were ready to leave.

The clamor outside increased, filling Stella with new and

equally terrifying fears. She climbed onto the driver's seat. "Bring weapons," she instructed. "Hoes, pitchforks, anything you can find."

Kosta crawled up beside her and took the reins. "Get in the back with your papá," he said.

She glanced into the hay-filled bed of the wagon. Giddeon could barely be seen, surrounded as he was with hay and the other men, who had taken her suggestion and now held farm tools to supplement their meager supply of ammunition against an enemy as feared as the Yankees: frightened, fleeing civilians.

"No," she replied. She had relinquished the reins, however, and now jerked a whip from where it was attached beside the wagon seat. The instant Carl threw open the door, she cracked the whip across the horse's rump; the animal bolted from the barn. At the last moment, Carl vaulted into the wagon bed and they entered the fracas outside the barn.

When at last Kosta's pleas to stop whipping the horse broke through Stella's muddle of fear, her arm felt like a limp rag, but her brain had somehow settled.

They had left behind the majority of fleeing people. Night had fallen around them, and the North Star shone above her shoulder.

"Why don't you climb in the back now, Stella?" Kosta suggested again.

"No. We must get him home to Mamá. How long will it take?"

His voice was gentle when he answered. "We won't make it at all if you kill our horse."

"Oh," she gasped. "I hadn't realized . . ."

"We'll get him there, don't you worry about that."

But the first time they stopped to let the horse water at a stream, she checked the bandages on Giddeon's leg and found them soaked. Without a word, Delos handed her his shirt, which she tore into strips. While she rebound the shattered leg, Delos took one of the strips to the stream and bathed Gid-

315

deon's face when he returned.

"Querida . . ." Giddeon called, his voice no more than a low moan. *"Querida . . ."*

The sound filled her with renewed panic . . . and anguish.

"He's delirious," Delos said.

"He is calling my mother," Stella said, scrambling to the driver's seat beside Kosta. "Come. Quickly. We must get him home."

Without stopping again, they forded the Nueces at the Santa Margarita Crossing and headed for Banquete.

"He is becoming more feverish by the mile," Delos said.

Stella looked at the sky; it was nearly high noon. "It is the sun," she retorted stubbornly. "Shield his body from the sun."

Kosta whipped up the horse. "If there's a doc at Banquete, we'd best stop and let him look at that leg. If it has to come off . . ."

"No!" Stella gasped. "We must get him home . . . to Mamá."

For the most part, Giddeon himself remained in a state of either unconsciousness or shock, Stella wasn't sure which. She hoped, whichever it was, it kept him from feeling the pain such a wound would surely cause.

Kosta didn't speak until the station house at Banquete came into sight in the distance. "We'll water the horse here, and get a bite to eat. And if a doc's in town . . ."

"No," Stella interrupted.

"You know, Stella"—the gentleness in Kosta's voice alerted her defenses—". . . you're the spitting image of your mother."

She turned to him, wary. "What do you mean?"

Kosta smiled, his eyes on the road. "Did I ever tell you about the day your mother told . . . ordered me would likely be a better term," he corrected, ". . . to build the bridge on top of the new casa grande?"

She studied him, wondering at his sudden urge to reminisce. "No."

316

He flicked the reins across the horse's back. "Giddeon had gone off to Mexico with a herd of mustangs; he'd taken about every able-bodied man on the ranch along, except me. Come to find out, it was your mother's doings."

"Mamá?" Stella questioned, still unsure where this story would lead.

Kosta nodded. "She kept me behind with a purpose. You see, your papá was bound and determined to leave her and the baby—that would be you—and head on back to sea; your mamá was just as determined to keep him at Los Olmos."

"I've heard that."

"What you haven't heard is the fire with which she went about it," Kosta said. "Desperate as she was to find some way to hold on to him, she decided to have me build a bridge atop the house. She was determined, I could see that as soon as she told me her plan."

"Why are you telling me this?"

Kosta drew rein in front of the station house in Banquete. He set the brake and turned to her. "Because, honey, it wasn't the bridge of a ship that would hold your papá on dry land . . . it was your mamá. Nothing more, nothing less. I admired her spunk, her determination; like I admire yours now. But I'll tell you straight out . . ."—turning he looked to Felix and Delos for support—". . . these men were there, they'll vouch for what I'm saying. Your mamá wants him home alive. Whether with one leg or two—if that's the choice—doesn't matter half as much as the two of them being able to live out their lives together."

Stella sat, scarcely breathing, while Kosta's words fell like a chilling rain over her fears. From behind her Delos and Felix mumbled in agreement. Finally, she lifted her face to the sky, sighed heavily, and squenched her lids against a rush of tears.

"If there's a doctor in town . . ." she agreed.

There was. Although since his black bag was empty of medicine and he possessed few tools of the trade, she felt sure Francisco could have done as well.

317

"You got him here in the nick of time," the doc, whose name she failed to hear what with the other urgencies surrounding them, told the somber group. He had unwrapped Giddeon's leg and washed it. When Stella looked at it, her stomach tumbled.

"These bones will never mend," he said. "They're splintered from the ankle nigh up to the knee."

"How much must you remove?" she asked.

The old doctor studied Giddeon's thigh at some length, pressing and prodding the muscles and the area around the knee joint. "I'll save the knee, that way he can get around practically good as new — with a peg."

Stella bathed Giddeon's face with a damp cloth and somehow kept her tears from spilling all over him. When the doctor seemed set to begin the surgery, she grasped Giddeon's hands in hers and pressed her lips against his fists. She tried to think of something to say, but she couldn't. She wondered desperately what her mother would have said.

She was grateful her mother wasn't here.

Giddeon was conscious enough that they made him understand what was transpiring; he tried to persuade Stella to leave the room, but since he was too weak to do anything about it, and since Kosta, Delos, and Felix regarded it as her right to be present, she stayed. Later, she was surprised he hadn't broken the bones in her hands, he squeezed them so hard at the moment of amputation.

Afterward, he passed out and slept fitfully through the next twelve hours.

When he awakened, she rushed to his side. She saw the pain in his eyes; she watched the questions form.

"How much . . . ?"

"Below the knee." Tears that she had been able to keep at bay until now gushed forth and streamed from her eyes.

She felt his hand tremble as he brought it to her face. "Don't, sugar. Don't." His voice was weak. Using her free hand, she wiped the tears from her face and concentrated on

318

holding them back.

"Your mamá always manages to have the last laugh," he whispered. "The first time she ever saw me, she thought I was a pirate, now I'll have a peg leg to prove her right."

They stayed on at Banquete for two more days, allowing the doctor to keep a close eye on his handiwork. Captain Wedemeyer left the second day, headed back to Titlum-Tatlum to survey the damage to his treasures.

The day before they left for Los Olmos, Stella sent Carl ahead with a message for her mother. Although she didn't specifically mention the amputation, she did say that Giddeon had been severely wounded, but was expected to make a full recovery.

To no one's surprise, Serita herself met them a little north of Camp San Fernando and rode the rest of the way to Los Olmos in the wagon bed with Giddeon.

"You were right," Stella told Kosta, beside him on the driver's seat. "How did you know?"

He grinned. "I may be nothing but a salty ol' bachelor, honey, but I ain't blind. I've been through more trying times than one shot-up leg with those two back there."

Stella cocked her head, studying him. "Why did you never marry, Kosta?"

After fidgeting a minute, he answered, "To be plumb honest with you, I never found a woman other than your mamá who was worth two cents, and your mamá was already taken. That is, of course, until you come along, and you're too young."

"Kosta," she teased. "I'm not too young for you. You may be crotchety, but you've got a lot of life left in you."

He laughed. "You're right as rain about that, honey, but . . . well, I guess you've always been somewhat like my own daughter."

She smiled.

". . . an' if what I hear is right, you're already taken yourself."

319

Stella felt herself blush under the warm spring sky. Of course, what Kosta meant by that statement and what she knew were two different things. "Papá talks too much," she laughed.

Once they got him home, Giddeon recovered faster than the doctor had expected. Those who knew him, however, were not surprised.

Being near the stagecoach route, they never lacked for news at Los Olmos, but the news they found awaiting them this time was not the news she longed to hear.

She had no word from Logan.

Other news, however, was abundant; foremost, Colonel Ford's progress down the Rio Grande.

"We've got the Yankees on the run now. They're headed straight for Brazos Santiago and the Gulf of Mexico!" Kosta enthused.

"Jorge joined the Cavalry of the West," Serita told them.

"I thought he was in charge of operations at Camp Casa Blanca," Giddeon said.

"He was. But you've witnessed the power of old Rip Ford. Jorge was so impressed with the colonel's new company, he joined up with the rank of captain."

Other, less welcome news, pertained to shortages: shortages of everything from salt—the Federals had taken El Sal del Rey again—to food and clothing, to medicine.

The last particularly affected Stella. She would not soon forget the agony her father went through during the amputation and afterward, for lack of adequate medicines.

"I'm sure a train of supplies is waiting at Laredo," she sighed one evening over supper. "I must make another drive."

The next day, news they received from two different sources confirmed her intentions.

The first was from Rio Grande City, where Colonel Ford was fighting the Federals. Jorge, the message said, had been wounded. Not seriously, but enough that he could not travel. He was confined to a military hospital.

Stella envisioned the lack of medicine. She must take another wagon train to the border for supplies. Kosta and Felix left for Rio Grande City to bring Jorge home.

The same day a message came from Harry Ransom in Alleyton saying he had a train loaded with cotton, but no drivers.

Stella and the vaqueros left the following morning.

She still had not received the one message she longed for above all others: word from Logan.

"If he comes while I am gone . . ." she told her mother.

"I will send for you, dear. At once."

Within two weeks Stella and the vaqueros had picked up the wagons—ten of them—in Alleyton and returned as far as the Santa Margarita Crossing on the Nueces.

"I remember last time we were here," Francisco mused that night after they finished eating.

"And I," she replied. "The idea of firing on that Yankee patrol boat still gives me chills. At the time it was the most horrifying experience I had ever been through. Now . . ."—she shrugged—". . . so much has transpired since then . . . and so much of it dreadful."

Francisco objected. "It is the way you look at it, señorita. The word dreadful should be reserved for the way things turn out. The things you have experienced have not turned out all that bad."

She thought about it in her bedroll that night. Francisco was right. They had been lucky. Even with Papá's lost leg and Alicia's death, things could have been worse.

Could yet be, she reminded herself, unable to keep at bay the one nightmare that had plagued her since the attack on the *Stella Duval:* Was it indeed the *Victory* that attacked them at Lamar?

And, if so, where was Logan? Had he been on board the *Victory* during the attack? Where was he now? Why had he not come to see about her? Had Dar Blakesborough at last carried out his vile threat?

When she awoke from her fitful sleep the next morning, Max was sitting at the campfire, drinking coffee.

She almost knocked him over in her enthusiasm.

"He's on board the *Victory*," Max answered her questions. "We'll catch up with him soon enough."

She sighed. There was little Max knew about "soon enough." She poured herself a cup of coffee with trembling hands.

The commotion aroused Francisco, who chastised the guard for letting a Yankee slip into camp.

"Max may be a Yankee, but he isn't an enemy," she assured her corporal.

"That is not what you told me about this man, señorita, after the way he betrayed us last time."

"Francisco, things change. I know it is hard to understand how a man can be a friend and a Yankee at the same time, but . . ."—she shrugged—". . . well, we won't tell him any secrets, if it will make you feel better. He will be a help on the drive."

Francisco snorted. "The only help we need from here on to . . ."—he paused deliberately, Stella knew—". . . for the rest of our journey the only help we need is from above, unless this . . . this Yankee can bring us rain to water our thirsty livestock."

Francisco remained adamant, not leaving Stella alone for a moment with the Yankee traitor. He did not, however, refuse Max's help in getting the wagon train on the road. It wasn't until noon that Stella found the chance—or the courage—to ask about the attack on Lamar.

"We came along three days later," Max told her. "The attacking ship was the USS *Constitution*." He tore off a large bite of tortilla wrapped around slices of jerky. "We picked up some of the *Constitution*'s crew. One of them had the nameplate from the blockade runner. Logan was fit to be tied when he saw your name, painted fresh like that."

"Where is he?"

"Logan thinks . . ."—pausing, he cleared his throat and ran a hand through his sandy hair—". . . ah, he *hopes* you and your father have been taken to Brazos Santiago with the *Constitution's* other prisoners. He set me ashore at Los Olmos Bay to get word to your mother."

Three days later, they pulled into Camp San Fernando and were engulfed by a wild celebration.

"Old Rip took Brownsville back from the Yankees!"

"We've got 'em running with their tails between their legs now, boys!"

"We'll whip 'em this go 'round!"

Max took the news hard, she could tell. He went off by himself and sat staring into the night.

Stella followed him. The sky was clear, and she immediately found the North Star, like a persistent guiding light. Always there, leading them onward. The only trouble was, they never got anywhere. If it was true that they had the Federals running and were whipping them, it would be wonderful, because it would signify the end of a war too long fought.

But she had heard that refrain before, and it was old. Like the chorus of a song sung after each verse. Would it never end? Would they never have peace again? Would the rest of her life be spent wishing upon a star?

Suddenly she knew the only thing that had any meaning for her was *when* she would see Logan again. Not for how long. Only when.

The idea of their living together . . . happily ever after, as he had said . . . appeared further away than ever. Early solutions to their other problems seemed as remote: the outcome of the war, always "around the corner," never was; neither was an end to the suffering, to the killing and maiming. In the overall sweep of the war, her simple contributions—taking an occasional train load of cotton to market and returning with foodstuffs and medicine—seemed woefully inadequate.

She recalled her despair at learning how little control she had over her life. Now, she was reminded of her own inadequacies again; this time in a matter of much graver concern.

At Brazos Santiago Logan would be in the middle of the Brownsville fighting, and all she could do was sit here and pray Francisco was right—that this would not be a dreadful experience, that when it finally ended, it would end all right. Giddeon's recent wound did not help assuage her fears, however.

She turned to Max. "He won't have cause to go ashore in Brownsville . . . will he?"

Max inhaled silently. In his efforts to reassure her, he hesitated a moment too long to be convincing.

Chapter Sixteen

By the time they arrived in Brownsville two weeks later, Colonel Ford's Cavalry of the West had reclaimed not only the city but much of the surrounding country, as well.

For days and miles before reaching Brownsville, they had been joined by flocks of people returning to their homes, by speculators returning to do business, and by soldiers hurrying to get in what they figured would be the last shots of the War for Southern Independence.

It wouldn't be long until they were proven right—about part of it, anyhow. For the time being, Stella and her crew enjoyed the camaraderie of like-minded citizens, all, of course, except Max. Stella teased him that he would be found out for what he truly was: a Southern gentleman at heart.

But it was another gentleman for whom she longed daily, hourly, by the minute. A dozen times a day she asked Max the same question: "Do you think he is all right?"

And Max always answered with the same statement. "I'm sure of it, Stella."

Then why wasn't she convinced? she wondered. Every time she asked, she listened to Max's tone of voice, to the inflection he put on each word; always he sounded confident.

More so as the days wore on, she noted. He'd had practice now. But she remembered the first time she asked the question—back at San Fernando when they sat beneath the stars and Max had hesitated before replying.

Surely, he could know no more about Logan's safety now than he had known two weeks ago. He was covering up his own anxieties for her sake. She was sure of it.

And she dreaded to learn the truth. In fact, the only thing she dreaded more was not finding Logan at all.

She tried to console herself with the notion that her worrying had no merit: that it stemmed from Papá's being shot, from Jorge's being wounded, that Logan was the most important person in her life, and she naturally worried more than necessary.

It didn't help at all, her rationalizing in such a manner. By the time they arrived in Brownsville she was in a tumbled-up state of mind. First, she would meet with Pryor Lea; then she would insist that Max take her to Logan.

First things first. The evening they arrived, Francisco took a message for Pryor Lea at the Confederate headquarters and was fortunate enough to run into the man himself. He arranged a meeting between Stella and Mr. Lea the following morning at the Confederate building on the plaza, after which, Lea would personally supervise the exchange of cotton for supplies.

"With the Confederates holding Brownsville once more, shipping cotton down the river to Bagdad will be an easy matter, according to Mr. Lea," Francisco reported.

They camped that night on the outskirts of town, amid the clamor and clatter of citizens returning home. Although the town had been retaken, skirmishes still were reported daily by soldiers hurrying to join the fight. Sporadic cannon fire from the direction of the Gulf confirmed their dreams — and Stella's fears.

They circled the wagons Indian-fighting fashion, and Francisco and Max made Stella place her bedroll in a wagon in the center. In addition, they posted a tight guard.

"We didn't come all this way to be robbed by our own people," Francisco muttered.

326

"Nor to have anything happen to you," Max told Stella. "Francisco and I would both be in danger of losing our heads were we to let something happen to you now."

She protested, but the loyalty they felt toward both her and Logan warmed her heart, and when she slept she dreamed of lying in Logan's arms.

Before dawn she awakened to find Max gone and Francisco ready to escort her to the plaza for her meeting with Pryor Lea, whom they met on the steps of the Confederate building as he was arriving for work.

Brownsville's central plaza was a lovely place, Spanish in tone, surrounded by graceful palms and punctuated with a multitude of brilliant flowers. Women, young and old, scurried about in traditional Spanish costumes, their heads covered with black rebozos or mantillas.

It reminded Stella of her own heritage, causing her to feel shabby and inappropriately dressed in her customary leather pants and boots. Although she had put on clean clothes and polished her boots, her shirt was wrinkled, and with the sun glinting from the surface of her oxblood boots, she saw how scuffed they were. She clutched the gray-and-black rebozo beneath her chin and stared across the street at the plaza, where black-attired ladies scurried about—some carrying bread from the panadería, some meat from the carnicería, a number exiting the church across the square after attending morning mass.

Pryor Lea followed her gaze toward the plaza. "Such a delightful morning. Perhaps you would prefer having our little chat beneath the palm trees."

Stella and Francisco followed the Confederate agent across the street, where she took a seat on the bench he indicated. Quickly, she turned her attention to the matter at hand. "We brought ten loads of cotton. Francisco told you that?"

Lea nodded. "Your supplies are waiting: medicine, clothing, and the salt you requested from the interior of Mexico.

327

Although I am sure you have heard — Colonel Ford liberated El Sal del Rey."

She listened, waiting to hear the one thing he did not mention. "Arms?"

He shook his head. "The French absconded with every shipment of armaments we tried to put aside for you. The battle between Maximilian's Imperialists and the Liberals under Benito Juárez is heating up." He shrugged. "Since the French are our allies, we can't very well refuse to sell them arms that are just sitting in a warehouse."

Although distressed to learn of her father's mishap, and sorry as well about the loss of the ship, Lea was enthusiastic about the opening of the coast for shipping.

"We will have plenty of time to secure more vessels now," he assured her. "You can bring cotton straight to the coast again. The only place we may have a little trouble is Brazos Santiago, and even there not for long."

Her heart quickened at mention of the place to which Max had said Logan sailed. "What is happening at Brazos Santiago?"

"My dear Miss Duval, we are in the throes of good fortune. Before the onset of autumn, we will have run the Yankees out of the Gulf of Mexico — Texas's portion of it anyhow. The coast will be firmly in our grasp."

She wanted to question further, but dared not. What did it matter? she wondered. Speculation from him was no more reliable than speculation from a Yankee.

She sighed. This war had made her a cynic. Standing, she shook hands with Pryor Lea and assured him Francisco would deliver the cotton to the docks before nightfall.

"And you, my dear. What are your plans?"

"I am taking the stagecoach back to Los Olmos," she said. "I'm anxious to see about Papá and my cousin Jorge."

Pryor Lea bent over her hand, brushing it with his lips . . . a slight contact, one that she did not feel, however, for her eyes had caught those of a vaquero whom she had noticed lounging against a tall palm during her talk with the Confederate agent. Now, he caught her eye, grinned, and tipped his sombrero.

Her heart tipped as well.

"May I escort you back to the wagon train, my dear?"

"What?" She drew her attention—half of it anyhow—back to Mr. Lea. "Ah, oh . . . no, I don't believe so, thank you. Francisco is here, and . . . ah, I think I will stroll around the plaza a bit . . . it is so . . ."

"But the stagecoach . . . ? When does it leave?"

"Thank you ever so much, Mr. Lea. I shall alert you when to expect another load of cotton."

When he still objected, she finished, "Don't give my plans another thought. They are in good hands. . . ."—her body tingled against her clothing—". . . the best of hands."

Max had not been able to find Logan until nearly daybreak, and that only after rowing out to the *Victory* and enduring a confrontation with Dar Blakesborough.

"Cafferty has sealed his fate this time," Blakesborough stormed. "When you find him, bring the bastard directly to this ship."

"Aye, aye," Max had shrugged.

Ensign Jacobs came into Logan's cabin, where Max rifled through papers, looking for some clue to his friend's whereabouts.

Jacobs closed the door behind him. "He'll be somewhere around the French legation in Matamoros. Look for a down-at-heel vaquero. He said to tell you to come dressed for action."

Max glanced at his own trail-riding attire. "Action means a fight," he grinned. "And a fight means Logan has zeroed in on the target."

Forewarned though he had been, Max passed Logan by twice in his search. Logan called to him.

"What the . . . ?"

"Español," Logan hissed. *"Hable Español."* He dragged Max across the street and around two corners before Max spoke again, this time in Spanish as Logan instructed.

"What have you got?"

"Not enough," Logan admitted. "They are meeting again tonight. That should provide us the evidence we need."

Max stared at the sky. "Let me take over. You need to get yourself over to the plaza in Brownsville, pronto. Stella is meeting Pryor Lea at the Confederate headquarters this morning."

Logan rubbed his three-day's growth of beard. "I'll find a place to clean up. . . ."

Max shook his head. "She'll be gone if you don't get over there . . . *pronto, en Español.* I'll take over here."

Logan calculated quickly. "We need to change bloodhounds, anyway. They'll be sure to recognize me before long."

"What time is Blakesborough supposed to arrive?"

"Six o'clock."

"Where can I find you if there's trouble?"

Logan considered briefly. "Valensuela Ropería in Bagdad." He grimaced at his clothing. "She'll hate . . ."

Max laughed. "No way, amigo. She won't even see your attire . . ."—he slapped Logan on the back, eyeing his face—". . . or feel your scraggly beard, if I wager correctly."

Stella's mouth went dry at the sight of Logan, lounging against the palm tree, looking every bit the part of one of her vaqueros—too long on the grimy trail. With great difficulty, she contained herself until Pryor Lea started across the street to the Confederate headquarters.

She couldn't run to Logan; not here within sight of every Confederate soldier in South Texas. She mustn't. Quickly, she looked around for Francisco, who came to her side from

330

behind.

She took his arm. "Walk with me. Slowly . . ." — she nodded in a direction that would take them past Logan — ". . . that way."

Francisco tensed at her touch. "Señorita . . . ?"

"Just walk," she encouraged, "walk . . . walk."

They ambled up one side of the square, Francisco balking, she exuberant. When they passed Logan, she gave him a surreptitious wink, and his wink in return nearly caused her to stumble.

She clutched Francisco's arm tighter and felt him relax a bit. They rounded the corner, made the next side of the square at a quickened pace, and proceeded to stroll down the far side from the headquarters building.

"Do you remember Logan Cafferty?" she asked Francisco.

"*Sí*," he responded.

"Did you see him back there beside that palm tree?"

"*Sí, señorita.*"

"When he comes up to us, let him take your place. Mr. Lea is expecting you at the docks with the wagons this afternoon. Take the supplies back, as usual." She reached into her leather pouch. "This is the list of where everything is to go. Be sure to stop by Los Olmos to see if they need some of the medicine. I will meet you at Los Olmos before our next trip. Tell Mamá where . . . ah, who I am with, so she will not worry."

They made the switch without missing a step. Logan came up behind them, Francisco inched ahead, and Logan took his place at her side. She glanced sideways across the plaza toward the headquarters building — it was hidden behind a covering of foliage and palm trees. Surely their little ruse would go unnoticed.

His grip on her arm sent fiery streaks through her body and erased thoughts of anything but this one man from her brain.

331

"Max told me I'd find a princess in the plaza," he whispered.

She trembled, giddy, not from his words, but from his presence . . . from his beloved presence.

"If there's a princess in this plaza, she is definitely in disguise," she responded, thinking now of her disreputable attire.

At the corner he guided her down a side street, away from the plaza. "She isn't the only one in disguise."

At his self-degrading tone, she turned and studied him. "We could both use a bath and a change of clothing." Lifting her hand, she touched his stubbled cheek. "But I'd have known you anywhere."

A carriage stood around another corner, and without hesitating, Logan pulled the door open and handed her inside. After issuing instructions to the driver, he climbed in beside her.

She swallowed, staring at him, inhaling the very essence of this man, her beloved Logan. The carriage bolted forward, but inside it, she entertained the crazy notion that the world stood still, holding its breath — as she held hers. She pursed her lips, recalling how when she was very young, Papá would come home from a long trip bringing her a package; she would stare at it for an eternity, allowing anticipation to build to unbearable limits, then finally, when she could stand it no longer, she would tear into the package, strewing paper this way and that.

At last she fell into Logan's arms, experiencing much the same vibrant expectancy . . . of strewing the world and its concerns this way and that, leaving the two of them free in a world of only themselves — their arms, their bodies, their hearts, their lips, their unrequited passion.

His tender, demanding, urgently caressing lips . . . his strong arms and hard muscles . . . his heart thudding against hers, beating out the rhythm of her soul: *I love you . . . love you . . . love you . . .*

Finally he drew back and sheepishly rubbed the stubble on his chin. "I'm scratching your face . . ."

She placed a hand over his, feeling his long, hard fingers and beneath, his stubbled beard and heated skin. "It feels wonderful. I've missed you so . . ."

He held her head in his hands. His fingers in her hair raised goose bumps on her scalp and down her neck. "I'm sorry about Giddeon," he whispered.

The reminder brought a catch to her throat. She pressed her lips together.

"Was it terrible?"

She stared into his troubled, loving eyes and nodded.

He kissed her, still holding her head as in a vise.

When he lifted his lips a hairsbreadth, she spoke in a trembling voice. "The worst part was thinking it was you."

Their fears passed between them as on a flood of memories streaming from their eyes. At length, he clasped her to him and held her tightly against his heart. "My God," he whispered. "How could you have thought such a thing?"

"If you believed Papá and I left Titlum-Tatlum by land, then you would have . . ."

"Shhh," he whispered.

". . . but you would have . . ."

"Don't, princess. It's all over."

Gradually she began to relax against him. "What happened at Titlum-Tatlum?" she asked.

He tightened his arms around her. "I talked Blakesborough out of bombing the island. Told him we were too close to the Confederate warships at Galveston. We went in by boat . . ."—she felt him chuckle against her—". . . found your *ship*. I told Max I'd wager it was your idea."

She smiled. "No, but it was a good one." The security she felt in his arms, the strength he represented, the love he offered her combined to replace her dreadful memories of the attack with memories that were not only affectionate, but growing more so with each passing moment.

She sat back and ran her fingers lightly over his chin, his cheeks. "Where are we going?"

Her fingers traced his eyes, his nose.

"Does it matter?"

Just before she thought to expect it, he captured her finger in his mouth.

Her breath caught at the acutely sensual gesture — at the memories it evoked, at the promise it bore.

"No," she replied. "Not as long as you are there."

He lowered his lips to hers. "You are definitely a part of my plans today, princess . . . and forever."

The carriage finally came to a halt, and when Stella looked out the window at a familiar dock on the Rio Grande, she questioned him again.

"I have a surprise for you" was all he would reply. Even after they boarded a steamer traveling down the Rio Grande River, he still refused to reveal their destination.

When the steamer docked just past noon, their destination still baffled her. "You have business in Bagdad?"

He squeezed her around the shoulders. "First things first," he commented. After which, he located a carriage, issued instructions, and a few minutes later told her to remain in the carriage while he went inside a haberdashery on the main square.

When he returned, he still offered no explanation, but at least he did answer a couple of questions.

"This is where I lodge when I'm in town on business," he replied to her first question, looking toward the second story of the establishment — Valensuela Roperia.

Inside he introduced her to the haberdasher, Señor Valensuela and his wife, the señora, who immediately took charge of Stella.

"Come along, dear, I have the niño heating bath water already."

Stella threw Logan an inquisitive glance.

"You do trust me to choose your clothing?"

"I suppose . . ." — she stared at the male attire displayed around the room — ". . . a riding skirt like last time would be nice." She opened the leather pouch to withdraw some money.

He winked. "Coming up. But this is on me. I owe you something for the mess I made of our last trip to Bagdad."

At the head of the staircase, Señora Valensuela stopped, then led Stella toward a wing of rooms to their left. She nodded across the stairwell. "Those are the colonel's rooms, over there."

The steamy water and luscious smells that greeted Stella inside a decidedly feminine room were quite a departure from the meager things she would have expected in this shanty seaport town. Señora Valensuela understood her dismay.

"With the French coming in droves nowadays, we are able to obtain more luxuries. We *pay* for them, of course."

Señora Valensuela handed Stella a couple of flannel bath towels. "Take your time, dear. I will bring up some fresh undergarments to go along with the clothing Colonel Cafferty chooses."

Stella thanked her, and after the señora left her alone, she hurried through her bath, all the while wishing she could slow down enough to enjoy the warm scented water.

But Logan was downstairs, and she hadn't seen him in so long. Her mind strayed to their last visit to Bagdad. Indeed, he had made it a disaster for her . . . or their situation had done so. She hadn't even had a chance to find La Paloma Cantina where Papá and her grandfather had played their infamous game of cards, with her mother as the stakes. Perhaps this time . . .

A knock came at the door while Stella, her body wrapped in one of the oversize towels, worked at drying her hair with the other one. At her call, Señora Valensuela entered, bearing an armload of clothing and a broad smile.

"You are a lucky young lady, señorita." She put the under-

335

garments on a table and held up a full gathered skirt and lacy blouse. "You have found a handsome man, who has very good taste in clothing, as well as in—"

As though stuck with a hatpin, the señora clamped her lips shut, then finished in a lame fashion, ". . . and in sweethearts."

Blood rushed to Stella's face, which she knew must be a bright, hot red. She drew a deep breath, fingering the fine embroidery on the white tiered skirt. What difference did it make if Señora Valensuela thought she was nothing more than a courtesan? With her short hair . . . and shabby clothing . . . to say nothing of the way Logan rushed her into the establishment and began buying her clothing . . .

She inhaled, held her breath, and tried to steady her racing pulse. "I asked for a riding skirt."

"Oh, he bought that, too, dear. And some new boots of the softest leather. But he wants you to wear this costume for—"

Again, the woman stilled her own tongue. Whatever she had intended to say, Stella was just as glad not to hear it. "To dine with us," Señora Valensuela finished, then rushed to the door. "I have preparations to attend to. The parlor is three doors to your right. The colonel said to meet him there."

By the time the señora left the room, Stella was fuming with anger, brought about by an acute attack of embarrassment. Hastily she donned the new white pantaloons, chemise, and corset; then the two white crinoline petticoats. No hoops, she saw. A wonder Colonel Cafferty hadn't forced her into hoopskirts, so he could . . .

She slipped the white blouse over her head and fluffed the delicate embroidered lace that encircled her shoulders. It was pretty, she admitted grudgingly, stepping into the white skirt that was fashioned of tiers of white lawn interspersed with ruffles of embroidered lace to match that on the blouse.

Her embarrassment heightened as she eased her feet into the black kid slippers. Everything was a perfect fit, of course. Her mind conjured up the image of Logan showing her with his hands how he had been able to purchase the riding skirt and blouse to fit her.

Fluffing her hair, she glanced in the looking glass and clasped her hands to her fiery red cheeks. *That bastard!* Of course, Señor and Señora Valensuela realized exactly how he knew her correct sizes! Courtesan, indeed.

The only purchase of Logan's she had yet to touch was a white silk mantilla, which, when she picked it up, seemed to melt in her fingers. He did have good taste, she thought. Exquisite taste . . .

She draped the mantilla over her head. What difference did it make what the Valensuelas thought? She loved Logan, and he loved her. If he chose to flaunt it in a socially unacceptable manner, she wouldn't complain. They only had snatches of time together.

On her way to the parlor she felt her embarrassment begin to fade with her growing anticipation to be with Logan.

She opened the door, her face still flushed, but only partially from discomfiture now. Logan stood across the room, staring at the door as though he had willed her presence. At the sight of her, he pushed away from the mantel and grinned with unabashed pleasure.

When he stepped toward her, she stood stock-still, waiting for him. He, too, had bathed, shaved, and changed. Now, in fawn twill trousers and short cropped jacket, he almost took her breath away.

"Princess," he whispered. Taking her hands, he looked her up and down with admiration.

"You chose well," she said. "Thank you."

His eyes glowed. He twirled her in a circle by her fingertips, then his hands tightened around hers. "My Mexican . . . princess." Drawing her hand through the crook of his arm, he escorted her into the room, where she became aware of the others present.

Señor and Señora Valensuela beamed; Logan introduced

the third person. "This is Judge Lara. He has come to marry us."

It was a civil service, brief and in Spanish, but Stella knew it would not have been more perfect had they wed in a cathedral with a full choir and high mass. And when Logan produced a small golden band from his pocket to slip on her finger, her hand trembled so, he had to steady it with both of his. His hands, she noticed, trembled, too.

Afterward, Señor Valensuela produced a bottle of wine to toast the bride. Señora Valensuela invited them to sit down to a wedding feast. The meal, she insisted, was already prepared, since Logan and Stella had arrived at the haberdashery precisely at dinnertime.

Logan paid the judge and thanked the señora. "I have our afternoon planned," he added. "We will return later."

They took a carriage, and four blocks down the street, they found a café. "I had thought to take you to La Paloma, but the place is too disreputable for . . ."—he winked at her—". . . for a princess."

She clasped his hand tightly, feeling her golden wedding band warm inside his palm. "That's all right, you don't need to win a wife. You already have one."

When Logan started to order, the proprietor stopped him. "You have only ten minutes until we close for siesta, señor. Perhaps you should return for the evening meal."

"We will eat whatever you have," Logan told him.

Over a meager meal of sopa de elote and tortillas, Stella's attention went from Logan to her shiny new wedding band and back to Logan. "When did you plan this?"

His eyes twinkled, sending rushes of pleasure coursing through her body. "Under the palm tree this morning."

She laughed. "But the ring? When did you . . . ?"

"I have had that ring a long time, princess. I told you, I was waiting for the first opportunity."

At his words, her left hand clutched her belly. Instantly, his eyes held hers, twinkling.

338

"Did we make it in time?" he asked. "Or have we begun our family?"

She shook her head. She should be glad, she knew, with the war still in full progress. But she wasn't. She was past ready to start a family . . . to bear Logan's child.

Wiping his mouth, he tossed the napkin to his plate and dragged her to her feet. "Come, maybe we can fix that right now. I think we've given the Valensuelas enough time to retire for siesta."

He led her up the back stairs of the ropería. Her senses reeled with so many emotions, she felt as though she were flying through the air: from pure pleasure to unabashed passion, from intense longing, to a deep, glorious peacefulness.

Once they entered the upstairs hallway, he put a finger to his lips and led her to a door that opened to his key. Inside she found a small parlor, furnished with sofa, chairs, tables, and a desk in the far corner. The desk was neat, but the table was laden with packages. And beside it stood a new pair of shiny oxblood boots. She knew they would be just her size.

Beyond the parlor, she saw another room, glimpsed part of a bed, and beyond that, a closed door.

She inhaled, smelling his own spicy scent in the surroundings. She heard the key turn in the lock. She felt his hands, like delicate wisps of air, brush her shoulders.

She turned and came into his arms. For a long moment she was conscious of nothing but their hearts beating against each other, resounding in her ears. At length, he held her back and stared into her eyes—admiring, loving.

"Can it be true?" she whispered. "I am really your wife, after all this time?"

With precise movements, almost majestic, he fingered the mantilla covering her head, arranging it down the sides of her face, over her shoulders. His fingertips grazed her skin in feathery strokes.

"As soon as all this is over we will have a church wedding," he told her.

She studied him solemnly, reveling in the delicious sensations with which his presence always filled her. "So I can promise to obey?" she teased.

He raised his eyebrows. "Not a bad idea, although I'm afraid you would never be able to fulfill such a pledge." Then he turned serious. "So I can vow to love, to honor, and to protect you."

As their gazes held he drew the mantilla from her head and tossed it to the table. He tousled her hair and ran his hands over her shoulders above the low-cut bodice of her blouse. Lowering his face, he kissed her, his lips plying hers with tender, urgent promises, with demands.

She reached for him, finding his waist, steadying herself by drawing him near. She was so happy she wanted to cry and laugh at the same time, and she never wanted to stop kissing him.

Lifting his lips, he kissed her face, while his hands pressed her closer to his aching body. "Princess," he mumbled. "My Mexican princess."

She sighed, her lips finding his. Between kisses she mumbled into his mouth. "I am definitely not a princess any longer. I have been promoted."

He looked at her, quizzing.

"I am now your *wife*."

He kissed her appreciatively. "And, I, Mrs. Cafferty, am proud to be your *husband*."

She stroked his cheek with her fingers and felt his arms tighten about her. "How much time do we have?"

Dropping his hand to her shoulders, he studied her with a twinkle in his eyes before easing his fingers inside the neckline of her blouse and pulling it farther over her arms, trapping them at her sides. Then, still holding her eyes with his, he ran his fingers inside the front of the garment and pulled it below her chemise-clad breasts. Forced thus to the top of her corset, her breasts fell in silky mounds into his hands.

"Enough time for me to love you as you have never been

loved before," he mumbled, moving his lips across her face, down her neck and chest, to her breasts, which he kissed through the thin layer of fabric, teasing her nipples, first one, then the other, alternately with his lips, then his fingers, until she didn't think she could stand still a minute longer.

But his promise strengthened her forbearance. With trembling fingers she pressed his head closer to her breasts, burying her lips in his hair. "I can hardly wait to see what that might be, Colonel Cafferty," she whispered. "I thought surely I had already sampled all your magic."

His body throbbed against hers and only with the greatest resolve was he able to keep from disrobing her in an instant, and himself, and taking her without further ado. But he had promised himself that regardless of what had gone on between them before, she would have a wedding night to remember, and he intended to keep that promise. Lifting his lips, he cupped her breasts in his palms and nibbled his way to her lips. The passion in his eyes caused her to gasp.

He grinned. "I promise you, Mrs. Cafferty, by tomorrow morning you will be so thoroughly ravished by my loving you will have to spend a week in bed from sheer exhaustion."

She laughed. "Then let's get started."

The instant their lips met, a knock came at the door. Logan ignored it.

The knock sounded again, this time a bit louder.

Stella tried to move her lips, but Logan held her fast. "It's only Señora Valensuela. She will go away."

But it wasn't Señora Valensuela, and the caller did not go away.

Max's voice startled them with its urgency. "If you're in there, Logan, open up and be quick about it."

"Damn it . . ." Logan muttered.

His expression changed from passionate to anxious.

"What's the matter?" she asked.

He lifted her blouse back over her breasts, arranged it around her shoulders. "I have to let him in." His whisper

341

sounded like something between an apology and a plea.

"Of course," she said.

Max stormed quickly into the room. "You've got to get out of here." He nodded toward Stella. "Both of you."

"What . . . ?" Logan began.

"Blakesborough . . ."

"He didn't show up?"

"He did, all right, but his aide, Herbert, found him before contact was made. He'd had Herbert and a group tailing you. They're on their way. . . ."

From below, the front door rattled. Behind them, the rear-entrance door burst open. Logan grabbed Stella's arm. Footsteps sounded on the central staircase.

Max peered into the hallway. Suddenly he flew back into the room, landing on his back in the middle of the floor. Stella stared at him.

"Got you, Cafferty. Caught in the act of consorting with the enemy."

She cringed. She would know that voice anywhere. It would echo through her nightmares for the rest of her life. It would call from the depths of hell in ages to come.

Turning, she stared at Dar Blakesborough, swelled up now like a bayou toad. Gun drawn, he grabbed for Logan with his free hand. Stella threw herself at him.

He rebuffed her attack with the flick of an elbow. "Don't exert yourself, reb. As soon as I take care of this traitor, I'll show you my appreciation for helping nab him."

Suddenly the room teemed with blue uniforms; they seemed to swell and sway, filling her vision. She moved toward Logan, but he was staring past her, behind her.

Then a powerful hand gripped her shoulders and forced her backward. For an instant the melee turned black. "Logan!" she cried. "Logan!"

Chapter Seventeen

Max's voice meant trouble. Logan sensed that the moment he heard it. It took longer, however, to convince his brain and body to switch from the aphrodisiac of Stella's sweet passion to a fighting mode, and by that time Dar Blakesborough had poked a gun in his gut.

Then Blakesborough flexed his elbow to ward off Stella's attack, and Logan was ready with a chop to the man's wrist. The pistol clattered harmlessly to the floor.

He followed with a swing at Blakesborough's jaw.

Blakesborough protected himself from the blow with his left forearm, punched with his now-free right fist, and Logan staggered backward.

In his peripheral vision he saw moving figures, heard voices. Regaining his footing, he focused on Blakesborough, landed a solid jab to the man's jaw, and followed with a swift punch at his midsection.

Blakesborough sidestepped with the grace of a two-masted sloop on its maiden voyage. He struck at Logan's chest, then stepped in with a backswing that gave Logan time to recoup.

Logan feinted to the left, stepped right, and felt confident he was about to land the final blow. This, he later acknowledged, was his biggest mistake since failing to realize Blakesborough would be followed by a regiment.

Although, the way things turned out it wouldn't have mattered much one way or another. The same moment Blakesborough read Logan's feint, a sea of blue uniforms surged into the room, as though a porthole had been left open during an angry storm.

Quickly, Logan glanced behind him, searching for Stella. Blakesborough had not come, even initially, alone. Ensign Herbert had followed him into the room, and was now engaged one-on-one with Max.

And there was Stella, in the thick of the melee. Stella, his princess . . . Stella, his wife . . . Stella, who, unfortunately, did not have a cowardly bone in her body, held a walnut tea table over her head, and just before Blakesborough dealt him another blow, he watched her smash it over the shoulders of Max's opponent.

Max stared from one to the other, apparently stunned by the collapse of his opponent from no action of his own.

Suddenly chaos in the form of Federal reinforcements burst into the room. "Get her out of here," Logan called to Max. Blakesborough hit him in the chest.

Although his voice swooshed from his throat as a result of the blow, he maintained eye contact with Max long enough to know Max understood.

Stella watched, dismayed, as the room filled with blue-uniformed men. She looked toward Logan, but he was staring past her.

Before she could turn around, a powerful hand gripped her shoulders and pulled her backward. For an instant the melee turned black. "Logan!" she cried. "Logan!" Her feet flew out from under her and she heard Max's voice in her ear.

"Come on, Stella. Run."

She struggled to free herself, helplessly watching the sailors pin Logan's arms to his sides. "Let me go. Why . . . ?"

By this time Max had dragged her into the adjoining bedroom. Without relaxing his hold, he closed the door between the two rooms, then opened a door on the opposite side of the bed. Peering quickly beyond, he dragged her into the empty hallway.

344

"This way . . ."

"Max! Don't leave him!" She worked to free herself, but he held her with a death grip.

The sounds of action came from the hallway around the corner, which opened into Logan's parlor. Max glanced the other direction, nodded toward a window.

"We'll go that way."

She skidded her heels along the floor. Her mind raced. "You can leave him if you want to, but I'm not."

"We're wasting time, Stella. If we don't get out of here before Blakesborough realizes you have slipped away . . ."

She jerked to free herself.

"Stella." His voice was firm. "If you stay, he'll fight to the *finish*."

She flinched at the inflection he placed on the word *finish*. "But . . . ?"

"Come on. I'll explain."

"Please, don't leave him," she begged, following him to the window.

In one swift movement he raised the window sash and propped it up with the wooden support rod. After a quick glance over the edge, he grasped her arms.

"Please, Max."

"He'll be all right if we are free to help him."

"If Francisco and my vaqueros were here . . ." Her words died quickly; Max's logic convinced her, reluctantly. She removed her slippers and scrambled to the windowsill.

"Careful, now. I'll hold your arms and lower you as close to the ground as I can. Prepare for a good drop."

Her white wedding skirt billowed above her head as she fell, and she wished for her riding pants and boots. She landed with a thud on the ground below the window; her slippers peppered down on top of her. Quickly, she jumped up and out of Max's way. Big as he was, he landed with the grace of a kitten.

Like a flash of lightning, he grabbed her arm, and to-

345

gether they raced away from the ropería, around a corner, and behind the protection of another building.

"I wish Francisco and your vaqueros were here, too," he gasped, when at last they stopped to rest.

"What will they do with him?" The pause in their flight gave her emotions a chance to catch up. "How do you know they won't . . . kill him?" The last words quivered out on a whisper, and Max took her by the shoulders. He shook her gently.

"Stella, listen to me. Blakesborough doesn't want him dead. He wants to humiliate him, to throw him out of the service in disgrace."

In spite of her efforts, tears formed like hot boils in her eyes. She wiped the back of her hand across her face. "But . . . we could have . . ."

Max shook his head. "No. If I hadn't gotten you out of there, he would have fought to the finish, regardless of the injury it brought him. You know he would never let Blakesborough take you prisoner again."

She inhaled a deep, quivering breath. Unconsciously she twisted the golden band around and around on her finger with her other hand. "I know," she whispered.

Max stared at the ring a moment, then he lifted her hand to his lips and kissed the ring. "Congratulations, Mrs. Cafferty. Stop worrying, we're going to get him back."

Near midnight they trudged into the vaquero camp to find Beto on guard. They planned an early morning departure with the supply wagons, he told them.

Francisco awakened, and the three of them sat around a stoked-up fire, drinking coffee, eating jerked meat, and discussing the fastest method to rescue Logan.

"That's why Logan had to be so secretive about his job," Max told them. "For almost a year the Gulf Fleet has been losing arms. Blakesborough was suspected, but with his father's position, the investigation had to be top secret. Since Logan and Blakesborough already had a feud going, Secre-

346

tary Wells figured Blakesborough would be too busy begrudging Logan a plumb assignment to see him as a threat to his own illegal dealings. Logan had Jacobs and me assigned to the *Victory* to help him."

"How much more evidence do you need?"

"Not much. In fact, we were closing in tonight. Blakesborough had a meeting scheduled in Matamoros — at the French legation there — with a Frenchman from the legation in Brownsville. Logan had been tailing him the last few days; when we got to town, I located Logan and changed places with him." He grinned at her, then pointedly looked at her hand. "I knew he had plans, but I didn't realize he intended to carry them out so soon."

Stella wrapped her arms about herself, squeezing in the warm sensations Max's suggestion recalled. Mrs. Logan Cafferty. How long she had waited for that name to be hers! Now that it was . . . "Look at the mess I got him into. If he hadn't come to see me he wouldn't have gotten caught."

"You aren't to blame," Max assured her.

"They followed us . . ." she objected.

"No. They had the apartment staked out. They knew he operated from there. That's a good indication Blakesborough still doesn't know we are on to him. His hatred for Logan drove him to close in tonight. Nothing more. I'd wager my life on it."

She twisted the ring on her finger; it was Logan's life being wagered tonight. "If I hadn't come to town, he would not have gone to the apartment. He would have remained on the stakeout, and by now you would have caught Dar Blakesborough at his dirty game. Instead, look what . . ."

"Stella." Max's voice with its calm warning brought her diatribe to a halt.

Then she finished. "It's true."

Max shrugged. "And it's done. Now we have to figure out how to get him back."

They sat in silence while the white smoke from the campfire circled upward. A scattering of stars glimmered from the black sky; she thought how, if Logan were here, the stars would be glittering and gay, shining on her wedding night. She wondered whether he could see them from where . . .

Suddenly she knew exactly where he was. "He's . . . he's in my cell . . .?" She stared questioningly at Max as she spoke, and when she paused, he nodded, solemn.

"Not for long." His confident tone gave her hope.

The golden band was hot on her finger from all her twisting and worrying. She rose and filled their coffee cups. Francisco accepted the refill without a word, and she could see he, too, was deeply affected by the turn of events. Replacing the pot over the coals, she returned to her seat on the log between the two men.

"What we must do," she said, "is finish the job he set out to do tonight. If we can obtain the evidence you need, then you can convince the admiral to set Logan free."

Max looked into the fire so long, she expected him to argue with her reasoning. But when he spoke, he agreed.

"To do that, we must find a way to get hold of Blakesborough's Brownsville contact."

"Who is he?"

"A Monsieur Leclerc. Do you know him?"

"No." She stared into the fire, concentrating until her eyes saw only a red haze.

Francisco had remained silent during their conversation; now he spoke. "You, Señor Max, do you know this man?"

Max nodded. "But the important question is, does he know me? Regretfully, he most likely does."

"Then you can go to him as a messenger from this man Blakesborough."

Max sighed. "That's too risky. If Blakesborough warned him about Logan and me, he could expose us. We'd put Logan in more jeopardy."

They lapsed into silence again. Stella got up and started to pour more coffee. Suddenly, she had an idea.

"You say Leclerc buys munitions and armaments?"

"To help Maximilian fight Benito Juárez," Max said.

Stella smiled, feeling more confident than she had in several hours. "I'll go."

In unison, the men objected.

"Listen to me," she cautioned. "Everyone in Brownsville knows I sell cotton for the Confederacy. They also know the Confederacy needs money; we will sell anything we can get our hands on to raise funds to fight this war. . . ."

"Everyone also knows the Confederacy *buys* armaments and munitions; they don't *sell* them," Max argued.

She nodded. "But Monsieur Leclerc will not be sure. If I approach him about a meeting of mutual importance, he will come. The French are desperate for supplies . . . and for political friends. I represent the Confederate States of America, France's ally."

"I cannot allow you to do this, señorita."

Stella studied Francisco, so faithful and loyal. She started to tell him she was no longer a señorita, but this was not a time to change topics — not when Logan's life hung in the balance. "I must," she said.

"No," Max replied. "Logan would slit both our throats if we let . . ."

"Nothing will happen to me," she insisted. "Monsieur Leclerc won't harm a person he thinks can perform a service for him . . . and for his emperor. I will arrange a meeting with him, that's all." She looked behind her at the sleeping vaqueros. "The rest will be up to you."

Max ran a hand through his sandy hair, thinking.

"What would we do with him, señorita?" Francisco inquired. "How could taking this man bring Señor Logan back to us?"

Max stared into the fire. "We could persuade him to send for Blakesborough, but . . . ?" He shrugged. "What then?"

Again, they studied the situation. Stella refilled their cups. Francisco rose and fixed a fresh pot of coffee. "Daybreak is near," he said. "The men will soon arise."

"In order to free Logan we must . . ." Pursing her lips a moment, she spoke again, enumerating the things necessary to accomplish their task. "First, we must get Blakesborough away from the ship. If we can lure him into a trap where he will be caught dealing with the French . . ."

"That's it," Max interrupted. "You arrange a meeting with Leclerc. Not on the plaza . . . it must be away from anyone who could come to his aid. . . ."

"I will say I must meet him here on the edge of town, since the wagon train is leaving this morning."

Max nodded. "Yes. He must be warned that the matter is sensitive, that he cannot let anyone else know, for the present. Therefore, he should come alone—" He sighed. "The man isn't a fool; he will never go for that."

"Yes, he will," Stella countered. "I'll see to it." She spoke slowly, methodically fitting together the pieces of the puzzle. "Instead of meeting with me, I will bring him here. I'll go to him . . . to make arrangements for a meeting with . . ."— her eyes brightened—". . . with Papá!"

"Perfect!" Max scanned the vaqueros. "Once here, we have enough men to detain him until he does our bidding."

"Which is to send for Blakesborough at once," Stella enthused.

"I still do not like this, señorita," Francisco said.

"It will work, Francisco. In fact, if you want, you can come along. I will take a carriage, and you . . ."— she looked toward Max—". . . both of you can follow in a separate carriage. Just be sure not to arouse his suspicion."

"I am not clear, señorita, on how this will help free Señor Logan."

Stella looked at Max, waiting for him to explain.

He shrugged. "First things first. Let's lure Blakesborough off that ship. Convicting him will come later. If we can't find a way to set him up in time to free Logan, some of us will detain him, while the others go on board and release Lo-

350

gan."

They agreed Stella should try to see Monsieur Leclerc as soon as he arrived at the legation, preferably before he entered the building. In the few hours remaining to them, her distress returned time and again, growing to near panic level before she was able to banish it. Tomorrow she would panic, she told herself. Tomorrow . . . if their plan did not work.

"It will work, señorita," Francisco assured her. "We will not let that Frenchman out of our grasp."

As daybreak approached she found her satchel in one of the covered supply wagons where she had left it early the previous morning. Climbing inside, she changed into pants and shirt, thinking wistfully of the new boots Logan had bought her that were lying back at the apartment—or even her old scuffed ones.

But the wistfulness passed with the ensuing idea, of her new and beloved husband lying most likely in the cell with which she was unbearably familiar. The darkness inside the wagon isolated her, and tears formed in her eyes; by the time she finished dressing, they streamed down her cheeks, and her shoulders began to shake.

Dar Blakesborough was a vicious, violent man. He had not harmed her because she had Ensign Jacobs to protect her with his inventive imagination. Was Logan as fortunate? Or had Blakesborough learned that Jacobs worked for Logan?

She sank to a pile of clothing and held her head in her hands, sobbing now, unable to keep at bay images of the horrors Dar Blakesborough was capable of inflicting on Logan. She could almost hear the crack of the flogging whip. When at last she dried her eyes and exited the wagon, the sun was lighting the sky to the east.

At the fire, she busied herself with plans for the day, hoping no one noticed her appearance. Max and Francisco, however, had been trained to keep an eye on her.

Max handed her a cup of coffee; when she took it, her

hand trembled, and he squeezed her shoulder. "We'll get him out today, Stella. I promise."

She bit her bottom lip to still its trembling. "I can't keep from thinking of what he might be going through."

Max cleared his throat. "Don't think about it," he said in a gruff voice. Then softer, he continued, "He'll hold up. He knows we're coming."

"How?" she demanded.

Max shrugged. "He's the one who told me to get you out of that apartment. Didn't you hear him?"

She squinted through the smoke of the campfire, shaking her head.

"He knows we're coming, rest assured of that. And he expects us today. So, we'd better get started."

Shelling and skirmishing around the waterfront were not uncommon; Colonel Ford's men kept up a constant barrage from the lighthouse area, firing toward Brazos Santiago in an effort to keep the Federals from mounting an attack.

Beto rode with them until they found a carriage to hire; afterward, he returned to camp with their horses. Stella, Max, and Francisco climbed into one carriage, intending to change to two before they reached the plaza.

At first Stella put her increasing tenseness down to the desperate situation she faced, and indeed, she knew, that played a big part. But something else was wrong. A restless air stirred in the streets. By the time they changed to two carriages and she arrived at the plaza, the place was buzzing with more than merchants returning to work, more than soldiers itching for a part in the fight.

The soldiers moved now with determination. She had directed the driver to stop at the steps leading to the French legation. From the darkened interior of the cab, she watched for the man Max described to her: of slight build, not over thirty years old, with bushy black hair swept straight back from an exaggerated widow's peak, always formally attired with waistcoat and cravat.

"He wears a top hat and carries an elaborately carved ivory cane. Fancies himself an ambassador," Max had said.

From time to time, she glanced across the street at the Confederate headquarters. Despite the early hour, scores of men, in and out of uniform, swarmed into the building and out again, all engaged in animated conversations.

Then she saw her man. At least, he fit Max's description. Surely, no one else carried such a cane. She moved to open the carriage door, but her hand froze on the handle. For one terrifying moment she stared out the window, watching the jaunty Monsieur Leclerc approach the carriage, headed for the entrance to the French legation. For one sickening moment, she sat frozen with fear . . . fear of failing Logan.

Leclerc took the steps. She watched him hook the ornate cane over his forearm and reach to open the door of the building.

Well, she would certainly fail Logan if she did not get out of the carriage! Frantically, she forced the door open and stumbled onto the brick walkway, calling the man's name.

"Monsieur Leclerc."

Turning, he surveyed her from the top step. His disdain renewed her fear of failure. Then she visualized Logan in Blakesborough's hands, saw the whip connect with his back. She stiffened her spine.

"May I have a word with you, monsieur?"

He frowned.

"I am Stella Duval. I am engaged in . . ."

His eyes pierced hers; recognition replaced a measure of his disapproval. "I know your reputation, miss, but I am a busy man. Perhaps your Confederate agent . . ."

"Actually, it is my father who would like to speak with you. Captain Giddeon Duval . . ."

"Captain Duval," he repeated. "If it is for permission to fly our colors, I am sure . . ."

She held panic at bay, prayed for wisdom . . . and patience. "My father must speak with you immediately on a matter of grave concern to your country."

Leclerc's frown deepened. "My days are filled with matters of grave concern to my country, Miss Duval. Perhaps you could be more specific . . ."

"Arms, monsieur."

His eyes widened. She saw a flicker of interest, then he laughed. "Indeed? Am I to believe Captain Duval has come into a shipment of arms he is willing to sell to France, rather than keep for the Confederacy?"

"Of course not," she assured him. "I have not explained very well. You have heard of the Dance Munitions Plant?"

Again she saw a flicker of interest. "Go on."

"The plant is completing an important order for the Confederacy. However, they find themselves in the critical position of not being able to finish the order without additional operating funds. They have invented this small cannon, which they are willing to sell. . . ." She clamped fingers over her mouth. "Excuse me, sir. I talk too much. The details are for my father to discuss, not me."

Leclerc averted his eyes. His head bobbed almost imperceptibly. "Tell him I will see him this afternoon."

She glanced to the curb where the carriage waited. "Pardon me, monsieur, but you must be aware of the price on my father's head. Why, the reward the Yankees are offering is enough to entice even a Confederate to turn him over to the Federals. He is not safe on the streets of Brownsville. I have brought a carriage. He awaits us at his camp."

Leclerc examined the carriage. Upon approaching the plaza, Stella had engaged a carriage around the corner from the French legation, after inquiring of the driver whether he regularly worked the street. He had assured her he daily carried passengers from that building.

Now, she was glad of her decision, for when Monsieur Leclerc caught the driver's eye, the driver tipped his hat.

"Mornin', sir."

Leclerc glanced apprehensively toward his building, then

back at the carriage. "I shouldn't . . ."

Suddenly Stella entertained the disastrous idea that the scheme might not work. "I realize you must be terribly busy, monsieur. If it were not for the fact that my father must leave town within the hour, he would not rush you." She turned toward the carriage, panic swirling hot and sickening in the pit of her stomach.

One thing was certain, she would never make a poker player. She thought of La Paloma Cantina, of the game played by her father and grandfather — of the stakes in that game . . . not only her mother's hand in marriage, but her very life and Stella's . . . their entire heritage. Wagered by two self-assured men.

The stakes today were no less vital: Logan's life, and with it, her own. Turning back to Leclerc, she suppressed her fear with admonitions for this moment only: a steady voice, a firm handshake.

Extending her hand, she smiled. "Of course, if you are not interested, we can go elsewhere."

In the time it took Monsieur Leclerc to call her back, her heart practically stopped beating.

At length, he shrugged. "I suppose it won't hurt to listen." He laughed, a confident, self-satisfied laugh that eased some of her anxieties. "Your reputation for loyalty is as high as your father's. Why, the two of you have become legends in this part of the world. To both the Confederates and the Federals, I might add."

Once convinced, Monsieur Leclerc settled into the ride with such enthusiasm, Stella would have regretted deceiving him, had Logan's life not depended on their plan.

After a few blocks, she again became aware of the great number of soldiers moving through the streets.

"They are traveling with such urgency . . . and all headed east, toward . . ." — she paused, as the direction registered in her brain — ". . . toward the Gulf. What is happening?"

"You have not heard?" Leclerc questioned. "The Federals

355

crossed Boca Chica inlet during the night."

"You mean there is going to be a battle?"

"Likely," he conceded, "but do not let it concern you. Your Rip Ford will not let the Yankees retake Brownsville."

By the time they reached the vaquero camp, they had left most of the soldiers behind. An uneasy sense of calm settled over the area. Max and Francisco had learned about the attack at Boca Chica, too. And they had a plan.

Max held back, however, until Leclerc was seated at the campfire awaiting the appearance of Giddeon Duval, and the vaqueros had surreptitiously surrounded him.

Max stepped into the circle of wagons, introduced himself, and Monsieur Leclerc's countenance changed from composed and confident to defiant and fearful, as quickly as the sun could hide behind an ominous black cloud. He looked at Stella with an expression of betrayal that caused her to cringe. His compliment about her loyalty rang a discordant note in her ears. Well, she was loyal, she countered. To Logan. To Logan, her husband.

Max took charge, and to no one's surprise, Leclerc adamantly refused to cooperate.

"Why should I write such a message?" he demanded. "Give me one reason I should betray a trusted ally." He looked Max over with a scornful eye. "You brand Captain Blakesborough a traitor, and in the same breath, you expect me to become one."

"We are wasting time, Leclerc. Valuable time."

"Humph! You had best become comfortable, because it will be—how do you say it over here?—a cold day in hell before I betray a valuable ally such as Captain Blakesborough."

While Max and Leclerc argued, Stella stood by and Francisco mobilized the vaqueros. Stationed at intervals around the camp, they stepped one by one to the edge of the clearing. A disreputable lot in their trail clothes, large sombreros, and crossed bandoleers, some held weapons in the open — rifles, Bowie knives — others their menacing demeanors enough to bring a shudder to the Frenchman's shoulders every time he looked their way. He did not waiver from his original decision, however.

He was a courageous man, Stella thought. She had to admire him for that. But his courage could keep them from rescuing Logan before . . . Suddenly a terrifying thought occurred to her — one she had not previously considered: What if the *Victory* sailed from Brazos Santiago before they were able to rescue Logan?

Emboldened by this new fear, she entered the bargaining herself. "Monsieur Leclerc, we need your help. We would not have stooped to such measures if your aid were not . . . imperative."

"Stoop is the correct word," he spat. "I should be ashamed, were I . . ."

Fueled by both fear and distress, she interrupted him. "You will be more than ashamed if you find yourself in the camp of Benito Juárez."

His eyes flew to Max's. "You would not dare . . ."

Max shrugged. "Like the lady says, your help is necessary to free an innocent man. The choice is yours."

It wasn't, of course, much of a choice. Stella filled a round of coffee cups, and they sat in a tight circle, staring at Monsieur Leclerc, awaiting his decision.

"Look at it this way, Leclerc." Max's tone changed from tough to placating. "There's a traitor for every hundred men. You may lose Blakesborough, but by day's end, you'll find someone to take his place."

"Not with his connections."

Max shook his head. "Dar Blakesborough has only one connection — his father — and that isn't going to be enough to save his hide. This letter will be of no consequence in the ultimate course of things, except to a man wrongfully im-

357

prisoned."

Stella could feel the minutes tick by, one by one, as surely as if she had a pocket watch implanted inside her heart. She knew Leclerc would cooperate, once they convinced him they would carry out the threat to turn him over to the very man his emperor was battling for control of Mexico. But could they convince him of this in time to save Logan? Anxiously, she glanced around at the vaqueros. She caught Francisco's eye.

The old vaquero wore the expression of a cragged stone. He stepped into the clearing with what could only be considered a purpose, stopping within inches of where Leclerc sat on a log. He squatted before the man and stared hard into his gray eyes.

Stella saw Leclerc's eyes shift uneasily from Francisco's eyes to his hands—to the razor-sharp Bowie knife the old vaquero flicked back and forth across a thumb. Light glinted from the polished blade.

She stood beside Francisco. "Now, you have three choices, monsieur. Benito Juárez's camp, Francisco's blade, or a simple letter."

The Frenchman made his choice in short order after that. Although his voice shook, the hatred in his tone was unmistakable. "What do I write?"

Max provided writing paper and pencil, and the words. "Tell him to meet you at a place called White's Ranch."

Leclerc's eyes darted from the paper to Max. "The devil, I will! That's where Rip Ford's headed with his damned Cavalry of the West."

"Don't worry about it," Max replied. "You won't be there. Once Colonel Ford captures the Federal captain who just happened to find his way into the battle, you will be free to return to the French embassy. No one—other than one lousy traitor—will ever know of your letter."

"Except us." Stella's voice held a quiet tremor. "And we will be forever grateful."

358

Chapter Eighteen

"The fighting at Boca Chica plays right into our hands," Max explained after he instructed Monsieur Leclerc to write a second letter. "At the same time, it plays havoc with our scheme to arrange for Admiral Farragut to arrest Blakesborough — and secure Logan's release — before the rebs get hold of him."

Stella gazed into the fire. "The admiral will have his hands full today." Her thoughts switched abruptly back to Logan, how to rescue him, what she would do when she saw him, how she dreaded the possibility he may have been flogged or otherwise mistreated.

"To ensure Blakesborough reaps his just rewards," Max continued, speaking now to Leclerc, "pen a letter describing your dealings with the captain."

Again Francisco came to the rescue, and the Frenchman's initial reluctance to sign his name to such a statement fled in the face of the stalwart vaquero's blade.

Stella couldn't claim to be disappointed that they would be the ones to rescue Logan. This only enabled her to see him sooner.

Max and Francisco had other ideas, of course, and it took her a while to convince them she would not — *would not* — be left behind.

The first real problem arose when they discussed going into Colonel Ford's camp to advise him of Blakesborough's imminent arrival.

By that time they had located the man at the French legation whom Monsieur Leclerc assured them he used as a go-between in dealings with Dar Blakesborough. The courier himself convinced them by his near collapse at the suggestion of what they would do with Leclerc, were he to fail to deliver the message.

After they shuttled him off on the mission, they turned their attention to the second concern: assuring Blakesborough's arrival would be expected at White's Ranch.

"We must get word to Colonel Ford. He will be glad for the chance to capture a Federal officer," Stella said.

Max agreed. "I would go myself . . ."—he scanned his worn vaquero attire—". . . I certainly look the part, but if they recognized my Boston accent . . ."

Stella laughed. "That's the first time you've mentioned your origins, Max. You are from Boston?"

He shrugged, noncommittal. ". . . or someplace."

She returned her thoughts to the matter at hand. "I am the perfect one to go. I've met Colonel Ford; he will surely remember me right away."

Both Max and Francisco objected, but she persisted. "I'm the only one he will recognize. We are wasting time. *I* am going. . . ."

Max sighed. "Not alone. I can't allow it."

"Nor I, señorita. I will ride with you."

She agreed and it was just past high noon when they set out from the vaquero camp, leaving two men behind to guard Monsieur Leclerc. Eight vaqueros accompanied Max to the Rio Grande to secure a boat to take them to the *Victory*.

"Meet us at Clarksville," Max told Francisco and Stella. "Do you know it?"

Stella nodded, and Francisco answered. "Across from Bagdad on our side of the river."

"We should arrive at the ship after sunset, but we must leave earlier—five o'clock?"

"We will be there, Señor Max."

"Don't go without me," she appealed, and he agreed. She couldn't bear not being among the group to free Logan . . . yet . . . what if she and Francisco were detained? What if they couldn't get to Clarksville by five o'clock?

"Max . . . ?"

When their eyes met, she knew he understood her concern. "If we have to leave without you, Stella, we will take him to the apartment in Bagdad. Can you find it?"

She nodded and they set off in opposite directions.

The afternoon was hot, the roads crowded, and in the distance they heard cannon fire. Added to her other anxieties, Stella felt the urgency inside her mount. She whipped up her horse.

Francisco kept pace and together they made their way through the bustling town of Brownsville, past the square and out toward the Gulf, following a steady stream of soldiers. She wasn't sure exactly where White's Ranch was located, so from time to time she asked a passing soldier.

Their answers were always the same. "Follow us!"

So, they did—Stella, armed with one rifle and limited ammunition; Francisco with his rifle and ever-present blade.

"The crowds have thinned now," she reflected aloud.

"*Sí,*" Francisco acknowledged. "The people are fleeing the battle. They recall the last time Brownsville was attacked by Federals, when Colonel Ford's own men set fire to the town."

"That will not happen again," Stella responded, uncertain why she was so sure of the fact, hoping she was right, knowing, all the while, the only thing that mattered to her was one single Federal officer.

"I do not think so, either, señorita."

Stella studied the old vaquero, a grin playing on her lips. "Francisco, I will tell you something, a secret."

He turned, waiting patiently, as always.

"I am no longer a señorita."

His eyes widened by degrees as her statement settled into his mind. "Señori . . . ?"

She held out her hand for him to see her golden band. "Logan Cafferty and I were married yesterday . . . in Bagdad."

Slowly, Francisco's weathered face broke into a broad smile. "Ah," he said. "Señor Logan — he is a good man." He tipped his sombrero. "La Señora Duval de Cafferty."

She laughed. "I have heard Mamá called la Señora Cortinas de Duval, but it sounds a bit old-fashioned today."

The words played in her mind, however. *Duval de Cafferty.* They meant she belonged to him, and she did, of course. "I suppose I will be known as Mrs. Cafferty."

"Whatever your name, señora, we will rescue your bridegroom. Do not fear for him further."

It took a good three hours to locate Colonel Ford's camp. As advised, they followed the river of soldiers and the gunfire, which seemed to explode closer and closer with each step of their horses. Anxious lest they spend too much time looking for the colonel, she persisted in stopping from time to time to ask the location of Colonel Ford's camp; and as before, they were guided each time into the melee of men and animals and battle cries.

When they arrived a new problem arose. The colonel's aide detained them for what seemed like an eternity.

"He ain't got time for civilians, ma'am. You're plumb loco to be running about a battlefield like this. Why, you could get yourself shot and nobody'd even know it."

Francisco slanted his rifle toward the young man, a casual gesture, but one the soldier did not miss.

When Colonel Ford greeted her with a bear hug, she felt vindicated at the look of surprise that spread across the face of the aide who had been so certain Colonel Ford had no time for civilians.

"A Yankee captain, you say? Coming directly into our camp? Ma'am, we are once more in your debt." He grinned, his eyes wide with curiosity, but she kept her silence.

He accepted this in his good-natured way. "I am not one to

look a gift horse in the mouth, mind you. A bit curious, perhaps, but you leave this Captain Blakesborough to us. We will see his detainment is a lengthy one."

"If you get tired of holding him, contact Admiral Farragut of the United States Navy. He will be looking to put Blakesborough behind bars, too."

"One of them, huh? No good to nobody?"

She agreed, shook his hand, and wished him well. Clarksville was no more than five miles farther, and they made it with time to spare. It, too, teemed with Federals. Francisco guided his mount close to hers. "Stay close, señori . . . ah, señora. This town is full of Yankees."

She grinned at him. "I am a Yankee's wife, Francisco."

He nodded toward the milling soldiers. "I do not think that would make a difference with them; in their eyes you are just another reb."

She had not given thought to what sort of vessel Max would commandeer—nor from whom. So, when she saw a Federal supply boat anchored offshore, she paid no mind, until the crew began waving and calling to her.

"Mrs. Cafferty!"

"Señora Cafferty!"

Her head reeled with the sound of her new name as Max helped her aboard. She studied the crew, a combination of her own vaqueros and an equal number of Federal sailors.

"Why did you take such a boat?" On board this vessel, her men were actually in Federal hands, an unsettling thought.

"It was the quickest way out of the harbor." He grinned. "What better disguise than a ship already loaded to supply our fleet in the Gulf?"

It made sense, she supposed. "Are these men trustworthy?"

"They'll do." He scrutinized her vaqueros with a smile. "In fact, I figured we needed a few real sailors to get us out of the harbor. Don't suppose many of your men are a hand at sailing?"

"I'm afraid not, but . . . what about later? Can you convince these Yankees to set my men free?"

"I told the crew they are *my* vaqueros, hired in Mexico." He laughed. "Besides, I have more authority around here than you realize. Since you and I have never been properly introduced, Mrs. Cafferty, you wouldn't know that I outrank all these men, and most on board the *Victory*—except of course your husband—by a bunch."

She considered him silently, realizing that for all the time they had spent together, she actually knew very little about this man—Logan's valued friend, and her own. "How much?" she questioned at length, teasing, yet serious.

"Colonel Maxwell Burnsides, USMC, at your service."

She thought about that as they weighed anchor and set sail for the Gulf waters. She was interested in Max, of course, but mostly she thought about it to keep from worrying over the condition they would find Logan in.

Although Max did not take the wheel himself, he stood beside the helmsman, and Stella stood beside him, holding the rail to support herself against the pitch and toss of the boat.

"With you and Logan both colonels," she wondered aloud, "why couldn't you have arrested Blakesborough earlier? He surely gave you cause, assaulting an officer, if nothing else."

"That wasn't what we were after. We wanted to put him away for good, and to do that we needed the kind of proof Leclerc provided us this morning. Secretary Wells figured, given time, Blakesborough would let his hatred for Logan override what little sense he had. He would begin to get cocky, careless; he would make a big mistake. When that happened, we'd be waiting. He was right."

"Right, yes," she agreed, "but a little too late to suit me."

"Me, too," Max admitted. "But don't start worrying now. We must keep a clear head about us."

Stella stared straight ahead, straining her eyes toward the

ships anchored in the deeper waters off the bar. A multitude of them: merchant ships from countries around the world, as well as military vessels, Confederate, Federal, French, and Mexican — each watching and waiting for the opportunity to close in on his own particular enemy.

"I don't see any fighting," she said at last. "Not even the sound of the battle."

"We're heading due east," he told her. "The fighting is to the north. The only fighting we're likely to run into will be on board the *Victory*."

As they neared the *Victory,* the sun sank low behind them, casting the ship in a haze of bronze. "Are we too early?" she asked. "Will they recognize us?"

Max shook his head. "They will recognize a supply boat, and that is always welcome."

With that he turned to the crew and began issuing instructions. "Unload your supplies in the usual manner. I want the vaqueros out of sight, behind crates and rigging, until we are secured to the vessel. I will follow our crew members up the ladder . . ." — he paused, stared at Stella — ". . . you stay back until I signal."

She nodded, stifling an almost overpowering urgency to rush on board the *Victory* and find Logan, with the sure knowledge that were they to succeed in freeing him, she would have to trust Max and follow his instructions.

The wait stretched interminably as she crouched with the vaqueros behind stacks of supplies and awaited Max's signal. They had docked at the *Victory* in the last rays of sunlight, with shadows falling in ominous hulks across the deck of the supply ship; as they waited the shadows spread like ink stains, until by the time she heard Max's voice again, she could barely make out the rungs on the rope ladder flapping against the side of the larger ship.

"Come as quietly as you can," he called down.

Quickly, she slung her rifle over her back, bandoleer-style, and began climbing the swinging ladder, thankful for a calm sea and adept sailors at the rail. She wished for her boots; the rope cut into her feet through the thin soles of her black slippers; the pain called to mind the dastardly things Dar Blakesborough could have inflicted upon Logan, and she hurried.

When at last she reached the top, Max pulled her onto the deck; he was the only person in sight. He motioned her behind a coil of rigging with a single greeting: "Blakesborough's already gone ashore."

She scooted behind the coil, relieved, yet still anxious. She glanced toward the stairwell that led to Logan's cabin and beyond to the galley, thence by another passageway and stairwell to the hold below decks.

One by one the eight vaqueros climbed on board, found their legs and scurried to hiding places Max indicated.

Suddenly footsteps thudded along the deck. "What's going on here? Haven't you got that boat unloaded by now?"

She watched Max duck his head into his collar and quickly look down the ladder. The feet came into view. Her breath caught, recognizing the man she had hit with the table at the apartment in Bagdad. Dar Blakesborough's man.

He moved toward Max . . . closer . . . closer. He peered over Max's shoulder; she watched him tense, then draw his pistol.

Before he could free his weapon from its holster, Max raised up beneath him, sending him sprawling backward. "What the hell . . . ?" he sputtered.

The deck was cast in the shadows of late afternoon, the time between sunset and the rising of the moon.

When Blakesborough's man scrambled to find his footing, Max lunged for his ankles. The two men rolled around on the deck; Stella gripped her rifle, alert for a way to help.

She couldn't fire the gun, she might hit Max. She cast about the deck — no vaqueros were in sight. She knew they, too, waited for the appropriate time to act. Fighting men, all, they would not enter an altercation without determining the whereabouts of the enemy. For that very reason, she could not call to them: Other Blakesborough compadres could approach from any direction.

Yet, she couldn't sit on her heels and let Max be tossed into the ocean, either. In the darkened corner, she rose stealthily to her feet. The men rolled this way and that about the deck.

She crept into the open. They scuffled, each fighting to gain his footing; she stared into the darkness, straining to keep sight of Max. She concentrated on one figure, followed him as he rolled beneath the other, kicked free of his opponent, scrambled to his feet—

Stepping in quickly, she heaved the rifle over her head and swung it down, walloping her target on the head. He fell limp.

Max jumped to his feet and tossed her a quick glance. "I owe you two," he whispered. "Let's get out of here."

She tensed at sudden footsteps behind them; then a man spoke. Ensign Jacobs.

"Welcome aboard, ma'am."

She wanted to hug him, she was so glad to see him alive and free. The implications of what that meant for Logan soothed her ragged nerves. "Where is he?"

"Come. We will leave the fighting to these men."

"Bring him back here," Max called after them. "We will take the supply boat back the way we came to avoid the battle at Boca Chica."

Jacobs spirited her through corridors familiar with memories. She pushed them all aside.

"How is he?"

"He'll pull through, ma'am."

She grasped his words, then gasped; quickly she forced her brain to settle down: Logan was alive, Ensign Jacobs said he would live, and she was here to see to it that he did. She would deal with everything else later. Right now, those were the only three things that mattered—plus the fact that she would see him within minutes.

They passed several sailors in the corridors, but none challenged them.

"Are we safe?" she whispered.

When Jacobs glanced at her, she read more in his eyes in the dim light of the galley through which they passed than in his quick nod.

She didn't speak again until they reached the steps leading to the hold. Jacobs took a lantern from a hook and motioned her behind him. "Stay in the shadows. Most of the crew hate Blakesborough and will be glad to see him get his due; those who support him are likely on deck fighting his battle. But to be safe, stay behind me. I do not know who is on guard."

The descent into the dungeonlike hold filled her with such repulsion she thought she might be sick before she reached the bottom step. Her hands trembled; perspiration beaded on the back of her neck and down her spine, cold and chilling.

Jacobs dismissed the guard and waited until the man cleared the steps before he moved toward the cell. "It's Jacobs, Colonel. Look who came to get you out of here."

Stella stopped at the door of the cell. Jacobs rattled the key in the lock. The hinge creaked like an old adversary, and the door swung wide.

"Logan . . . ?" Her throat constricted over the sound; she was certain there was no one else on the face of the earth for whom she would step inside this cell . . . no one except . . .

"Princess . . ."

His voice was rough from disuse. Something made of metal touched her hand.

"Give him some water," Jacobs suggested.

She took the cup and moved toward him. Jacobs held the lantern higher, but still she was unable to see him well enough to suit her.

His hands closed over hers, sending tremors through her soul, bringing tears of thanksgiving to her eyes; she guided the cup to his lips. After a long pull, he released her hands. She reached for him.

"Not in here," he mumbled. "I don't want you in here."

She grasped his arm and pulled him out the cell door. The acrid stench below decks was stifling, as before, but it did nothing to dampen her happiness at finding him alive and mobile. Now to get him off the *Victory*.

"I don't want you in here, either," she said, "so let's go. Max has a boat waiting."

It wasn't as easy to get him up the stairs as she had expected, a fact that added to her urgency. With Logan supported on either side by Stella and Jacobs, his feet dragged limp on the steps, but between them they managed to pull him onto the main deck and drag him toward the starboard side of the ship unmolested by Blakesborough's sailors.

A thousand questions pummeled her senses, but she didn't ask them; Logan wasn't up to answering, and she didn't want to ask Jacobs in his presence. At that moment the only imperative was to get him on the supply boat and away from here.

"We were saved by the all-around bastard Blakesborough is," Max told her when they reached the rail where he waited. He looked Logan over as he spoke. "The only man aboard who gives a damn about the captain is Herbert, and you took care of him . . . Mrs. Cafferty."

Much to her distress she was forced to stand aside once more and watch helplessly while the crew, at Max's instructions, lowered Logan to the supply boat by way of the net with which they hoisted the crates of supplies. She began to scramble down the ladder, determined to find a comfortable place for them to lay him. If only there were enough daylight for her to inspect him properly.

While she concentrated on the rungs of the swinging ladder, she heard Max address the crew on the deck above her.

"Ensign Jacobs will be in charge. Anyone who questions his authority will be thrown in the hold."

She heard him pause, then continue, "Admiral Farragut will be out in a few days, after things have quieted down on shore, to . . . ah, to issue new assignments."

The only suitable bed was a long row of crates, over which she hastily spread a tarpaulin one of the crew members handed her. They laid Logan on it, and she knelt by his side, gripping his hands in her own. The damp night air settled over them; the salty sea sprayed in her face.

She recalled Logan asking, *Was it terrible?* of the attack when Giddeon was wounded. Although she had not yet managed a good look at him, she knew his treatment at the hands of Dar Blakesborough had been terrible. But he was alive, and from what she could see, unmaimed. What had Francisco said? Things weren't *dreadful* if they ended all right. With Logan alive and free, things were beginning to end all right.

He stirred, and she reassured him with soft kisses to his forehead. "You are free now. We're going home."

Home? she thought. Like a Spanish word, it had tripped from her tongue without design. *Home.*

"Home . . ." Logan whispered, his voice faltering, weak, wonderful. He squeezed her hands.

"Home," she whispered, kissing his lips lightly, afraid to hurt him, wanting him desperately. Salty tears ran down her cheeks and mingled with the sea spray.

Max came to kneel beside them. "How is he?"

"I'll make it, friend," Logan managed, though his voice was still rough and weak.

Max pressed an open palm to Logan's forehead, then turned to Stella. "He'll be fine, now he's got you."

They sat thus in silence, letting the whipping of the sails and the creak of the ship moving through the night waters drift over them. They weren't out of danger, she knew, but since she did not hear cannons or gunfire, she began to relax.

As they sped through the night Logan's grip on her hands strengthened, and she thought how Max's words were true for both of them. They would be all right, now that they had each other.

When the lights of Bagdad came into view, Max cleared his throat. "Stella, I learned something on board the *Victory* you should know."

She felt him shrug beside her and realized what a familiar gesture that had become. "What is it?" she asked. Before he could answer, she added, "Nothing you have to tell me can dim my happiness, now that Logan is safe."

"I know," he replied. "But . . . well, this is a horse of a different color, as you say in Texas . . ." — again, he cleared his throat — ". . . General Lee surrendered to General Grant over a month ago. Word just arrived today."

The sea spray spit at her cheeks, stinging in its sudden intensity; her heart thudded against her ribs. She felt Logan's hands tighten in warm support around her cold fingers. Her brain felt chilled, as though someone had opened her head and filled it with icy sea water. Her only conscious thought was that her words to Max were untrue: His news did dim her happiness.

She thought of Colonel Ford and the soldiers congregating at White's Ranch to wage battle with an enemy who had already defeated them. "What about Colonel Ford?"

Again, Max shrugged. "That battle doesn't matter one way or another now. The rebellion's over."

Reaching, she smoothed back an imaginary strand of hair from Logan's forehead, resting her hand on his damp skin. "Except to the men who will die there."

The war's over.
The rest of the way to the port at Bagdad Max's news pounded in her head, but the words rallied no patriotism, marshaled no protest, no feelings of betrayal or anger or

371

even joy, reminding her simply of a ram buttressing futilely against a barred door. *The war's over.*

Once they carried Logan to his apartment above the ropería, however, and she inspected his beaten body in the light of Señora Valensuela's lamps, her brain took up a different chorus.

Was it terrible? And those words did bring feelings: horror and pain and anger and disgust. How terrible she discovered in graphic detail: his multihued battered face, red and black and blue . . . and swollen almost beyond recognition; his fists, covered with dried blood . . . his own and that of others; and his back, flogged to a welted mass of crisscrossed wounds.

Señora Valensuela brought water, clean cloths, and turpentine, and Stella cleansed and doctored as best she could. He didn't speak, but she knew he was conscious, because he flinched when she worked below the surface of dried blood and dirt to the bare flesh.

After bathing his back, dousing the injuries liberally with turpentine, and dressing him with clean strips of cloth, she laid him back on the crisp linens of the bed that was to have been their wedding bed and tended his hands, leaving his face until last. Señora Valensuela brought fresh water and more turpentine, and Stella made a cold compress for his swollen face. Tenderly, she held the cloth in place, keeping her tears back by reminding herself that he was free and would recover.

But when he raised a battered hand and caressed hers against his face, running his finger back and forth across her golden wedding band, she was unable to hold back. Tears poured from her eyes and fell onto the cloth.

From beneath it, he spoke. "It's over, princess. We made it."

She sat close by the bed, holding his hands, until at last he fell asleep and she could no longer keep her eyes open. Blowing out the one remaining lamp, she crawled into bed beside him, knowing she should change from her grimy clothing, unable to muster the strength to do so.

Señora Valensuela awakened her the next morning with a tray of coffee and empanadas de calabaza, soft pockets of sweetbread filled with pumpkin.

"I also brought fresh clothing for you," the señora said. "I will sit with him while you bathe." When Stella protested, she continued. "You do not want him to awaken to such a sight."

Stella rushed to finish her bath before Logan awakened. But once she dressed in the calico morning gown with fresh undergarments and clean skin beneath, she was glad she had taken the time. For when Logan opened his eyes and smiled into her face, she was glad it was clean; when he reached to tousle her short curls, she was glad they were soft, and when she bent to kiss him, she was glad she smelled like a woman instead of like a trail driver.

Señor Max had gone to Brownsville to confer with Admiral Farragut, Señora Valensuela told Stella, but she did not know where Francisco was.

That afternoon Max, attired in the splendid uniform of a United States Marine Corps officer, came bearing the news they had craved. "The admiral is pleased," he told Logan. "He's recommending you for a medal and a promotion. He will come in a few days to fill you in personally."

Relief washed over Stella. "So, they took Blakesborough into custody?"

Max nodded. "Colonel Ford transferred custody to Admiral Farraqut as you suggested to him, Stella."

When Logan spoke, his tone was bitter. "I'd like to have struck the final blow at that scoundrel, damn his soul."

Max grinned. "You'll get your chance at his court-martial, friend. As things turned out, we all had a hand in his downfall, and in the last battle of the rebellion. Colonel Ford captured Blakesborough; Ford won the battle, but when his prisoners informed him of Lee's surrender and the

373

subsequent orders for all Confederate troops to surrender, he evidently decided the better part of valor rested in surrendering himself and his men on the spot."

"I don't understand," Stella said. "We were told the Federals attacked Boca Chica. Why did they do that if they knew the war was over?"

"They didn't attack," Max told her. "The rebels thought they were attacking. They were carrying out orders to take control of the territory."

"What will happen now?" she asked.

Max shrugged. "No one can predict, yet. According to Admiral Farragut, plans are being laid for General Kirby Smith to surrender the Trans-Mississippi Department. Of course, that will take a while. Looks like most of the higher-ranking Confederates are coming over here."

"Here?" she questioned.

"Mexico. They seem to figure fighting for Maximilian will be better than living under Federal rule."

She turned her head toward the window; distress filled her body and mind. Would the conflict never end?

"I sent Francisco to Los Olmos with the wagons," Max told her. "With the instability in the area, I figured the vaqueros should get away from the coast."

"Thank you," she whispered without turning around.

Logan had listened, propped against a pillow. He now reached for her and pulled her against his shoulder.

Instantly her worries left political strife for more immediate concerns. "Don't . . . I'll hurt you."

He chuckled beneath her shoulder. "Never, princess."

Max stood from where he had sat beside the bed; he leaned forward and kissed Stella on the cheek. "Looks like you two can make it without me for a while. I'll be heading out to the *Victory.*"

Logan stopped him. "Has the admiral decided who gets command of the *Victory?*"

Max drew to attention, clicking his heels and saluting Logan. "Colonel Maxwell Burnsides, reporting for duty as acting captain of the USS *Victory*."

"A leatherneck captaining the *Victory?*" Logan asked.

Max laughed. "Only until they find a true-blue navy man to take charge. I suggested Jacobs."

Logan healed quickly, and by the time Admiral Farragut called a week later, he was able to receive his commanding officer in the parlor with Stella by his side.

She protested at first, thinking that she, a "known rebel" as it were, would not be welcomed by this high-ranking Federal officer.

"This is Mexico," Logan had replied. "He has no jurisdiction here. Besides, you are my wife, and I want you present. I promise you, it will be an interesting meeting."

His words called to mind another promise he had made her in the parlor of this apartment, and she reminded him of it.

He grunted. "I could never be injured badly enough to forget such a promise to my wife."

But although they lay beside each other at night, and exchanged kisses frequently during the day, the most intimate advance he made toward her was to tousle her curly head. It was a promise he intended to keep to the letter, she knew: the promise to give her a *wedding night* she would never forget.

The morning after Max came to call, she returned from her morning bath, carrying a tray of nourishing broth and goat-cheese quesadillas, to find him sitting at the desk finishing a letter.

When she scolded him for being out of bed, he waggled his eyebrows and replied, "That bed is no longer a sickbed."

His reminder only made her hunger for his touch all the more. She set the tray on the table. "Then come eat and get well," she said. "I am tired of waiting for that promise."

He sank to a chair, drank the broth, and finished the

quesadillas. Afterward, she unwrapped his back and examined the wounds. "You are healing quickly," she admitted. "There is no sign of fever."

He pulled her face to his. "The fever is what's healing me." He whispered kisses across her face, teasing, tempting. "Rebel fever, deep inside, burning with desire."

"Me, too," she mumbled, wanting to tell him she would settle for less than perfection — much less. But she didn't, because the anticipation of his promise beckoned her with a sensualness she had not imagined possible, certainly not since she had shared his bed so many times already.

The admiral sent a messenger ahead to advise them of his visit, so they had time to prepare for it: she, attired in a crisp morning gown of violet chambray; Logan in his marine uniform, supplied by Max in a crate load of his possessions from the cabin on board the *Victory.*

Stella poured tea, then sat back to listen. Admiral Farragut caught them up on what they were calling reconstruction activities, designed to bring the rebelling states back into the Union with a minimum of turmoil. She did not say so, but she knew, even if he refused to admit it, such a situation would never be possible.

"Eventually, we'll hold open elections so the people of each state can choose their own governor. For the time being, a provisional government will be set up. That's what I have come to discuss with you, Colonel."

"Before you proceed, I'd like you to read this." Logan reached into the drawer of the parlor desk and withdrew an envelope that bore the name of the ropería on the outside.

"What is it?"

"Read it, sir; then I will explain, if explanation is necessary."

The admiral scanned the few lines scrawled on white parchment paper. Afterward he stared silently at Logan a few moments longer. When he spoke his voice held a noticeable tone of regret. "Your resignation from the United States

Marines Corps? I need you now more than ever, Colonel."

Stella caught her breath at the admiral's words. They hadn't discussed the future; Logan should recover first, she had thought. She turned toward him, waiting, as did the admiral, for his explanation.

He looked at her when he answered. "My wife needs me more, sir."

She pursed her lips to still their trembling. The admiral asked the question that was on her own tongue.

"What will you do?"

Logan grinned, sheepish. "I'm not sure. We haven't discussed it, actually." He turned back to the admiral. "My wife's father was badly injured in this . . . ah, in this *war*— lost a leg, as a matter of fact. We must help him out in whatever way we can until he fully recovers. After that . . ."—he shrugged—". . . who knows?"

Admiral Farragut drained his teacup and set it back on the tray. He wiped his lips with the linen napkin and placed it carefully alongside the cup and saucer. Then he looked frankly at Logan. "I won't say I'm not disappointed to lose you, Cafferty. You're too good a man for that. But we're going to need good men . . ."—turning, he nodded toward Stella—". . . and women on every front in the days to come. Men and women like yourselves, like your family, Mrs. Cafferty. It's going to take all we can round up to heal the wounds left by this . . . *war*."

After the admiral left, Stella carried the tea tray to the señora's kitchen. She had been surprised at his resignation from the service, surprised and pleased. He knew how much it would mean to her, and as sick as he had been, he had planned to tell her in this special way. Her heart swelled with the love they shared, her mind swirled with questions.

Questions that faded like a rose in the heat of a South Texas summer when she found him in the bedroom changing clothes. He had already removed his jacket and shirt. She stopped short in the doorway, her heart pounding.

He turned. His trousers, unbuttoned, hung precariously on his hips. Unconsciously, she chewed the corner of her lip.

"Come, princess." He held out his arms. "Let's work at curing this rebel fever boiling inside us."

She stumbled toward him, fell against him, and wrapped her arms about his head. Her heart pounded furiously. Her arms trembled.

"I'm as giddy as if this were the first time," she whispered.

He removed his tongue from the recesses of her ear and filled the space with words. "It is . . . our first time as man and wife."

She didn't remind him of his promise; she didn't have to. He went about loving her with a thoroughness that set her on fire. Rebel fever, as he called it, consumed them both and the more they loved the hotter it flamed.

He kissed her with deep, wet, exploring kisses that reminded her how empty she was — all of her — for him — all of him. Only the thought of Señora Valensuela's chagrin over a ruined gown kept her from tearing the garment from her body.

And only the thought of his tender new skin kept her from tearing at his, as well.

Logan held her to him, ran his hand along her trussed-up back, molded her form to his, reveling in the feel of her breasts — even shielded from his touch by layers of clothing — as they nuzzled against his chest. This was what had kept him sane through the floggings and later in the cell, the same cell in which she had been held, he was sure. Love for this woman. Not hatred or thoughts of reprisal against Dar Blakesborough. Funny, now that he thought about it, Blakesborough had rarely crossed his mind, then, or later here in the apartment.

This woman, his wife. His love for her had filled his heart and his mind so full he had no room left for Blakesborough. His love for this woman, his wife.

She wriggled against him, struggling, anxious. Yet, as

badly as he wanted to feel her skin against his, he was wont to turn her loose—even for the necessary task of disrobing. Eventually, he did, of course, and working together, he with hands clumsy from their recent battering, she with fingers slowed by her desire for haste, they soon found themselves disrobed and lying together on the large walnut bed.

His lips suckled and caressed her own, stoking the fire inside her to unbearable limits. She moved against his body in rhythm with his stroking hands. His new skin felt rough against hers, toning her senses, leaving her wonderfully alive and desperately near expiration at the same time. His body's rigid projection rose between them, hot and hard, pressing against her . . . near, mere inches from the place she yearned for it to be. She struggled to accommodate him, but he held her back.

By the time his lips found her breasts, her nipples were already aching and rigid and she pressed herself closer, closer, and he opened his lips to fill his mouth with more of her sweetness.

Still it wasn't enough.

Neither for her, nor for him.

Splaying her palms against his sides, she let the heat of his body travel through her arms to her very core, firing her still, when she had thought such was not possible. Quite unconsciously she reached between them and grasped him in her palm, shifting to move him closer to where her desperate yearning focused. He groaned at her touch, and she felt as though she had grasped a sunbeam as light and energy flashed through her, hot and brilliant and ethereal.

He moved back, propped himself on an elbow and studied her a moment, catching his breath. "You don't . . . know . . . what you're doing to me." His words whished out on ragged breath, taking hers with it as on the same beam of light.

Together they looked down at his body. . . at her hand . . . and together they returned to look into each other's eyes.

The ordeal etched in lines around his eyes; if he concentrated, he told himself, he could hold out. If he concentrated . . . Tenderly, he reached a hand to push a wayward curl back from her eye.

"It's about grown out," he whispered.

She stared at him without turning loose, and his mind, most of it, stayed with her hand.

From her forehead, he trailed his fingers down her face, her neck, plied her rigid nipple, watched her eyes smolder, felt himself on the edge.

From her breast his fingers trailed over her hip, around her own arm, which hadn't moved an inch, and down to the silky liquid heat between her legs. He watched her still, concentrating on maintaining control of his own body, while his fingers slipped inside hers, into her heated core, as into the very mouth of a volcano.

His fingers began to move, and still he held out.

She tightened around his moving hand.

Still he held out.

Her smoldering green eyes begged.

And still he held out. His heart raced, his breath came from no more than skin deep. He felt as though he were drowning in her fiery liquid, in her eyes, in her passion.

He watched her jaws tighten; felt her body begin to convulse around his hand.

Then she opened her legs and with her hand guided him to the place they had both longed to be for so long.

"Home," he whispered.

"Home." She lay back, pulling him on top of her, and together they completed this short, tumultuous yet unbearably sweet journey.

"A perfect wedding night," she sighed into the recessed crook of his shoulder.

Drawing her back, he pulled at the curly ringlet over her eyebrow. "Night?" he teased. "The sun hasn't even set yet, princess. This was just for practice."

She quivered against him at the fervor in his words. He squeezed her.

"I have a feeling, Mrs. Cafferty, this malady called rebel fever will prove incurable."

"I certainly hope so, Colonel."

Author's Note

I first became interested in the Cotton Road after reading accounts about it during research for *Texas Gamble*. The Cotton Road, Lifeline of the Confederacy, followed what was known as the "Old Matamoros Road," used by the Spaniards on their entradas into Texas, by countless settlers and traders before and since, by General Zachary Taylor for his invasion of Mexico in 1845, and by the Confederates to ship cotton to market during the American Civil War. The Cotton Road passes La Hacienda de los Olmos of these stories. Since I wanted to write a follow-up story to *Texas Gamble,* the Cotton Road, with its intrigue and historical significance, became the obvious choice.

But, of course, the story of the Cotton Road could not be told without including stories of the Union blockade of the Texas (and Southern) ports, the coastal defense of Texas during the Civil War, and the conflict between the blockaders and the blockade runners.

Civil War students will immediately recognize the liberties I have taken with (among other things) the timetable of the war. I decided to begin this story after the fall of Vicksburg on July 4, 1863, when the Union strengthened the blockade, making the Cotton Road even more vital to the survival of the South; I wanted to end the book with the battle at White's Ranch, considered by many to have been the last battle of the war.

The problem arose in dramatizing history: The Federals

under General Banks withdrew from the Texas coast after the Caney Creek incident in early February 1864. From that time until mid-May 1865, when the actual battle at White's Ranch occurred, war-related events along the Texas coast were scarce. The blockade runners and the Cotton Road traffic moved in relative safety. After Caney Creek, however, my story had warmed up for the finish; I could not afford the luxury of a year's lapse in activity; therefore, I squeezed history to fit the dramatic timetable of my story. If you are interested in reading how it really happened, may I suggest several of my favorite books on the subject.

Texas Treasure Coast by Tom Towsend, Eakin Press. A true account of ships, shipwrecks and treasure along the Texas coast from the 1700s through 1964.

Why Stop? by Claude and Betty Dooley, Gulf Publishing Company. A compilation of Texas's Historical Roadside Markers. My husband and I used this book to follow the Cotton Road, as nearly as one can today, what with interstates and pasture fences obstructing some of the route. We learned a lot of Texas history and had a terrific time in the process.

Wild Horse Desert by Brian Robertson, New Santander Press, Edinburg, Texas. A history of South Texas (the setting for both this book and *Texas Gamble)* beginning in 1519.

The White Castle of Louisiana by M.R. Ailenroc, reprinted in 1986 by Louisiana Library Association. The diary of one of Mr. Harry Ransom's daughters.

My thanks to Dan Parkinson, author of numerous Zebra Western Novels, for teaching me how to plant a deadman.

If you enjoyed the story of Stella and Logan, check your bookstore in a few months for their daughter Marina Cafferty's story. The granddaughter of Giddeon and Serita

Duval, Marina grew up hearing tales of her grandfather's sunken ship, the *Espíritu Estelle,* and its mysterious cargo (related in *Texas Gamble).* The spirited descendent of both her mother and grandmother, Marina has long dreamed of salvaging the ship and discovering its true contents, which her grandfather gave up for love of her grandmother.